Not Quite Mr. Darcy

A NOVEL

KIM GRIFFIN

Copyright © 2023 by Kim Griffin

Visit Kim Griffin's website at KimGriffin.org

ISBN- 979-8-9884389-1-5 (Paperback edition)

ISBN- 979-8-9884389-0-8 (E-book edition)

All Rights Reserved. No part of this publication may be reproduced in any form or by any electronic or mechanical means, including photocopy, recordings, information storage and retrieval systems, without permission in writing from the author. The only exception is by a reviewer, who may quote short excerpts in printed or electronic book reviews.

This is a work of fiction. Unless otherwise indicated, all the names, characters, businesses, places, events and incidents in this book are either the product of the author's imagination or used in a fictitious manner. Any resemblance to actual persons, living or dead, or actual events is purely coincidental.

Cover Design by Hannah Linder

Editing by Heather Wood

Scripture quotations are from The ESV® Bible (The Holy Bible, English Standard Version®), copyright © 2001 by Crossway, a publishing ministry of Good News Publishers. Used by permission. All rights reserved.

Content Warning: This book contains infertility, miscarriage, dementia, cancer, infidelity, and loss. In all of these situations hope is shown.

Dedication

In memory of my mom, who shared her love of Jesus Christ and exemplified how to show that to others. Her mind was gradually taken over 14 1/2 years before she succumbed to Alzheimer's. I rejoice that when I see her again, her mind will be whole. She loved the image of a butterfly because it represents a rebirth, which beautifully depicts what happens when a person becomes a Christian. The picture below was painted by my daughter for Mother's Day after my mom passed. I am beyond grateful for my mom and her legacy.

Therefore, if anyone is in Christ, he is a new creation. The old has passed away; behold, the new has come.
2 Corinthians 5:17 ESV

And he who was seated on the throne said, "Behold, I am making all things new." Also he said, "Write this down, for these words are trustworthy and true."
Revelation 21:5 ESV

Contents

Chapter One

It is a truth universally acknowledged that Mr. Darcy does not exist.

Taking a deep breath, Kate glanced at her phone. Fifteen minutes of her train trip from St. Pancras Station in London to Dover Priory Station remained. Her eyes drifted to the bright green rolling hills out the window as her thoughts wandered.

Moving to a country on the other side of the Atlantic Ocean seemed so much more romantic at the age of fourteen when Kate and her best friend, Jennifer, first started making plans for their future. Those plans included visiting England to see the places enshrined in Jane Austen's books and find their very own Mr. Darcys, but as often happens, life intervened.

At twenty-nine, Kate was just now realizing that dream, minus the search for Mr. Darcy and the best friend co-traveler. Now that she was a grown woman with experiences beyond her years, she knew better than to waste time searching for the nonexistent Mr. Darcy. As for Jennifer, it wasn't like her friend abandoned her. Jennifer was now married, pregnant, and mother to three-year-old Emma. Moving them from

Memphis, Tennessee to England wasn't practical. So much for teenage plans.

Kate frowned, remembering that she wouldn't even be here herself if it weren't for the death of her husband, Mark, nine months earlier. Biting her lip, she refused to let tears escape, and focused again on the quickly changing scenery outside of the train. This was supposed to be a time of refreshment and renewal, not a time to be stuck in her head. She was finally experiencing things she'd long thought were out of reach. *This will be good*, she silently assured herself. *A chance to leave behind the pain.*

If only she could convince Jennifer that she wasn't here to find her true Mr. Darcy. Kate stifled a chuckle at the thought. Ever since high school, Jennifer had been intent on ensuring Kate had her Mr. Darcy.

The first time Kate saw her then-future husband walk into her high school French class as a new student, all the girls swooned. He was so tall and handsome.

Later that year, when Mark and Kate started dating, Jennifer insisted he was Kate's very own Mr. Darcy—tall, dark, handsome, and from a very wealthy family. He even seemed a bit snobbish at first, though that quickly passed once he felt comfortable at the school.

Kate always said that Mark was not quite Mr. Darcy because he didn't have the accent. Now it was very clear the two of them wouldn't get the happily ever after Jane Austen intended for her characters. Jennifer assured Kate that her Darcy was still out there somewhere, and with the relocation, she would finally find him—accent and all. A sad smile emerged as she remembered those happy, carefree high school days —a sharp contrast to her current reality—and there it was again, that ever-present pain trying to rise to the surface. Nine months of counseling couldn't make it go away; perhaps an ocean of distance could.

The murmurs of surrounding passengers drew her back to the moment and brought a small smile to her face. She wondered if she would ever get used to the various British accents.

As Kate's gaze moved from passenger to passenger, no one gave her the sad eyes, and it was blissfully freeing to be an ocean away from everyone who knew, or at least thought they knew, of her pain. She'd told her new employer, Tracey, about her husband's death but had requested that she keep it to herself. This was Kate's chance to get away from the constant reminders of what she'd lost. Thankfully, her soon-to-be patient was unaware of Mark's death, and Kate planned to keep it that way.

Once the train stopped, Kate's chest tightened as she stood and gathered her things. This was it. She was really doing it—living and working in England. Pulling her suitcase behind her, she scanned the station for Tracey while anxiously moving towards the exit. The station was tiny and neglected compared to the large bricked St. Pancras station where she had boarded the train.

"Kate!" Tracey waved from a few yards away.

At the sight of Tracey's smile, Kate's apprehension faded away.

Tracey was an elegant woman, tall and thin, just like Kate imagined from their FaceTime conversations. Though sleek and classic, Tracey's white bob was the only thing that gave away her age.

"So good to finally meet you in person. I just . . . " Her lips pressed together and she leaned in to squeeze Kate's hand tightly between both of hers. "I just cannot tell you how much this means to me. From the first FaceTime, I knew you were the one to help my mum." She laid a hand over her chest. "The past few months have been so surreal for us. I never imagined Mum would have these issues."

Nodding, Kate patted the top of Tracey's hand. "I understand. I've seen so many families in this same position, including mine, as you know. I will do everything I can to help make it easier on her and you."

Her heart went out to Tracey. She'd seen the pain and sadness of families as they slowly lost their loved ones to dementia. Her own grandfather had gone through the same thing, which had directed her choice of specialty as a nurse. Eventually, the loved ones' minds deteriorated so much that they were no longer bothered by their state, but that was when it became the hardest for the families—watching their loved ones live barely aware and not able to recognize or communicate with them as they waited, sometimes years, for them to pass.

Kate's long hair whipped around her face, and she shoved down her negative thoughts as she followed Tracey to the car. This was her opportunity to pour into the lives of others as they traversed the difficult path ahead. "Such a windy day," she called out, tightening her jacket.

"Oh, this is nothing. It picks up a bit in the winter months."

A flash of worry passed through Kate as she thought about the eighty-degree weather she had just left behind in Memphis. When she checked the weather forecast for Dover earlier, it said sixteen degrees. Granted, in Celsius, that meant something completely different, but with the wind and her light jacket, it didn't seem far off.

"Did you enjoy your stay in London yesterday?"

Before Kate could answer, the quaint Priory Hotel across the street caught her attention, and she was reminded of all the reasons she'd chosen to move to England. She snapped a picture.

Chuckling, Tracey spoke again. "You'll get used to it. Nearly everything around here is old compared to what you're used to in the U.S. That particular building is rather new by our standards. Late 1800s. Train travel really didn't become popular until then, and that's when this area built up. So . . . London? Did you enjoy your brief visit there?"

"Oh yes. It was amazing! I look forward to going back when I have more time and I'm past the jet lag. I took a hop-on hop-off bus, mostly staying on, then a water cruise on the Thames. I got a great overview of the city and probably took a hundred pictures. So many iconic buildings that I've only seen photos of—Big Ben, Tower Bridge, Shakespeare's Globe Theatre. I love all the old architecture." She'd always appreciated the historical aspects of her late 1920s home in Memphis, but even these "newer" buildings here held so much more history than the home she'd sold months before.

"And you were lucky. Yesterday was one of the rare sunny days." Tracey pointed. "My car's over there. Let's get your bags in the boot."

After loading the bags, Tracey walked up to the front left door and held it open while Kate continued towards the other side, only stopping herself when she saw the steering wheel.

"Oops! I forgot. This is going to take some getting used to."

Tracey chuckled. "We have a taxi service lined up for you to get around with, but with a little practice, you may feel up to driving the car soon."

"Hmm, we'll see." Kate tried to keep her expression neutral, but seriously doubted she would ever be willing to tackle driving on the left side of the road.

Once buckled in the car, she recognized it as the same type of Mercedes that her husband had wanted to buy weeks before his death. He'd just been promoted to a junior partner in his law firm and was looking for a status symbol, but she'd convinced him to wait until they could save some of the money. After all, junior partners didn't make *that* much.

She'd given in on their historically-preserved midtown home when the firm that had hired him straight out of law school offered to loan them the down payment. The house had left her with sticker shock, and if the firm hadn't paid off his law school loans, too, she would have said no to it.

Her husband had been a charmer, that's for sure, always talking her into something or other. It was why he had been such a good lawyer; he could convince people to believe almost anything. Financial issues were the one thing she could resist him on . . . sometimes. Glancing around, she silently agreed the car was an impressive piece of machinery, but was thankful she had stood her ground and hadn't been tasked with selling a barely-used Mercedes. It had been stressful enough finding the right buyer for their home.

"Kate? Are you okay?"

"What? Yes, sorry. Just remembering something my husband did a few weeks before his death."

Tracey glanced at Kate warily. "I'm just going to mention it this one time. I know you've asked me not to tell anyone about your husband's death. I get that you don't want to be faced with that constantly, and I won't tell a soul, but . . . if you ever need to talk, know that I'm here for you."

Working to hold back her frown, Kate nodded. She could tell that Tracey meant well, and truthfully, there may come a time when she would want to talk. She just couldn't imagine it being anytime soon. Maybe she shouldn't have mentioned her husband just then, but she wanted to be truthful and not seem like a flake staring off into the distance for no reason.

"On to business then." Tracey pulled out into the traffic. "Mum is at the cottage with Chloe, so now's the time if you have something you'd like to ask without her around. Her mind may be in and out, but she can still hear everything."

Smiling, Kate pictured Mrs. Corbyn listening in on their conversation.

Mrs. Margaret Corbyn, the patient, was an eighty-four-year-old widow in the early stages of dementia. As a registered nurse who had worked in a nursing home dementia unit for the last five years, Kate was mostly prepared for this job; however, this would be a new challenge since she'd be living with Mrs. Corbyn twenty-four hours a day. The family had managed Mrs. Corbyn's care on their own for several months since discovering her dementia, but it was too much with their busy schedules. Since they lived in London and Mrs. Corbyn desired to stay at her home on the Kingsdown coast in familiar surroundings to keep a sense of independence, this was the best solution.

Together with Kate, they had worked out a plan to allow Kate various breaks during the week, and the family would periodically come to town and help as well. All in all, it was a perfect situation for Kate. She would get time to see the country she'd dreamt about since reading her first Jane Austen book and be able to work while doing it. Both would be a good distraction from Mark's death. Several FaceTime chats with Mrs. Corbyn and Tracey had shown Mrs. Corbyn to be delightful and still very coherent with only occasional confusion. Tracey said that there had been a couple of evenings when she was more confused than normal, but that it was easily manageable. It was a challenge Kate was ready to take on.

There was barely time to discuss anything before they were in Kingsdown, rounding the corner of a little gravel coastal road. It was lined with homes and apartment buildings of varying sizes that Tracey explained were mostly built in the early 1900s.

Suddenly, the two-story whitewashed hip-roofed cottage she'd seen in the pictures Tracey sent was before them. Balconies lined the upper level, facing the English Channel, and a low brick fence enclosed the front yard.

Tracey pushed a button, and an iron gate slid open for the car. They pulled into an unattached garage. "Are you ready?" She gave Kate an encouraging smile.

"I am," was all that Kate could reply as she prepared to step into her new life.

Chapter Two

Before they had even grabbed Kate's bags, Mrs. Corbyn was at the door, waving them in. "Come through! Come through!" She looked like a much older, slightly withered version of Tracey and had a broad, welcoming smile. "Katie! It's so good to finally meet you!"

"It's Kate, Mum." Tracey appeared embarrassed.

"Oh, Katie's fine too." Kate glanced between the two women.

Mrs. Corbyn's brow rose and her hand flew to her cheek. "I'm sorry. Yes, Kate. I just . . . I had a friend named Katie growing up."

"No, really, Mrs. Corbyn, I'll answer to either."

"Margaret." Her smile returned, and she extended her hand. "Please, call me Margaret."

"Okay then. Margaret." The moment she stepped through the door, the smell of bacon and eggs hit her. "Smells delicious." According to the time on her phone when they arrived, it was almost 9:30 a.m., and her body was still so confused with the six-hour time difference that she felt famished.

"We've put together a full English breakfast for you," came another voice from further in. "Welcome, Kate. I'm Chloe." A beautiful woman with pale blond hair emerged from the direction of the delicious smells.

"It's great to meet you! You must be exhausted. Let me show you to your room upstairs so you can freshen up before eating."

"So good to finally meet you too!" Kate glanced at the stairs behind Chloe. "Actually, if you can just show me to the ladies' room?"

Chloe's head tilted and her brow rose.

"Toilet? Yes, it's right here, dear." Tracey pointed to a door under the stairs.

"We also call it the loo," Chloe added, "but you can call this a bathroom or washroom since it has a walk-in shower."

Kate shook her head. British English would require a bit of a learning curve.

Once she finished in the bathroom, she joined the ladies in the dining room. The English breakfast consisted of fried eggs, Irish bacon, sausage, black pudding, mushrooms, sautéed tomatoes, toast, baked beans, and English breakfast tea. Baked beans for breakfast seemed strange, and the black pudding scared her when she found out it was sliced and fried sausage with blood in it. She was determined to try some of everything and had both, though one small slice of the black pudding was all she forced down. It was good, but the thought of blood in her food was a little too unsettling.

Following breakfast, Chloe gave her a tour of the upstairs and showed her to her room, pointing out what had been Margaret's room across the hall. "With Gran's dementia came loss of balance, and she's been struggling with stairs lately. These past few months while we had her in London, we had the downstairs bathroom here remodeled and converted a downstairs study into her new room." She opened the door to Kate's room. "And this is you."

Kate's room was filled with antiques and looked perfectly cozy, but she was drawn to the picturesque view of the English Channel through the large window along the side wall.

As Kate peered out the window, Chloe dropped to the end of the bed and let out a sigh, causing Kate to turn from the window. "Are you okay?"

"I guess . . . not really. It's just hard . . . scary, all this going on with Gran. She's been the glue that held us all together forever, even when

Pop was still alive. She's the one we all turn to when things go wrong in our lives. She's one of the kindest, smartest, most well-spoken women I know, and it's strange when she forgets the simplest words. Like at our meal earlier, she forgot the name of the tea. It was English breakfast. How could she forget that? It's practically like forgetting her own name."

She wiped a tear and looked sideways at Kate, who had settled beside her. "I'm sorry. You've been through this too with your grandfather, right? How did you get through it?"

Thinking back to her own experience, Kate frowned. Walking Margaret's family through the process was going to be an important part of this job, both for Margaret's benefit and theirs.

"It was different for me. My grandfather had mid-stage Alzheimer's from the time I was young, so I never had an opportunity to develop much of a relationship with him. It was hard when he couldn't even remember who I was. But I did see how difficult it was for my mom. They had been close, and I know she felt like he had been taken from her long before he actually died. I don't know what to say other than to visit her every chance you get while she's still aware of who you are. It's so much harder to bear once they don't recognize you.

"But I'll also say that what you guys are doing by letting her have her autonomy and stay at a place that holds memories is good for her. It will help slow down the process. When people place their loved ones into aged-care homes too early, they typically have a rapid decline. This process can last for years or it can go quickly. Making sure she has good care and keeping her out of an institution for as long as possible is going to help all of you feel better."

Chloe smiled through her watery eyes and nodded. Once she was able to regroup, they continued their tour of the upstairs. In addition to Margaret's old room, there was a guest room where Chloe and her mom were staying for the weekend and an enormous bathroom. Chloe explained that there had been another bedroom and a tiny bathroom in its place, but the family remodeled it years ago. It now contained a claw-foot tub with a showerhead on a pole at one end and a curtain that could be pulled around it when using the shower. It also had a bidet next to the toilet. All of the fixtures looked antique and went well with the look of the cottage. Kate could envision herself in the dreamy room, taking a bubble bath surrounded by candles while reading a good book —probably *Pride and Prejudice.*

Just before Chloe led Kate back downstairs, Kate noticed another set of stairs going up. "Where do those stairs lead?"

"Oh, those. They're just to the attic. I mean, we can go up there if you want. It's certainly not off-limits, but there's nothing special in there."

"No, that's fine. We should get back down anyway. I'm sure your mom and grandmother are wondering if we've gotten lost."

Kate and Chloe joined the others to chat, and soon after, they served her cream tea—tea, scones, and clotted cream—during what they called "elevenses." The rest of the afternoon was spent walking along the pebble beach and through the neighborhood, then preparing "high tea" for the evening. The women insisted that being her first visit to England, Kate needed the full tea experience, and promised that they would take her for afternoon tea the following day to compare the three.

Kate felt like an outsider looking in, watching the three women work together in the kitchen with their easy conversation and loving respect for one another. It wasn't that they left her out. They constantly included her in both the conversations and the chores, but it was clear that they had a tight bond. That thought made Kate lament that her grandmother had died when she was young. She barely remembered her, but her mom spoke often about how close they had been, much like Kate and her mom were. The distance from her mom was probably the hardest thing about being so far from home.

With four women working together, it wasn't long before everything was ready. The high tea was less fancy than Kate had imagined, and when she asked about it, Tracey told her that afternoon tea was the kind with finger sandwiches and pastries that Americans often associated with an English tea. This high tea had heartier food and fell closer to the time that Kate considered dinner time. A spread of a ploughman's platter, shepherd's pie, and salad accompanied their tea. If she wasn't stuffed after that, the banoffee pie did her in. She decided it was worth it, though.

"I know we're going to be fast friends." Margaret reached over and squeezed Kate's hand.

A smile found its way to Kate's mouth. At least for now, she could feel like a part of this beautiful family with three generations of women. It would help distract her and ease the painful hole in her heart.

Chapter Three

"I can't wait until you make it back to London with Gran! The HOHO bus is nothing compared to a tour with me." Chloe hugged Kate goodbye as if they had known each other for years and not only a weekend.

Kate looked between Chloe, Tracey, and Margaret and nodded, unable to speak while feeling moisture fill her eyes. Where did that come from?

She'd come to England looking for an escape from what had become her new normal. She'd needed a distraction, but here she was only days in and finding so much more. Not only a grandmother of sorts, but Chloe, though eleven years older, felt like a sister. They had stayed up later than the others watching movies, giggling, and swapping stories. The shared experience of losing grandparents to dementia bonded them as well.

Clearing her throat, Kate managed to force words out. "I can't wait either. I'm looking forward to meeting those two boys of yours."

"And they'll be ecstatic to meet Aunt Katie." They both laughed, and Margaret just smiled. The name had stuck.

"Don't hesitate to ring me if you have any questions Mum can't answer." Tracey embraced Kate and leaned closer. "Or anything else you need to talk about."

"Thank you." Kate leaned back and looked Tracey in the eye. "I'm feeling much better about things." When Tracey raised her brow, Kate nodded and whispered, "Honestly. England seems to be the best medicine I've found for my broken heart."

"Good. That's as it should be, and I have to say, I'm feeling better about things too." Tracey's eyes moved to her mom. "I know she's in good hands, but . . . this is hard . . . leaving her to others and knowing this is only the beginning."

Kate nodded. She could see the sincerity of both thankfulness and concern in Tracey's eyes. The weekend had only confirmed the feeling she'd had since landing in London. This move was a good decision for her and for them.

"Katie? What should we do this evening?"

Kate's eyes followed the Mercedes as it vanished into the distance, then turned towards Margaret. "Take turns reading your book?"

Margaret reached forward and touched Kate's long hair. "Did you change your hair, Katie? I thought it was red."

"No, ma'am. My hair has always been brown. I keep these blond highlights in the front, though. I've been doing that since high school. Do you like it?" It was the dementia talking, and though Margaret knew of her illness, it was not always helpful to remind her of it. The conversation confirmed how important it was for her to be there with Margaret.

"Is Corbyn coming tomorrow to see me?"

"Corbyn?" Kate looked up from the book she'd been reading out loud and tried to process what Margaret meant. Margaret's last name was Corbyn. Did she mean her deceased husband, Graham Corbyn? Surely not. That would likely be one of the last things she'd forget.

"My grandson, Corbyn."

"Oh, right, sorry." Tracey, an only child, had named her son Corbyn to keep the family name going. Where was Kate's mind this evening? Maybe it was early-onset Alzheimer's like her grandfather. Although she knew how unlikely that was at the age of twenty-nine, sometimes being around people with dementia made her doubt her own memory. The fact that she'd not met Corbyn or spoken with him yet surely played a part in her forgetfulness. Also, she still associated the name Corbyn with the last name of Margaret and Tracey, who went by her maiden name for the sake of running the family business.

"Tracey said he's working at the Paris office and it will be a few weeks before he's back at the London one."

"He needs me. He's . . ." Margaret's brows furrowed, and Kate waited patiently for her to continue. "He's . . . sensitive."

"Sensitive?"

Margaret nodded her head.

It was an odd way to describe her grandson. Maybe that wasn't what Margaret meant. At some point, Kate was sure to meet him; then she could decide for herself.

"Let's tuck you in, shall we?" With the way Margaret's eyes drooped and her speech had slowed, Kate could tell that it was time for Margaret to call it a night.

"Your hair . . ." Margaret reached up and ran her fingers along the length of Kate's hair. "Different."

"Um." Kate touched her hair and recalled the earlier similar conversation. "Goodnight, Margaret." She smiled, then glanced to make sure the room monitor was on before shutting off the light and leaving. As she had hoped, Margaret instantly forgot about her hair.

After checking that all of the doors were locked, Kate set the alarm for downstairs only so she could go out on the upstairs balcony. With Margaret's dementia, it was just as important to make sure she didn't wander outside as it was to make sure someone unwanted didn't come in.

When Kate reached her room, she smiled at the view through the French doors. Digging through her things, she found the few books she'd brought. There was always the Kindle when she was ready for more. *Pride and Prejudice* lay at the top of the pile, and she chuckled recalling how Jennifer insisted the book travel with her to England. "After all," she'd said, "it's this book that started you on the road to England." It was in fact the very copy of the book her mother had given her in high school that piqued her interest in England.

"Sorry, Jane," she said softly and set the book aside. "I'm not quite ready for romance in my life again."

Truly, she wondered if she would ever feel like her heart was mended enough for that. Her collection of Sherlock Holmes stories caught her eye. Now that was more like it. Something to keep her mind busy, and set in London, no less. Maybe she'd pick up on some of the locations mentioned.

With the book, the monitor for Margaret, and the soft blanket from the chair in her room, she turned on the balcony light and settled into a rocker outside. The breeze from the Channel and the moon reflecting in the ripples of the water made it hard to open the book. The scene before her was mesmerizing. It seemed to pull the stress and sadness she'd tried to stifle for the past eight months to the surface. When her vision became blurry, she realized she was crying, which certainly wasn't the plan for the evening, yet somehow left her feeling lighter. It released some of her pain, but would it be enough?

"Maybe there really is something special about England," she spoke into the wind with hope.

Chapter Four

From her balcony, Kate viewed the perfect cloudless morning sky. It filled her with energy for all that lay ahead with her new job and home. She dressed and ate with anticipation while waiting until time to wake Margaret.

At eight a.m., Kate hurried to check on Margaret and get her ready for their day with Margaret's knitting group. Kate wasn't required to participate in Margaret's activities other than getting her there and back, but this first week, she planned to attend everything with her so that she could make connections with the other people in Margaret's life and see how she functioned in different situations. With that, she would be better equipped to make suggestions to help Margaret maximize her capabilities and give her friends a better understanding of how to help as well.

She had to admit, though, that today wasn't just work, and she was looking forward to learning the basics of knitting. Maybe she'd join Margaret there regularly.

By Wednesday, Kate agreed to let Margaret spend most of the day with two of her friends while Kate explored the area on her own.

Today, she planned to tour Walmer, a town just north of Kingsdown. It was the place to go shopping since Kingsdown had very few shops.

Kate couldn't stop grinning as she wandered around the winding streets with their mishmash of brick roads, asphalt, and pavers, along with the hodgepodge of one-, two-, and three-story shops all pressed tightly together. People may have thought her perpetual smile strange, but it was hard to stop smiling when she'd imagined doing something like this for years.

Each old building held so much character, unlike most of the carefully planned and uniformly designed buildings in many of the shopping centers around her old home. Different colored brick, beautiful wood trim, windows of various shapes and sizes, doors that drew one in —she loved it all. But if it weren't for her GPS, she would easily get lost. There was definitely no planning or organization to the layout of the roads.

The variety of shops intrigued Kate. The funniest sight was Claire's, the ubiquitous emporium of cheap jewelry found in strip malls across the U.S., here in a quaint little building situated alongside an adorable shop of upscale women's clothing.

She also discovered an exercise studio and signed up to take a class the following Wednesday, though she might need to fit in some other exercise before then. Especially considering the nearby bakery with the most wonderful treats had sent her off with a box of goodies and directions to a nearby pub. She was told the pub served the best food in the area.

As with most of the buildings, the pub had its own unique charm, and upon her entrance, the delicious smells settled any doubts she had about eating at a pub. The bar was packed with customers standing about, and she noticed many of the booths and tables were filled. Glancing around for someone to assist her, she was at a loss as to whether she should seat herself or wait to be seated. Finally, she caught the eye of a man who had just delivered food to a table.

"You look a bit confused, luv. Are you looking for someone?"

"Um." His term of endearment threw her. "I was told you had the best lunch in the area. Do I just seat myself?"

His eyes twinkled, and the side of his mouth curled up. "Ah. A yank. Have a seat." He pointed to a booth, then squeezed between the crowd at the bar before returning with a menu and laying it on the table, leaning against the bench opposite Kate.

"First time in a pub, luv?" She nodded slowly, still bewildered by the overly familiar language. "In most pubs, you order and pay for your food at the bar, then find a seat. Some snooty places that think their food is extra special and call themselves gastropubs will seat you, but they're just regular restaurants with a bar, if you ask me. I'm Aidan, owner of this fine establishment. Take a look at the menu and let me know if you have any questions, Miss . . ."

"Oh, Kate."

"Kate." He smiled. "Welcome. Just passing through, touring the area?"

"Actually, I just started working in Kingsdown."

"All the better. I hope you'll decide to make Rose and Crown your go-to lunch spot." He winked and began describing his favorite dishes.

She ordered the chicken tikka masala, which he raved about and she secretly found amusing. It never occurred to her that Indian food would be so popular in England, but this wasn't the first time that someone had raved about curry. She enjoyed it immensely, and when he suggested strawberry fool, she had to order the dessert just out of curiosity.

"You seem to like the strawberry fool, luv."

Kate looked up to find him watching her scrape the last bite of strawberries and cream from her bowl, and she felt her face heat. "You've caught me. It's delicious."

He leaned down. "I'll tell you a secret, luv. It's a splash of Grand Marnier that makes ours stand out."

Miming zipping her lips, Kate said, "Your secret's safe with me. I'm a fan and will certainly be back."

"Hopefully it isn't just the strawberry fool that brings you back next time." Aidan winked.

"I . . ." Kate blushed and looked down at the spoon that was still filled with the remains of her dessert.

"By the way, your meal's on me."

"Oh, no. I couldn't possibly—"

"I insist. It's not every day we get an American beauty like you living in the area. Seeing you return soon will be payment enough." The bartender waved Aidan over. "Excuse me, luv. Duty calls."

Kate watched as Aidan solved the bartender's problem, then mingled with the customers. Between the delicious food and the friendliness of the owner, she would definitely be back.

"What are you running from, Katie?"

"Hmm?" Kate looked up from the blanket she was knitting. Hers lacked the quality of work done by the more experienced women in the knitting group, but she felt more confident in her skills after practicing. Now that she knew the basics, she could help Margaret along when she got confused and needed help correcting a mistake.

"I know I don't always think straight anymore, but I can tell you're running from something . . . or someone." As Margaret looked at Kate, her eyes sparked with focus instead of the slightly confused look she often had this time of the evening.

Kate held her gaze while she decided how to respond. Her brow furrowed as she considered how much to share. Was she ready to face it so soon after leaving? "I . . ." She fiddled with the knitting needles. "I *have* left things behind, and it's not that I don't trust you, but . . . I just don't know if I'm ready to talk about it yet." Or fully face this new reality.

Margaret nodded and continued to knit. After a few minutes of silence, she spoke. "Have I told you about how Graham and I met?" She twisted the engagement and wedding rings on her left hand.

Kate swallowed the lump in her throat and shook her head. Was it possible Margaret guessed her problems had to do with a man, or was she just reminiscing?

"I can still remember the first time I saw him like it was yesterday. I was just seventeen." Margaret smiled dreamily, and Kate tried to imagine her as a young woman. "I had just moved to London with my dear friend Katie. I told you about Katie, right?"

"You've mentioned her." Kate smiled back.

"Yes, well, she's been my best friend since primary school. We both went to London for work directly after college and roomed in a flat together. We had so much fun." She stopped and looked at the blanket she was knitting. "Oh." She looked up at Kate and furrowed her brow.

"It's okay, we'll fix it." Kate reached across for the blanket and undid some of the last few stitches before handing it back.

"Thank you, dear." Margaret picked up her knitting, then laid it back down. "What were we talking about?"

"When you first met your husband."

"Oh yes. I first met him at his office. He was so handsome—the most handsome man I had ever seen. Did you know he was ten years older than me?"

Kate shook her head.

"He seemed so mature and polished. He interviewed me for my first job, and I became a secretary at his new publishing company." She sat up straighter, seeming energized. "I was a writer, you know, that's why I wanted to work at a publishing company. That night, I told Katie I'd met the man I would marry." She giggled almost like a little girl.

Kate couldn't help but be transported to the day she'd first met her own husband. She'd said almost the same thing to her best friend, Jennifer. While Kate sat in French class on the first day of spring semester her sophomore year, Mark walked in with one of the office assistants. After speaking with the teacher, he was introduced as a new student. She found him mesmerizing from the moment he entered the room, and she was sure that she'd never seen a man more beautiful. When he placed his things in the row just across the aisle and winked at her as he sat down, it took everything in her to keep from sighing out loud.

What made her day, though, was when he asked her name once the bell rang. It was a miracle that she could walk to her next class, and she might not have if it weren't for Jennifer finding her and walking with her. That was when Kate announced to her friend that she had found the man she wanted to marry, not truly believing it would ever become a reality.

"And we were married when I was nineteen. He was twenty-nine. I had a hard time believing he had been single for that long. God had saved him for me." Margaret had a faraway look, and Kate felt guilty for zoning out so long. Thankfully, Margaret didn't appear to notice. She had started knitting again; the stitches were quite messy, but Kate knew that came with the territory as her memory declined.

Kate smiled at her companion. Every day, the pain she'd left in Tennessee seemed a little further away.

Chapter Five

Wiping sweat from her face with the long-sleeved shirt she'd removed halfway through her beach run, Kate slowed and approached the gate to the house.

"Are you renting Mrs. Corbyn's place?" a voice called from the porch of the house next door. Kate had not seen anyone there in the two weeks since she'd arrived in Kingsdown. "I haven't seen her in months. Has she given up the place?"

Kate changed directions as the man descended his stairs. "No, she was staying with family the past few months. I'm her live-in nurse." At that, his brow drew up. "She has dementia," she explained.

"I had no idea. She's said odd things here and there, but knowing she was getting up in years, I didn't think much of it." He held out a hand. "Kieran Davies. This is my place, but I'm mostly in London for work and have a flat there."

Kate wiped her sweaty hand on her shorts. "Kate Thomas."

"Kate." He smiled and was slow to release her hand. "You're from the U.S.?"

She nodded and chuckled. "The accent always gives me away."

"I imagine. Care to join me on the porch? I can get you a bottle of water, juice . . . I have some bottled smoothies, or even a lager if you're up for it."

"I, uh . . ." She glanced at her watch.

He held up his hands. "I won't bite, I promise. I'm just being neighborly."

"Okay, yes, I'll have a water. I just can't stay long since I need to do some things before Margaret gets back."

He nodded and disappeared into the house while she found a seat on his porch.

"So what's going on with Mrs. Corbyn?"

After she explained her job, he told her about his own as an app developer. It required him to travel some, and he mostly worked out of London for meetings and convenience to the airport. But when his schedule was clear, he liked to work from his Kingsdown home.

Aware of a chill from the breeze, Kate reached to pull her shirt back over her tank and noticed the time. "I'm sorry, but I really should get going. It was so nice to meet you."

"I assure you, the pleasure is all mine." He stood as she did and shook her hand, his grip lingering. "Since I'll be in for the weekend, you and Mrs. Corbyn should join me for dinner tomorrow evening."

"That sounds wonderful, but Tracey and Chloe will be in town as well, and I couldn't possibly expect you to cook a meal for all four of us."

"Nonsense." Kieran smiled easily. "I was thinking of grilling seafood, tossing some potatoes in the oven, and rounding it out with a salad. Nothing could be simpler."

Kate tried to get a read on his sincerity, but it was difficult with someone she'd met only twenty minutes earlier. "If you're sure then. We won't be too boring for you?" He didn't look much older than she was, and she couldn't imagine that he wanted to spend his evening with four women who were not dating material. She certainly knew she wasn't, and the only other single woman was eighty-four.

"Absolutely." His smile seemed sincere.

"Maybe I can get the girls to go out to Walmer, and we can pick up desserts from the bakery."

"Sounds perfect."

"You're a lucky woman to have caught Kieran's eye!" Chloe giggled, seeming younger than her forty years. "He's so-o-o good-looking!"

Kate's eyes widened. "I don't think that's what it is. He was just being neighborly." She found herself repeating his words. Surely that was all it was. She tried to think back to her time with him. Admittedly, he was good-looking, but she felt nothing and couldn't imagine that part of her heart stirring for a long, long time. "Anyway, you're married."

"Yes, but I'm not blind. I'm just saying, it's great for you. He's quite the catch. Did you know he developed some app that he sold for millions at the age of twenty-four? He could live off his investments, but keeps working because he's just that brilliant."

"And maybe a little cocky if he told you all that."

"Actually, it was all over the news. He's a really down-to-earth guy." Chloe studied Kate. "You've met him. Wouldn't you agree?"

After she shrugged, Kate nodded. "I guess you're right. We didn't speak long, but he didn't come across as the bragging type." She smiled but was hopeful things wouldn't become awkward with Kieran. He did seem like a nice guy.

Throughout the evening at Kieran's place, Chloe played matchmaker. Kate appreciated the thought, but without explaining her situation, she didn't know how to make Chloe see it was an impossibility. Several times, Tracey looked on, clearly feeling bad about it.

Kieran was the perfect host, and Kate could see he would be a good friend to have in the area, making it even harder. She didn't want to rebuff him completely, and what if he really was only trying to be neighborly?

The women insisted on cleaning up after the meal, and Kieran pulled Kate aside to give her his number if she ever might need it. "When you're in London, be sure to contact me. I'd love to take you out to one of my favorite restaurants," Kieran offered as he entered his number into Kate's phone.

Should she say something? And what would she say without sounding presumptuous and ungrateful after he had just opened his home to them and been so thoughtful? "How kind of you." Perhaps she could wait to cross that bridge once she came to it.

"Oh, he's such a dear. Reminds me of my Graham."

Margaret's voice carried from the kitchen, and Kate locked eyes with Kieran and chuckled. "You've certainly made her day."

"Hopefully yours as well."

A strange feeling settled inside, and Kate hesitated to respond.

"I'm sorry, that was too forward of me. You've only just met me this weekend. I would like to get to know you better, though."

Kate smiled dolefully, wishing he had not said more and knowing she would have to explain herself. "I've only recently gotten out of a . . . very serious relationship." She wasn't ready to be tagged as a widow. Was it bad that she didn't share that information with a man she barely knew?

"I get it. No worries. My offer still stands when you're in London, though. I imagine you can use a friend."

In theory, it had seemed so simple to leave America and all her pain behind, yet she had the feeling she would need to work through it sooner than she imagined. It felt as if part of her died soon after her husband, yet how did the hurt continue to resurface if that part was dead? And why did a man looking at her and talking to her about his desire for more than friendship send her into a tailspin?

Chapter Six

"You look tired," commented Kate's new friend Hayley as they left their exercise class.

"Thanks a lot. With friends like you, who needs enemies?" Kate crossed her arms and gave a little smirk.

"Kate! I didn't say it to hurt your feelings. You just don't look like yourself. Is everything okay?"

"Yep. I'll be fine. I've not been sleeping well. Probably still having a hard time adjusting to the huge time difference."

"After nearly three weeks? That doesn't sound normal. Maybe you need to go to this herbal place not far from here. They make all kinds of tinctures and teas that can do wonders. I bet they have something that will help you sleep."

Kate rolled her eyes. She loved hanging out with Hayley, but she was a bit of a hippie, and Kate questioned her judgment on certain things. "Don't worry. I'm sure it will get better soon." The real issue was her heart problem. Ever since turning down Kieran, she'd been troubled. Not because she felt bad about turning him down, but because of the reminder of why she had to. She hoped that internal tension would fade.

After they freshened up, she took Hayley to the Rose and Crown, where Aidan treated them like queens. It was a welcome distraction.

Hayley had an infatuation with Aidan and said that she stopped by there regularly since she worked at the coffee shop just around the corner.

"This is the most I've ever spoken to him." Hayley wriggled excitedly in her seat. "Usually he's all business. You should come this weekend to hear one of the bands they have playing. There is a different one every Friday and Saturday night."

"I'll have to pass this weekend because neither Chloe nor Tracey can come to stay with Margaret. I can go next week though. Do they do it every weekend?"

"They do, but that's got to stink—not getting to go out at night."

"I'm really fine with it." Having been married since the age of twenty-two, she had been out of that scene for a while. In fact, the only late-night thing she'd done in years was going to events at the country club and posh hotels where they would see other couples from her husband's law firm or schmooze with local politicians. It was quite different from hanging out at pubs and listening to bands.

Hayley made a face. "Just because you live with an old lady doesn't mean you have to act like one."

"Hey now."

"Keep hanging with me, and I'll help you break out of your doldrums. I have a feeling there's something wild inside of you waiting to break out, Kate Thomas."

Kate covered her mouth, trying to hold back laughter. "You definitely stretch me, Hayley." She could tell Hayley would keep things interesting and help distract her from other thoughts.

"Somebody's got to, Miss America."

"Miss America?" Aidan drew closer after dropping plates off at the booth next to them. "I can see that."

Kate shook her head. Hayley had taken to calling her Miss America since she was from the U.S. "You two are funny. Pageants are definitely not my thing."

"I'm trying to get Miss America to join me here this weekend for the live music."

"She's right, come. You'll get a taste of the local sound. You're from

Tennessee, right? Country music? This is different, but I think you'll like it. Most bands we host have a Celtic flair."

"I do like Celtic music, but I told Hayley I'll have to wait another week to come. I have to help with Margaret this weekend. By the way" —Kate placed a hand on her hip—"Memphis, the part of Tennessee where I'm from, is known as the home of the blues and the birthplace of rock 'n' roll. You know, Elvis? Country is in Nashville. Not my thing."

"I stand corrected. I guess Tennessee is just full of musicians . . . and also Jack Daniel's. We sell that here if you need a taste of home."

"Not my thing either, but thanks." Kate chuckled.

"Music and alcohol aside, you work too much if you can't get away for a weekend evening. Doesn't she, Aidan?" Hayley huffed, but her eyes sparkled. "Seriously, though, I hate that you can't come this weekend. I don't know how you do it."

"It's not too much. I'm here with you, aren't I? Most weekends, they plan for someone to be with her to relieve me. This is just not one of those weekends. I'll be fine, I promise."

Warm sun on her face, breeze blowing, and pebbly sand between her toes, Kate momentarily closed her eyes and imagined her life was different, with no pain from her husband to dampen the future. A sharp rock underfoot brought her back to reality, and her eyes caught onto Kieran's home.

She didn't know if Kieran would be back in town this weekend, but this same time the week before, he had stopped her for a chat. Though he seemed like a nice guy, something about him bothered her. He reminded her too much of her husband with his flashy car, his talk of clubs, golf, and tennis, his impeccable taste in clothes—and even his home. It was a fine example of history on the outside, yet the inside exemplified modern perfection. It all pointed to a lifestyle focused on money, and that had become a point of contention between Kate and her husband, who constantly lived beyond their means.

Why couldn't she separate things in her mind? She should have the maturity to be a friend to a man and not stress over the fact that he invited her out.

"Katie, you've not been acting like yourself. You can talk to me, you know." Margaret moved closer to Kate.

"Oh, I just stepped on a rock." Kate reached down and rubbed her foot.

"No, not that. It's been days. I may be an old woman who's not always in my right mind, but I see things. I see you're in pain, and I'm not speaking about the rock you stepped on."

How did a woman with dementia have the ability to read minds? If Kate answered her, would Margaret say something to others? Sometimes Margaret forgot what was appropriate or confused parts of what she'd heard. She might forget if Kate asked her not to speak about it to others. "You're right. There is something. I just don't feel ready to open up about it yet."

"I can understand that." Margaret stopped and seemed ponder. "Tell me, Katie, are you a born-again Christian?"

Kate glanced sideways at Margaret, wondering if she was having one of her episodes with the sudden subject change.

"I do know what I'm saying right now." Margaret raised a withered brow.

"Yes, of course. I was born a Christian." That's just the way things were in the South where she was from. Most people she knew back in the Memphis area considered themselves Christians.

Margaret blinked at her twice, then averted her gaze. "I see."

"What do you see?" Surely Margaret wasn't thinking straight.

Coming to a stop, Margaret placed a hand on Kate's arm. "No one is born a Christian."

"What? But you asked me if I was a born-again Christian. Isn't that what you meant? I attended church quite a lot as a child, though not as much since high school," she added softly.

"It's okay, dear. I'm not the one you need to talk to about it."

Kate waited for her to go on, only to notice her pointing up at the sky. "I need to pray?"

"Yes, talk to God about it. That's what prayer is, you know."

"Well, yes, I guess I do know. What should I talk to him about?" This conversation was getting stranger by the minute, and she hadn't prayed since she was a child. Prayer was mostly for preachers, wasn't it?

"If you have excuses for not going to church, you need to talk to him about it, but that's not the point. The point is that you need to know what a Christian is."

Thinking back to her time at church, Kate tried to recall what she'd learned. "I need to believe that he's God and that he loves the world and saves the Christians so we can go to heaven when we die." There was something more she couldn't quite recall. "Oh, and for some reason, he sent Jesus, who was perfect, to die for us on a cross. To show us how much he loves us, maybe?" Though when she thought about it, that seemed kind of extreme.

"Hmm." Margaret tilted her head and studied Kate. "How does sin fit into that?"

"That's right, I knew I was forgetting something. We're all sinners and have to do our best not to sin too much so we can get into heaven." Kate watched as Margaret's brow furrowed. How was this old woman with dementia making her feel like she didn't have a clue? She was born in the "Bible Belt" after all, where a church sat on practically every corner. From what she'd seen in England, churches were few. Did this eighty-four-year-old woman think she could school her about church?

"I think it's time for tea."

Was Margaret serious? Kate felt sure that Margaret's dementia was causing issues today. "Yes, we can head back for tea."

Margaret nodded.

By the time the tea brewed and they sat, Kate felt confident the God talk was forgotten, and she breathed a sigh of relief. Not that she didn't believe in God; she just didn't see the purpose in talking about him, especially considering the events of the past year of her life. The last time she heard a pastor talk about God was at her husband's funeral, and that was not a happy memory.

When she filled out the initial form for this job, it had a box to mark if she was a Christian, so of course she did. If Margaret liked to talk about God, Kate would make the best of it.

"So, sin . . ."

Kate's eyes went wide. How was it possible for Margaret to remember what they were speaking about fifteen minutes earlier? In her observations over the past three weeks, Margaret sometimes remembered facts she was told, but she'd not continued a conversation after such a long interval. "Yes?" She was curious if it was a continuation of the same conversation.

"Even our smallest sin—well, small in our eyes—keeps us separated from God and unable to go to heaven. We can never be good enough. It's not something we can earn."

Wow, she *was* still talking about the same thing. But what on earth could she mean? "I don't understand. If we can never be good enough, then how does anyone get to heaven?"

"Precisely!" Margaret lifted her teacup and slowly took a sip.

Kate wanted her to explain and hoped she hadn't forgotten what they were talking about.

"Jesus. That's where he fits in. He is God in human form, perfect. His death wasn't just a stunt to get people's attention. It was the price for our sin. We all deserve to die. Like when you disobey a law and are supposed to have some predetermined punishment. Death is the price for sin, so God made a way for us to avoid eternal death by substituting Jesus for us. Only he who was perfect and sinless could pay for our lives with his own."

Jesus was a substitute? It all sounded so different from what she remembered as a child. Was it possible she had misunderstood things all these years? It piqued her curiosity, but maybe after she slept on it, she'd realize it was just a lot of rambling from an old woman. "But everyone dies."

"Our earthly bodies die, but our souls continue, and at the end of this world, we get new bodies, and there will be a new earth without sin and brokenness. We can live forever, but those who haven't accepted Jesus are thrown into the fiery pit of hell and separated from God for all eternity."

"Um." The conversation was getting morbid, yet Kate was still curious. She wondered what she could do to ensure she had a chance at that forever life if it did exist. "I'll try to go to church with you most Sundays. I just wasn't up for it last weekend. I plan to go this week." Church attendance might please this God that Margaret spoke about, if he was real. It had been so long since she'd attended regularly. The previous Sunday, she had told the ladies she had a headache to avoid church. Maybe lying wasn't the best idea. Would God hold it against her?

Why was she even letting this bother her? It seemed obvious that God didn't care what his creation did or what their lives were like. What if God was just a fairytale Margaret and others told themselves in hopes of something better? The reality was that bad things happened. Why would it be any different when they died? Since her husband's death, sometimes dying actually seemed preferable to living.

Margaret smiled. "That's a start."

Just as Kate grew tired of the conversation and began feeling edgy, Margaret started talking about her garden. Beautiful blooms of all kinds filled it. Margaret liked to clip the flowers and set them in vases around the house, yet she couldn't keep it up like she used to, so the lawn service helped her with that. It was getting a little unkempt, but Kate didn't dare attempt to do anything with it lest she kill all the plants with her black thumb.

As Margaret appeared to fall asleep, Kate quietly removed their tea things and slipped into the kitchen to tidy up. When she returned, Margaret was awake, reading something she had written in her little notebook. Kate had helped her make sections where she could write things she wanted to remember. There was a section called "New people," one called "Things to remember," and Margaret had insisted on one called "Prayer." Kate wondered what Margaret was reading but didn't dare peek at it. That would be like looking into someone's diary, which wouldn't be right.

Margaret looked up and gave her a sad smile. What must it be like to know that you were slowly losing your memories and ability to process thoughts?

"Margaret, what would you like for dinner?" Kate gently reached for her hand to guide her into the kitchen, and Margaret's smile brightened.

"Thank you, dear. You . . ." Margaret stopped mid-sentence.

"Would you like me to show you what I was thinking about making?" She pointed to the pantry, and Margaret nodded.

The simplicity of the evening was satisfying, but their conversation about God stirred both confusion and questions in Kate.

Chapter Seven

Kate punched in the alarm code before turning to Margaret and guiding her out to the car. For their Saturday activities, she planned to take Margaret to Walmer, now that she was becoming familiar with it. She even discovered that Walmer Castle had a lovely garden and tea room, both of which Margaret would enjoy. As they backed out of the driveway, Kate's gaze drifted to Kieran's home, and she wondered what he was doing this weekend since he had not returned. A pang of remorse hit her, yet she knew it was best that she didn't lead him on.

"That Mr. Davies seems like a very nice man. He's had that home for several years and has always been a kind and considerate neighbor." Margaret smiled at Kate.

Kate's mouth curved into a smile. "I can see that about him." She looked ahead at the road but could see Margaret still watching her in her peripheral vision.

"And he's a nice-looking man too. Quite the catch."

"That's exactly what Chloe said. Are you playing matchmaker, Margaret?"

"Who, me?" She shook with mirth.

"Are you comfortable, Margaret?" Kate placed Margaret's feet on a small footrest and arranged the blanket on her lap. The Walmer trip had left Margaret exhausted.

"I'm fine, dear. Just needed a sit-down."

"We've had a busy morning. I'm going to run upstairs and get a book to read, then I'll be right back down to join you."

"Very nice. I'll be here resting my eyes."

Margaret appeared to be drifting off already as Kate turned away. Once upstairs, she stopped first in the bathroom, but then movement in the backyard garden caught her eye. Drawing closer to the window, she saw a man trimming the plants. He wasn't someone she recognized from the lawn service. They always called ahead and wore blue shirts with the name of their company. She'd not received a call, and this man had no shirt.

She couldn't tear her eyes away as his tanned, well-muscled arms and back flexed with his work. When he turned to lay the trimmings to the side, she caught a glimpse of his angular face and square jaw. He stopped and wiped his brow with his arm, pushing dark blond hair away from his face. Kate continued to stare, unable to move away. His face lifted, and his eyes moved towards the second floor of the cottage. She jumped back from the window with a gasp.

Gathering her thoughts, she decided to confront this stranger in the yard. Quickly, she descended the stairs and peeked in on Margaret before hurrying out the back door.

At the sight of the man, Kate froze on the porch. "Ahem." She tried to get words out. "Excuse me . . . sir?" He didn't respond, so she moved off of the porch and approached him. "Sir?"

As the man turned, his blue eyes found hers, and a smile formed on his lips. He was the most beautiful man Kate had ever seen.

"Um, excuse me, sir. Who—" As she spoke, he laid his tools down and pulled out earpods.

"You must be Kate." He smiled broadly. "I'm Declan." He reached out his hand, then examined and withdrew it. "Sorry. I'm sure you don't want to shake my hand in this state."

For some reason, she didn't feel bothered by the dirt and would have been happy to shake hands. The accent alone sent her heart racing. "Um . . ." Her mouth didn't work properly now that she was face to face with this man named Declan.

"I'll take a break and come chat with you ladies."

"Wh—" Before she could get a word out, he slipped on a gray t-shirt and walked into the house. Kate hurried to follow him in and found him embracing Margaret. She was relieved to see Margaret knew him, since she had ineffectively prevented someone she believed to be a stranger from entering.

"Let me look at you. It's been too long," Margaret announced as Declan stood back and she scanned his face adoringly. "Katie, dear, you've met this handsome man?"

"Um." Her eyes moved between Margaret and Declan. "Just now, he introduced himself outside. I found him working in your garden."

Margaret smiled and reached up to pat Declan's arm. "Ah yes, he's so good at that. What would I do without him? You look like you need a cool drink, dear. Go get something and come back to sit with me."

"Yes ma'am. I need to wash up, and I'll get you some water too." Declan turned towards the kitchen. "Kate, would you care for something?" he called back.

"Um." Why couldn't she get out a sentence without starting with "um"? "Actually, I would love some water. D-do you need some help finding things in the kitchen?"

"I've got it. I know my way around in here."

"Oh okay." Who was this guy, and why, after months of lifelessness, was her heart about to beat out of her chest? Kieran, a good-looking and wealthy man, had asked her out just a week ago, yet she couldn't get away from him fast enough. How did she go from that to this so quickly? Men were not on her agenda when she left for England, despite Jennifer's encouragement. She needed to shut these feelings down. It could only end in disaster with her emotions so unstable, and she should know better than to be drawn in by a man's looks.

Hopefully, this guy wouldn't stay long. He was making her uncomfortable in a completely different way than Kieran.

"So how are you adjusting to England and your new job, Kate?" Declan settled into a seat directly across from her.

"I'm starting to learn my way around and have even gotten used to driving on the wrong side of the road." It felt awkward sharing with a stranger, handsome or not.

Declan chuckled. "I have to drive on the wrong side in many countries, and it does play with your mind. So this lovely woman is treating you well?" He reached across to pat Margaret's hand.

"Of course. You garden for a living?" Her face heated as she recalled him standing outside shirtless. She felt like a schoolgirl who hoped her crush didn't guess her thoughts.

Both Margaret and Declan laughed. He glanced at Margaret before speaking. "Actually, I work for the company, Corbyn Publishing. The only gardening I do is for this special lady."

"Oh, I-I'm sorry." Kate's brows knit as she wondered if he took offense, though he'd laughed it off. He looked like an outdoorsy type, so she thought he could have been a gardener.

"I do enjoy it, but don't have as much time as I'd like. What about you? Do you have a green thumb?" Declan raised a brow.

"No, definitely not. It seems that every plant I touch dies." She could feel the heat rising to her cheeks again as Declan held her gaze.

"Then by all means, leave the garden to me. We wouldn't want anything to happen to the plants." One side of his mouth lifted. "So, where would you ladies like to go to dinner? My treat."

Kate looked at Margaret, silently questioning if they should go to dinner with Declan. She'd hoped he would be on his way out by now, and dinner was still a couple of hours away. This was becoming dangerous for her emotional health.

"You should surprise us, dear. You're always so good at finding the best places." Margaret leaned towards Declan.

"Great. I'll leave you ladies to yourselves then while I finish up outside. It shouldn't take much longer than an hour, then I can pop into the shower and we'll be off."

"Wonderful!" Margaret clapped her hands. "How long will you be able to stay with us this time?"

"Through tomorrow afternoon. I've got to get back to the Paris office for a Monday morning meeting."

Kate tried to hide her shock and pasted on a smile though her insides swam. Thankfully, Declan was out the door before he could notice what was likely a grimace. *This time?* It seemed that Declan visited Margaret's home regularly. Why did it simultaneously make her heart soar and her stomach plummet?

Sitting in church, trying to keep from falling asleep, Kate recalled the dream that had woken her in the night. It began with Mark picking her up for their first date when she was a high school sophomore. He took her to the Asian and French-inspired seafood restaurant in midtown Memphis. She could almost taste the roasted sea bass. Somewhere between sea bass and crème brûlée, Mark morphed into Declan, and Declan was the one who drove her home and gave her that first kiss. The dream kiss had startled her awake and caused her mind to swirl in confusion. Meanwhile, the man disturbing her thoughts slept down the hall.

As they had prepared to leave for church that morning, Kate could hardly glance in Declan's direction without the memory of the dream kiss coloring her cheeks. She'd wondered if he could sense her thoughts when he looked her way. Thankfully, Declan currently sat two seats away, on the other side of Margaret. At least she had this reprieve during church when she didn't have to face him. Lunch, however, might prove more difficult.

All too soon, the pastor said the closing prayer and dismissed the congregation. As they passed him on the way out, he stopped Declan. "So good to see you, Corbyn. How have you been?"

Everything else the pastor said faded into the background as Kate tried to comprehend the pastor's greeting. This was Corbyn? Margaret's grandson? Chloe's brother? She'd imagined Corbyn to be older than Chloe, who was forty. Hadn't Chloe mentioned he was older? She'd spoken about what a protective brother he was, and how he had stepped up to help with Margaret since her husband's death. But this man, Declan, couldn't be much older than she was, if at all.

Without even registering what was happening, she had shaken the pastor's hand, nodded at him in answer to some question, and they were in the car.

"Kate, are you okay?" Declan looked back at her from the driver's seat.

"Corbyn?" That was all Kate could bring herself to say.

"Yes?"

"You're Corbyn?"

He looked at her in confusion and nodded.

"Why did you tell me to call you Declan?"

His worried look morphed into amusement. "Sorry, it's just my family and business associates who call me Corbyn. It's my middle name. To everyone else, except the pastor, I'm Declan, and that's how I introduce myself."

Kate was at a loss for words. Clearly, she wasn't family.

As if reading her mind, he answered her thoughts. "It's nothing personal. My family likes to call me Corbyn for the sake of the company, to carry on the family name. It's the same reason my mom uses her maiden name. As the head of the company, it helps keep the fact that it's family-owned at the forefront of people's minds, but when I'm outside the office, I prefer to be Declan, an everyday guy, not the corporate executive of Corbyn Publishing."

"Oh . . . I see." She did, but it sounded so foreign. He was second in charge at one of the top publishing companies. She was used to people reveling in the power and respect that came with a well-known name, yet he intentionally avoided that. Now it was for a different reason that she asked herself, *Who is this man?*

Over lunch, she looked at him with fresh eyes. Respect overpowered the embarrassment of her dream yet heightened her feelings of attraction to him. Ironically, the thing he hid from people outside of work revealed his humility and made her more interested in him. She longed to know more about what made this man tick but scarcely knew what to ask without seeming impertinent.

Throughout his visit, he was the perfect gentleman with both Margaret and Kate, and the way he cared for his grandmother said a lot about his character—and yes, the accent made him seem like Mr. Darcy incarnate. If Jennifer were here, she would say, "I told you so." Kate held back a chuckle with a fake cough into her hand as she anticipated her next conversation with Jennifer.

Later, when Declan had gathered his things to leave, he shook Kate's hand. Her eyes landed on their hands, and she wondered how and why her heart fluttered.

"Call me if you need anything. I'll try to be here on weekends when Mum or Chloe can't."

"Thank you, Declan. I do appreciate that."

He turned and hugged Margaret. "Gran, I love you."

"I know, dear. Next time, bring the lovely Alexandra."

"I'll try. She wanted to come but had too much on her plate this weekend."

Once he'd gone and they had settled in the sitting room, Kate turned to Margaret. Before making assumptions, she had to know. "Who is Alexandra?"

"Alexandra? Oh, she's beautiful. She's Corbyn's fiancée."

Kate froze, thankful she was seated. "Fiancée?"

"Yes. They've been friends since primary school. Isn't that sweet? She's a writer but also works at Corbyn Publishing. They remind me so much of me and Graham when we were younger." Margaret sighed and closed her eyes.

Kate forced a smile. "How nice for both of them." With her clouded mind, she hardly knew what either of them said for the rest of the evening.

After finally shutting herself in her bedroom that night, she threw her hands to her face and let out a muffled "Gah-h-h!" then flung herself on the bed. "Kate, you are so stupid! How could you fawn all over a guy you barely know? Of course he's taken." What had she been thinking? Clearly, she hadn't been thinking at all. "So embarrassing!"

Could she have been any more obvious with all the tripping over her words and ogling him for the past two days? All these months, she'd felt nothing for a man, then decided to let her mind wander with a man who was completely unavailable. *But he's so dreamy! And so kind, and humble . . . and so perfect for someone named Alexandra.* Her hands flew to her face again.

She had to snap out of this quickly. She barely knew the guy. It could be weeks or months before she saw him again. Why was she even entertaining these thoughts when she had turned down the perfectly nice and handsome Kieran last week? What was wrong with her? She was doing just fine before she met Declan. She didn't have an interest in any relationship two days ago. Determination had brought her this far, and it could get her past this too.

Chapter Eight

"**S**o the totally hot guy that you're interested in turns out to be engaged?" Hayley asked for confirmation as they walked to the Rose and Crown.

When Kate nodded and blew out a breath, Hayley forged on. "Well then, you just need to find another distraction!" She wiggled her eyebrows.

"I'm really not in a hurry to date." *Maybe won't ever be ready for another relationship.*

Their usual booth was open, and Kate began to think Aidan purposely saved it for them every Wednesday to use after their exercise class.

"How are you two lovely ladies?" Aidan was by their side before they were fully seated.

Kate offered the usual pleasantries. "Fine, thank you."

"Liar." Hayley shook her head. "She needs a date."

Aidan's eyes widened. "Somewhere in particular?" He looked from Hayley to Kate while Kate's eyes shot daggers at Hayley across the table.

"No, just in general. She needs a man to ask her out."

Kate's face reddened, and she looked everywhere except at Aidan.

"Well, that's perfect then. I know just the person." He smiled at Hayley while Kate stayed silent.

"Great! Is it someone she's met?"

"Of course. Me." Turning to Kate, he tried to get her attention as her eyes flew up to his before landing on Hayley. "Kate, luv, I'd planned to ask you out soon. Hayley here just gave me the kick I needed."

Kate furrowed her brow, and she started to open her mouth.

"I'm sure she'd love to, Aidan. Give me your phone, and I'll give you her details. I think she's too happy for words."

Aidan handed over his phone with a wide grin before excusing himself to take care of some business. Meanwhile, Kate shot lasers across the table with her eyes.

"Hayley! What are you doing? You totally have a crush on him. I'm not going to date him." Kate folded her arms.

"Yes, you are. He is so into you, and I've been able to tell that from the first time we were in here together. He's never shown much interest in me. Just because I think he's cute doesn't mean I'm going to keep both him and you from something that could be wonderful."

"Hayley, that's breaking the girl code. I am not going to ruin my relationship with you, my only real friend here, just so I can test the waters with a guy."

"While I appreciate the sentiment, we're not teenagers, and I think I can handle it." When Kate shook her head and started to speak, Hayley threw up her hand. "I don't want to hear it. It will not bother me one bit. What will bother me is if you turn down that nice guy over there and hurt his feelings."

Kate followed Hayley's gaze, and Aidan smiled. "Ugh. Hayley . . . you're putting me in a tight spot."

"I don't know about that. You seem to have plenty of room." Hayley tilted her head and looked across the booth, grinning. "Hopefully I've made you see reason."

By the time they left, Kate had a date for the next night and was a nervous wreck. After she agreed, it occurred to her that this would be her first date in fifteen years. Not only that, but she'd only ever had one first date, and it was with her husband. What was she thinking? The one thing that eased her mind was that she had to return to the cottage by seven thirty p.m. before Margaret got back from her church event.

"I have a date . . . with a guy named Aidan," Kate confessed to Margaret over dinner that night.

"That's nice, dear." Margaret's unfocused gaze confirmed that she had hit that point in the day where she couldn't quite comprehend what was being said or what was happening around her. Normally, she would have been more interested.

Kate's nerves were frayed. She was glad the date was the very next day, or she might chicken out. Her first date with Mark had been as a teenager, and she had no idea what to expect on a first date as an adult. She'd wanted to talk about how nervous the upcoming date made her, but that wouldn't be possible in Margaret's current state.

At times like this, she felt sadness for each moment that Margaret's family missed out on. Kate's plan to take her to London for the weekend somewhat assuaged her heavy heart. It wasn't as if the family hadn't tried to have Margaret in London and avoid this situation, but Margaret had made them all feel guilty for keeping her from her home. She'd told them it held her last memories with her husband. In the end, Margaret got her wish, but it had its drawbacks.

This London visit held much more promise than Kate's one night and HOHO bus tour weeks before. From the moment she arrived at Tracey's lavish historical Belgravia townhome, she felt welcome. Tracey's husband joined them, as well as Chloe and her husband and teen boys. Everyone planned to stay at the enormous townhome for the weekend to maximize their time with Margaret.

The home sat in an amazing location near several beautiful parks. If it wasn't for the lack of land around the home itself, the building would have seemed more like a country estate. It had been in the Corbyn family for one hundred and fifty years. With her American sensibilities, Kate could hardly fathom a home that old, especially since it was so well-maintained. Though originally built in the 1820s, the six-bedroom home had been updated with all the latest amenities. They had even modernized the inside of the mews house behind it. Comparable to an American carriage house above a garage, the mews house added another apartment to the family's property.

With the five floors plus a terrace at the main house, Kate imagined they were thankful for the elevator Margaret and Graham had added years ago. They'd even added a sauna and hot tub that Chloe and Kate planned to enjoy over the weekend.

After dinner the first night, Chloe insisted that Kate join her and unwind in the hot tub. Her recent date with Aidan became the topic of conversation. "So what's this Aidan guy like?" Chloe asked as she sank deeper into the water.

Kate shook her head and smiled. "It's funny. He's not at all like my usual type." Actually, her one and only type. "Personality-wise, he's similar, but it's his looks and job that are a sharp departure for me. He's probably a few inches shy of six feet, and he's really muscular. Looks like he spends half his day in the gym-kind of muscular." Kate waved a hand through the water as she thought about Aidan. "Oh, and he's got tattoos on both arms. Lots of them. He also owns the pub that I go to for lunch on Wednesdays."

"Nice! So I take it you normally go for a more bookish type?"

"That is correct." Kate chuckled. "Office guys, suits, that sort of thing."

"So if this doesn't work out, maybe Kieran? He's a good-looking, bookish type—well, computers actually, but he's got that look. You could date them both and see who rises to the top."

"That's the furthest thing from my mind. I wasn't even thinking about dating since I just recently got out of a relationship. My friend coaxed me into it." Maybe it wasn't the furthest thing from her mind when it came to Declan, but Kate was determined not to tell Chloe how she felt about her brother. Why bring up the impossible?

Kate's reaction to Declan made her wonder if dating might help with her loneliness. While she enjoyed spending time with Margaret, with her in and out of awareness, her need to be heard wasn't always satisfied. She also realized that she missed the companionship of someone of the opposite sex. Despite her loneliness and need of a distraction from Declan, she was surprised to find herself having a conversation about dating two guys after nearly nine months of no romantic inclinations.

Chloe frowned. "I'm sorry. I had no idea. Do you want to talk about it?"

Shaking her head, Kate looked down at the water. *Just recently got out of a relationship?* She hated telling half-truths to these people who had welcomed her into their homes and lives, but she wasn't ready to bare her soul about her troubles. How long should something like this take to heal? Her therapist had told her there was no timeline; everyone was different. So far, England had been all that she'd hoped for in distracting her and removing the constant reminders of her past and her pain, but a dark ache still lingered deep down. Eventually, she would fully face it, but she wanted to be a stronger person first.

Changing the subject, Chloe talked about her family. They were a tight-knit bunch, which Kate envied. She was close to her parents and brother but didn't see them that often. Her brother lived in Birmingham, Alabama, which made it hard to get together, and though her parents lived across town, they rarely saw one another either. Funny how life got busy and she didn't make time for those she loved.

She imagined being part of Chloe's family. It could be possible through Declan. That would be a happy life.

But where had her mind gone? She was not *that* woman—the kind that stole men away. How could she think such thoughts!? Aidan . . . Aidan . . . Aidan. That's where her mind needed to focus. He was interested in her, nice, good-looking, and most importantly, available. Their first date had gone well enough.

Dating was still a difficult subject. Kate wanted to talk to Chloe about the awkwardness of having her second first date at the age of twenty-nine, but again, she wasn't ready to delve into that other part of her life.

A flash of her life the year before Mark's death came to mind, and she remembered the numerous Saturdays out on a boat at Pickwick with other couples from her husband's firm. Sometimes Mark made it for the full day, but other times client meetings kept him away and he didn't show up until dinner at one of the partners' lake homes. The wives never made her feel bad when Mark failed to attend. They were all familiar with that aspect of the job. Though hard at times, it had been a comfortable life, but it was no longer *her* life.

The hot tub water splashed on Kate's face, camouflaging the moisture seeping from her eyes and bringing her back to the present.

The London getaway flew by too quickly, and Kate had promised Aidan another date on the following weekend.

"You seem quieter tonight than you were on our last date. Is everything okay?" Aidan peered across the table with concern.

Kate smiled at the handsome man, searching for the right words. "I was really nervous and rambling last time, and honestly can't remember half of what I said." She didn't mention the real reason for her pensiveness.

Kieran had watched them from his front porch when Aidan picked her up. She had no idea Kieran would be back in town. He'd nodded at her and held her gaze until they backed out of the driveway and she could no longer see him. It left her unsettled.

Aidan grinned. "Are you saying I make you nervous? We talk at the pub all the time."

She turned her thoughts back to Aidan. "I know, it's just . . . I've only recently gotten out of a very serious relationship, so the whole getting-to-know-you first date kind of thing is . . . it's been a while."

He reached for her hand. "I'm sorry. No pressure. I just enjoy spending time with you."

"I'm enjoying it too." She nodded and smiled back. He couldn't have been more accommodating and thoughtful with her.

"I almost don't want to share you with others, but I know you promised Hayley we'd meet up at my pub to catch the band." He raised a brow, and she got the feeling he wanted her to say it was fine for them to skip out and do their own thing.

"Yeah, Hayley's having her first date with a guy she met at the coffee shop and made me promise. She didn't want it to be like a regular date until she got to know him better."

Half an hour later, they sat in a booth at the Rose and Crown across from Hayley and her date, Erik. Aidan and Erik heatedly debated the best type of lager.

"If you blokes don't give it up, Kate and I will have to hire a solicitor to end this dispute." Hayley winked at Kate. "I think you Americans just call them lawyers, right?" When Kate nodded, Hayley explained the difference between barristers and solicitors. Hayley's last boyfriend was a solicitor. Kate didn't mention that they had that in common.

With that, Kate's mind drifted to when Mark took his bar exam. He had studied so hard, then they'd had to wait three months for the results. When they found out he'd passed, the firm celebrated at one of the partners' homes. She remembered being so excited that she rented a little bed and breakfast down in Oxford, Mississippi, for the next weekend. When he finally got away from work, she'd had his bags packed for the surprise, but he had been upset that she'd made plans without asking.

"Kate?" Hayley was standing up, reaching for her hand. "The loo?"

"Oh. Sure." She reined in her thoughts and looked at Aidan, who nodded.

"So how's it going? Less stressful than the first date? He seems totally enamored with you."

Kate chuckled. "It's good, he's a great guy. But you know that. What about you? That Erik guy seems nice."

Hayley shrugged. "Meh. I don't know if I'm feeling it."

As the night went on, Kate understood why Hayley wasn't interested in Erik. He was hard to talk to and very argumentative. When

Aidan suggested that they stand on the edge of the crowd to watch the band, Kate and Hayley couldn't get up fast enough.

Aidan stood behind Kate, wrapped his arms around her, and pulled her close. She closed her eyes and relaxed into that comfortable, secure feeling of having a man care for her again.

When she opened her eyes, she noticed Hayley looking at Aidan longingly, and that comfortable feeling vanished. That was why she hadn't wanted to date Aidan in the first place. Why did Hayley keep insisting that she was fine with Kate dating him? Aidan's arms no longer felt right. What was she thinking? It had only been nine months since everything with Mark happened. Deep inside, she knew what she had to do.

Chapter Nine

"I can't believe you told Aidan you can't date him anymore! He's the greatest guy ever! Now he's going to be so sad."

Kate pulled the phone farther from her ear and winced before bringing it back to speak. "Maybe not. Especially if a certain girl named Hayley turns up the charm and is there for him during this sad time."

"I thought you liked him?"

"I do, Hayley, but not like that. I think I'm still not ready for a relationship." She'd enjoyed her time with Aidan, but maybe it was just having *someone* that was nice. It wasn't like she couldn't live without him in particular, and that wasn't fair to him or Hayley. Who knew? Maybe Hayley and Aidan had a chance.

"How long has it been since your last relationship?"

Kate hesitated to tell Hayley because it might bring up more questions, but the thought of trying to remember another lie sounded impossible. "Just over nine months."

"Okay. So you've had some time. You won't know if you're ready if you don't try."

"If you're really worried, then I'll let you in on something . . ." Is this really what she wanted to say?

"Kate? Are you still there?"

"Yes." Kate's mind had wandered back to the steely gaze of her neighbor the night before. "Margaret's neighbor is an app developer who lives in London, and this is his weekend home. Anyway, he's really good-looking, and he made it clear that he's interested in me. I told him I wasn't ready, but he still said he wanted to get to know me. It just so happens that last night he saw me leave for my date, and I think he was jealous." Kate couldn't bring herself to admit she'd been married.

"You've been holding out on me."

"Not really. Nothing much has happened. I met him one weekend, and he invited all of us over for dinner. Then he's been MIA for the last two weekends. Well actually, I don't know about last weekend since I was gone, but either way, I hadn't seen him until the incident last night when I was leaving with Aidan."

"Okay, I guess I'll let you off the hook with Aidan since you have another prospect. When are you going to make your move?"

"There's no move to make."

"Yes, there is. You should just pop over and check on him or make some cookies and drop by. You know, the way to a man's heart and all that."

"Whatever. I think I'll just let things happen organically."

"You mean you won't do anything. If I hadn't pushed you with Aidan, you never would have gone out with him. Dating is good for you. It will help you get over whatever it is that you don't want to talk about with your ex."

"Mm-hm."

"You're not going to do anything, are you?"

"Maybe." *Doubtfully.*

"Okay. I'm giving you a chance to redeem yourself this week, and by next weekend, if you've made no progress, I'm stepping in."

"Yes, Dr. Hayley. Thank you very much for your clinical diagnosis."

"Aidan was everything you described him as, Kate. Quite good look-ing." Chloe wiggled her eyebrows as they walked along the beach.

"Aidan? Do I know him?" Margaret looked at Chloe.

"We met him last night, Gran, when Kate left for her date." Chloe gave her grandmother's shoulder a squeeze.

"Oh." She frowned with embarrassment. "I've forgotten. Is he a nice man?"

"Seemed that way. Kate will have to tell us. She had a date with him last night." Chloe grinned across at Kate.

"Katie! That's wonderful." Margaret clapped. "Do you like him?"

"As a friend." Kate turned to Chloe. "I told him I just want to be friends. That I'm not ready for a relationship right now."

"Oh really?" Chloe's voice rose along with her eyebrows. "That's unfortunate."

"Okay." Chuckling at Chloe's odd response, Kate pulled out her ponytail holder and rebound her hair that had worked loose. Before she was finished, she felt a firm hand on her shoulder.

"Hello, ladies."

Without turning, Kate recognized the deep timbre of the man approaching.

"Kieran! Come to join us on our walk?" Chloe grinned.

"I came to invite you up to the deck for a drink and some biscuits."

"That sounds wonderful." Chloe began steering Margaret towards his house.

Just as they approached his gate, Chloe stopped and snapped her finger. "Actually, I just remembered, I've got to check on something at the house. Come on, Gran."

"Mm-hm." Kate crossed her arms.

"Okay, ta-ta." Chloe waved, and Margaret looked confused as they turned away.

Chuckling, Kieran led Kate up to the balcony. "Join me in the kitchen while I throw some things on a tray?"

Nodding, she dropped onto a stool by the bar and looked up to find him watching her. She held his gaze while trying to decide what she wanted from him. She'd just turned Aidan down, but it *had* been a pleasant distraction. Not that she was ready for anything serious, nor did she trust herself to choose wisely. Maybe if she kept her relationships with men superficial, she could have male companionship without the heartbreak. Then she wouldn't have to worry about that niggling thought in the back of her mind that she couldn't trust Kieran.

"How'd the date go? He seemed eager to please, flowers and all."

Kate bit her lip and felt heat rise to her face. He had seen the flowers too? They were beautiful but felt like a little much. Especially after she told him no more dates. "He's a great guy."

"I sense a *but* coming."

"But I told him I wasn't ready to date."

"Ah, same thing you told me, so I shouldn't take it too personally."

"Yeah." How could she convey what she did want? "I'm just looking for friends right now."

"I can do friends. I'd like a chance to get to know you better."

"I'm honestly not that interesting." *In other words, please don't ask really personal questions.*

"I beg to differ. With that American accent, you are all kinds of interesting. I've done my research on Memphis, so I know you were raised around the blues and barbecue, along with a beautiful historic hotel that keeps ducks in the lobby fountain during the day until they parade them up to their rooftop mansion. That's quite interesting."

Kate bit back a smile. "You *have* done your research. What else have you learned about my home?"

"I hoped you'd fill in the rest." He placed two glasses on the counter next to a tray of cookies and slid a stool closer to her.

If Kieran didn't rush her into a relationship, he might be the perfect diversion from Declan . . . and eventually more.

Chapter Ten

Nearly a week had passed since Kate had seen Kieran. They'd hung out well into the evening Friday. He took her on a date Saturday night as "friends," of course, and by Sunday, it was a given they would spend time together. Though he returned to London Sunday, they texted each day and spoke twice. He was a busy man but promised to come in from Saturday to Sunday this weekend. Kate was glad for that, since Declan would be in, and she needed an excuse to get out of the house. Not that she didn't want to see Declan, but she found him much too attractive and *too* engaged to torture herself.

Unfortunately, or perhaps fortunately, when Declan entered the cottage Friday afternoon, he wasn't alone. It was difficult enough knowing that the handsome man was unavailable, but seeing his stunningly gorgeous fiancée added salt to Kate's wounds. Alexandra had long, silky black hair, mile-high legs, and was dressed to perfection. She could have passed for a runway model. Even when introducing herself, Alexandra showed perfect poise, and Margaret clearly adored her. Considering how much Declan respected his grandmother, that was high praise in his eyes.

Minutes after meeting Alexandra, Kate could see that she and Declan made a perfect couple. It was painful to watch as he doted on her. They finished each other's sentences and seemed to anticipate just what the other needed. It reminded her of what she'd had with Mark at one time, what she'd lost, and what she doubted she would ever have again. There was also a little bit of good old-fashioned jealousy thrown into the mix.

Somehow, in just one weekend, Declan had made a lasting impression on her. Even when he was doting on his grandmother and fiancée, he still made Kate feel seen, and it was wonderful. Every time Declan's eyes found hers, it was like he could see into the depths of her heart and intended each look and word to heal it.

Her time with Kieran had felt so different. With him hoping for something more, rather than healing, it had left her exhausted.

That night after dinner, Declan stayed in the kitchen to clean with Kate while Alexandra caught up with Margaret. He washed, she dried, and she felt alive with his nearness.

"So . . . Kieran, huh?" He'd stopped washing, and she could feel his eyes on her.

Meeting his gaze, she responded with a shrug. "We've started hanging out when he's in town. As friends."

"Good." His eyes didn't waver from hers as he searched for the truth.

"Good?"

"Yes, good that it's only as friends. I've known him since he bought the place, and we're friends, but when it comes to girls . . ." He shook his head.

Kate laid down the towel. "What are you not saying?"

He pursed his lips and seemed to struggle with how to respond. "You could say he gets around, and he's not usually satisfied with just one woman at a time. Since he's gone during the week, there's no telling who else he's with."

Her breathing slowed. How was she supposed to respond to something like that? She wasn't even sure how she felt about dating or about Kieran. She had said he was a friend, but knew it could turn into something more. His time away had seemed good since she didn't want to be pressured into a relationship too soon.

Declan continued to watch her and added, "You're worth more than that."

Was she? Why did he care? With the way things had ended with the "love of her life," she sometimes questioned if she was worth it.

He squeezed her shoulder. "Hey, I don't mean to tell you what to do. Just trying to look out for you."

"Thanks." Kate's tangled thoughts kept her from saying more.

After finishing up in the kitchen, they rejoined the others. Declan took a seat by Alexandra on the settee, and Kate sat on the sofa across from them with Margaret in her favorite chair in between. Alexandra and Declan filled Margaret in with stories about the Paris office.

Kate's eyes fell to the diamond ring on Alexandra's left hand. It was unusual for an engagement ring, but unique with a wheat design and the solitaire offset from the center. Her thumb rubbed against her own ring finger. It still felt bare without her rings.

"Tomorrow we're taking Gran to Leeds Castle. You should come, Kate. It's a lovely castle, and I think you'd enjoy it. Don't you agree, Corbyn?" Alexandra seemed sincere.

Kate contemplated lying. "I'm supposed to do something with Kieran tomorrow." Her eyes moved from Alexandra to Declan with worry after their conversation. Though she might still go out with Kieran, she didn't want Declan to think badly of her, but it would be rude to cancel her plans with Kieran at the last minute. Declan's jaw clenched as he watched her.

"Well, bring him along, or he could meet us there on his way in from London." Alexandra looked between Kate and Declan and laid a hand on his leg. "You're friends with Kieran. Why the face, Corbyn?"

Finally, his eyes pulled away from Kate's as he refocused on Alexandra. "It's fine, sorry." He rubbed a hand down his face. "I'm just going to . . ." He pointed upstairs as he stood and walked off.

Alexandra didn't miss a beat as she started right back up with the conversation.

"They believe King Alfred the Great claimed the land and had buildings here in the late 800s, but they would have been built of wood, and there are no remains from that time. The first recorded buildings on the land weren't listed until the late 1000s. From the late 1200s through the early 1500s, its ownership rotated between the King of England and his queen. That building"—the Leeds Castle tour guide pointed to the right—"is the main castle, and that part"—she pointed to the structure on the left—"is called the Gloriette. It was the Ladies' Castle. During medieval times, the women would have their meal there and watch the hunts, since it overlooked the woods."

As Alexandra, Kate, and Kieran toured the property on Segways, Declan and Margaret went to the dog collar museum on the mobility bus. Alexandra filled the group in on additional history and facts about the property. She knew as much as the tour guide, maybe more. Kieran had been to the property several times before and likely knew most of the information, but to Kate, it was all new and fascinating. In fact, when she found out her ticket would allow her access for an entire year, she began trying to figure out the next time she could visit.

Parking the Segway, Kate pulled out her phone to photograph the castle in the distance. The weight of an arm settling across her back caused her to jump.

"Sorry to startle you," Kieran's voice rasped next to her ear.

"No problem. I'm just trying to capture all of this." Kate waved a hand towards the castle. "I know this is an everyday sight for you, but this is amazing for me. We don't even have buildings from the 1200s in America."

"I can see you like it. You haven't stopped smiling since we got here." At Kieran's comment, Kate covered her mouth, but he pulled her hand away. "No, don't. I think it's cute."

Cute wasn't her aim. He was starting to grate on her nerves. Ever since they had met up at the castle, he'd acted like a different person from the Kieran she'd been getting to know. He'd boasted about his work to Declan and acted quite possessive over her, even though she had not agreed they were anything more than friends.

Those things might not have been so bad if she hadn't seen him flirting with a worker in the gift shop where they paid for their Segway tour. She had been on the other side of the shop with Alexandra and seen the whole thing. He even gave the woman the same smolder he'd given Kate numerous times. She didn't know if she should be mad or thankful that Declan had warned her of his concerns about Kieran. She didn't think she blew his interaction with the woman out of proportion.

Trying to keep her smile from turning to a grimace, she turned back to continue taking pictures.

By the time they finished the tour and met back up with Declan and Margaret at the café, Kate was famished and glad to have Declan there to talk with Kieran. She needed a break from him. Why had she thought this was a good idea? Oh yeah, the weekend before, she'd really enjoyed their time together.

Strange how seeing Kieran in a different environment and knowing his history with women changed that. Unfortunately, Declan was still just as much of a gentleman as ever. *Sigh.* That he would forgo the Segway tour and do the slow walk through the dog collar museum with his grandmother—which sounded as interesting as watching grass grow —spoke volumes about his character.

"Have any of you guys done the Knight's Glamping here?" Kate spoke after finishing one of her tea sandwiches.

Except for Margaret, who looked confused, all the others shook their heads.

"It does look lovely, doesn't it," Alexandra offered. "I'm not usually one for camping, but their setup makes it look appealing."

"Exactly what I was thinking. I may see if my friend wants to go with me one weekend. I'd love to come back and spend more time on the property." Kate looked at Declan. "Of course, I'd wait until a weekend when you or someone from your family could be with Margaret."

"That sounds quite wonderful, dear." Margaret perked up and patted Kate's hand.

"A friend for your weekend getaway, eh?" Kieran wiggled his eyebrows at Kate, then lowered his voice and whispered, "I think I can make time for that."

Acting like she didn't hear him, Kate turned away and grabbed the sugar dish to add another cube to her already sweet tea. Anything to avoid acknowledging him at the moment. She could feel the burn from Declan's stare even though she looked down. The tea in her cup was extraordinarily interesting.

Following their full day at the castle, Kieran had everyone over for curry at his home. After eating, Margaret was tired, and they began saying their goodbyes. However, Kieran insisted that he needed to speak with Kate "briefly." Declan seemed hesitant to leave her, but Kate urged them on, deciding she should stay and say what needed to be said rather than put it off.

Ways to be honest without being hurtful spun through Kate's mind. When she arrived just over a month ago, she'd never dreamt she would find herself turning down two seemingly nice Englishmen over the course of two weekends. Though Kieran was making Kate uncomfortable, she realized that most of her anxiety was rooted in unresolved feelings about her husband. She never should have jumped into dating so quickly. She was nowhere near ready.

"Finally, I have you all to myself." Kieran smiled slyly and wrapped an arm around her back to guide her into the sitting room and onto the sofa next to himself.

As soon as they were seated, Kate tried to slide away, but his arm still circled around her. "I'm glad you were able to join us today. It really was a beautiful place." Maybe glad wasn't the right word choice for what she intended to convey. Her southern roots had ingrained in her to always be kind, and sometimes that required a touch of exaggeration, but this was a time to speak the truth, even when it might not be what someone wanted to hear.

Before she could continue, he placed his other hand on her cheek and leaned closer. "Yes . . . beautiful."

"Yes, well . . . Kieran . . . I'm so glad to have made a friend like you here."

He continued to stare into her eyes and caress her cheek. "Yes. I can see us becoming good friends."

This wasn't going as she'd hoped. "I . . ." She couldn't think with him touching her and looking at her like that, so she reached up to pull his hand from her face, but it only ended with him lacing their fingers together. "What I'm trying to say"—she stopped to clear her throat—"is that I really don't feel ready for more than friendship right now." The dark look in his eyes threw off her train of thought. "It's not you, I just . . . I've tried it twice now, and the timing doesn't feel right."

He nodded and released her hand before sliding away. His face was unreadable.

"I'm sorry." She twisted her fingers together and stared at them, ashamed for leading him on. "I thought I was almost ready." She shook her head and then stood up to leave when it hit her that she would have to see him time and again. "I do hope we can still be friends. I . . ." She decided to leave it at that. "I should go. Goodnight."

Just as she exited the room, she heard his footsteps behind her. "Goodnight, Kate."

Stepping into the sitting room, Kate found Declan on the settee, looking at his phone. His eyes caught hers, and he placed a finger on his lips and then whispered, "Alexandra is helping Gran go to bed." When

Kate nodded and sat in a chair close to him, he raised a brow. "I thought you would be at Kieran's a while longer."

She shook her head. "I heard what you said and decided it wasn't worth risking my heart."

"What did you say to him?"

"I told him all I want right now is to be friends."

"I'm sorry for intruding on your personal life. I didn't mean to ruin things for you. Who knows, maybe he's ready to settle down."

Kate pressed her lips together, thinking about how much to say. "No, this will be best in the long run. Today I saw him flirting with a girl at the shop where we paid for the Segway tour. It's possible I've blown it up more than I should, but I'd rather not constantly worry if he's seeing someone else behind my back. That's a big deal to me, and truthfully, I'm not ready to date. I don't know what I was thinking. I keep trying for something I'm not meant to have and just messing things up in the process."

"Don't beat yourself up over it. I'm sure Kieran will snap back easily enough."

Kate frowned at the thought that she was so easy to get over, but what did she expect at this point?

"Sorry, that came out wrong. I seem to say all the wrong things when you're around."

"No, it's fine. I'm a big girl and can take the truth."

"Kate, back so soon? Is Kieran okay?" Alexandra curled up next to Declan, who was trying to shake his head subtly at her. "Oh sorry, sensitive subject, I suppose. So . . . will you be going to church with us tomorrow?"

Looking between the two, Kate wanted to say no but remembered how disturbed it had left Margaret the time she'd missed. It really wasn't that bad; not at all what she expected of a British church attended by an eighty-four-year-old woman. The contemporary church didn't have the liturgy of standing up and down, saying creeds and prayers. Not only that, quite a few younger people attended. The church she had gone to as a child was much more formal than Margaret's, which was surprising. "Yes, I'll join you."

As they chatted about the day, Kate couldn't help noticing the easy, caring relationship between Alexandra and Declan. She knew what it felt like to be that in love and to have every confidence in her relationship and in the future, but she also knew how fast it could be snatched away.

Jealousy and anger began to form in her heart. In the middle of the conversation, she excused herself before her tongue slipped and she regretted more than just how she ended things with Kieran. They seemed surprised but were courteous, as always. Goodnights all around, and she was free to work through her feelings without an audience.

Chapter Eleven

Two little boys tossed a ball while their baby sister and mom looked on. Margaret grinned as she watched from the park bench where she and Kate sat.

"We never intended for Tracey to be an only child, you know." Margaret turned towards Kate.

"Really?" The look on Margaret's face spoke of sadness, and Kate hesitated to ask why.

"Yes, after Tracey, I had three miscarriages. Then my endometriosis worsened, and they told me it was causing infertility. Nothing they tried helped. Eventually, they had to do a hysterectomy. I had thought four would be a perfect number." She smiled sadly. "Graham said we could have as many children as I wanted." She shook her head. "God had other plans. Now I'm blessed to know my great-grandchildren."

Kate's heart clenched as she thought about all the negative pregnancy tests she'd taken herself, the hormone shots and medications. Somehow, at the age of twenty-nine, the girl who had gotten married right out of college found herself unmarried and childless. That was never how she'd seen her life. She squeezed Margaret's hand. "You have a wonderful family."

"I do, and I have truly had a wonderful life. It was a chance to learn to trust God and view him as enough." Margaret stopped and looked at the children. Kate thought Margaret had lost her train of thought until she spoke again. "I can see that something troubles you, Katie. Give it to God. Find peace in him."

Kate nodded but was at a loss for words. It sounded so simple yet impossible too. Maybe it worked for Margaret, but all the broken pieces of Kate's life couldn't be mended so easily.

"When I let go of the things I thought I needed, I became more satisfied with the things I had. I never wanted Tracey to feel like she wasn't a blessing, but there was a time after my hysterectomy when I acted that way. Thankfully, God helped me to let the loss of my plans go, and I turned things around before causing emotional damage to her." A bird landed on a nearby tree, and Margaret pointed at it. After watching it fly away, she commented, "The—" She stopped and looked at Kate and shook her head. "Beautiful."

"Yes, the bird was beautiful." Kate struggled to reconcile the woman who had just been speaking about deep feelings and thoughts with the one who couldn't remember the word "bird," but times like that were increasing for her. Dementia was such a strange disease, taking away words here and there, sometimes more, sometimes less, and gradually progressing until a person could no longer communicate with or understand the world around them.

Kate's mind drifted back to their previous conversation. Would she ever find peace? How would that even be possible in her situation? Since she was a young girl, she'd longed to be a wife and mom. Now, even if she got married again, being a mom seemed unlikely. Sure, there was adoption, but she wanted the swollen belly, feeling little kicks from inside, and later to look down and say, "He's got my eyes," or "She's got his nose." Before Mark's death, she'd felt anything but peaceful each month when she found out they were unsuccessful again.

Kate blinked back the moisture building in her eyes. Yet when she looked at Margaret, she saw peace in the midst of a hopeless situation. Margaret had nothing better to hope for. Her dementia would continue until it took everything, yet here she sat, knowing all of that and smiling. What must that feel like?

"Margaret, where's the book you want to read to the class?"

A local primary school had set up a day for Margaret to come read one of her children's books to students. She used to read to them regularly before dementia began making it difficult. After speaking with Tracey, Kate agreed that she could accompany her with an extra copy of the book and assist by showing the pictures and stepping in if Margaret froze up or got confused. They hoped that this way, she could continue with the reading program for a while longer.

"The extra books are in the attic, dear. I believe the children's books are in light blue plastic bins." Margaret's excitement was contagious.

Kate smiled and nodded before going up the two levels to the attic. It was clear that the reading program brought Margaret joy, and Kate would do everything possible to make it happen. A well-organized space in the attic greeted her—shelving filled with plastic bins, furniture on one side covered in plastic, and a circular window at the end. The uniquely-shaped window drew her closer, and as she peered out, she recognized the side yard down below and some of Margaret's flower bushes. She couldn't hold back her smile as she remembered that first day meeting Declan.

Moving back to the shelves, Kate found the light blue bins and searched through them for the book Margaret requested.

"I didn't know you'd written so many books." Kate called out as she returned from the attic. "I'd like to look through the others you've written. Would you mind if I read some of them? I'm assuming all the bins are filled with your books."

"They are, and you are welcome to read any of them." Margaret twisted and pointed to the built-in bookcase behind her chair. "First prints are all on those shelves."

Kate approached the bookcase and found it filled with leather-bound books. Nothing like the standard colorful hardback children's books in the bins upstairs. Her fingers ran across the gold-embossed design on the front cover of one.

"Each time I came out with a new book, Graham had three of them leather-bound—one for the office, one for our home, and one for Tracey." Margaret's smile became a grin, and her eyes stared into the distance. "Of course, he didn't do that for all of his authors."

Turning back to the bookcase, Kate was even more awed by the man who had made his wife feel so special. Graham sounded like a rare find. A set of books that all said *Willowland* and were numbered one through twelve caught her attention. On the front of the first one was a beautifully-embossed willow tree with a girl and boy sitting on the ground beneath.

"That's from my *Willowland* series. Those were some of my favorites, with the adventures of Mary and Sam. They are young people who . . . well, you should just read and see. I don't like to give anything away." Margaret winked.

"I think it went fairly well, Tracey. Before your mom read, she answered a few questions that the school sent us ahead of time. I had typed out her answers, which helped. She had a couple of hiccups with that, but I kept her on track. Early on in the book, she missed a few words here and there. It wasn't until the last third of the book that I needed to take over. Both she and the children responded well to that, and I think it seemed almost as if we'd planned it."

"I'm so glad she could read at the school again. It's always meant a lot to her, and thank you, Kate, for making it possible. Whenever you think something is too much, just be honest with her."

"Yes, I will. Margaret's been a joy to work with—always willing to do whatever is necessary and not feeling like she has to cover up her dementia. That's when it's the hardest, when a patient doesn't want people to know."

"I imagine so."

"I will say that after lunch, she is starting to slip more and earlier. Also, I noticed in the book that she reads with her book club, she's gone from highlighting key points as I taught her to highlighting nearly every word. That tells me she's having more difficulty comprehending what she reads."

There was a pause before Tracey responded. "I knew she would gradually lose more of her abilities, but that doesn't make it easier." Tracey sighed. "This is such a difficult disease."

"It is. I'm sorry. Though there is not the physical pain that many other diseases have, the emotional pain and suffering is extreme. Especially for the family." *And can last for years.* But she knew Tracey didn't need to be reminded about that.

"I can't thank you enough for all you do, Kate. It has given my mom more time to enjoy her life before she no longer can. I'll be there this weekend. We'll just keep taking it one day at a time and adjust as needed. When she can't participate in most of her usual activities, maybe she'll reconsider living with us in London."

The sea breeze and sounds of the ocean lapping against the beach had Kate sinking into the lounger outside her bedroom balcony. Since Tracey arrived for the weekend, Kate had taken a solitary walk on the beach at sunset, called her parents, and was now beginning the second volume of the *Willowland* series.

The first book reminded her of the Chronicles of Narnia. In it, the two main characters fell asleep at the base of a willow tree and woke up in a land reminiscent of the Garden of Eden in all its lush perfection and natural beauty. At the close of the first adventure-filled book, the young people woke up at the base of the willow tree. It ended as a cliffhanger with no mention of whether they both remembered being in the curious land or if it was all a dream. She was anxious to find out, but Kieran's car pulling into his driveway drew her attention away.

He and a woman stepped out and joined each other in front of the car, where she wrapped her arms around him before he pulled her into a kiss. When he released her, she giggled, and they headed towards the house. Just before they were out of Kate's line of sight, Kieran turned, looked up at Kate, and winked.

She sat there, mouth open, staring at the empty space where Kieran had just been. He knew she was there and put on that show? And to think, she had actually considered that in the future, she might be ready for more than friendship with him.

Kate: Your friend Kieran came home with a woman just now. I'm out on my balcony and he pulled her into a kiss, then winked at me!

Declan: I'm sorry. That's a real jerk move.

Kate: Right?! And she looks like a floozy.

Declan: Floozy?

Kate: Like she's only there for one thing.

Three bubbles popped up then disappeared.

Declan: I'll take the train in tomorrow and talk with him.

Kate: No, I'll be okay. Thank you, though. And thanks for trying to warn me. I should have taken you more seriously in the first place.

As Kate stared at her phone, bubbles popped up and then disappeared again before her phone rang. "Declan?"

"Are you okay? Really?"

"Yeah . . . yeah, I'm fine." She tried to convince herself. Not that Kieran was so great a loss, but it felt like a reminder that maybe she wasn't enough or worthy of pursuing. "I'm just glad I already have plans for tomorrow night in case he's still around."

"You should take a day trip somewhere, or an overnight. Didn't you mention a friend you wanted to take to the glamping site at Leeds Castle?"

"That's a perfect idea. Thanks. Surely we can come up with someplace to go if the glamping thing doesn't work out." Her mind flitted through ideas. She even had a list of locations from *Pride and Prejudice* —places mentioned in the book and filming locations.

"I'm still going to say something to Kieran. He should be looking out for you ladies, not torturing you." Declan paused. "Do you think maybe you've been going on dates with these guys because you're lonely and missing home?"

That caught her off guard. Could there be some truth to that?

"I'm sorry. I shouldn't have said that."

"No. It's something for me to think about. My parents are coming for a visit in a couple of weeks, though, so if what you said is true, that should help. I don't think I miss my home itself, just possibly my parents." It had been a wise decision to get away from Memphis, hadn't it? Memphis held too many reminders of her past.

"I'm glad you'll see them soon. How long are they staying?"

"They're going to spend about three weeks in the region, but most of that will be touring other places in the U.K. They plan on staying with me about five nights, then going to Paris for two or three days, then coming back to see me before leaving."

"Brilliant. You should join them when they come to Paris. I can show all of you around. I'm sure my mom or Chloe can stay with Gran for the weekend."

"I wouldn't want to impose on you. I don't—"

"Don't be silly. In fact, you guys can stay at my place. I have two rooms, and I can stay at Alexandra's place. You wouldn't be imposing. If you come to Paris and don't stay at my place and let me show you around, I'll be offended."

"You drive a hard bargain." She looked across at Kieran's home. "How did we get from me complaining about Kieran to my parents and me staying at your place in Paris?"

"I suppose you have a way of drawing me in with your American wiles." Declan laughed.

If only it were that easy to draw him in. He was such a perfect gentleman, ready to help whenever the need arose. If she were ready for a relationship, she could only hope to find someone like him. "Alexandra is so lucky," she murmured under her breath.

"What's that? Sorry, I couldn't really hear you."

"Oh, um. Ducky. It's just ducky that you're helping me out." Why did she keep saying such stupid things? It was like her brain short-circuited around him.

"Is that another American saying? You have some interesting ones. Floozy and ducky?" He chuckled, then asked her about how the week had been.

Glancing at the time, Kate realized nearly an hour had passed, and she felt guilty for monopolizing his time. "I'm sorry. I'm sure you have better things to do on a Friday night than console me." Her mind went to Alexandra, who was likely waiting for his attention. "I need to contact Hayley anyway if I'm going to try to set something up for tomorrow."

"True, I suppose you do, but it has certainly not been a burden to talk with you. I hope tomorrow is a success for you and your friend."

After their goodbyes, Kate contacted Hayley and booked one of the glamping tents before sending a quick text to thank Declan again for the idea and letting him know she'd worked it out. Once she spoke with Tracey about the plans, she was ready to curl up in bed and read until she drifted off. Dreams of knights with blond hair and blue eyes awaited.

Chapter Twelve

"So there they were, the knight on the black steed in full armor and the knight on the white steed. The horses flew towards each other as the knights held their jousting lances. The knight on the white horse easily knocked off the knight on the dark horse, and when they removed their helmets, it was revealed that the white knight was Declan and the dark knight was Kieran. At the command of the king, the white knight approached, and the king offered him the hand of the princess in marriage. I, of course, was the princess in the dream, and the king looked surprisingly just like my father. The king's tent looked very similar to the glamping tent we're staying in."

Kate turned to take in the scenery of the Leed's Castle property as she and Hayley continued their walk.

"You dreamed this last night after Declan swooped in and saved the day?"

"Well, he didn't actually swoop in. I texted him, and he ended up calling me, but yeah, he made me feel a lot better after seeing Kieran and that girl."

Hayley tsked. "You've got it bad."

"Tell me about it."

"So what are you going to do about it?"

"What do you mean?"

"Are you going to show him that you're worth his consideration?"

"He's engaged, you know that; and I am not *that* woman."

"Shame." Hayley shook her head.

"I thought I could handle it, but the dream felt so real. My feelings for him were so intense in it."

Hayley grinned. "Intense feelings for the knight jousting for you?"

"I know it sounds weird, but I think it was my real feelings for Declan coming through. There's just something about him that draws me to him."

She wanted to compare Declan to Mark but still wasn't ready to share that part of her life. Mark had been a flirt and could say the right words, but he was a busy man with no follow-through. Not only that, Declan seemed to get her. He didn't put her off with simple answers when they spoke, and he wanted to know what was driving her and how she really felt. He took the time to ask the tough questions. What meant more than anything was the way he encouraged her and tried to protect her. "Did I tell you Tracey said Kieran sent flowers? I'm sure it's because Declan spoke to him. He told me he would."

"Wow, he's obviously made a huge impact on you in what . . . two weekends?"

"And some texting and a couple of phone conversations."

Hayley pulled out her phone. "Is he on Insta?"

"Not a personal account, but he's in a lot of the posts for the publishing company. I'm sure whoever is in charge of social media realizes what a draw he is for the female population."

"I'll say. Ooh la la!" Hayley wiggled her brow as she scrolled through the Corbyn Publishing feed. "Yep, I'd be trying to convince him he needs to reevaluate his wedding plans."

"Nope. Not happening. Women who steal other women's men are awful."

"You're right. I don't truly mean it. I just . . . I don't know . . . guess I was hopeful for you that maybe his engagement would fall through, and maybe I'm living vicariously through you." Hayley's foot slipped on the root of a tree on the path they were following, and Kate caught her by the elbow. "But hey, there are lots of other fish in the sea for both of us. We'll find our people at the right time. Yeah?"

"Yeah." *Doubtful.* "Oh look, isn't this a nice view of the castle?" Kate pulled out her phone to snap a picture.

"Here. Let's do a selfie." Hayley leaned in as she grabbed the phone and adjusted it. As she clicked, a text popped up from Kieran.

Kieran: Sorry about last night. That was uncalled for. I may bring women home sometimes, but I won't flaunt it in the future . . . that is, unless you're the woman.

"Ooh. Now there's a development."

"Um, no. I seriously have no interest in someone who takes relationships that lightly. I really will be fine not dating. Anyway, we have other things to do besides worry about my lack of love life. We've got a maze to get lost in. Ready to head that way?"

As they turned, a feeling of emptiness overcame Kate. Even in the midst of all her busyness and the adventure of new experiences, she felt like part of her was missing and wondered if that would ever go away. *Keep moving forward*, she reminded herself as the brush crunched under her feet.

Storm rages like tempest deep inside
Ever eluding hope it would seem
Night darkened leaves nowhere to hide
Smiling, pretending it was just a dream
Pain
Loss
Sorrow
Devastation
I look for peace in you
And find the will to live
Like the morning dew
Hope only you can give

As Kate read the words of Margaret's poem, she guessed it was written after one of her miscarriages. So far, the book of poetry had worked through being wooed by Graham, falling in love with Graham, their marriage, the birth of Tracey, and now this—the first dark spot in the book.

It brought back a rush of feelings from Kate's own struggle with infertility. She'd never completely or even partially worked through the disappointment, pain, or sadness it created.

Kate's eyes moved to the bottom of the page.

Oh sing to the LORD a new song; sing to the LORD, all the earth! Sing to the LORD, bless his name; tell of his salvation from day to day. Declare his glory among the nations, his marvelous works among all the peoples! For great is the LORD, and greatly to be praised; he is to be feared above all gods. Psalms 96:1-4

How could Margaret put such a joyful quote on the same page where she mourned her miscarriage? Even now, after having multiple miscarriages, she seemed fine with it, and the grace with which Margaret handled her latest disappointment, dementia, was difficult to comprehend.

For the rest of the week, Kate devoured the poetry book each night after helping Margaret go to bed. She looked for answers, hoping to find the key to unlocking and conquering her own sadness and hurt. It contained more sad poems about other miscarriages and a few less traumatic things, but so much happiness and joy flowed through most of Margaret's poetry.

When Kate broached the subject, Margaret was very open about how the miscarriages affected her and how God pulled her and Graham through each time, actually bringing them closer through their sadness. Margaret showed Kate a list of Scriptures she'd compiled through the years to help with praising God in the hard times, and each night, she had Kate read out loud from it. "They're to uplift the soul and help turn our mind away from our troubles and toward God, our greatest treasure. He's the one who makes all other losses seem unimportant as long as we have him."

Being raised in the Bible Belt of America, Kate was familiar with people who were really into God, but she'd never been close to anyone who was. From a distance, she'd always thought they were hypocrites and wanted no part of that. Not that Kate didn't respect God—at least the idea of Him—or occasionally go to church. It was something nice to do now and then, especially at Christmas and Easter.

Margaret poured so much of her life into working with her church to make things happen for her community. She was earnest about reading her Bible and praying, and kind towards everyone she met. It made Kate wonder if she had misjudged those who were so serious about their faith in Christ.

"Count it all joy, my brothers, when you meet trials of various kinds, for you know that the testing of your faith produces steadfastness. And —" Kate looked up just as Declan joined them in the sitting room.

"Let steadfastness have its full effect, that you may be perfect and complete, lacking in nothing. James 1 . . . I forgot the verse numbers." He finished reciting and grinned down sheepishly at the two women.

"Two through four. You have it memorized. Impressive." Kate wondered how much more of the Bible he knew. She hadn't expected him until later that day but was more than pleased to see him arrive early, as evidenced by her racing heart.

"Gran made sure we learned her special verses." His grin could melt the frostiest heart, and Kate imagined a young Declan reciting Scripture with Margaret. "Enough about me. How are you ladies doing this afternoon?"

The next morning, somewhere between wake and sleep, Kate found herself in a hospital delivery room with Mark beside the bed, holding her hand. A doctor delivered their baby and then handed it to Kate, but no noise escaped from it, nor did it move. Mark's face became angry, and before Kate could respond, he and the baby faded away.

As Kate watched the image of Mark disappear, he was replaced with

Declan smiling down, then leaning in to kiss her forehead. "You've got this, beautiful. She'll be in your arms any minute." This time, a doctor delivered a healthy, crying baby girl. "Look at what we made." Declan kissed Kate on the lips as he wrapped his arms around her and the baby.

Kate overflowed with feelings of joy and love as she looked between their daughter and Declan, who pulled her close. She tried to form words, but nothing came out, as if she'd become mute. She tried again to no avail, but Declan wiped a hand over her brow and kissed her again.

"It's okay; you must be so tired." Once more, she opened her mouth, but a loud clang startled her, and she blinked . . . then blinked again.

As her eyes focused on her surroundings, she realized she was in Margaret's beach cottage, not a hospital. Reality began to dawn, and disappointment set in. There was no baby, and Declan was not her husband. Her hands went to her lips, where the kiss that had felt so real still lingered. The way he had looked at her held so much love and happiness. Moving her hand to her chest, she swallowed down the sadness. Neither Declan nor a biological baby could ever be hers. Maybe if she closed her eyes, the dream and happiness would return for a little longer.

Eventually, Kate forced herself awake and headed to the kitchen, where she found the source of the clanging that disturbed her sweet dream. Declan was at the stove cooking eggs.

When he turned and their eyes connected, Kate felt heat rise to her face as she remembered his kiss in the dream. He was an engaged man. She shouldn't linger on thoughts like that, but he awakened things within her she'd thought might never awaken again.

As Declan watched her, his eyes seemed to ask a million questions that she didn't dare answer, but only one came out of his mouth. "Hungry?"

Kate's shoulders tensed and she nodded, hoping he couldn't see the things left unspoken.

At the end of the day, after a Canterbury Cathedral visit with Margaret, Kate and Declan put Margaret to bed, and Kate found herself in the sitting room with him. Her heart still raced every time she was around him, but at least he couldn't read her mind. The thoughts about him that kept creeping in made her feel guilty. She hoped she could keep a blank face. The realistic nature of her earlier dream made it hard to stop imagining what it would be like if they were more than friends.

Her eyes turned to the hallway, and she wondered if he would think her rude if she left. Just as that thought passed, he sat down and asked if she would stay and talk.

As she started to open her mouth, Declan spoke. "Are you feeling okay after . . . well, what happened with Kieran last weekend?"

Her eyes caught his, and she remembered his concern the previous week. How could she walk away from someone so kind? She sat. "I'll be fine. Did you have anything to do with the flowers he sent?"The side of his mouth curled up. "I might have mentioned that flowers can help smooth the way when a woman's feelings are involved. But I also warned him off of you." He bit his lip. "I hope you don't mind."

"I don't." She shook her head. "Now that I've seen for myself what he's like, any interest on my part has disappeared. I wouldn't want to date someone who leaves me wondering if he's spending time with other women. Though I don't think he took your warning too seriously, since he suggested that I could be one of the women he brings home."

Declan's jaw ticked. "I'm sorry. About most things, he's a stand-up guy, but women are his weakness. If you get into anoth—a relationship, you deserve someone who will treasure you."

Kate's eyes went wide. What was he trying to say? He fiddled with a book he'd picked up from the table beside him.

Anxiety gripped Kate, but she stayed silent. She didn't have a response about Kieran, and didn't want to continue talking about him.

Neither did she want to sit here looking at the man she'd dreamt about that morning.

"I . . . I know that you lost your husband this past year." His eyes lifted from the book in his hands.

Of all the things she expected him to say, it wasn't that. Conflicting emotions rose up. Her brow furrowed, and she fisted her hands. "Your mom promised she wouldn't—"

"No," he interrupted, sitting up and laying the book down. "She didn't tell me. She wouldn't do that. I had you investigated on my own and discovered it." He shrugged at her shocked look. "This is my gran. People take advantage of the elderly, especially those with dementia. I couldn't take a chance on that, so I had someone in America check up on you." Seeing her continued frown, he added, "I'm sorry if that seems invasive, but I'm sure you can understand where I'm coming from. My mum, she's a good businesswoman, but sometimes with personal issues, she's a bit naive."

What could Kate say to that? She wished he'd not found out about her husband, but she would feel the same need to know in his position. It had worried her that an engaged man was so attentive to a woman who was not his fiancée. Now she understood why he had gone out of his way to be so kind to her. It both relieved and saddened her.

"I brought it up because I wanted to tell you that I understand. I lost someone I loved suddenly too. She was my fiancée." When Declan saw the confusion on Kate's face, he smiled sadly. "Yes, I've been engaged twice. I realize it's not quite the loss that you had after years of marriage, but . . . it was hard. It left me lost and confused. Thankfully, Gran was there for me. She helped me get back on track and reminded me of what was important."

The thought of his loss brought tears to her eyes, and Kate blinked them back. So many emotions swirled through her mind. "I'm so sorry. I had no idea. I guess I just thought that since you and Alexandra had been friends since you were young that it was only ever her."

Declan chuckled softly. "No, as soon as I had those sorts of thoughts about girls, I wanted to be with Alexandra, but for the longest time, she just saw me as a friend. I had to watch as she dated one guy after anoth-er." Kate flinched at the thought. "It's true. It wasn't until the end of college that she finally began to view me differently. We have an unusual relationship, but it works for us."

Kate nodded, but she didn't really understand. Who could pass by the adoration of someone like Declan for even a short time, and why were they waiting so long to marry? If she were Alexandra, she would have locked him down fast. What a strange thought. Not what she would have anticipated feeling ten months ago just after Mark died. "Where is Alexandra this weekend?"

"She had some things scheduled, or she would have jumped at the chance to come visit Gran. But back to you. My mum mentioned that you don't want people to feel sorry for you, and you want to put it behind you. I won't press, but I'm here if you need me. You seem to be handling things really well. From personal experience, I know you can feel like everything is fine, and then it hits you out of the blue."

This time, there was no holding back the tears. Declan moved to the sofa next to her and rubbed her back as she started to shake. "It's okay. Let it all out."

Frantically, she wiped the tears from her face, but they came so fast, it didn't help. Eventually, the tears slowed, and her breathing evened out as she leaned into him. Once she regained her senses, she pulled back, suddenly feeling self-conscious. She wanted to tell him more, but something held her back. "I . . . I should go to bed. Thanks for sharing with me and offering a shoulder to cry on."

"Will you go with us to church in the morning?"

Kate responded with a nod, and Declan's eyes lit up. "Great. See you in the morning. Goodnight, Kate."

Chapter Thirteen

The following night, Declan read Scripture from Margaret's encouragement list. "For he has said, 'I will never leave you nor forsake you.' So we can confidently say, 'The Lord is my helper; I will not fear; what can man do to me?' Hebrews 13:5-6." He looked up and smiled at Kate before noticing that Margaret was drifting off to sleep. "Gran, let me help you to bed."

Once again, Declan urged Kate to join him in the sitting room after Margaret went to bed, and she felt powerless to refuse. Before he even sat down, she found herself speaking. "How did your fiancée die?" She hoped it didn't offend him that she asked something so personal. Surely not, since he was the one who had dug into *her* personal life.

A muscular hand rubbed over his face before he leaned back into the sofa and blew out a breath. His eyes held hers for what felt like ages before he spoke. "Car accident. A drunk driver." Kate gasped. "Yeah . . . it was bad, but they think Victoria died instantly."

Now it was her turn to comfort him, and she reached to place her hand over his but then withdrew it.

The corner of his mouth drew up. "I won't bite."

Trying to hide her embarrassment, she forced a smile and quickly patted his hand before withdrawing it again. "I'm sorry. I know when I found out my husband was shot, it devastated me."

"By a legal client, right? And then the guy shot himself. That had to have been hard to accept."

Kate stared at her folded hands in her lap and nodded.

"I imagine you're like I was and have had a hard time forgiving the person who caused you so much pain." His words drew her eyes up, and she nodded again. "Even though he's dead. Maybe especially since he's dead and you can't confront him."

A tear slipped from her eye, and she reached up to wipe it and nodded. He was going to think she was a mess, crying all the time.

"Hey. I'm sorry. I keep making you cry. That wasn't my intention." He placed a hand on her shoulder.

"It's not your fault. I'm the one who started this conversation, but yeah, I have had a hard time with forgiveness. I don't know how to let go of the hurt and anger, so I just keep shoving it down deeper and deeper." When their eyes met, she knew he understood her pain. "I . . . I guess that's part of why I didn't want anyone to know. It's easier to not face it."

"I get it. I went through all the stages of grief, and it wasn't pretty. The anger stage held me hostage for a while. I was mad at God. I was mad at the driver, who walked away with nothing but a broken leg. Yeah, he got prison time, but he killed my fiancée. It was Gran who kept pursuing me and loving me, even when I was not very lovable."

"So one day you just decided to stop running?"

"Gran kept pointing me back to God. She said she prayed for me every day, and every time she saw me, she prayed over me. She gave me her list of encouragement Scriptures, and it sat in my nightstand untouched until one day, Victoria's birthday, I was so broken and angry that I cried out to God, saying I wanted to die. I actually thought about getting drunk and driving into a lake, but the thought that I might leave someone else in the same mess shook me out of it. God reminded me of the list, and I read the verses over and over until I passed out that night. The next morning, I felt different. I opened my Bible, and the first verse I looked at said, 'Forgiving each other as the Lord has forgiven you,' from Colossians chapter three verse thirteen. It hit me hard. Even though I was angry with God, I still wanted His forgiveness. How could I hope for that if I couldn't forgive someone else?"

Kate felt an onslaught of emotions. Where to begin? "I have no problem forgiving some things. But this . . . I don't know. I mean, say for example, someone cuts in front of you in a line. That I can get over and forget fairly easily, but killing someone—like your fiancée"—she motioned towards him—"that's on a whole other level. I imagine it's the same for God. You've got people who make little mistakes that he forgives, but some get to go straight to hell when they die."

"It would seem that way, but the Bible says it's different for God. The thing is, we all deserve to go to hell. He is so perfect, so holy, that even what we think of as small sins keep us separated from him and unable to get into heaven and his presence. Nothing we can do is good enough to outweigh those sins or earn our way into heaven."

"But I thought . . . then how . . . ?" Kate was thoroughly confused. Part of her wanted to shut this conversation down, but another part wanted to know what made Declan who he was. Also, she enjoyed hearing him talk—that accent—but truly, what made him the kind, compassionate man that she couldn't stop dreaming about?

"That's why Jesus, God the Son, fully God and fully man, came down to live and be sacrificed on the cross. He, perfect and holy, paid the price for the sins of every person past, present, and future who would accept him as their Lord and Savior. Everyone since Adam and Eve is born a sinner. Here." He grabbed a pen and scrap of paper from the table and scribbled something. "Read this tonight or in the morning, and we can talk about it."

She looked down and read, "Romans 5:12-21."

"It talks about how Adam brought sin and death into the world, but the free gift through Jesus Christ brings justification and life."

"Justification?"

"Viewed as righteous before God, forgiven for our sins."

"Oh." Kate looked from the paper to Declan, feeling overwhelmed by the conversation. "I should . . ." She nodded towards the stairs. While she loved their deep conversations, this was the second night he'd left her feeling unsettled.

"Can I pray for you first?"

"Um, sure."

Declan laid a hand on her shoulder. "God, I thank you for Kate. She is so kindhearted, compassionate, and thoughtful of others. I pray that you would heal her heart, help her draw near to you for strength, and enable her to see you more clearly. Help her be honest with herself and you and let out all the hidden things in her heart so you can take care of them. Show her what she needs to see in your word. Help me be the friend she needs and know how to encourage her. In Jesus' name, Amen."

His hand on her shoulder felt so intimate, but not in a romantic way. It was a feeling Kate couldn't quite explain but felt in the depths of her soul. He was sharing something so personal and offering it to her. She couldn't recall ever having such a meaningful conversation with Mark, and the things he said about her in his prayer—he seemed to think highly of her, not just feel sorry for her. It made her want to open up more with him. It was freeing to think she could finally let go and share her deepest pain with someone.

That night as she got ready for bed, her mind was filled with reminders of the beautiful cathedral they had visited the day before with its stained glass depicting sacred images, its vaulted ceilings and stone arches. Did God dwell there? "God, who are you?" she said, feeling awkward and unsure. "Do you hear me? Do you really care about the details of my life? If you do, show me. Give me a sign or make things clear. Amen."

She felt silly. Was she just whispering to walls? Something within her longed to think God cared. She thought he might be real. It seemed obvious that the world didn't come from nothing. The intricacies of every living thing, even the planets and stars themselves, pointed to careful planning by a higher power. But Kate had always imagined God as making his creation, then leaving them to fend for themselves. Maybe that happened after Adam and Eve. Who could blame him for wanting to desert mankind? Supposedly, he told them they could eat from any tree but one, and of course they had to have that one.

Shaking her head, Kate chuckled under her breath. Wasn't that the way it often was for men? They wanted the one thing they couldn't have.

Lying down with the Bible Declan gave her, she read through the Romans Scripture listed on the paper. After reading, she wrote out her questions for Declan. He did offer to talk with her about it. Hopefully he really meant it.

The next morning, Kate hurried downstairs, wanting to speak to Declan before Margaret woke, and she found him just coming in from a run. He seemed embarrassed when she suggested they talk before he showered, so she waited patiently while preparing breakfast.

"Mmm. Smells good."

Kate turned from the stove, and her breath caught at the handsome man standing there with his piercing blue eyes and blond hair still damp. As they ate, he walked her through some questions she had about the Romans verses. He answered most of them but said he'd get back to her on one thing. He'd even written more verses for her to read.

The morning flew by, and that afternoon, she had more questions to ask Declan, even though he'd only left a couple of hours earlier. That night when she texted him her questions, he called. They talked more about forgiveness and sin before discussing plans for when her parents came. As she snuggled into the bed, she felt peaceful. Something she hadn't felt in a long time.

Chapter Fourteen

"Kate, dear, I can't wait to tell you about all our adventures." Kate's mom encased her in a hug, then turned and whispered in her ear, "I hope you're feeling okay this week."

When Kate pulled back, she looked at her mom and nodded. Kate's parents had been her anchor through it all, especially her mom, who knew many of the details her father didn't.

Kate's dad stepped up and joined the hug. When they finally released her, she reintroduced them to Margaret. "Margaret, do you remember my parents? Brett and Abby?" She had met them two weeks earlier.

Margaret hesitated. "Yes, Katie, but . . . they've changed." Her eyes squinted, and Kate guessed she was confusing her and her parents with her old friend Katie and her family. With Margaret's dementia escalating, she wasn't sure if Margaret even thought of her as different from her old friend anymore.

Throughout the afternoon, Kate's parents regaled them with stories of their time in Scotland, Wales, and the countryside of England.

Her mom was a presence wherever she went. There was no mistaking when Abby Thomas was in the house. "Did you know that throughout Wales, castles dot the countryside and are often no more than a day's horse ride apart, so if there was an attack, they could ride to another and get help? Of course, a day's ride was only about twenty miles away. As small as Wales is, it has over six hundred castles. More per square mile than any place in the world. The history there is so amazing!"

Her parents had arrived in London two weeks earlier. Kate had taken Margaret and met up with them for the weekend before her parents left on their tour of Great Britain. They'd kept in touch, but it was hard to share everything through calls and texts.

Later that night, her parents joined her on the upstairs balcony. "Tell us about this young man we're staying with," her dad questioned.

The pressure in Kate's chest felt heavy, and she looked out towards the sea as if it held answers. She longed to say that he was something more than a friend, but that was only wishful thinking. A kind of thinking that she'd not been able to correct so far. She settled for speaking of what Declan actually was to her, and hoped that they couldn't read between the lines and see the longing in her heart.

"He's Margaret's grandson and a friend who is working at their Paris office and offered for us to stay at his apartment. Declan's also going to play tour guide and show us around. He and I have been working on a list so he could make a schedule for us."

"Sounds like you two have grown close. You said his name is Declan?" Her mom had a way of getting right to the point.

"Yes, Declan, and we really are just friends. He has a fiancée." It wasn't getting any easier to say that, but it needed to be said before her mom imagined something going on between Declan and Kate.

"Oh." Her mom frowned and looked disappointed, but when her dad looked at Abby pointedly, she smiled and added, "Anyway, I'm looking forward to you showing us around here this week, before our Paris weekend."

"It's 31.35 miles long and opened in 1994. Although it says that plans for it started in 1802, work on it didn't start until 1882 and was abandoned until 1988, when it started again." Kate's father read an article on his phone about the Chunnel under the English Channel as they rode the train through that very place.

"This is so fun." Her mother beamed. "I've not been on a train since you were little, Kate. Remember the Chattanooga Choo Choo? Of course, that's nothing compared to a train ride between countries and through the Chunnel!"

"I wonder why they stopped in 1882? I guess they didn't have the materials and technology we do now to make it work." Kate was just as impressed at the amazing feat as her parents.

There were no stops on this train, and it would take them to the center of Paris. Kate had found that the train systems and subways made it much easier to get around Europe without a car compared to the U.S. Once in Paris, they merely needed to get on the metro, which was in the same building as the train station. It would take them close to Declan's apartment. How much simpler could the trip be? They'd had a ten-minute Uber ride to the Dover Priory train station that morning, and three and a half hours later, they would be in Paris—another dream come true.

Mark had always been too busy for long getaways, saying he had to prove himself to the partners at his law firm. Kate had wanted this since high school, when Jane Austen introduced her to the English country-side. Finally, here she was, living that dream.

Kate's eyes fell on her parents as her mom snuggled into her dad's side. She silently sighed at the realization that she might never have that again. As much as she longed for a relationship to fill the emptiness, the fear of taking a chance and being hurt overshadowed that longing. Maybe that was why Declan was so tempting. He was already taken, and there was no genuine worry that anything would come of it. That relationship would stay in her imagination, because one thing she knew with certainty: she wouldn't get involved with a married—or practically married—man.

As seriously as Declan took his relationship with God, it didn't seem likely that he would ever risk infidelity. That thought made her more comfortable around him. He had his head on straight and was much more emotionally in touch than Mark had ever been. Most of the time, Mark was all business with Kate until he wanted his physical needs met. Then he would turn on the charm. Sometimes it frustrated Kate, but usually, she was so starved for his attention that she took anything she could get.

Once they started having trouble getting pregnant, things got tense in that aspect of their lives too. The physical part of their relationship began to feel like a job and had been lacking the last couple of years before his death. Kate felt her heart rate slow as she remembered the painful things tied to her marriage. If only she'd been more aware of what was happening between them. No, she wouldn't let her mind go there again.

God. That was where her focus should be. Declan had said that God turned things around for him and brought healing to his brokenness. She closed her eyes, feigning sleep before her parents questioned why she was staring into space.

What would it mean to become a Christian like Declan and Margaret? Not just someone who claimed Christianity when it was convenient, but someone who had a relationship with God. She remembered him saying in one of their conversations that a two-way relationship was the difference in a real Christian. God wasn't far off and impersonal like she'd imagined. But was that true? Could she trust God? Would that mean she would have to make changes in her life or act differently? Would she really find healing? It didn't seem possible.

She had memories of going to church regularly for a couple of years when she was in elementary school. The Sunday school teachers had been kind, and she made some friends—guys and girls. Although a few of the girls were snobby, overall, she had good memories of it.

Some stories they taught seemed quite fanciful, like a young boy killing a giant with a stone from a slingshot. Goliath—that was the giant's name. Then there was the one of Noah and the flood. Of course, most people had probably heard of that one. Maybe she should look them up in the Bible Declan had given her. She wondered how similar the Bible's words were to the tales she remembered. Did Declan believe those stories were true?

Her eyes popped open. "Do you remember when we went to

church for a while when Cameron and I were little?" She looked between her parents and they nodded, looking curious about the sudden question. "Why did we start going?" After that time, they had only taken them occasionally for Christmas or Easter, so it didn't seem to hold much significance to either of them.

Abby looked at Brett, then back at Kate. "Your dad worked under a man who attended that church, and he was trying to make an impression on the higher-ups at FedEx. We also thought it would be good for you and your brother to learn the basics about God." She shrugged and looked at her husband for confirmation, and he nodded.

"Remember that church softball team you were on?" her dad questioned, and flashbacks of picking daisies in the outfield flashed in her mind. "My superior, Tom, was the coach and asked me to assist because he knew I'd played baseball in high school. I felt like we should go to the church if I was going to be coaching, and I made some good contacts there too. I'd say it was a good experience. What made you think of that?"

Kate gazed at the contour of the French countryside that had emerged after they exited the Chunnel. "I've been attending church with Margaret."

Did she want to get into a conversation with her parents about God? They might think she was just desperate for something because of all she'd gone through. Maybe she was. Part of her also wanted to hide the fact that she'd been talking with Declan about God. That was a personal thing they shared, and she wanted to keep it hidden from others. Looking back at her dad, she shrugged. "It just reminded me of when I was younger." Although Margaret's church was quite different, not as formal as the church she'd visited as a child, it still stirred those memories.

From the few times she'd sat in on the service when she was little, she recalled a lot of standing to recite things that everyone seemed to have memorized. They also sang old-fashioned hymns.

Regardless of those past experiences, church with Margaret seemed different. Ever since Declan had started sharing with her about his relationship with God, she'd listened more intently, and the things she heard moved something deep inside her. Whatever it was, it left her wanting more.

Excitement raced through Kate as they approached Gare du Nord in Paris. Excitement to see the city, but also an excitement she wouldn't speak out loud—to see Declan. What would it hurt to enjoy his company as long as she kept things platonic? He was making a difference in her life, and she respected and appreciated him. Not just his physical appearance, which was beyond measure, but even more who he was inside.

Declan had suggested Kate download the Citymapper app, and it successfully directed them step by step through the journey to his apartment. They easily found their way to the metro on the lower level, then one stop later, they were two blocks from Declan's apartment in the second arrondissement. It had only taken ten minutes once exiting the train. She smiled to herself as she texted Declan to tell him they were off the metro and almost to his apartment.

From the moment they stepped out of the metro at Chatelet les Halles, Kate noticed a completely distinct atmosphere from England. It wasn't just because they were in a city and she'd spent most of her time on the English coast. Paris felt different from London too.

She saw no signs of the pervasive Georgian style found in London. From what she learned, the designers of London favored the regularity of roads and architecture. When planning their trip, however, Kate had noticed that irregular and often narrow roads filled Paris. The architecture also was more varied. Some buildings looked ancient, with others influenced by Renaissance or Rococo styles. It all worked together for a more romantic atmosphere than that of London.

Kate couldn't wait to drop their bags and start touring. She noticed the café across the street and imagined herself sitting outside, sipping café au lait while eating a croissant. *Perfect.*

Sleek-looking Parisians bustled past, and more casually-dressed tourists stopped for photos, but she hardly noticed them as she gaped at the buildings. Kate would look just like those tourists the rest of the weekend, camera in hand, trying to capture every detail to reminisce over later.

When they turned down Declan's street, she found it just as beautiful as the others she'd passed. Charming buildings pressed up against one another. Shops filled the lower floors. Iron balconies decorated with flower pots added pops of color above them. A boulangerie, a couple of clothing stores, a home accessories store, and other shops she couldn't quite make out from their names lined the street.

"Christian Louboutin?" Abby pointed to the red shop just ahead of them, and Kate's mouth fell.

"I knew this had to be a nice area since it's only a short block and a half from the Louvre and three to the Seine, but I didn't realize this was such a high-end area."

"His family business must do very well. Are you sure he's seriously engaged?" Her mom winked.

Kate tensed, and her dad stepped in. "Abby, don't tease our daughter. She doesn't mean that, dear."

Just as Kate regrouped, she looked up to see Declan leaning against a building, looking at his phone. Handsome as ever. As if he sensed her, he raised his head and waved, a smile taking over his face. Kate felt as if the air around her stilled and the surrounding buildings faded. Her body moved towards him without another thought. "Hi."

He pulled away from the wall. "Hi."

Chapter Fifteen

"You must be Declan." Brett stepped forward and shook a nodding Declan's hand. "We're Kate's parents, Brett and Abby."

Heat crept up Kate's face. How could she forget that her parents were standing right behind her?

"So great to meet you." Declan shook Abby's hand, then reached down for her suitcase. "Here. Let me help you." He turned to punch a code into a security box, pulled the door open with his free hand, and leaned against it to hold it open.

Kate passed him, and he snatched her bag as well. When she shot him a questioning look, he shook his head. "I've got it."

Leading them to a tiny elevator, he set their luggage in it and offered for her parents to ride it while he and Kate took the stairs to the fifth floor. The elevator barely held her parents and the luggage.

When the doors closed, Kate turned to Declan. "Declan, I can't thank you enough for all you're doing! I just know—"

Looking down, he squeezed her shoulder, then stiffened before quickly moving back. "I'm glad it worked out. This way." He turned and pointed to the stairwell entrance.

Kate noticed his reddened face as he directed her up the stairs. She tried to take in the elegant though small stairwell, but his presence and thoughts of him were distracting. He obviously didn't mean anything by the shoulder squeeze, but she feared her awkwardness gave away the feelings she was working to hide.

Breathing hard when they reached the fifth floor, Kate approached her parents to get her suitcase, but Declan beat her to it.

"It's just down this way." Declan led them farther down the hall and unlocked his apartment door. "Did you bring an extra key with you from Gran's?" He looked at Kate as she entered.

"I did, thanks." The words got stuck in Kate's mouth as they passed through the entry hall into the living room.

Beautiful didn't begin to describe it. Her eyes darted around the room, absorbing every detail—wood floors in a herringbone pattern, ornate ceiling and wall molding, crystal chandeliers, several sets of French doors that opened onto separate iron-enclosed balconies, a carved marble mantle, and fireplace surround. French antiques covered in updated neutral fabrics filled the room, while the draperies appeared to be made of silk and bolder colors. It was more perfectly French than Kate could have imagined. Every detail screamed elegance and style.

Her parents appeared equally impressed with the apartment. When Abby commented on the excellent location and beauty of the building, Declan explained that his grandparents had purchased it in the early sixties to use as a getaway and for business on the continent.

"I guess it's like Americans buying lake houses, except in a different country."

"True," Abby replied. "How nice to have such an interesting city just a quick train ride away. We truly appreciate you showing us around. It will be a great help since our visit here is so short."

"I hope so. Speaking of, we should leave if we want to keep to the schedule I have planned for this afternoon." Declan looked at the time on his phone. "Let me show you to your rooms so you can freshen up, then I've got a picnic packed to eat by the river before we go to the Louvre."

Within minutes, they were sitting alongside the Seine eating a baguette, cheeses and meats, fruit, and the most elaborate pastries Kate had ever seen. She watched the water as the tour boats floated under the bridges, and remembered that Declan had scheduled them on one the following night at twilight. He said the lights of the Eiffel Tower would come on just as they approached in the boat. It gave Kate chills just thinking of it.

"What's that building?" Abby pointed across the water to the enormous but beautiful architecture.

"A library. It's part of the Institut de France that works to preserve the arts, literature, and science. The building was originally a school and first built in the mid-1600s."

"Wow. And to think, the U.S. wasn't even a nation then. So much history. How do you keep track of it all?" questioned Abby.

"I certainly don't keep track of it *all*, but since this is such a large building and close to my apartment, I know about it." Declan chuckled, then offered to take pictures of Kate with her parents by the river.

"You could be a professional guide." Brett patted Declan on the shoulder after they entered the Louvre through the less crowded lower-level mall entrance. They had all seen the long line for bag check at the main entrance on the ground level and were thankful that Declan knew a better way. "These museum passes have already paid for themselves since we avoided the ticket line."

"Too bad we didn't have someone like you on the U.K. portion of our trip," Abby mused.

With the same efficiency, Declan led them to some of the key points of interest in the museum—Michelangelo's *Dying Slave* statue, *Winged Victory of Samonthrace* statue from the second century BC, the famous *Liberty Leading the People* painting that commemorated the French Revolution and inspired the Statue of Liberty and Les Miserables, the statue of *Venus de Milo*, and the enigmatic smile of Leonardo da Vinci's *Mona Lisa*. All the masterpieces were set against the backdrop of a lavish French palace, with the artwork adding to its elegance.

"It really is smaller than I had imagined when I was younger," Kate commented on the Mona Lisa while snapping some photos and taking a selfie. "After researching the painting, I knew to expect it, but it still caught me off guard. It looks dwarfed compared to most of the paintings here."

Declan nodded and smiled before checking his watch. "There are a couple more things in here I'd like to show you, then we'll walk through the Tuileries Gardens on our way to Musée de l'Orangerie, where they have Monet's Water Lilies collection." He watched as Kate lit up.

"I've always loved his work. The way it captures the colors and mood as though through a hazy glass." Kate closed her mouth when she realized she was drawing attention. It delighted her that Declan made it part of their tour. She motioned for her parents to follow so they could move on to the next pieces of artwork on Declan's list. The sooner they finished here, the more time she'd have perusing Monet's paintings.

"You mentioned your interest in Monet when we were working on plans for this weekend. You'll love the installation of his work at the Orangerie. They have a specially designed oval room with walls and ceiling height proportioned specifically for his series of eight Water Lily paintings." Declan guided them through the museum crowd.

On their way to the exit, Kate's eyes darted around the palace, trying to take everything in. The Louvre itself was a beautiful piece of artwork. A palace that started as a fortress and through the years was changed and enlarged. It had become not only impressive in design by mixing a variety of French styles but also impressive in size as it consumed the equivalent of several blocks.

If the elegance of the building wasn't enough, upon their exit past the modern pyramid, they traced a path through numerous formal gardens. Kate looked down at the limestone gravel that covered the path, giving it an old world feel, especially against the backdrop of the many marble statues.

Kate's eyes trailed to where Declan was standing with her parents, and her heart picked up speed. If only her heart didn't feel so drawn to him. Every time they spoke, whether in person, by phone, or text, he encouraged her. The things he was teaching her about God were changing her perspective about Christianity. He had created a hunger in her to know more.

She moved to where the others stood and looked at Declan. "Will Alexandra be joining us for dinner?" If she had to watch the two of them together, that would help snuff out some of her longing.

Declan frowned as he turned to Kate. "She said she was sorry to have missed time with you. She especially felt bad that she couldn't meet your parents, but she already had plans in London for this weekend before she realized you were coming."

"I'm sorry. Did we mess things up for you? I had no idea you had previous plans." Kate realized she should have followed up to make sure he didn't feel obligated to them.

"Oh, no. Her plans don't involve me. I would have told you if there was something I needed to do. It was important for me to be here. You are doing so much for us. This is the least I could do. I want this to be a memorable weekend for you."

It hurt a little to think he was doing this because he felt like he owed her. She thought he wanted to because of their strong friendship. When he pointed out the entrance to the Orangerie, she let herself fall behind, needing a minute to refocus.

Declan wasn't exaggerating when he said the Orangerie had a special place for Monet's work. The unique curved walls drew her eyes around the room as if the paintings were 360-degree windows looking out over a pond. In person, they appeared much more vivid than any book or reproduction she'd ever seen, and she stood soaking it all in until a presence behind her sent chills up her spine and drew her from her reverie.

"What do you think?" said the all-too-familiar voice of the man she could hardly stop thinking about.

"It's everything you said and more," she responded without turning toward him for fear the feelings his nearness evoked would be apparent.

He squeezed her shoulder and leaned down to her ear. "I'm glad you like it."

When she finally caught her breath and turned, he had moved several feet away and was in a discussion with her father.

"Mmm. How do the French stay so skinny with all this delicious food everywhere?" Abby swallowed a spoonful of chocolate mousse and placed a hand across her chest.

"It's probably because everyone walks everywhere, and though they do indulge, they often keep the portions small. Then again, they're not eating processed foods, but rather, handmade pastries and breads." A smile overtook Declan's face as he looked up at the man approaching. "Claude, it was delicious as always."

"So glad, my boy." The man named Claude switched to French as he looked at the others around their table.

Declan responded by speaking in French as well before saying, "Meet my good friend Kate, along with her parents, Abby and Brett."

"So good to meet you. Friends of Declan are friends of mine. I hope you've found everything you dreamed of. Declan, did you make sure they were well-fed? Only the best for your friends."

Declan chuckled. "Relax, Claude. There is nothing they could eat here that would not be the best. I made sure that all of your specialties were brought to the table."

"The chateaubriand and coq au vin?"

Declan nodded.

"French onion soup, spinach soufflé?"

Again Declan nodded. "As you can see, we have the crème brûlée, chocolate mousse, and crêpes suzette."

"Good. That is good." Someone came from the back and called Claude. "So glad to meet you all. I'm sorry we don't have longer, but I must take care of this." He took Abby's hand and kissed it before bidding them *au revoir*.

When the door to Kate's parents' room clicked shut for the night, she felt on edge. She and Declan were alone, and he wasn't making any move to leave. All day, his presence had tempted her, yet she'd kept her head on straight. Sitting alone with him might be her undoing, but she did want to talk with him about the things she had been reading in the Bible.

Declan had suggested that she read the first eleven chapters of Genesis alongside the book of John to get a grasp on God's greatness and the salvation he provides.

"In the beginning was the Word." Kate's voice drew Declan's attention. "That's Jesus? He was there when God created the earth and everything?"

Declan pressed his lips together, but his eyes were smiling. "You go straight for the difficult things." She bit her lip and shrugged. "Jesus is a person in the Trinity—the Father, Son, and Holy Spirit—and though there are three, each is equal yet different in their tasks. The Spirit was there, in the beginning, hovering over the waters in Genesis 1:2."

"That's right, I had forgotten that. Let me go grab my Bible." Heart pounding, Kate hurried away. Once she sat down, Declan moved closer to point out the verses in Genesis they were discussing. Her breathing slowed as he used his Bible app to explain how the same Hebrew word used throughout the Old Testament meant wind, breath, and spirit. He also showed her the New Testament Greek word that was the equivalent. He pointed out that the Holy Spirit was shown in Genesis 2 as God breathing life into Adam.

"Switching back to Jesus, the most amazing revelation was the promise in Genesis chapter three verse fifteen that God would put enmity between Satan and the woman's offspring, and that he would bruise Satan's head." Declan told her Jesus was that offspring to come.

"Whoa. God was giving a prophecy about Jesus on the cross way back in the garden of Eden?"

"He was. You're a quick study. So you understand that Jesus dying to pay for our sins, then rising to life, proving he is God, redeemed all mankind and is the death blow to Satan that verse refers to. Right now, Satan is on borrowed time until Jesus returns and finishes him off."

"I'm hazy on the 'finish him off' part, but I read all of John a couple of times. The part where Jesus said 'It is finished' stood out to me, and I did take it to mean he had released mankind from sin."

Declan's grin grew wide.

"What? Why are you looking at me that way?" She wanted to continue making him smile like that.

He shook his head, still grinning. "You're impressive. You keep studying and reading the Bible like that, and you'll be teaching me soon."

"Hardly. This book is enormous!" She smiled, feeling flattered but humbled at the prospect of knowing even half as much as he seemed to. "I can tell there are so many layers of details in it that a lifetime wouldn't be enough to learn it all."

"That's a keen observation, and that's why I read and study my Bible every day. You could study a passage one day, and on another see additional things that God shows you. It's the Holy Spirit working to reveal things to us. The same Holy Spirit that gave many men, through hundreds of years, the words to write the Bible in order for God to tell the story about salvation through Christ from Genesis to Revelation."

"See, that." Kate waved her hand in a swirling motion. "All of that with the Spirit. I feel like I'm just barely scratching the surface of the things pertaining to the Holy Spirit. It's some deep stuff. I thought I understood about Jesus until I learned that he was there in the beginning when everything was created in Genesis." She tried to stifle a yawn, and Declan grinned.

"On that note, I should leave. We have a busy day tomorrow."

Kate looked at the time on her phone and frowned. "Are you sure you'll be okay going out this late? Maybe you should stay here. I can sleep on the sofa. I feel bad that you're giving up your home."

"It's not a big deal. Alexandra's place is only a block away, and the streets stay busy well into the early morning hours. Midnight is nothing, and I wouldn't have offered my place if I didn't mean it. It is truly no trouble to stay at Alexandra's."

Though Kate was sincere in her offer to sleep on the sofa, she was thankful he'd not taken her up on it when she curled into the comfortable bed. She'd just settled down to read when her mom tapped on the door and joined her on the bed.

"Can I see your phone, dear? I'd like to get copies of the pictures you took." Abby pulled out her phone, and her eyes fell to Kate's reading material. When Kate handed her the phone, she said, "Thanks.

I've not been able to get settled tonight. I'm just so excited about this little Paris visit."

Laying aside the Bible she'd been looking at, Kate picked up her Paris guidebook and started flipping through it. She casually glanced at the pictures her mom was looking at, noticing several with Declan as the focus.

"He's a good-looking man." Abby zoomed in on Declan's face. "Are you sure there's not something going on between you two?"

"Yes, Mom. You know how I feel about having a relationship with someone who is taken."

Her mom watched her for a moment before nodding. "I know, dear, but you've been through a lot, and you're emotionally fragile. The way you looked at him today . . . it just seemed like there was something more there." She took a deep breath. "And truthfully, he looked at you the same way."

"There's nothing going on. I promise." Was he really looking at her the same way? Surely not the *same* way. "He's been in love with Alexandra for years, and if you saw them together, you would know she's in love with him too."

"Well, just be careful. I don't want you to get hurt, and whether either of you cares to admit it, there is something happening between you two."

"He knows about Mark's death," Kate blurted out, hoping her mom would stop pushing the subject.

Abby reached over to squeeze Kate's hand. "What does that have to do with anything?" Abby's brows rose.

"When he told me he knew about Mark's death, he also admitted to me that he had been engaged before, and his fiancée died."

"Oh how awful!"

"Yeah. So he feels like he can relate to me, and I think he feels sorry for me."

"I don't think the look in his eyes was him feeling sorry for you, but that's beside the point. Please be careful. I'm not trying to tell you what to do, but sometimes when people are vulnerable, they'll mistake comfort from someone for love. Your father and I love you so much and don't want to see you hurting more. You've had enough pain in your young life."

"Thanks, Mom." She leaned into her mom's waiting arms.

"You know we would love to have you back with us if things get to be too much."

"I know. I'll be fine, and I really do like it there with Margaret. It has been a good distraction."

Her mom's eyes shifted to the nightstand. "You're reading the Bible?"

"I am. De—" She stopped herself from saying Declan was talking to her about it, not wanting to increase her mom's worry that they were too close. "It helps me."

"That's good. Religion can be helpful in getting through hard things. That's another reason your dad and I took you to church when you were younger, so you could learn some things that might help you later."

"But you stopped going?"

"The man your dad had been working under moved away." She shrugged. "We didn't see any reason to continue." Abby studied Kate's face as it fell. "But if that's something you're interested in, it's fine. I know you've mentioned going with Margaret, and you seem to be more settled, so maybe that's just what you need for now."

Kate tried to smile, but it didn't reach her eyes. The contentment Declan had wasn't from attending church. It wasn't from "religion."

"Relationship" slipped out of her mouth. She didn't intend to say that, but maybe it was what her mom needed to hear. "There seems to be a difference between going through the motions of religion and actually having a relationship with God." Her mom's brow furrowed. "That's what I'm seeing in Margaret's family. They attend church not only to be encouraged by others and learn things, but to worship the God they love and talk to every day. They read the Bible and pray every day, not just to store up more facts, but to better understand how great God is and gain God's direction and encouragement for their lives. Sunday is a weekly celebration of what they've been doing the rest of the week, not a standalone experience." Even as she spoke the words, she felt something come alive inside.

"Hmm." Abby's smile faltered, but then she reached out to hug Kate. "It sounds like this is really helping you. I love you. We should get to bed. I'm sure Declan has another big day planned."

"Goodnight, Mom." She wished her mom was more responsive when she spoke about God.

"God, what does this mean for me?" she softly called out and wondered what came next. Was she ready for something more? For *that* kind of relationship with God? What would it cost her? Her parents seemed fine without it. They were good people, but Kate felt a longing for something more, and not just because her previous life had fallen to pieces, but because there was something inside of her drawing her to God.

Chapter Sixteen

"Oh my goodness. This is the most delicious thing ever." Kate covered her mouth while trying to swallow a mouthful of a delectable pastry. "I know we had this conversation, but how does everyone not weigh a ton? All those beautiful pastries at the patisserie. It would take months to try them all." A breakfast of French pastries made the early morning wait in line to enter Notre-Dame Cathedral much more enjoyable.

"She's right, Declan. I don't understand either. Every single pastry in those cases looked divine. I can't imagine turning any of them down if offered one." Abby opened her photos and looked at the pictures of the patisserie case.

Declan grinned and looked between the two women.

Brett nudged him. "For both to be so excited about desserts, I think they manage to maintain beautiful figures."

Declan's cheeks reddened. "If you all turn to face me, I can take a picture of you with Notre-Dame in the background."

"Good idea. Thank you, son." Brett looked at the women and motioned for them to turn. "Kate, dust off your cheek. You missed a spot with your napkin, dear." His hand motioned to the side of her face.

Before Declan had finished taking their picture, a woman in line behind them offered to take a picture with him in it as well. He squeezed in next to Kate, and she felt all her determination to emotionally distance herself from him fly away. Gorgeous looks aside, he was a good man, the kind of man she had always hoped for.

Even when Mark was alive and she thought everything was fine, he did not have half the character Declan did. Mark would never have given up his apartment over the weekend for an employee and their parents. He certainly wouldn't have given an entire weekend of his personal time to show those same people all the busiest places in Paris. Places that he'd seen so many times, he had all their historical facts memorized. He definitely wouldn't have given up weekends to watch his ailing grandmother.

No, Mark was always busy with things that pleased Mark and things that improved his image. Kate, as his wife, had been good for his image, but that wasn't enough to get him home at a decent time during the week or keep him from working, golfing, and who knew what else on the weekends. The deep conversations she'd had with Declan during their brief acquaintance probably topped the total time Mark had spoken with her in the last five years of their almost six-year marriage. That was a painful realization.

Kate felt Declan's hand touch her back, and she looked up at him as he winked when they entered Notre-Dame. If only that wink meant something more and he were single, he would be the man of her dreams.

Even with the stone walls and hard surfaces inside the cathedral, there was a respectful hush. A sense of awe fell upon Kate the moment she entered the nave and looked up at the beauty all around. Grand Gothic arches that reached toward the heavens, intricate stained glass windows, statues, and icons had all been designed to inspire worship of the Creator of all. It took her breath away.

"And to think, the holy city in heaven will be more beautiful than this," Declan spoke softly into Kate's ear.

She turned, and he was so close. "You really think so?"

"Read Revelation 21." Declan pointed Kate and her parents to the exit. "This way, and we can see the exterior."

Kate nodded and silently repeated, "Revelation 21." She didn't want to forget to read it before bed.

A heaven more beautiful than this? Her heart raced.

"These are the flying buttresses that were added to the design later in construction when the height of the cathedral became too much for the thin walls." Declan pointed out the unique architectural element that had become an iconic exterior feature of the cathedral.

Historic architecture had always intrigued Kate. People of the past put so much more time and effort into making many of the significant buildings into works of art, meant to last. Learning history through architecture was becoming one of her favorite pastimes since coming to Europe.

Moving farther into the garden, Kate attempted to capture all of the structure at once in her photo before closing in again to zoom in on the details.

"Did you ever consider a major in architecture?" Declan leaned in as she framed her shot.

Smiling, she clicked, then put her phone away and turned to him. "It's a hobby. I knew I wanted to be a nurse working in memory care too much to give that up, but I definitely enjoy this."

He held her gaze before calling out to her parents, "Anything else you want to see back here before we move to the side of the building? After this, we'll go to Sainte Chapelle. It's only a couple of blocks away."

The way he looked at Kate was unnerving, but she tried not to let her imagination run away, and focused on what he had just said. "I can't wait to see that. The pictures online are unreal. It looks almost as if the walls are entirely made of stained glass. If this was hard to support"—Kate waved at Notre-Dame—"I imagine that must have been even more of a challenge. How did they do it?"

"You'll see," Declan answered. Kate's excitement was contagious, and he grinned back at her while leading them around to the side of the building.

While stepping back from the building and snapping another photo, Kate was jostled by a group of people running past. As she turned, Declan threw an arm in front of her to protect her from what was escalating into a screaming mob running from the cathedral.

"What's going on?" he called out to a man running in their direction.

"Gunshot in the cathedral!" the man shouted and continued to flee.

"Stay together!" Declan commanded Kate and her parents while he watched the crowd. "As soon as there's a break in this mob, run that way!" He pointed to a side street. Seconds later, a gap opened, and he grabbed Kate's hand, pulling her forward while watching behind them to make sure her parents could keep up. They made it to the end of the street and turned left before stopping. The eerie sound of French police sirens surrounded them.

Wide-eyed, Kate looked up at Declan just as her parents pulled her into an embrace. Her shoulders relaxed, and her racing heart slowed.

Brett reached out an arm. "Come here, son." He pulled Declan into their group hug, and now Kate felt her face pressed against Declan's chest.

Once again, her heart rate picked up as she listened to the rapid beat of Declan's.

"Dear Father," Declan prayed out loud, "Thank you for protecting us. If there is anyone injured, I pray that you would get them the help they need to keep it from getting too serious. Father, I pray for the person who shot the gun, that you will convict their heart of their sin and change their heart. God, please give us peace as we try to continue with our day. Help us not be fearful. In Jesus' name I pray, Amen."

"Thank you, son." Brett gave Declan's shoulder a squeeze before releasing him and Kate. Abby continued to cling to Brett and looked around with worried eyes.

Declan hesitated before pointing the way to Sainte Chapelle. Just as they approached, a man emerged from the entrance with a sign announcing that they were closed.

"Closed?" questioned Brett.

"For security reasons," the man replied, and a man dressed in black military garb holding an automatic rifle joined him.

Kate gasped, and Declan grabbed her hand, pulling her away as he spoke. "Thank you, sir. Maybe we'll check back later."

"Was he part of some sort of SWAT team?" Kate's voice came out shaky.

"No. That's a typical police uniform."

"With an automatic rifle?" Brett hoped to calm his worried wife.

"Yes, that's standard." Declan tried to appease them. "Really, those guns are perfectly normal. The police seem to have everything under control. We'll just head off the island to get away from all this." Sounds of sirens still swirled around the area.

Declan had a way of calming Kate, which helped after the Notre-Dame incident. As they walked past the beautiful architecture of Paris, it seemed to have lost its appeal. All she could think of was getting away from the island and the police sirens. Once they safely crossed the bridge, the heaviness in her chest lifted and buildings came back into focus, but still something niggled in the back of her mind.

Musée D'Orsay, Musée Rodin, Tour Eiffel, Rue Cler—the endless art, architecture, and culture kept Kate and her family so busy that the events of the morning faded like a distant memory. By the time they were seated on the sunset river cruise down the Seine, they were all exhausted, though happy with how the day turned out.

As the boat turned a corner, the Eiffel Tower came into view and lit up. The lights had a sparkle effect, and Kate couldn't snap enough pictures. Seeing the Tower this way was something she had imagined for years since she'd first heard about it.

As the boat neared the dock, Brett and Declan were in a deep discussion. Abby wrapped an arm around Kate and spoke softly. "I'm going to miss you, dear. I know this is what you need, but it pains me to know all that you've gone through and to have you so far away."

"I'll miss you too. But this has been good for me, I promise. I know you're only a phone call or FaceTime away."

"Yes, even if it's the middle of the night for me." Abby's eyes held regret and sadness as she squeezed her daughter tighter. They shared a look. Her mom was the only one in her life who knew the full extent of all she'd gone through. "I believe you truly are doing better. There's hope in your eyes that wasn't there before."

Kate nodded and tried to smile, then her eyes flickered to Declan, and she found him watching. Though she'd never shared the extent of her suffering, something in his expression made it appear that he knew there was more than she'd admitted. Her gaze shifted to the buildings along the river. She wanted to tell him everything. He was the first person other than her mother she felt comfortable discussing it with, and she felt it would bring her closer to healing. Though it would be embarrassing, she knew he wouldn't think less of her, but first there were other things she needed to talk to him about.

As if Declan knew she wanted to talk, he followed them up to the apartment and lingered at the door. Kate hesitated to invite him in. She didn't want to have this conversation in front of her parents, and with them leaving in the morning, she had little time left with them.

"Brett and I have some packing to do before bed so there won't be so much in the morning. Goodnight, you two." Abby looked knowingly at Kate as she pulled Brett into the apartment.

"Um . . ." Kate bit her lip while searching for what to say. "I . . . would you come in for a few minutes?"

"Of course." Declan smiled down at her as if he'd been waiting for this.

They both settled on a sofa in the living room.

Declan spoke at the same time Kate did.

"What's—"

"I want to become a Christian."

His eyes lit up. "That's great news!"

"After the gunshot at Notre-Dame, I couldn't stop thinking, 'What if I died without becoming a Christian?' The funny thing is that when I first came to England, I was so certain I was a Christian. Now I know how far off I was from the truth." She turned her head back toward the bedrooms. "I'm sure that's what my parents think about themselves as well." She frowned. "Hopefully once I'm a Christian, they'll see something's different about me. Anyway, what do I do? I can't tell from the things I've read."

"It's really pretty simple, and it sounds like you have already made the choice. You just need to voice it." He pulled out his phone and clicked around before showing it to her. "Read this."

"Because if you confess with your mouth that Jesus is Lord and believe in your heart that God raised him from the dead, you will be saved. For with the heart one believes and is justified, and with the mouth one confesses and is saved," she read Romans 10:9-10 out loud. "That's really all there is?"

He eagerly nodded. "Obviously, God knows if you're sincere or just going through the motions. If you really mean it—truly trust that Jesus is the only way to God and that he is not only God but your Savior from sins through his death and resurrection—then it's going to change your life. You're going to want to talk to him every day, read his words in the Bible, and be part of a local church so you can encourage and be encouraged by other believers. You'll even want to share the good news with others, just like what you mentioned with your parents."

"Yes, I want all those things. I believe all those things. So I'm a Christian?"

"You are. This would be a good time to pray and tell God those things."

Kate felt heat rise to her cheeks. "I've never prayed in front of anyone before, though I have been talking to God these past few weeks."

"Just do that, talk to God. I promise I won't judge you." He reached over and gave her hand a squeeze.

Once Kate finished praying, he pulled her into a hug, and she momentarily froze before hugging him back. The fact that it made her feel things that were wrong set her on edge. She tried to push those thoughts away. This should be a happy time, and she didn't want anything to take away from it.

He pulled away before she could fully wrap her mind around the conflicting feelings. Was that God reminding her it was wrong? "Alexandra," she mumbled, unable to hold back any longer.

"What?"

"Your fiancée, Alexandra."

Declan's brows drew together. "Alexandra's not my fiancée."

Kate moved back farther and frowned.

"Not anymore. It's been a while," he added.

The news shocked Kate, but left her hopeful. "But how? Why? She seems to really love you." Kate thought back to the engagement ring she'd seen Alexandra wear when they met nearly two months earlier.

Declan shrugged. "I guess she does in her own way, but I think I'm more like a brother to her. You've heard how close our families are. We've been doing things together for ages."

Kate opened her mouth to ask how it ended, but stopped herself before sounding rude.

"I'm okay about it. Really. She and I weren't meant to be, and I've come to grips with that."

Kate's heart raced, and her mind reeled. Not only was she now a Christian, but the man who had her heart racing again was no longer engaged. She hoped she was successfully hiding her elation at his news. Kate knew the process of a relationship ending. He wouldn't be ready to have another woman in his life for a while.

A gentle smile began to form on his face. "Back to important, happier things. You becoming a Christian is so great. I already planned to urge you to attend church in the morning after your parents left. Now you have to."

"Perfect." Her smile turned to confusion. "Wait, a church here in Paris? Do they speak French?" He seemed to understand and speak the language fluently, but her little bit of French from school would leave her lost and confused in a church service.

"No, no." He chuckled. "I attend an English-speaking service. We are a church within a church. We meet in a French-speaking church's fellowship hall. Most of us can speak and understand French fairly well, but there's something about hearing God's Word in your heart language that seems to make a difference."

"Okay then. I'd really like that." She wanted to say more. It was all so close to pouring out. What would he think? Would he comfort her? But now was not the time. It was late, and the things she had to say would take time. She didn't want to risk her father overhearing either. She and her mom were determined to avoid telling him everything. It would be too much for him. He would feel like he'd failed her. No, that conversation was best saved for later.

"Thank you for taking so much time to talk to me about God. I never would have gotten to this point without it."

He gave her a humble smile and looked at her earnestly. "God would have worked on you even if I had not been willing, but I'm so glad I could be part of this. It's the most important thing you can ever do."

Kate pondered that. "God would go to so much trouble for me?" She didn't mean to speak it out loud.

"Yes, God would. He died for you. He would leave the ninety-nine to go after the one." When she gave him a funny look, he added, "Read Matthew 18."

That night, Kate dreamed about a lost sheep and the shepherd leaving the flock to find the one. Over breakfast, she was torn. She wanted to tell her parents her good news, but what would they think?

Halfway through their meal, she couldn't take it any longer and told them. As she'd anticipated, they were confused. They thought she was already a Christian and believed they were too. Kate had believed the same thing when she first arrived.

In their minds, someone who believed the God of the Protestant church existed and didn't follow some other religion was a Christian. They didn't fully grasp who Jesus was as part of the Trinity and why he had to die. They were still trying to earn salvation, and Christianity was more of a label than a reality in their lives.

Inwardly, Kate promised God she would do everything possible to help them see the difference, even with thousands of miles and an ocean between them. Her parents were the most important people on earth to her, and she couldn't bear the thought of heaven without them. As soon as that thought worked its way through her brain, she understood that God felt the same way about her. Goosebumps made her shiver.

Was that the Holy Spirit speaking to her? Declan had talked about the Holy Spirit being the part of God that resided in every Christian. Tears threatened to spill out. The day before had been wonderful when she became a Christian, and yet it was as if something more awakened—a better understanding. All of God's love filled her and overflowed through her. Every pain and hurt that she'd suffered over the past year and before no longer seemed important. Would it always feel this way?

Kate glanced around the fellowship hall of the French church. A contemporary congregation had bought the old, abandoned church building several years earlier. The architecture was stunning.

As they sang, their voices rose and the high ceiling amplified them, creating a harmonious effect. She wondered what it would sound like in the vaulted main sanctuary she had seen on the way in.

A palpable joy filled the space. Was the congregation as joyful at Margaret's church, or had she missed it because she wasn't a Christian before?

When the service ended, Declan introduced her to so many people, she couldn't remember their names. A British couple from the church, Hannah and Luke, joined them for lunch at a nearby café. Kate learned that they had moved there two years earlier for their jobs. They had met at university, and both became Christians through a ministry on campus. It was a romantic story made sweeter by Hannah's new pregnancy. Amazingly, Kate didn't feel envious. She knew better than to think becoming a Christian made all of her sinful urges disappear. Instead, she realized her joy refused to be extinguished by such petty thoughts. That awareness brought her more joy.

"Thank you so much for everything," Kate said effusively as they walked back to Declan's apartment.

"I'm truly honored I could show you and your parents around."

"It has been a great weekend, and I still can't believe you gave up your apartment for us, but I'm also thanking you for helping me understand God better. There's still a lot of . . . baggage I have to work through, but now it doesn't seem so important. My burden feels lighter."

He pulled her into a side hug, and she took a last look around, feeling content next to him.

"Thank you for letting me share that with you, Kate. Speaking of sharing things . . . I know you were baptized as an infant, but if you'd like to have a believer's baptism, we could try to set that up at Gran's church next weekend. Maybe Mum and Chloe can come in as well. Of course, I wouldn't miss it."

"That's right, baptism." She thought about what she'd read in the Bible and recalled people getting baptized to acknowledge the decision they'd made for Christ. "Yes, I think I'd like that. Can you help me set that up?"

He grinned down at her, wrinkled his brow, then pulled his arm away. "I'd be honored. I could go back with you today and get started setting things up."

"What? No, that's too much. You already gave up your Friday and weekend." He frowned at her refusal, but she continued her insistence. "I would feel bad. If you want to help, you can work on getting your sister to come."

A guilty feeling welled up, and she added, "I'll talk it over with your mom when I get back to Kingsdown. Though I'm a little embarrassed, after telling her I was a Christian when she interviewed me."

"No worries. Mum will definitely understand. She'll be so happy for you, as will Gran. I hope Gran's having a good day so she can fully celebrate with you." Moisture gathered in his eyes.

Reaching over, Kate started to wrap her hand around his arm, but at the last second just patted it. "I've really missed her this weekend. She's easy to become attached to. I can see why she's so special to you."

He smiled through his sadness. "She's lucky to have you, Kate Thomas. We all are so thankful you came."

Everything that led up to today hit her at once. The lows of the last year, and the high she'd felt becoming a Christian. Her voice was strained. "Me too, more than you know." *It saved my life*, she wanted to add.

He held her gaze as if he could see her turmoil from the past year. She no longer wanted to hide it from Declan. Her hidden pain would be safe with him. One day soon, she hoped to get the chance to tell him.

Chapter Seventeen

As the train flew past the French countryside, Kate's mind drifted off to the prior year. It felt like she'd aged decades rather than eleven months.

It was hard to reconcile what her life had been like one year ago compared to now. She had a somewhat happy marriage with issues that she believed could be worked through, a job with regular hours, weekends at the country club with wives of the other lawyers from Mark's firm, her parents and Jennifer close by. But she always looked towards a future when things would get better with Mark—when they would get pregnant, when he would have more time, and when he would make partner in the firm.

Now, after months of devastation and being an ocean away from everything familiar, she was happier than she'd ever remembered being. She felt hopeful, and her happiness didn't depend on any particular circumstance in her life. No husband, baby, or even job could give her the feeling of contentment that she currently had.

As angry as she'd been at Mark when she first arrived in England, and as much as she'd wished he'd never entered her life, now she could honestly say all the difficulties had a purpose. Without them, she wouldn't be here now—seeking and loving God with all her heart. With that thought, she relaxed into her seat and drifted off.

"I won't be home until late tonight."

Kate frowned and turned to Mark. "Again? You were at the office all weekend and stayed late every night this week."

Dumping his coffee in the sink and placing the cup in the dishwasher, he shrugged. "A lot going on at work, especially with this big trial coming up."

Pushing back from the kitchen table, Kate turned towards him and spoke softly. "But I'm supposed to be ovulating. We can't miss this chance."

Mark's hand slammed down on the counter, and his eyes narrowed. "Kate, everything doesn't have to be about you getting pregnant. That's all you care about anymore."

"Me? I-I thought it was what we both wanted." She fought hard to keep the tears back.

Without a glance back at her, he jerked up his leather briefcase. "I can't do this right now. I'm going to be late." Seconds later, the door to the garage slammed.

Kate jerked awake in her seat, and her eyes bounced around the train car. Did a door slam? Her hands shook, and her chest tightened. Then it came to her. She'd been dreaming about the last time she saw Mark, the day he was shot. Clenching her hands, she pushed the memory back into the recesses of her mind. *I will not be plagued by the past today.*

Hayley insisted they eat somewhere other than the Rose and Crown for lunch Wednesday. The café seemed nice, but Kate already missed the variety of Paris. "Why are we here and not Rose and Crown? What will Aidan think?"

"Well . . ." Hayley bit her lip and twisted her face. "Aidan asked me out." She awaited Kate's response.

"That's wonderful. You've been interested in him for a while." Kate smiled genuinely.

"Yes, but I didn't want to go out with him if there was a chance you had any lingering feelings for him."

"No. I think he's a great guy, but there was never any real chemistry between us. I'm sure he realized that, too, and that's why he was ready to ask you out so soon. You should definitely go out with him."

"You're sure?"

"Absolutely. It would make me happy if you did."

"Well then, I think I will." Hayley grinned. "So, tell me about your weekend."

"It was perfect; everything I'd imagined." Her heart raced as she recalled the food, beautiful architecture, and most importantly, the decision she'd made to become a Christian. "We should go to Paris one weekend. I'm already craving the pastries from this cute little patisserie Declan introduced us to."

"Love that idea! It's been ages since I visited. So . . . you had your handsome tour guide . . ." Hayley wiggled her brow, then chuckled at the face Kate made. She put up her hand. "I know, I know, he's taken. You have eyes, though, and can still admire him. Anyway, tell me what you did."

While giving Hayley the rundown of her weekend, Kate shared the news of Declan's single status, but avoided telling her anything that might make her continue to assume there was anything more than friendship between her and Declan. Maybe one day something could happen between them, but he needed time to heal, and so did she. "Back to you and Aidan. When are you supposed to go out?"

"Saturday. He wants to take me out for the day and to lunch." Hayley practically bounced in her seat. "I'm not sure what he plans for the day. Maybe it will last until evening and I can go with him to Rose and Crown and hang around while he does his boss thing and the band plays."

"I'm happy for you. I hope it goes great and lasts all day just so you can keep that giant grin longer."

Hayley tried to hide her smile but couldn't. "Hopefully, I'll have better control by then. I don't want him to think I'm a crazy person."

"He already knows you and knows you're crazy." Kate broke out in laughter.

"All right. That's enough. Are you going to meet me there Saturday night if I stay?"

"I don't think I should. I don't want it to be awkward."

"It won't—"

"But don't stay out too late Saturday night. I want you to come to my baptism Sunday morning. I became a Christian on Saturday." Now Kate was having to keep from grinning like a crazy person. Just thinking about her decision brought that feeling of peace and overflowing joy back.

"Yeah? Somehow, I thought you already were a Christian."

Kate made a face. "I did, too, but I started reading the Bible and realized I had made Christianity and God up according to what I thought they were, not what they really are."

This was a chance for Kate to tell her friend how different it was to have a relationship with God compared to just imagining him being far away and doing his own thing. She was so excited that she couldn't hold it back. Hayley listened and didn't seem put off by the conversation. She even agreed to go to the church service to see the baptism.

Just as Kate had Margaret settled in her chair, the sound of the back door being unlocked sent a thrill through her. She'd been looking forward to Declan's arrival all day. Throughout the week, he'd called her several times and texted the other days with words of encouragement and Scripture.

"I think I hear Declan coming in," Kate remarked to Margaret's confused look towards the back of the cottage.

"Who?"

"De-Corbyn."

"Corbyn," Margaret repeated with a smile.

"Mm-hmm. Let me see if he needs help with anything. I'll be right back." Kate practically skipped to the door, not holding back her grin.

"Alexandra!" Kate struggled to keep her smile. He'd not mentioned she was coming. Of course she would come; they might not be engaged anymore, but she was like family. She stared at the intimidating beauty before her, trying to gather her thoughts. "You-you had a good trip?" Kate's eyes went to Alexandra's ring finger and found it bare. The hope she'd been stifling rose ever so slightly.

"It's a dull ride, but I had Declan and a good book to keep me company. Isn't that right, darling?" she questioned Declan as he entered with two overnight bags.

"What's that?" His eyes caught Kate's and didn't waver as Alexandra spoke.

"I was saying I had you and a good book to keep me entertained on the train. Hello." She patted him on the cheek twice before he turned to her.

"Oh yes, quite right. A good book to pass the time. How are you, Kate?" He set the bags down and started to reach for Kate, but dropped his arms to his sides.

"Good. Great. Um . . . your gran is in the sitting room." To Kate, Alexandra wasn't treating Declan like a brother.

"Perfect. I-we're glad to be here for your special weekend." As Declan stuttered over his words, Alexandra pushed past Kate.

"Gran!" Alexandra called out. Her next words were muffled through the walls of the rooms.

Kate and Declan stood in the back hall staring at one another.

Shifting on his feet before lifting the bags, Declan grinned and commented, "I guess I should get these put away."

"I'll just . . ." Kate pointed towards the sitting room but didn't move. Declan's curious gaze finally brought her to her senses, and realizing she blocked Declan's path, she turned to join Margaret and Alexandra.

His presence unnerved her. During the past week, they had become close, not only sharing a bond of losing a significant other, but now both being Christians. She'd not had a close friend who was a guy before, and she wondered how to act, especially in the presence of Alexandra and the family. What was the protocol for that type of thing?

The following day, she would have bowed out of their visit to a local garden if she hadn't already promised Declan she'd go. That had been before she knew Alexandra planned to join. Kate liked Alexandra well enough, but noticed a new tension between them and felt responsible.

When Tracey and Richard arrived in time to join the group, Kate's concern eased. At least there would be more people for her to interact with.

The garden sparked something in Margaret. "So pretty," she commented as they approached each new flowering plant.

Concern on Tracey's face drew Kate from Margaret's side. "What is it?"

Tracey glanced at her mom, then shook her head. "Her mind is really slipping. In the past, she would have named every plant and explained how to care for it. Maybe even described the various other kinds of similar ones. But today, all she says is 'So pretty,' and it's only ten thirty in the morning." She wiped moisture from her eyes before it escaped. "I knew she was getting worse, but this has caught me off guard. It seems significantly more advanced than last weekend when I stayed with her. Do you think her medicines need adjustment?"

"Maybe. We can certainly take her in and try that. I have noticed more confusion this week, but I'm guessing it's also more apparent at a time like this when tasks require higher-level thinking." Kate watched as Tracey's brow furrowed and she nervously rubbed her arms. "I'm sure you're worried that this means she's going to lose her abilities rapidly now, but that's not usually the case. More often, there is a large change, then it levels back off for a while at a slower pace. We can reevaluate her weekly activities before you leave."

Tracey's face relaxed some, and she led them farther away from the rest of their group. "Okay, thank you." Her voice shook as she added, "This is so hard. My heart breaks a little more every day."

Placing a hand on Tracey's arm, Kate wished there was something more she could do. "She's a beautiful woman, inside and out. Hang on to every memory of the way she was."

Absentmindedly touching a flower, Tracey nodded, then turned back to Kate. "Do you think it's time for her to be moved into the memory care facility?"

Kate thought of the facility only blocks from Tracey's London home that she'd visited with Tracey when last in the city. The ideal arrangement contained individual "houses" on separate floors that provided each patient with a private bath and room. The attached fenced-in garden had hooked Tracey instantly.

"No. It's still too soon. As nice as it is, while she is very aware of who everyone is in her life and where she is, it would be an enormous setback for her."

"Okay. You're right. I just don't want to do the wrong thing. It's so hard to know."

"It is. Every patient is different, both in how they react to things and in how quickly or slowly the disease progresses. We've made a good basic plan, and we'll keep communication open about her progress so we can figure out when the time is right." She tried to soothe Tracey with her words, but the future held so much more tension and sadness.

It saddened Kate as well. Over the past few months, she'd grown quite attached to Margaret and her family. Though Tracey had worked out a deal with the memory care facility for Kate to work there once Margaret moved into it, it would differ from what they had living together. At that time, she would need to consider returning to her life back in the U.S. That thought sent unwelcome chills through her body. Though she had healed much since her move to England, she still couldn't imagine being ready to go back for a long time. "We have to take each day as it comes and enjoy each moment."

"You kids should go out tonight."

"None of us are anywhere near what could be called a kid, Mum, but I agree that it's a good idea. What do you think, Kate? Are you up for it?"

Still feeling uncomfortable around Alexandra, Kate's first instinct was to say no, but she knew him well enough now to realize that if she said no, he would have them all stay home. He was just that thoughtful.

"Actually, my friend Hayley invited me to the Rose and Crown pub to hear the band tonight. We could join her." At least if they went there, she would have someone else she could talk with and diffuse any awkwardness with Declan and his ex. Though she wondered if they would reunite after seeing the googly eyes Alexandra had made at Declan all day. As much as she wanted to give Hayley and Aidan time without her, Kate knew that Hayley would be excited to have them.

Chapter Eighteen

"You said this place belongs to a friend of yours?" Alexandra asked as they entered the Rose and Crown with Celtic music filling the space.

Kate nodded just before being attacked by a wide-eyed, animated Hayley.

"Oh my gosh! He's hotter than I imagined," Hayley whisper-yelled into Kate's ear with the band in the background. "But I've got your back." She glanced over at Alexandra.

Kate's eyes followed Hayley's and she was thankful the others appeared unaware of Hayley's comments. She grabbed Hayley's arm and pulled her to where Declan and Alexandra stood.

"Hayley, meet Alexandra and Declan." Introductions were barely complete before Hayley moved them toward the booth Aidan had saved them. "How was the date?" Kate questioned Hayley.

Hayley's entire face lit up. "So good." Then lowering her voice, she added, "We'll talk later." She turned to Declan and Alexandra. "Tell me about yourselves." The band had stopped between songs to say something, and they used the time to get acquainted.

"You made it!" Aidan called out just as the band was beginning its next song. Edging his way through the growing crowd, he leaned over to hug Kate.

"I did, and I brought friends—Alexandra and Declan."

Aidan grinned and threw out his hand toward Declan.

With a clenched jaw, Declan eyed the tattoos peeking out from Aidan's shirt while shaking his hand. "How do you know Aidan, Kate?"

Aidan bit back his amusement and let Kate answer while Declan glared his way.

"He's my friend who owns this place. I told you about him."

Declan only grunted an acknowledgment.

"By the way"—Aidan rested a hand on Kate's shoulder—"I'll be there for your baptism tomorrow. In fact, you should bring your group back here for lunch after. I'll set aside the party room for you."

"Are you sure?"

"Absolutely, and *your* meal's on the house. Plus, I'll throw in desserts for everyone."

"Yum. You do have some really good desserts." She looked across at Alexandra and Declan. "You think that would work for your family?"

Declan shrugged. "It's your day."

"Okay. Plan on . . ." She counted on her fingers. "Eleven." Looking back at Hayley, she questioned, "You'll come to lunch too, right?"

"Of course. Wouldn't miss it." Hayley smiled up at Aidan, who silently watched her.

Someone called to Aidan, and he winked at Hayley before disappearing back through the crowd. With him gone, the focus at the table turned toward the band. Declan's response to Aidan, especially his gruff reaction to the lunch plan, confused Kate. Declan was normally so friendly, even with strangers.

One of the band members began playing a dulcimer. Kate found it intriguing to watch and a welcome distraction from the workings of her mind. It wasn't until Hayley started pushing to get out of the booth that Kate fully returned to the present.

"Let's go dance." Hayley pointed to the line forming and dancing like the Riverdance performances she'd seen on TV.

"Wow. Yeah, looks fun, though you have to promise not to laugh at me. Alexandra, Declan?"

Alexandra didn't move and shook her head. "I think I'll sit this out."

Kate nodded, then motioned Haley out of the booth. As soon as she and Hayley were out of their seats, Hayley dragged her to join in the dance line. She'd always felt like she was a fairly good dancer, but this was unlike anything she'd done before. It looked like a variation of tap dancing, which she'd never tried. Hayley linked arms with the last person in line, then linked her free arm in Kate's.

Even though Kate wasn't doing the correct steps, she picked up the rhythm and bounced around in time with the others. She couldn't hold back laughter as she tried to imitate the movements. Just as she began to get the hang of it, she was startled by an arm linking with hers. A sideways glance revealed Declan, and if her face wasn't already red from all the dancing, his presence made it so. What must he think of her ridiculous imitation of the dance? His friendly smile erased most of her worry, and seeing that he was inexperienced himself removed the rest.

Before the dance was over, Aidan had squeezed in between so he could be next to Hayley. All was right. At least until Declan held her elbow as they moved back to their seats, all the while frowning and clenching his jaw.

Declan remained quiet as he drove them back to the cottage. Though Alexandra was chatting away, Kate felt tension in the air.

"Kate, it seems like you have an admirer. Kieran will be jealous." Alexandra turned her body toward the back seat so she could see Kate.

"Oh." Her eyes caught Declan's in the rearview mirror before turning to Alexandra. "Kieran and I . . . that didn't last long. I told him I wasn't ready for anything, and he showed me his true colors by bringing a girl home the next weekend and making out right in front of me."

Then she remembered the other thing Alexandra said. "What did you mean by 'admirer'?" Her face heated, and she fought the urge to look back at the rearview mirror. Maybe she should have ignored that comment. Had it bothered Alexandra that Declan danced with her?

"Aidan. He seems quite taken with you."

Now her eyes did shoot up to the mirror. Declan was watching her. "What? No, it's not like that. I—"

"Are you sure? He was quite chummy with you."

"Well, yeah, we're friends. I mean, we did go out a couple of times." The car suddenly felt stuffy. "But that was ages ago, and I realized I could never have *those* kinds of feelings for him."

"I think he's still hopeful."

"No, really, he just started going out with Hayley. He and I are only friends."

Alexandra's words made her think back through all of her interactions with Aidan throughout the night. Surely it wasn't what Alexandra thought. The way he winked at Hayley and danced with her. Something inside of Kate reminded her that Declan had danced with her—well, next to her—with linked arms. So maybe that didn't mean anything. Her throat tightened, and she tried to swallow as she leaned back farther into the back seat, wishing that Alexandra hadn't cast doubt in her mind. "Even if he were interested, I'm working through some personal things right now."

As soon as the last words were out, she regretted them. Alexandra always put on a nice front, but something about her made Kate feel the need to hold back. She found it ironic, since it was so easy to speak to her former fiancée. Declan made her feel like she could drop all of her defenses and pour out her soul. She was surprised she'd been able to hold back this long from telling him the hard things that plagued her.

"Personal things. What's going on?" Alexandra pushed, but even as she asked, Declan reached over and squeezed her leg, then shot her a look. Alexandra hesitated a few seconds before turning back to face the front.

Silently, Kate thanked Declan through the rearview mirror.

Unfortunately, Alexandra was sharing a room with Kate that night, since Declan's mom and Richard were in and needed a room as well. She hoped Alexandra wouldn't use the opportunity to push Kate to say things she'd been holding back for nearly a year. She was ready to talk about them, but she felt Declan would best understand her. Kate trusted him.

It was no surprise that even without makeup on—and dressed in an oversized shirt and sweats—Alexandra's beauty could light up any catwalk. She and Declan had made a beautiful couple.

Alexandra was quiet when she returned to Kate's room after preparing for bed in the bathroom. Kate quickly turned out the bedside light, hoping that Alexandra had forgotten the earlier discussion.

"When you find someone who is there for you, caring for you in the good times and the bad, don't let them slip away." Alexandra's voice was soft but clear.

"Aidan and I really aren't that close."

"Maybe not now, but I can see he cares. I . . . I used to see Corbyn like a friend, pushing him away time and again. I missed out on years because I was too caught up in other things to really see him. I don't want to keep doing that." Alexandra chuckled. "We could already be married and have little ones running around if I wasn't so slow to figure that out."

Was Alexandra just playing games with Declan's heart? She made him think she didn't care, but then said things like that. Was she jealous of Kate's friendship with Declan? It was not a topic Kate wanted to discuss with Alexandra, whom she was starting to mistrust. "Aidan's dating Hayley, my friend. That's what matters. It would be selfish of me to mess that up for someone I honestly don't have those kinds of feelings for." Maybe Alexandra would catch the subtle hint.

"I just had to say my piece. You should keep that in mind before letting something good pass you by."

"Goodnight." That was all Kate could manage. She wasn't letting anything pass her by, and she didn't plan to let Alexandra ruin her excitement about her baptism the following morning.

A knock on the door drew Kate from her dream, or rather nightmare, of searching for Declan in a field of lavender, only to find him holding Alexandra in his arms.

"We've got breakfast waiting for you. I figured you would want to get up, since this is your big day."

The voice of the very man she'd been longing for in her dream sent a pang to her heart, and she internally chided herself for her weakness before glancing at the clock and seeing it was 9:27.

"Oh wow, I didn't mean to sleep this late. Thanks." She'd not slept this late since . . . she really couldn't remember. Her fitful night of sleep must have thrown off her internal clock.

She glanced around and noticed Alexandra was already out of the room, then hopped out of bed, swaying as she pulled on a robe before heading for the bathroom. Throwing open her door, she slammed into a wall that she instantly recognized as Declan. "Sorry," she muttered and hurried off, worried he'd noticed her morning breath.

He chuckled and went back downstairs.

Before going downstairs herself, Kate decided she needed help since she would soon have the whole congregation watching her. Pulling out her verses compiled from Margaret's list for encouragement, she found a verse that would be perfect for today.

Philippians 4:6-8—Do not be anxious about anything, but in everything by prayer and supplication with thanksgiving let your requests be made known to God. And the peace of God, which surpasses all understanding, will guard your hearts and your minds in Christ Jesus. Finally, brothers, whatever is true, whatever is honorable, whatever is just, whatever is pure, whatever is lovely, whatever is commendable, if there is any excellence, if there is anything worthy of praise, think about these things.

Looking down from the baptismal pool toward her friends, Kate was struck by the way God provided more than she could have imagined when she first left home just over three months earlier. Hayley and Aidan, Tracey and Richard, Margaret, Chloe and her husband and kids, Declan—they all sat on the front row for her.

The pastor held the microphone up to Kate so she could announce to the whole congregation her decision. "Thank you, God!" she called afterwards, thankful not only for her salvation, but to have shared her testimony without stumbling over her words.

As she waited for the pastor to dunk her, she noticed someone else moving to kneel by the pool. Her heart raced once she realized it was

Declan. When did he leave his seat? The pastor announced that Declan would be baptizing her. As she thought about it, she realized it couldn't be more perfect. Other feelings aside, after Margaret first had Kate questioning if she was really a Christian, Declan had been there to answer her questions and encourage her in her search for truth. He had gently nudged her along and explained things when she was unsure.

After the pastor explained baptism, Declan reached over and placed an arm behind her. "I baptize you in the name of the Father, Son, and Holy Spirit. Buried in the likeness of Jesus' death"—he lowered Kate, then lifted her out of the water—"and raised in the likeness of his resurrection. Second Corinthians 5:17 says, 'Therefore, if anyone is in Christ, he is a new creation. The old has passed away; behold, the new has come.'"

Thankfully, the water dripping down her face when he lifted her disguised the falling tears. The emotions that had built up all morning finally found their release. This was what the peace of God felt like. Regardless of her past or the struggles she knew awaited her future, God would get her through. He would be there for her. Always.

During lunch at Aidan's place, the staff treated Kate like a queen, and when Aidan pulled out a chair for her, she couldn't help but look towards Alexandra. Alexandra wasn't watching, but Declan was. Throughout the meal, though Hayley was sitting beside her and Aidan on the other side of Hayley, Kate still felt self-conscious every time Aidan spoke directly to her. Although she did notice that there was plenty of conversation happening between him and Hayley. That should have set her mind at ease. Funny how someone's offhanded remark could send a person's mind spiraling.

Chaos ensued once they said goodbye to Hayley and Aidan, then everyone else descended on Margaret's cottage. Ten people in the cottage, two of whom were boisterous teenage boys, felt cramped, yet somehow Kate loved it. They had all come to celebrate her. Even her parents, who had watched the baptism online, FaceTimed her to say "Hi."

"Thanks for letting us be part of your day." Alexandra set her overnight bag down in the kitchen and reached for Kate's hand.

Kate looked from Alexandra to the handsome man standing there, and her heart rate picked up. Alexandra had a blessed life. She'd been careless with her heart for years and still ended up with one of the best men Kate had ever met wanting to marry her. How could she take that so lightly and toss him aside? "I'm glad you both could come too." She schooled her expression for fear they would see things that were better left unsaid.

"You know I wouldn't have missed it for the world. Are you sure you don't want me to stay?" Declan looked around at the mess in the kitchen. "I can help you clean up. I hate for us all to leave you with the cottage in this state."

"No, it's fine. The cleaners come tomorrow and are great about doing extra when needed."

"If you're sure then."

"I—"

"She said she was fine, and I can't miss this train, Corbyn. I've got a morning meeting."

"Right." He looked back at Kate with concern before saying his final goodbye.

Kate had so much to be happy about. That was what she wanted to dwell on as she watched them pull away—not the stirring in her heart.

Chapter Nineteen

Peace and joy were fickle things. To say that life went back to normal over the next couple of weeks wouldn't begin to describe the tumultuous thoughts going through Kate's mind.

Everything seemed normal on the outside, even good. She and Margaret had their routine, and Kate had started helping out with some of the church's ministry work during the week, but periodic texts and calls from Declan sent her world spinning off-kilter.

Every time Kate saw Declan's name pop up on her phone, she found herself back in that moment when Alexandra told her how much Declan meant to her. She could still hear her words. *"When you find someone who is there for you, caring for you, in the good times and the bad, don't let them slip away."*

Over the past two weeks, whenever he texted her, she waited hours and sometimes even overnight before responding, hoping that he would give up. As much as she wanted to talk with him, how could she? She needed to make sure Alexandra had every opportunity to reconcile with him if there was a chance. Instead of him giving up, his texts became more frequent and urgent as he worried about her. She eventually started answering his texts more regularly to assuage his concern.

Today was the first day she thought he might have taken the hint, since he hadn't texted all day. It was Friday afternoon, and she expected

Tracey around five. That gave her about thirty minutes to finish the casserole she'd prepared for dinner before she joined her friends at the Rose and Crown.

Margaret sat at the table reliving some trip with Graham from ages past while Kate finished layering the vegetables and cheese. The sound of the back door opening startled them. "Hey, Tracey! How was the traffic?"

"No traffic to worry about on the train, and from Dover Priory to here was an easy ride."

The sound of the deep voice she loved made her heart simultaneously race and almost stop. With a hand over her heart, she jumped back from the counter. "Declan! What are you . . . we weren't expecting you. Did you come to meet up with your mom? She'll be here any minute."

"No, Kate, I came here to spend time with Gran and to check on you." His eyes never moved from Kate's as he walked toward his grandmother.

"I know you!" Margaret struggled more than usual today. Her earlier story about Graham had started when Kate said Tracey was arriving by train later.

"You do, Gran. It's me, Corbyn." He looked up at Kate with a furrowed brow.

"Corbyn? Do you know Graham? He'll be here soon. He's taking the train."

Kate followed him to the kitchen table. "I'm fine. You didn't need to come. Your mom was already coming." She wasn't fine. Did he really come knowing how much she would need him this weekend?

"My mum isn't coming. I told her I wanted to take this weekend."

She stopped and looked at him closely. His sad, sweet eyes were full of concern. *When you find someone who is there for you, caring for you, in the good times and the bad, don't let them slip away.* The words echoed in her mind. "Okay . . . well, I'm going to be out tonight. I'll stick this casserole in the oven for you two, then I need to go get ready."

Declan's face fell, but Kate rushed off before he could respond. She sent the group a text to see if anyone wanted to meet her early for dinner. Regardless, she wasn't eating with Declan.

It was hard to enjoy her night with constant thoughts of Declan and the picture of his hurt look running through her mind, but she stayed out until she could barely keep her eyes open, hoping that he would be in bed. She quietly entered the cottage and made her way toward the stairs only to be startled by Declan's groggy voice.

"You're home. Come, tell me about your night."

Once her heart resumed a somewhat normal pace, she looked back into the sitting room to where he sat on the sofa, running his fingers through his hair. Even with messy hair, he was the most handsome man she knew. "It was fun. Did the Rose and Crown thing. I'm going to head to bed. I can barely keep my eyes open."

Not wanting to see his response, she looked down before saying, "Tomorrow . . . actually later today, I guess, I have plans with friends." She'd cobbled together plans for the day while at Rose and Crown. Knowing the sparks that flew between them, it would be dangerous to spend the whole day with Declan.

"Oh. I was hoping we'd have some time together. You'll be home for dinner?" He sounded so hopeful.

"No. Goodnight." As she rushed up the stairs, part of her wanted to go back and explain herself, but what could she say? This was best for both of them.

The next day, Kate listened for sounds of Declan and made sure to avoid him before leaving. Maybe it was childish, but she couldn't bring herself to face him this weekend. He had caught her off guard, and she wasn't prepared.

Once she had left for Hayley's, she pulled over and sent him a text letting him know she was gone. As she continued to drive, she heard her phone blowing up. Upon arriving at Hayley's, she checked to find three texts, two missed calls, and a voicemail from Declan. Kate worried something had happened to Margaret. Instead, the texts and voicemail told her that Declan was worried about her and concerned he'd done something wrong. Kate rubbed her temple, feeling a familiar tension coming on.

Kate: I'm fine. I'll be home late tonight.

She started to add, "Don't wait up," but that might give him more reason to hassle her about her avoidance of him. Hayley was in a chipper mood since things with Aidan had been going wonderfully. In fact, Hayley and Aidan were having dinner later.

Without Hayley available for dinner, Kate made plans with Mira, another friend Hayley had introduced her to. Mira reminded her of her friend Jennifer from back home. She was that friend with the perfect marriage to her college sweetheart—the marriage that made all of her friends envious and hopeful that they, too, would find their person one day.

Kate had a full day ahead to distract from the confusion brewing in her heart. She helped Hayley organize her kitchen, then Hayley treated her to a manicure and pedicure. That afternoon, they went to their exercise class, then shopping with Mira and some other friends from class.

Two other friends joined them for dinner, and halfway through the meal, Mira proclaimed that she had a big announcement. From the gleam in her eye and her giddiness all afternoon, Kate had a good guess. "I'm pregnant. Can you believe it? Tom and I are going to be parents. We were not even planning to have a child for a while, but here we are."

"Oh my. So you really are excited?"

"I'll admit, at first, I panicked. It kind of messed with my mind as far as my ten-year plan, but Tom and I talked about it and decided to embrace it. It's meant to be."

A sense of déjà vu came over Kate, and of all days for this to happen. She smiled and gave the expected congratulations, but her mind went back to a similar conversation at a work event with Mark just over a year before.

After another negative pregnancy test just that day, it had been hard to hear about someone getting pregnant who had not even wanted to be. Kate had been polite, but then quickly escaped the conversation and moved across the room, only to have her husband accuse her of being rude. He gave her the cold shoulder the rest of the night, saying she'd embarrassed him in front of colleagues.

For some reason, that memory pushed her over the edge. She was already so tightly wound after being surprised by Declan's arrival and not sleeping well because of the significance of the day that she didn't have the emotional energy to withstand more. Her original plan had been to meet up with Hayley at the Rose and Crown, but she sent her a text saying she didn't feel well and would head home after dinner. The rest of the meal, she smiled and nodded, but by the end, couldn't recall what was discussed after Mira's announcement.

The drive back to the cottage went much the same way. She remembered getting into the car but not the drive. That night with Mark had been playing on a loop in her mind. Somehow, she stumbled her way into the cottage. Maybe she could slip upstairs unnoticed.

"What's going on? Kate? Why are you crying?" The familiar male voice from her dreams stopped her forward movement.

Kate touched her face and looked at her fingers. Tears? When did that happen? "I . . ." Was she ready to share the things she'd been holding back? She covered her face in shame. What would he think of her? This wasn't like telling her mom. "You don't want to hear all my baggage."

"I do, and I know that today is the anniversary of Mark's death." He stepped forward and touched her cheek, wiping a tear. "I'm here for you. No judgment, I promise."

Sincerity was written all over his face. Maybe she could trust him with her broken pieces. Where to start? She tried to slow her breathing and focus her thoughts as she sat on the sofa. "You remembered."

He nodded.

Kate hesitated before taking a deep breath. "You know that I was married and that he died. Was murdered."

Declan nodded again, slowly.

"But there are other things." She took a deep breath and stared at her hands. "I have PCOS, polycystic ovarian syndrome, and it made it difficult for me to get pregnant."

Declan laid a hand over hers.

"We didn't start trying until we had been married a couple of years. When we first started trying, we weren't in a rush, but the last few years of our marriage, it became stressful—more and more tests, hormone injections, clomid. It began to cause tension between us, as it worried me more than Mark.

"In fact, there was a time only a few weeks before his death when we were at one of his office functions. Earlier in the day, I'd had another negative pregnancy test. When one of the other wives at the event announced she was pregnant, then proceeded to complain that they had not wanted to start their family but would make do, it hit me the wrong way. I smiled and said the right things, but had to get away. When I did, Mark got angry with me. He berated me for embarrassing him in front of his coworkers, then ignored me the rest of the night."

Tears started again as she recalled slammed doors once they arrived home and Mark sleeping in the guest room that night.

"Oh Kate, I'm so sorry. He never should have said those things. It's not your fault. Was that a habit of his?"

"What?"

"Making you feel bad about your difficulties getting pregnant."

She shrugged. "For the last year or so of our marriage, it was. Before that, he just acted nonchalant about the whole thing. He didn't comfort me about it, but he didn't make me feel bad either. The last year, though, it seemed I could do no right, and that included not getting pregnant and how I handled each letdown. We argued about that very thing the morning of his murder. Our last words were in anger. I actually felt guilty until . . ." It felt as if her throat was closing off. How could she go on? Maybe she should wait to tell the rest.

"Never mind. Today . . . today I was having dinner with friends." She winced as she recalled it. "One of my friends, Mira, has a perfect marriage. She's a wonderful, sweet young woman, and at dinner, she announced she was pregnant but gave the caveat that it wasn't part of her plan, and at first she was upset. It hit me wrong. Inside, I lost it—at least I hope it wasn't apparent outwardly. Everything from my past that I've been able to mostly avoid for months while here hit me all at once—my infertility, Mark's attitude towards me . . ."

Tears ran down her face, and Declan reached up to help wipe them. "I'm so embarrassed. I know I should let those things from my past go and I shouldn't envy her and all that, but it's so hard."

"God doesn't expect you to be perfect." He pulled her into his chest and wrapped his arms around her. "That's why Jesus died. You have been through a lot, and your past doesn't just disappear. As far as feeling envious, it sounds like you are happy for her, but your longing for a child is tangled up with that. You can pray that God will help you keep the two separate." Kate continued to sniffle in his arms.

"Now, what was the part you skipped over? You said you felt guilty about your last words being in anger until . . . but you didn't finish."

She stiffened. Part of her had wanted to tell him for a while, but now that the opportunity was here, she didn't feel ready. What would he think of her? The curry from earlier threatened to come back up, and her mind began spinning as the fight within grew. "I-I . . ." *Can't.*

"Kate, whatever it is, I'm here for you. Let go of whatever is torturing you."

Pulling back, she felt the loss of his heat, but kept her hands tight around his arms lest she lose her courage. "It . . . it was a couple of weeks later . . . after Mark died." Her voice was faint. "When I was finally able to bring myself to go through the bag of personal items they had taken off his body when he died." A rush of emotion hit her as she recalled things hidden deep in her mind only to surface occasionally, as if they'd happened to someone else.

"There was a phone—phones, not just his, but also another that I didn't think was his. Except I realized it was his when I charged it and there were multiple messages on the day of his death from a person listed only as 'B,' asking where he was. The person said they were waiting for him . . . in bed, along with some other inappropriate things I won't repeat. There were missed phone calls from the same person. He was"—she began to shake—"cheating."

Declan gasped, and she saw all of her own pain and anguish reflected on his face. "It was so obvious, even though I could only see part of the texts and there were initials in place of the name. I knew. Things began to make sense." Now that she had started, there was so much she wanted to say. "I didn't know the passcode to open it, but found I could pull the messages up on his laptop. The messages from the woman had been going on for almost four months. They included pictures . . . pictures of her that I've tried to erase from my mind." Flashes of skin appeared in the edge of her consciousness, causing her to flinch.

"That wasn't the worst." She blinked back tears. "There were messages from other women, and they went back several years. I can only imagine there would have been more if the phone had been older." Her face heated as she confessed things she had hidden in shame from everyone except her mother. Kate could no longer look Declan in the eyes, but instead found some point on his chest to analyze.

Declan removed his arms from behind her back, and she prepared for his rejection. He didn't even know the worst of it, but before she could move away, she felt his hands cupping her cheeks.

"I'm so sorry. I can't imagine how Mark could ever look elsewhere when he had you." Declan's thumbs began wiping away her tears as they caressed her cheeks.

In that moment, Kate felt heard, wanted. Her eyes flitted to his mouth, then she felt instant shame. He needed more time. Redirecting her thoughts, she continued confessing. Kate took courage as she bore more of her heartache. "Months after his death, I saw a high school acquaintance, and when she noticed I wasn't wearing my wedding ring, her first comment was, 'He cheated, right?'"

Kate could still remember her shock and confusion. "When I questioned her, she explained that it was common knowledge that he was cheating on me all through high school. She and others thought I knew but chose to stay with him anyway."

Her mind drifted back to high school, when they first started dating. Her parents wouldn't let her go on proper dates, but he would come over for meals or take her to his place for dinner. He always had her home early, and her parents thought he was such a gentleman. He continued to have her home early her junior year, too, even though by then, her parents allowed him to take her places. "Apparently in high school when he would drop me off or leave my place, he would go meet up with other girls."

It sickened her to think of how many women he had been with during their time together. If only she had known what he was back then, she never would have married him. "How could I have been so blind . . . so stupid?"

"Kate, look at me."

Her mind didn't want to, but her heart could not help but obey.

"There is nothing wrong with you. Don't place blame on yourself. It is all his."

A dark chuckle erupted from her. Here this man was comforting her after she had ignored him all weekend. "Don't you see? My whole life was a farce." The image of teenage Jennifer announcing Kate had found her Mr. Darcy now seemed absurd. "There is no Mr. Darcy!"

Confusion filled Declan's face before he pulled Kate into a tight hug. "I don't know Mr. Darcy, but you don't need him. I've got you. I've got you." He patted and caressed her back.

His kindness knew no bounds, but she had to give him a chance with Alexandra. She remembered the conversation when her mom said that when people are vulnerable, it's easy for them to mistake comfort for love. Was that happening?

"I . . . thank you for being here for me. I should try to get some sleep." She looked around. "Margaret? Is she asleep?" The whole weekend, she'd only considered her own worries. How could she have been so thoughtless?

"She started falling asleep, so I put her to bed even though it was early." Seeing Kate's concern, he added, "I don't think anything is wrong. Just a busy day."

Kate looked at him, not wanting to say things that would cause pain, but truth brought understanding and preparation. "That's normal as her disease progresses. She'll sleep more and more. I'm sorry." Because of Margaret's faith and that of her family, she knew they had hope. Margaret would one day be healed and they would be reunited, but that didn't stop the day-to-day sadness. If Kate could take that from Declan, she would.

"Thanks for being here with her, and thanks for helping me understand. It really does help. How did you get through with your grandfather?"

"It was hard. I did a lot of reading about it since I didn't know anyone with answers. The nursing home where he was didn't . . ." He was stalling her. "Goodnight." Tomorrow he would leave and take temptation with him.

Declan reached for her hand. "Kate, you've let me in this far. Please don't shut me out."

Her eyes fell to his hand, and she felt her determination waver. "It does feel good to let some of my pain out. I can't thank you enough. I'll see you in the morning." She forced a smile and pulled away at the sound of his sigh.

"Goodnight."

He released her, and instead of feeling satisfaction, her heart sank. *Traitorous heart*!

Chapter Twenty

Kate woke with a heavy heart. Declan's words and touch had been a balm to her soul. Over the past year, she'd had her pain so deeply hidden that healing had been impossible. Her old pain was far from gone, but she knew that her conversation with him had opened the door to healing.

But even as she felt the mending of her past begin, knowing Declan would not likely be part of her future opened new wounds. Speaking to God, she questioned why she had to exchange one pain for the other, and heard God say, "My grace is sufficient for you." Though she was unsure of her next steps, she would trust God to continue to provide.

Church went by quickly, and the selfish part of her wished time would slow. At lunch, she found Declan observing her more than once, but Kate averted her eyes lest he think she was staring back.

"What time do you need me to drive you to the train station?" Kate questioned once they returned from lunch.

"In a hurry to get rid of me?" He chuckled, but the look on his face said he was anything but amused. "There's still more to be said pertaining to last night's conversation." He finished seating Margaret in her favorite chair before settling on the sofa himself.

Margaret watched the exchange between the two and smiled, but Kate frowned, wondering what he had planned.

"Don't you have work tomorrow morning?" Kate questioned, feigning indifference as she stood stiffly across the room by the bookcase.

"Nothing that can't be done from my computer."

Kate nodded and gathered her courage. If Declan remained much longer and continued to insist on being so attentive to all her worries, she was in danger of falling in love. Perhaps it was already too late.

"Relax." Declan's close proximity caused her to jump. "I promise nothing you say will make me think less of you." She turned to him in disbelief. "In fact, your strength in such difficult circumstances has increased my regard for you beyond what was already there."

"Who else knows?" Those were the first words Declan spoke when Kate returned from helping Margaret to bed.

"Who else?"

"Yes. Who else knows the things you shared with me last night?"

She knew what he meant, but somehow imagined by stalling, she could avoid the conversation altogether. "My mom," Kate replied as she reluctantly settled into a chair.

"Only your mom? No one else, not even your father?" When she shook her head, he questioned her further. "But you and your father are close. I'm sure he would want to be there for you."

Kate twisted her fingers together as he spoke. "I know he would." She swallowed hard. "But he would also want some kind of vengeance for what was done to me."

"But your husband is dead, and so is the man who killed him, since he turned the gun on himself, according to what I read about it. Who else could he take vengeance on?"

Kate stared at him, weighing her words. "Partners in my husband's law firm."

"What? Why?" Anger flashed across his face.

"They knew." Her voice was practically a whisper as she recalled the humiliation she'd felt months after his death upon finding out their complicity. "My husband's legal assistant told me several months after his death. She'd known about the affairs and was paid nicely to keep his private life private, even from me. What you wouldn't have found in your research is that Mark was killed by a previous client whose wife he was most recently having an affair with. It was the woman who had been messaging him the day he was killed. His assistant was paid to keep her mouth closed so they could play it off as just a disgruntled client.

"The legal assistant finally had enough and left the firm after seeing how much I suffered and that the partners continued to invite me to firm events and treat me like they cared. They were really just trying to ensure I never found out the truth to turn it back on them. That's when she contacted me and told me the truth. She said the whole good ol' boy environment there was toxic and she couldn't stand for me to be fooled by it any longer. In fact, even though she's only in her fifties, she decided to retire early to get away from the firm. According to her, most of the partners have women on the side, and they all cover for one another. It's just sick. I wanted to tell the other wives, but she warned me that they had threatened her, and she actually feared for her life. Who does that? Just so they can keep cheating on their wives. It's awful." Kate looked down and realized her hands were shaking.

Declan's expression changed several times as he listened to her story. He started to speak, then shook his head and closed his mouth.

"Yeah. Not much to say about all that, is there? You can imagine why I don't want to risk my dad getting involved. These are powerful men. They have the ears of judges and law enforcement, as well as deep pockets to make things happen."

"You didn't know the law firm was involved until months after his death, and you didn't feel the need to tell your father before then?"

She shook her head adamantly. "I had enough trouble dealing with my own pain, and couldn't bear to see it reflected in his eyes too. I couldn't keep it from my mom. She reads me like a book and saw me soon after I found out. I did plan to tell Dad eventually, but it's too late now."

Declan pushed a chair next to Kate's and reached for her hand as he tried to school his expression. "I'm sorry, Kate. I'm sorry if you look in my eyes and see your pain reflected. I'm trying to remain calm, but these are hard things to hear."

Her eyes began to water, and she could see that his were too.

"I wish I could take some of this from you. I'll say it again: you're a very strong woman."

A half smile emerged on Kate's face. "Thanks."

He looked at her somberly. "What can I do? I understand why you didn't want to tell your dad. I, too, would like to make those men pay." He paused, the tension on his face growing. "I'm sorry. I'm not setting a very Christ-like example, but I wish I could at least expose them."

"I know you mean well, but no. I wouldn't want you to risk yourself either. Enough people have died in all of this. I just want to put it all behind me. That's why I haven't told people the truth. I don't want to be that person they always feel sorry for. My friends here don't even know I had a husband, much less any of my other horrible life details."

"What about Hayley? You two seem close. Sure, at first she may act a certain way, just like me. Though once I process this, I promise I'll stop looking at you funny." His lips quirked. "I bet before long, it will be the same for her. If you don't want to go into all the details about the firm, that's okay, but at least she would know where you're coming from. It's hard to be a good friend to someone when you don't know key elements of their life. It means a lot that you've shared this with me. I think it would mean a lot to Hayley too . . . and also your dad. He needs to know, Kate. And as much as you worry, he should know everything, if for no other reason than it will keep him from saying something to the wrong person."

Kate sighed. "I don't know. It scares me. I still can't believe I told you." She squeezed her eyes shut, then opened them to find him watching her. "But I have to admit, part of me feels better already from telling you."

His furrowed brow relaxed. "Can I pray for you?" When she nodded, he tugged her other hand with his free one and bowed his head. By the time he said "Amen," they were both choked up.

Declan wiped a stray tear from her face, and she couldn't help herself when she wrapped her arms around him for a hug. Almost as quickly as she did, she caught herself and pulled away, but he held onto her arm. "Watch a movie with me?"

She raised her brows, but he shrugged. "I think we both could use a distraction, and I found a Christian comedy that looks cute. It's a film from the U.S. called *Heaven Bound*. They even filmed it in your home state."

He patted the spot next to him once it was set up. "Join me on the sofa?" His puppy dog eyes made it hard to say no, and one and a half hours later, Kate found herself curled up next to Declan, sharing a warm throw and smiling.

"Did you know . . . about the main character's wife having Alzheimer's?"

Declan shook his head. "No, kind of uncanny isn't it? Or maybe God is trying to show us something. I'm sure Gran would love to think her story could bring others to Christ, like in the movie."

"It did. If it wasn't for her dementia, I wouldn't have become a Christian."

"Of course! I don't know why I didn't think of that. It makes all that she's going through seem worth it. I know Gran would feel that way if she could fully understand."

"I am truly thankful for coming here and especially for being introduced to Christ through you and Margaret, but her dementia is still heartbreaking."

"Indeed." He looked thoughtful. "The movie was meant to lift our spirits, but I'm afraid it's not been completely successful."

"I wouldn't say that." She smiled and searched for the right words to explain what was on her mind. "It helped put things in perspective, which is better than a momentary distraction. Regardless of what we watched, once in bed, I'll be sifting through our earlier conversation. Now I imagine I'll process those thoughts from a more hopeful perspective. So thank you for that."

"I'm glad you think so, Kate. I liked the tenderness the man showed when talking about his wife, almost as if she was still living. He treasured their marriage."

The wistful look on his face reminded her that Alexandra wanted to patch things up between them—as if Kate could ever forget it for long. "I'm sure you will have a marriage like that too."

"You think? I hope so." The smile forming on his lips as he spoke made Kate both happy for him and sad for herself.

"I should head to bed so you can get on with your dreams of matrimonial bliss while I dream of telling those close to me how unblissful my marriage was. I always said Mark was not quite Mr. Darcy. Now they will know how unlike him he was."

"You've mentioned Mr. Darcy before, and I'm still not sure who he is."

"A British publisher not familiar with Mr. Darcy? He's from Jane Austen's *Pride and Prejudice*."

His eyes went wide, and his cheeks turned pink. "I know Jane Austen, but am embarrassed to say I've not read any of her books. It seems I should read *Pride and Prejudice* at least so I can better understand."

The thought brought a smile to her face. The manly Declan reading the romance that women had swooned over for the last two hundred years. "Yes, you should."

"Are you ready for your knitting group today?" Kate arranged a napkin on Margaret's lap before sitting to eat her own breakfast.

"Knitting." Margaret smiled. "I like knitting." Then she frowned. "They are trying to make it hard. New things."

"It will be fine. It's a time for you to enjoy your friends. Don't let it worry you if it doesn't come out right." Kate hoped she wouldn't become too stressed over it and have to give it up yet. If she started giving up her activities with friends, most of the benefits of staying at the cottage would be gone. They would need to consider moving her back to Tracey's home. Kate forced herself to smile at Margaret, who was moving eggs around her plate.

"Thank you, dear." Even in her confusion, Margaret had an air of dignity. Declan walked into the room, and Margaret's eyes lit up. "You!" she said brightly.

"Yes, me, your Corbyn."

His hair was wet, and he looked as tired as Kate felt. "Just getting up?"

"No, I went for a run, then took a shower."

"That must be why you look so tired."

"Actually, I was up most of the night praying." Kate's brow rose at his confession. "For you," he added softly while looking at her with concern as he filled a plate.

"Thank you." She looked to see that Margaret was still playing with her food. "I think I made some decisions about what steps to take next."

Declan relaxed. "That's good. We can talk about it after we get Gran off. I'm waiting to take the afternoon train."

"You're right. I need to tell those close to me. I need to share and be vulnerable." After staying up much of the night thinking, praying, and even arguing with God, Kate had come to that realization.

Declan looked over at her from his lounger on the porch and grinned.

"No need to gloat." He kept grinning, and Kate shook her head while chuckling. "Seriously though, I think I'll tell Hayley first. I'm hoping that will get me warmed up before I tell my dad. He will be the most difficult, because I think it will hit him the hardest." A seagull caught her eye and drew her attention to the beach.

"I can't begin to imagine the range of emotions I'd feel if my daughter told me those things." He blew out a breath. "It hit me hard enough as it is. But don't stress over it. From what I've learned of your father, he's not only strong enough to handle it but also not prone to rash decisions."

"You're right. Thanks for the reminder."

Declan raised a brow. "Another thing I'm right about? Careful, Kate, I might start to think you like me."

There was no disguising the heat that rose to her cheeks. "After my dad, I'll need to tell my best friend Jennifer." That was another conversation she dreaded, and Kate hoped she would forgive her for waiting so long to tell her. "Jennifer is due to deliver in just over a month. Please pray that this doesn't overly stress her. I feel so guilty."

"If she's as good a friend as you think, I'm sure she'll forgive you."

"I hope so. She's been like a sister to me since we were little. I don't know what I'd do without her."

Standing and stepping in front of Kate, Declan pulled her up from her lounger and into a hug. "I'll be praying for you every step of the way. If you text me before you tell each of them, I can be praying."

Kate pulled away. "I'm so glad God brought you into my life, Declan. You've helped me in ways I never thought possible."

"That almost sounds like you don't plan on seeing me again anytime soon. I'm only three and a half hours away, and I will be checking in on you. I won't leave you to go through this on your own."

He was too close to the mark. She nodded but had no words.

"What about my sister? Did you plan to tell her?"

"Yes, I got distracted and forgot to mention her." *Distracted by your presence.* "I think I'll wait until she comes this weekend. I'd like to tell her in person. And your mom. She only knows he died, not about the cheating. I guess I should FaceTime her this week before Chloe comes." She took a deep breath. "I'll tell my brother after talking to my dad. He'll be angry at Mark. He never liked him. I wasn't sure about telling Margaret, though. I'm worried it might be confusing to her at this point. Especially since Mark is someone she's never seen."

"True. I don't think that knowledge is necessary for her."

"Right." Stomach churning, Kate leaned on the railing. How did she find herself in this place?

He reached out for her hand. "Why don't we spend some time in prayer and reading Scripture before I have to leave?"

"Okay." Once she agreed, he pulled her into a hug, and she inhaled deeply. He smelled of comfort, hope, and protection. She took in his scent, determined to hold on to every memory. She'd keep them tucked away until the coming days when she needed strength as she told everyone her truth.

Chapter Twenty-One

Shame. Like cancer, unseen from the world, it can eat away at the good. It spreads and ruins everything in its path, replacing the good and healthy with death.

Truth. It could stop the shame, but was as dreaded as chemotherapy. The thought of telling people the truth made Kate sick, and it wouldn't be a quick process.

Thankfully, Hayley could meet Kate for lunch Tuesday. Waiting another day might cause the beginning of a stomach ulcer. One foot shuffled in front of the other as Kate entered the café. *Smile. Greet Hayley.* She went through her mental checklist.

"Hey. What's up that couldn't wait until tomorrow?" Hayley stopped and frowned. "Oh, that bad? I'm here for you, Kate. What's got you down?"

"Thanks." She smiled warily, wondering if Hayley would still feel that way once she knew how long Kate had been hiding who she really was—a widow, rejected and scorned. "I want to tell you about some things from my past. Some things that will help you understand me better."

Haley's eyes went to the waitress walking towards them, and she nodded. "Why don't we order first?"

"So this woman's husband killed yours, and your husband's partners want to keep it hidden?" Hayley had been shaking her head in disbelief since Kate began. She scooted her chair closer to Kate and pulled her into a hug. "I'm not normally a hugger, but I think you need one. Or maybe I need one after hearing all you've been through. Kate, you are the strongest woman I know."

"I have a therapist and a doctor who would probably beg to differ."

"Oh Kate, I can't even imagine. Anyone would need therapy after that." Hayley shook her head and rubbed her brow. "What made you decide to talk about it now? Has something happened?" She leaned back and her eyes went wide. "Mira!?"

Kate nodded.

"Should you and I go do something else Saturday instead of joining Mira and the girls for the outing?"

"No. I'm going to have to get used to this sort of thing. I'm hoping with practice and a lot of prayer, it will get easier."

Nearly an hour and a half later, Kate walked alone along the beach behind the cottage. She smiled to herself, recalling how kind and supportive Hayley had been. With two more important people in her life aware of her past, she felt the millstone loosen from her neck. Retelling her story to those she cared about was not as painful as she'd anticipated. Would it keep getting easier?

Kate stopped and pulled her jacket tighter to brace against the late September chill rolling off of the water. Taking a deep breath of the salty air, she smiled up at the sky just as the clouds broke apart. The sun warmed her face and peace filled her. *Thank you, God.* As her gaze followed the rays of sunlight downward, she was struck by the beauty of its reflection on the water and pulled out her phone to capture it. Before putting it back in her pocket, Kate sent the picture along with a text to Declan to let him know about her successful conversation with Hayley.

When Margaret's friend brought her home from their seniors

church outing, she seemed happy yet tired. Kate helped her get comfortable at the kitchen table while she finished dinner. Margaret had a more difficult time communicating when she was worn out like this, and Kate filled the silence by talking about her day, minus the specifics of her conversation with Hayley.

"Give thanks in all circumstances." Margaret spoke out of the blue. "God loves you."

Lifting her eyes to the older woman, Kate wondered at the message. Margaret smiled brightly at her. "Thank you." Moments like these reminded Kate what a special person Margaret was. Even in her confused state, love poured out of her.

After studying her Bible regularly, Kate recognized that it was Christ in Margaret. She'd studied about the fruit of the Spirit in Galatians 5—love, joy, peace, patience, kindness, goodness, faithfulness, gentleness, and self-control. Being able to have those things, even in difficult times, was a sure sign that they were the fruit of the Spirit and not character qualities that came naturally. Day after day, she saw peace, patience, and joy radiating from Margaret, even when she had every reason to be angry and frustrated with her mental decline. Would Kate ever get to that point? Presently, her emotions seemed as erratic as a small boat caught in a storm.

By the time she had Margaret in bed, Kate could no longer push aside thoughts of her coming conversation with Jennifer. A sense of guilt ate at her. As she cleaned up the kitchen, she tried to reason through what to say. *How do you tell your best friend, who has been there for you all your life, that you hid one of your biggest trials from her?*

In high school, Jennifer never had a boyfriend, yet ironically, she was the one happily married with one child and another on the way. Jennifer used to lament that by the time Kate and Mark were married and had a houseful of kids, she would be known as the crazy cat lady. When Jennifer started dating Ryan, her husband, in college, Mark mocked him, calling him a computer nerd. He said they would never make it as a couple because Ryan didn't have a clue how to romance a woman. The tables had turned, and Kate had no husband because of his unfaithfulness, no children, and the last time he'd romanced her was years before his death.

For the past few weeks, Kate had been explaining to Jennifer the things she was learning about God and how they differed from what she'd previously thought. Jennifer seemed interested and considered visiting the church where her daughter went to preschool. Once she found out what Kate had kept from her, she might think Kate was just another hypocrite.

Kate scrubbed at the pot she was washing as if getting every last stain off it would cleanse her past mistakes. Some stains refused to come clean and were clearly beyond her abilities. She laid it aside. The pot would still efficiently cook. She just needed to stop focusing on its imperfections.

The buzzing phone startled Kate, and her mind immediately thought of home with worry. Relief flooded her when she saw Declan's name on the screen.

"Declan."

"You did it. One down."

"Yeah," she said flatly. It didn't feel like a success now that she compared it to telling Jennifer. She turned off the kitchen light and eased past Margaret's room to the stairs while lowering her voice. "Just a minute." Once she got to her room, she curled up in a chair and spoke. "At first it felt so great. It went easily, and Hayley was so understanding."

"I hear a 'but' coming."

Kate sighed. "But once my mind got past that and I got Margaret to bed, the thought of telling Jennifer hit me full force. I don't think it will go as smoothly. In fact, I imagine she'll be quite angry with me. How can she not be? We've known each other forever, and I kept this from her. She's like a sister to me."

"I wish I could do this for you. I wish I could somehow take away this worry and strain."

Kate chuckled weakly. "Thanks. I wish it could be that easy. I got myself into this mess of having to backtrack and tell people. That's my own fault. I should have been more thoughtful about how it would make them feel."

"Kate, you were dealing with enough. I can only imagine the depression your later discoveries threw you into. When you're in a bad place emotionally, there's no capacity to figure out how your actions affect others. My mum is in a good place now with my stepdad, but it wasn't always that way. When my dad told my mum he was having an affair and wanted a divorce, I was only six, but I saw how broken my mum was. I promised myself I would never do that to a woman. Gran moved in with us to help for a while, because my mum was depressed and unable to take care of us. My sister was sixteen and handled it in her own way by staying busy with friends, but I was lost. I'd really looked up to my dad and didn't understand why he was hurting Mum, and it hurt my feelings that she pulled away from me. It took my mum nearly a year to get a grip on what happened, and she wasn't also dealing with a murder like you."

Kate's hand went to her mouth, and she squeezed her eyes shut. "Declan, what if Mark hadn't been killed? I would have either eventually gotten pregnant or we'd have adopted. Then when I found out about his cheating, that poor child would have gone through so much, just like you. I would have ended up a single mom. Who knows how much longer it would have been before I discovered his unfaithfulness? Maybe . . . as awful as it sounds, it's a good thing that he died young."

She grimaced. "Not that I wanted him dead," she rushed to add, "but it probably saved me from a lot of other things. It's kind of twisted, but I guess I can see that as a positive."

"I guess so. There's no right way to go through trauma and loss. Don't feel like you have to rush or justify it. To be honest, I feel like I've only fully been over Victoria's death a few months, even though it's been years since she died."

"I . . . sometimes I forget you went through that." His recent relationship with Alexandra made it easy to forget he'd been engaged before. Moving to stretch out on her bed, she felt more relaxed after talking things through with Declan.

"You know, Mark's parents are divorced too. They divorced when he was a freshman in college. His dad left his mom for his secretary. The thing is, though"—Kate chuckled darkly—"Mark had been cheating on me since high school, and rather than learning from it, he kept on doing to me what his dad did to his mom." A yawn escaped, and she tried to hide it.

"You should get some sleep. It sounds like all these emotional trappings are exhausting you."

"I guess so. Thanks for being so encouraging to me. I feel like I'm dragging you down. You've got other things to worry about besides me."

"Hey, I called you, remember? I wouldn't have if I didn't want to hear these things. I wasn't expecting a fairytale story about how everything in your life is now perfect."

"Okay . . . thanks. I'll talk with you later." Even as she said the words, she felt guilty for thrusting him into the middle of all her stress. Yet she couldn't think of anyone she'd rather talk it over with.

After they said goodnight, her thoughts lingered on Declan. In her dreams, he was the hero.

Chapter Twenty-Two

"You look exhausted, dear!" Tracey said almost as soon as she walked through the door. She looked at Kate while hugging her mother. "I'm sorry, I should never say that to a fellow female. But it does worry me." Her eyes scanned Kate. "I can set something up for Mum so you have more time off than just this weekend."

Kate forced a smile, thinking back through the events of the week. "No." She glanced over at Margaret. "It's not that; it's mental exhaustion. I-I've been dealing with some personal issues."

"Well, that too can require time off. It's really no—"

"No, I'm fine—well, I will be fine. It will be taken care of this weekend. In fact, I'll explain everything to you later this evening."

Tracey gave a knowing look. "Okay, then. I still might insist you take some extra time. You absolutely deserve it."

The conversation with Jennifer had been hard in a different way than Kate expected. Jennifer burst into tears and was so distraught by the fact that Kate had not allowed her to help her through the suffering. Looking back on their discussion, she wondered if pregnancy hormones had heightened Jennifer's response. Their conversation did not end well and left Kate feeling worse than before. The next evening, they spoke again and things were better, but they were not back to where they had been. With Jennifer due in only a few weeks, Kate felt an urgency to fix things. The thought of not getting to FaceTime in on the delivery as they'd originally planned broke her heart.

Sleep eluded Kate the night before Tracey arrived, and the stress of the week caught up with her. Surely things would go more smoothly with Tracey. She couldn't bear the thought of disappointing anyone else.

Thankfully, Tracey was more than understanding. Her own first husband's unfaithfulness left her sympathetic to the plight of a fellow woman whose husband cheated on her and treated her badly.

"You and Declan have both been so kind and encouraging to me. He made me see how important it was to let those close to me know all that I've been through."

A mixture of pride and sadness passed over Tracey's face. "Corbyn is a good man. When I was in the midst of my own sadness after the divorce, unable to care for him as I should have, he doted on and protected me as if he was the parent and I was the child. He knew sadness and grew up in a way no one his age should ever have to. Most younger sons are wild, but he has always been so measured and temperate, making sure everyone around him was cared for."

Biting her lip, Kate nodded in agreement. She'd never met a better man in her life. "I can see that about him."

"There's no timetable for processing your pain, and no set way to do it." She reached out and squeezed Kate's hand. "Thank you for letting me in. I'm here for you if you ever need to talk. Can I pray for you?"

As Kate prepared for bed later, she anxiously glanced at her phone. She'd not heard it ring during her conversation with Tracey, but after speaking to Declan every night since telling him about Mark's unfaithfulness, it felt like a necessity. She hoped he would call again. Almost as if he knew her thoughts, the screen lit up with his name.

Declan: Just wanted you to know I've been praying for you. I won't call in case you're still talking with Mum, but I promise I'll pray.

Kate immediately dialed him, then realized maybe she shouldn't have.

"Kate, did you talk with Mum? How did it go?"

"Sh-she was . . . wonderful." Kate found herself blinking back tears.

"I knew she would be. She's been there. If anyone can encourage you through this, it's Mum."

Kate smiled to herself and imagined having him there in person so she could watch the way his cheeks dimpled when he smiled or the way his eyes brightened when he felt intensely about something, or even how he—

"Kate? Are you okay?"

"Huh? What?" Had he asked her something?

"I asked what time you planned to call your dad. Is everything all right?"

"I . . . yes, sorry, I guess my mind was wandering. Yes, my dad . . . I plan to call him tomorrow after a walk on the beach and then a nice long bath."

Declan sucked in a breath.

"Sorry, TMI?"

"N-No. That sounds like a very relaxing day."

Kate quietly chuckled at the fact that she had caused Declan to trip over his words. Usually, she was the one who couldn't think straight around him. "Hopefully it will help me relax before telling Dad. He's the other person who has me in knots." Her mind flew to Jennifer, and she silently asked God to intercede there. Again the tears threatened, and she tried to sniff them back.

"Kate." Declan's voice was soft and soothing, and he seemed to know just what she was thinking. "Things will right themselves with Jennifer. You two have been friends for so long, she'll surely forgive you. I imagine your dad will initially be hurt, too, but you're his baby girl, and he won't be able to maintain a grudge."

"Thanks. I have my doubts about Jennifer, but I do think my dad will come around. Especially with Mom there to champion my side."

"Then you'll only need to tell Chloe?"

"Yeah, and your mom was so thoughtful. She worked it out for me to go to London next weekend, so Chloe and I are going to take an overnight trip while exploring Windsor Palace, Oxford, and the Cotswolds. That should give me plenty of time to explain everything to her."

"Sounds wonderful. The two of you are leaving Friday?"

"Actually, Friday I'm visiting the memory care facility that your gran will eventually go to so I can confirm I'll be working there as Margaret's assistant on weekdays once she's in. That will help with her transition."

"So . . . you are planning to stay in England long term?"

"I really haven't decided, but I would like to help her transition. I think having someone familiar with her will keep her from the rapid decline people usually have when moved to a new environment with new caregivers. I had hoped to be here at least a year."

"But she might need to move in before then? That's what you're not saying. Right?"

"I'm sorry. It's starting to look that way."

Declan breathed a heavy sigh.

"Hey, Dad."

"Hey, sweetheart. Is everything all right? Your mom said you wanted to talk to me."

"It's actually about some things that I've known for a while but kept from you because I felt like I needed to protect you."

"Protect me? What's going on, Kate? You're my baby girl; I'm supposed to protect you."

"I know, and you've always been great at it, but this is something you couldn't protect me from." Kate proceeded to tell her father everything she had held back from him, along with her desperate plea for him to not try anything with the law firm.

"Dad?" He had been eerily quiet the whole time she explained things. "Are you mad? Can you forgive me?"

"Kate, of course, I forgive you, and no, I'm not mad. At least not at you." He sighed. "I'm mad at that poor excuse of a husband you had and at the law firm. Kate, I really am sorry. I feel like we failed you. I failed you. I was supposed to protect you from things like this."

"Dad. It's not your fault. There's no way you could have known.

Mark was hired by one of the best law firms in Memphis because he can convince people of nearly anything. That's not something he learned in law school. He was always very persuasive with his magnetic personality and ability to make even the most ludicrous idea sound logical." Anxiety flared as she remembered some of their arguments, but the sound of her dad taking a deep breath brought Kate back to the present. "You're really not mad at me for not telling you sooner?"

"Honey, I wish you had, but no, I can't hold a grudge over how you decided to handle this. You've been through enough. You don't need me adding any more baggage to your already heavy burden."

"Dad." Kate let out a breath. "You can't know how much that means."

"Since you're serious about religion now, this seems like a good time to pray."

Kate wasn't sure how to take that comment but did like that he acknowledged her faith. If only he understood she was serious about a relationship with God, not just about religion in general. "I . . . yes, I've been praying every day and have others praying too." She recalled Tracey's prayer over her the night before and smiled.

"I wish I were there to comfort you. It's hard to give a hug through the phone."

At the mention of a hug, Declan came to mind. Kate had never thought of herself as touchy-feely, yet every touch from Declan not only comforted her but made her long for more. The sound of her father's soft chuckle reminded her of his comment and spurred an idea. "Let's FaceTime. Your smile will be comforting."

"Anything for you, Pumpkin."

Relief filled her at his easy forgiveness and hearing his childhood name for her. If only Jennifer could find it in her heart to understand and forgive as well. Her father's reaction gave her hope.

Chapter Twenty-Three

"Join me on the beach for a morning walk?" Liam, Declan's cousin, had come with Declan over the weekend to help with Margaret.

Initially, Kate was disappointed that she would have to share her time with Declan, but Liam proved to be a pleasant distraction, and it was probably for the best that she had less time alone with Declan. He was becoming an addiction.

She looked towards the kitchen where Declan sat alongside Margaret, making sure she ate all her breakfast. Lately, she'd become so easily distracted that it wasn't uncommon for her to eat a few bites of a meal before leaving the table, and whoever was with her had the chore of helping her return to her meal.

"They'll be fine," Liam added, sensing her hesitation.

She nodded and followed him out the door while pulling on her jacket.

Liam watched her as they crossed over to the shore. "Don't get swept up by his good looks."

Kate felt heat rise to her face. "Pardon?"

"I've seen that look before. Girls swoon for Corbyn everywhere we go."

Frowning, Kate examined Liam. He was nice enough looking, though he'd not left her flustered upon their first meeting like Declan had. Was he envious of his cousin, and had she not been careful enough to hide her feelings for Declan? "Why would you say that?"

"Only to protect you. It's always been Alexandra. Even when he was with Victoria, I had a feeling they wouldn't make it if she had not died. I imagine they'll get back together soon."

Though the entire conversation made her insides wrench, Kate needed to hear these things. In the two weeks since she had told Declan her secrets, they had become closer than ever, to the point that she felt dependent on him. They spoke every day, and she missed him in the hours in between.

"You think so?" Alexandra seemed attached to Declan, but Kate didn't think he felt the same anymore.

"Yes. Once they do, things will happen very quickly. He's always been quite private about their relationship and evasive when I try to ask him particulars. He's a lucky man, though. He has everything a man could want—money, status as future head of Corbyn Publishing, looks, and the love of a beautiful woman who he's been best friends with forever.

"I thought I had all that mattered, but five years into marriage, my wife decided I would never be rich enough for her, and she left me for the CEO of the company where she worked. Never mind that he was twenty years her senior."

Kate realized her mouth had fallen open and tried to school her expression. "I'm so sorry. I understand how hard that is."

Liam stopped walking and looked at her. "How would someone as beautiful as you know about that?"

Blushing, she wondered out loud, "Did Declan not mention anything about my previous husband?" When he raised his brows and shook his head, she proceeded with a brief summary of Mark's murder and her discoveries, minus the law firm's involvement.

With so much in common, they spoke with ease until Liam's phone buzzed. "Sorry, that's my reminder to head back. I've got to take the train back to Paris." He frowned and held her gaze. "I'm sorry our time is being cut short. I've truly enjoyed getting to know you."

"I'm sorry too. I had thought you and Declan were staying through Sunday afternoon. He's not discussed leaving early with me." She would have to bow out from meeting her friends at the Rose and Crown in the evening.

"That's because he's staying. He needs me to get back to attend a book signing with one of our authors since the person assigned is sick." At her surprise, he shrugged. "It's his privilege as VP and future president of the company to send me back instead of himself."

As they walked up the steps into the cottage, Kate stumbled, and Liam wrapped an arm around her waist to steady her. "Thank you." She smiled at him.

Upon entering, she caught sight of Declan holding two glasses of water. He grinned, but his smile faltered when his eyes moved to the place where Liam held her. The warmth that she felt at seeing him quickly dissipated at his change in demeanor. How was it that Liam's arm around her had no effect on her, while one look from Declan had her body and mind in a riot? Declan nodded their direction and continued to the sitting room, where Kate heard Margaret acknowledge him.

"You're packed, I take it, Liam?" Declan's voice was clipped.

"Yes, everything's ready."

"Pleasant walk?" He continued to question him.

"Of course, and with excellent company." He smiled at Kate, but she held hers back, sensing the tension.

"Wonderful." Declan stood abruptly. "I'll transport you to the station, and we can go over some work things en route." His voice softened as he turned to Kate. "Do you mind staying with Gran for a bit while I run out?"

"Sure, no problem." She waited until Declan went upstairs for his wallet before speaking with Liam. They exchanged numbers and were saying their goodbyes when Declan returned and wasted no time urging Liam out the door.

Liam gave Kate a look before drawing near and whispering, "Protect your heart."

As the car pulled out, she recalled their earlier discussion about Declan and Alexandra. "As if I needed reminding," she muttered. "Margaret, it's such a beautiful day outside, isn't it?" They both could use some redirecting, she decided.

Margaret's face lit up. "Katie!"

It was a rare day now when Margaret could remember names. Kate was glad Declan had let her stay there so she wouldn't miss this opportunity to chat with Margaret during one of her more lucid times.

When Declan returned, he still seemed somewhat out of sorts. "I had intended for Liam to stay with Gran tonight so I could go with you to the Rose and Crown. I'm sorry that didn't work out."

"It's—" She read a text from her phone. "Jennifer's having contractions! She's still two weeks early!" Quickly dialing her friend, she realized how thankful she was that Jennifer had forgiven her a few days after her confession. It had been terribly hard waiting and praying she would.

"Jennifer, what's going on?" Kate questioned the moment her friend answered. Feeling her seat shift, she looked up to see Declan had joined her on the sofa.

"It may only be Braxton Hicks contractions, so don't get too excited. I'm going to drink some water and lie on my side and see if it subsides. I'd like to go another week if I can, though according to the doctor, this little guy should be all right if he comes early."

Kate blinked, realizing that she and Declan had been watching one another. "I . . . that's great." What had Jennifer been saying? "I'm just hanging out at the cottage tonight, so I'm expecting you to check in with me every hour or so. Okay?" Declan's eyes lit up at her announcement.

"I will. I couldn't do this without you. I can't believe I even thought I could cut you out of my life. Let me tell you, these pregnancy hormones have wreaked havoc with my emotions. Moreso this time than last. Poor Ryan, he's never going to want to get me pregnant again. Oh my, another one is coming on. I'm going to let you go so I can relax through it. Love you!"

"Lo—" Pulling the phone away from her ear, Kate saw that her friend had indeed hung up. Shaking her head, she realized Declan was smiling and still watching her.

"I think I may be having a godson very soon." Kate could hardly contain her enthusiasm.

The dimples on Declan's cheeks appeared. "Everything is going okay?"

"Seems to be. The doctor said the baby is fine coming anytime now. I can't believe she's having another baby."

Margaret clapped. "A baby!"

Declan seemed more hesitant. "You're okay?"

"Yes. Of course." In truth, the reality that Jennifer was on baby number two and Kate was currently not even in a relationship brought forth a familiar ache. How could Declan be so in tune with her feelings? He placed a hand on her arm and continued to watch her closely. "At least . . . I will be." She couldn't lie to him about this.

He didn't hesitate before praying for Jennifer, the baby, and Kate. When her heart began to race, she forced deep breaths, and by the time he ended the prayer, she felt better and hoped she looked calmer.

"So I get to hang out with you tonight after all?" One corner of his mouth curled up.

"Looks that way." Kate bit back her smile. It was going to be a long night. "Why don't we play some games? It seems like a good day." She tilted her head towards Margaret, hoping Declan would get her meaning. They had some simplistic kids' games that Margaret could do on her better days. *Hi Ho Cherry-O*, *Candy Land*, and *Chutes and Ladders* were her favorites. None of them required strategizing, and if she forgot what she was doing, they could easily help her along.

They were actually able to play all three games once each before Margaret began to struggle. If Kate hadn't already been in love with the man, she would have been after watching how patient and caring Declan was with Margaret. Not many men would willingly explain how to use the rainbow trail three times or point out the difference between Lord Licorice and Queen Frostine during a game of *Candy Land*. Throughout the games, she held back sighs too numerous to count. It was a good thing she only saw him every few weekends if what Liam said was true.

After dinner and reading, Margaret went to bed, which left Declan and Kate alone. It felt like a mixed blessing. Jennifer's contractions continued, though they were still irregular. Kate had mentioned to Hayley that if the contractions stopped, she would still meet her and the others at the Rose and Crown, but that wasn't looking like a possibility.

"What's the plan for Gran?"

Declan hit Kate with the question as soon as she returned from helping Margaret to bed. Her heart sank at the thought of the impending changes. "Right now, we're just taking it a week at a time, but your mom is hoping we can keep her here until December before making a permanent move to London."

"That's two months away. Do you think that's feasible?"

Kate rubbed her forehead. That was the very thing she'd been fretting over. "Right now, it doesn't seem like it. It's just so hard to know. It might be good to go ahead and move her so the family can have time to make memories with her before she's completely gone."

"That would be nice. Mum and I have worked it out for me to take over as president and move back to London at the beginning of December so I can have that time with Gran, and Mum will have more free time for her. Mum will stay on part time as I transition in."

"That's good. I had no idea, but I'm so glad you'll have that time too." She really was, but her insides fluttered at the thought of seeing him so much.

He nodded, then seemed thoughtful. "By the way, Kieran is in this weekend and came by looking for you while you were out walking with Liam this morning." Declan smirked as he spoke. "I told him that you were out with my cousin. He's met Liam before. Hopefully that will keep Kieran away. That is what you want, isn't it?" His look turned worried. "After hearing all you've been through with Mark, I'm guessing a guy like Kieran should definitely be off your list."

She shook her head. "I have no interest in him. I think he'll get the idea." She hadn't thought of Kieran in weeks and was glad he'd not spent much time at his beach house lately. Soon she wouldn't have to worry about seeing him at all. Looking around the room, she felt a flood of emotion.

"Are you okay? Did Kieran hurt you in some way?"

"What?"

"Your eyes are watering."

Kate touched the corner of her eye and felt the moisture. Her initial reaction was to school her expression, until she recalled Declan was nothing like Mark. Anytime Kate showed weakness around Mark, he pounced, tearing her down further. When she revealed her true feelings to Declan, he had only ever helped her and comforted her. "It has nothing to do with Kieran. I was thinking about what happens when we move your grandmother to London. I'll miss this place. I've been able to find so much peace and healing over the past few months."

Her brow furrowed and her gaze dropped to the ground. Could she trust him with more of her past?

"Last January was when I found out from the assistant who Mark's most recent mistress was and also about the law firm's involvement. I had a breakdown. It was just too much. Like I told you, I'd still been spending much of my free time with the wives of the partners, and of course attended their parties, so I was often around the partners. I felt like the partners had made a mockery of me, and it was so embarrassing. The realization that I would have to cut off those friendships, combined with all of the other trauma from the previous months, pushed me over the edge, and I . . ." Her heart raced, and the words caught in her throat. "I—"

When Declan's hand covered hers, she lifted her eyes to his and saw compassion and safety. Her voice fell to a whisper. "I planned to kill myself by overdosing." Declan's eyes widened, but he remained silent, letting her explain at her own pace. "My parents were at a friend's house watching a ballgame, and my mom came home early. She found me in the bathroom pouring out various pills and knew immediately what I was doing. I checked myself into in-patient treatment for a couple of weeks, then graduated to counseling sessions several times a week."

Declan sucked in a breath.

"My point is, I was at such a low place, but this"—she waved her hand, gesturing, towards Margaret's room—"this opportunity seemed like a chance to leave my pain behind when my previous manager told me about it. I couldn't have dreamed up a better solution. The constant reminders of the life I once had—or thought I had—are left on the other side of the ocean."

Declan squeezed her hand. "God was working in your life even before you acknowledged him. He knew just what you needed. I'm so glad he spared you and brought you here."

A lump rose in Kate's throat as she nodded. "It amazes me how perfectly he has cared for me, yet I have to confess, I currently feel lost."

"Lost?" Concern was etched on his face.

"I've felt so at home here that it is hard to imagine finding similar peace in London, but I don't feel ready to go back to the States either—permanently, that is. I'll still be visiting for Christmas and other occasions."

He watched her warily. His concern changed into something she couldn't read. "Kate, you've become like family to us. We will do everything in our power to ensure your happiness and comfort. True, London is more fast-paced, but once you have a routine and get to know people at work, church, and elsewhere, it will seem much smaller. There may not be a beach to stroll along, but my parents' home has a lovely park and pond nearby. Even the Thames isn't far."

His attempt to comfort her brought a small smile to her mouth. "Thank you. That is some comfort, but I can't stay at your parents' home forever. Once Margaret is in the care facility, I will need to find my own place."

"I promise we will make it as easy as possible. My parents won't be in a hurry for you to leave their home. It has plenty of room, and when you're ready, we will use our connections to find you someplace you love."

Kate looked up and silently begged him to stop endearing himself to her. "Thank you."

Reaching for her shoulder, he gave it a squeeze. "Promise that if you have anything you're worried about, you'll talk it through with me? You're not on your own, Kate, and I don't want you to get in your head with worry. Promise?"

Easier said than done. She nodded, but he raised an eyebrow. "Yes, I promise."

The beeping phone next to her head startled Kate. Blinking awake, she noticed tension in her neck and felt a weight on her legs. Looking around, she recalled falling asleep on the sofa while Declan held her legs in his lap and they watched television. Across the room, the television had been turned off, but Declan was still at the end of the sofa with his feet propped up on the coffee table and his head resting on a pillow. Her phone lit up again, revealing the latest text from Jennifer.

Jennifer: Over two hours since any contractions. If you're awake, please go to sleep. We'll let you know if they start back.

It was almost twelve thirty in the night. Still groggy, Kate vaguely recalled a text at about ten that said the contractions were slowing down. She began to push up to sitting on the sofa but stilled when her eyes landed on Declan. Her heart began to race. He was the most handsome man she had ever seen, and his kindness made his beauty even more arresting. He may not ever be hers, but she could still appreciate all that encompassed Declan Corbyn Fitzgerald.

Chapter Twenty-Four

"Asher Green—I like it. And he was only six days early. That's great," Declan commented when he called Kate as soon as she texted him the news of Jennifer's delivery a week after the false alarm.

"Yes. Seven pounds, eight ounces and twenty inches is a nice size too. Did the picture I sent go through?" Kate's grip tightened as she held her phone, anxiously waiting for Declan's reply. "Don't tell me he looks like every other baby either. That's my godson, and I think he's adorable. He has Jennifer's eyes."

"Got it. He is adorable."

The breeze on the cottage porch blew through Kate's hair, and she pulled it behind her shoulder. "I can't believe I have to wait over two months to see him in person. He's going to have grown so much. I told Jennifer we have to FaceTime every week, not just talk."

"That's hard. I'm glad I was around when Chloe's children were babies. They do change quite quickly."

"I was there for all of her daughter Emma's big milestones. I don't know what I would do without video chat."

"Do you need to get away before Christmas for a visit?"

"Oh, no. That would be too stressful. I'll wait, I just might whine about it a bit."

Declan chuckled. "I guess I can put up with that."

"Anyway, with Margaret so close to going back to London for good, I feel like I need to be here to closely monitor things and help her prepare to transition."

"Thank you for making her a priority even when other important things are happening in your life."

"She's become an important part of my life too now. All of you have." Kate felt heat rise to her face as she admitted the fact. "Sort of a surrogate family. You know how it is. You're changing your whole life for your gran, too, by moving back to London."

"It's not a huge sacrifice for me. Don't make me out to be a martyr. It was the plan all along. I'm just moving it up a bit."

"Still, you're making changes for your family. That's honorable."

"Thanks."

"By the way, Liam mentioned he was taking over your position at the Paris location. He seems excited about the promotion." They'd kept in touch sporadically since his visit. Gradually, their conversations spread further apart. It was slightly disappointing since she was glad to have a distraction from Declan, but the fact that it was only slightly disappointing was a sure sign that it wasn't meant to go further.

"Yeah. He said he'd been talking to you. He's a good guy, I just . . . I thought you'd decided not to get involved with anyone right now."

"I did, but since becoming a Christian, I've realized I need to be open to what God's doing in my life. Nothing's happening with Liam anyway. He made it pretty clear that his focus is on work right now, and a long-distance relationship would be too distracting for him."

"Hmm. I see."

What does he see?

"Oh my goodness. Hey, Asher. It's Aunt Kate. Can you give me a smile?" Kate cooed and spoke in a soft baby voice as she watched her phone for Asher's response. Asher wiggled in his mother's arms and smacked his lips. "Oh Asher, you are too adorable. Jennifer, I can't stand not being able to squeeze those precious cheeks."

"Two and a half weeks down. Less than a month and a half to go."

"Thirty-eight days, but who's counting? At least I have this beautiful view for a while longer." She switched her camera around so Jennifer could see her balcony view of the Channel. Kate's phone began to vibrate, and she saw the name Elsie pop up. "Jennifer, I've got to let you go. One of Margaret's friends is calling. Something may have happened with Margaret."

"No problem. I hope everything is okay."

"Thanks. Love you. Bye." Switching to the incoming call, Kate tapped her finger on the side of the lounger anxiously.

"Kate, dear, this is Elsie. Please don't worry."

That's how all bad news starts, Kate thought.

"Margaret's fine; she's just tired. After we had our book club, we went outside to walk around Hilda's garden. Margaret had seemed tired all through our discussion, so we sat her on a bench in the middle of the garden and took turns sitting with her. She ended up falling asleep on Peggy's shoulder. Poor Peggy couldn't move for fear Margaret would fall over. Thankfully, Hilda's husband was home and able to help get Margaret to my car, so I wanted you to know I'm bringing her home. I think she needs some rest. Hilda and her husband will follow to help me get her in. If you're home, that's fine; I just didn't want to catch you off guard. Oh, and I can stay with her if you have other things to do."

"Oh my. Thank you for taking care of her. I'm home for the afternoon, so you don't need to stay. Go ahead and bring her home. I'll call the travel doctor and have them come check and make sure it's nothing serious."

"One more thing." Elsie lowered her voice. "During our book time, Margaret suddenly lifted her shirt to adjust her bra. Thankfully, it was just us women, but I know she would be embarrassed to death if she were thinking clearly. That's a new behavior for her. I just thought you should know."

Three hours later, Margaret was awake and staring at the television. The doctor had said everything appeared fine and took blood and urine samples to check as well. It had already been a hard week for Margaret. She'd been confused multiple times and easily agitated. Kate had spoken with Tracey about it on Tuesday, but it was time to discuss it more seriously. Earlier in the week, it seemed it might be a fluke, and today, the doctor even said it was possible that she had a urinary tract infection that could cause confusion, but his office had just called and confirmed no infection. All her blood showed nothing abnormal. It was unlikely this would go away.

Tracey agreed to come to the cottage the following day so she could see her mom and make a plan. The afternoon seemed to simultaneously go too fast and too slow. Kate wanted to capture every moment with Margaret in the cottage and bottle it, but her mind wouldn't stop racing with all the possibilities of how the transition to London should go. Once Margaret was in bed for the night, Kate called Hayley to tell her what was going on.

Chapter Twenty-Five

Margaret's closest friends had already decided to have a low-key luncheon at Violet's home. That gave Tracey and Kate a couple of hours to hash out a plan for the timing of the move to London. Before talking things through, Kate and Tracey worked together in the kitchen on a simple lunch of sandwiches. Looking around the now-familiar room, Kate felt nostalgic. Every little thing made her heart ache, even the kitchen cabinet that creaked every time she opened and closed it.

"This place grows on you, doesn't it?" Tracey questioned.

"It has begun to feel like home."

Tracey gave her a motherly smile. "I promise we'll be back for visits. Besides, you're family now. You have access to the cottage anytime you want."

"Thank you. That means a lot. I'm sure London will be great, but this will always have a special place in my heart."

Once they began to talk things over, it became clear that it was time for Margaret to make the move. They decided to give Margaret through Wednesday to say her goodbyes to friends, although depending on what kind of day she was having, it may be the friends saying all the goodbyes. Thankfully, Tracey planned to stay until the move so she could help with packing and preparations.

"I guess I'll get started packing," Kate said while putting away her dishes after they'd finished their discussion. When no response came, she looked back to see Tracey hunched over the table and shaking. "Tracey?" Within seconds, Kate was by her side, and when Tracey looked up with red, glassy eyes, she understood.

"Taking this next step seems so real . . . so final. I'm not ready to lose her, but she's already becoming someone else." Tracey shook her head. "I'm supposed to hold it together and be the head of the family, encouraging everyone else, but the reality is, I'm falling apart inside."

"It's okay, Tracey. You don't have to be strong for us. We'll all work together on this and get through it. This disease is draining because it can last so long. This is a marathon, not a sprint, so we're going to be careful to save our emotional energy. Part of doing that means you have to allow yourself to mourn throughout the process." She wrapped an arm around Tracey.

"Thank you," came a whispered reply.

For the next hour, Kate worked on gathering items to pack. Somehow she'd managed to leave her own books, jackets, and knick-knacks all around the cottage. In the sitting room, an oil painting of Chloe and Declan playing in the cottage garden as children caught her eye. She had walked by it hundreds of times over the last few months, but never studied it so closely. Declan looked about three years old, which would have meant Chloe was thirteen. Even though he was so small, she could still recognize his piercing blue eyes that seemed to hold answers to the world's problems. Those eyes were joined by his playful smile, the same one she'd seen quite a few times. The painter had done a wonderful job of capturing it all.

Kate's thoughts drifted to their first meeting in that very garden, when she'd believed he was the gardener. Laughter tried to bubble to the surface, but she stifled it, not wanting to break the serenity of the afternoon. She never would have imagined how close she would become with the "gardener." With a sigh, she turned away.

"I can't believe you're leaving so soon." Hayley frowned into the drink the waiter just delivered.

"You'll have to come to town and visit. I can come here some too. Anyway"—Kate glanced from Hayley to Aidan—"you don't need a third wheel."

"Kate, how can you say that? This guy means a lot"—she interlocked her arm with Aidan's and gave it a squeeze—"but I still need my best girlfriend."

"You're just trying to make me cry." She and Hayley had become close, but she was glad things were working out so well for her and Aidan, and they would still have each other.

"She's right; even before you told us about this sudden change, Hayley was lamenting this day, knowing it wasn't too far away. I'll miss you too. I'll forever be thankful to you for helping me get to know this one." He tweaked Hayley's nose and blushed.

Kate smiled up at Aidan. Hayley brought out the softer side of the burly man. They were perfect together.

"Tomorrow night, we're inviting the whole gang to Aidan's pub to celebrate you." Hayley glanced at Aidan and he winked and nodded.

"I want to say it's too much, but it sounds like a lot of fun." Kate couldn't hold back her grin. As sad as she had been about the sudden move, she was glad to have good friends who made her feel special.

"Good. Now that is settled, let's enjoy our dinner!" Aidan leaned back as the waiter approached with their food.

"Look!" Kate pointed toward the children's shop window as she and Hayley strolled down the sidewalk after their exercise class. "Aren't those blue baby outfits adorable? Let's go in. I'm dying to pick some things out for my precious Asher. Only six more weeks. My fingers are just itching to hold him. Isn't he just the cutest?" Kate flashed the latest picture of him that Jennifer had sent.

"Yes." Hayley chuckled. "He is cute in all one thousand pictures you've shown me."

"Okay, okay, I get it. Maybe fewer pictures, but you have to admit, he is really cute." Something deep down inside her wondered how much stronger these feelings would be if he were her own child. A pang of sadness followed that thought.

An hour and a half later, Kate was loaded down with baby gifts that she hoped would fit into her luggage when returning to the States for Christmas. Thankfully, most of the items were clothes and wouldn't take up much space. She carefully balanced her bags and purse in her arms so she could carry them all into the cottage in one trip. As she stumbled through the door, her arms were gripped by firm hands.

"Whoa there. You okay?"

Staring into blue eyes, Kate felt a familiar flutter as she searched for her voice. "Declan, yes." She looked back at the door. "I guess I stumbled over the threshold. I didn't know you were coming this weekend."

Pulling bags from her arms, he grinned and shrugged. "I figured I would check in with Mum in person before heading to the city." His eyes scanned over the bags. "What's all this?"

"Gifts for Asher."

"Should have guessed with all that blue."

"Do you think it's too much?"

"Certainly not." His grin was lopsided. "I've been known to be a bit excessive with two boys myself, much to Chloe's chagrin." His face turned more serious, and he glanced towards Margaret's room. "They're out visiting friends, so we can speak candidly. How are you handling all of this?"

"With Margaret and the move?" He nodded. "Apparently by shopping." She waved towards the bags he now held. "Really though, even with the feeling I had that this would happen sooner than planned, it still is hard. You can never fully prepare yourself emotionally for these things. What about you? She's your gran, and you're moving between cities too."

"Yes, but at least this way, I'll be able to see her more. I've lived in London most of my life, so it's just going home for me. I knew Paris wasn't long term." He paused and seemed to contemplate. "The hardest thing for me is going through a new sense of loss every time her mental state takes a sharp decline."

Kate nodded. "After working with dementia patients for so many years, I thought I was somewhat numb to it, but it's been different since I've grown so close to your grandmother. It's like losing another family member."

"Even though she's not completely herself, I can tell she feels close to you as well. Thank you for going through this with us, and with her."

"I feel like you thank me every time we speak, but as hard as it is losing her so soon after getting to know her, I can't imagine my life if I hadn't had this chance. I've needed her as much as she's needed me at this time in my life."

"For such a time as this . . ."

"What?"

"It's from the book of Esther in the Old Testament. Esther was an Israelite who was made queen of Persia when they were under Persian rule. Through her position and the favor she had with the king, she was able to spare the Israelites from destruction. Esther's cousin told her, 'Who knows whether you have not come to the kingdom for such a time as this?' You should read it. It's a fairly quick read. Anyway, it seems that you are here 'for such a time as this.' Like Esther, it benefits yourself and also many others."

"For such a time as this," Kate softly repeated. Maybe when her mind started wandering and thinking romantic thoughts about Declan, she could remind herself that it didn't matter if he wasn't in her life that way. God placed her here to get through "such a time as this."

"Your mom and I were working on packing up some of Margaret's extra clothes. Care to help?"

"Love to. Lead the way." He motioned her forward towards Margaret's room.

"Actually, they're upstairs in her old room. We've been rotating them periodically since she doesn't have much storage in her current room."

After following Kate upstairs, he stopped in the doorway. "What's the plan here?" Declan looked around at the piles of clothing and boxes they'd already sorted through.

"Right now, we're focusing on cold weather clothing." Kate walked in and pointed to a pile of clothing sitting on a chair. "These things we've kept out to rotate to her room downstairs over the next few days, but those two boxes on the far wall are being filled with cold weather clothes from the closet and chest. Your stepfather will bring a truck to pick up all the boxed clothing as well as her favorite chair, books, and some other things like furniture for her care facility room that are going last minute."

"Okay. I think I can handle that. So, the cupboard and chest of drawers?"

Kate hesitated, then nodded once she remembered a cupboard was a closet.

"Got it. Just point out any drawers you've already finished."

Working alongside Declan was exhilarating and nerve-wracking at the same time. When he was turned away, she found herself watching how the light accentuated his broad build and square jaw. *For such a time as this,* she reminded herself. Looking down at the clothes in her hands, she tried to refocus, but seemingly without her permission, her eyes kept drifting towards Declan.

Once he looked her way, causing her to mumble some nonsense about fuzz in his hair. *Fuzz in his hair?* Now she felt like a middle-schooler fawning over the cool guy but too inept at conversation to know what to say.

Sitting so close to him as they completed their domestic task had her on edge. Every now and then when their hands bumped each other's, he caught her gaze and smiled. It came so naturally for him. He could go about his work as his friendly, unaffected self, while she held onto every detail—the sound of his breathing, the flex of his arms as he reached for more items from the drawers, his masculine scent of bergamot and something woodsy. It became a chore to regulate her breathing so he couldn't tell she was sniffing him. So embarrassing. Recalling the bones in the human hand from her anatomy class could be a good distraction.

Somewhere between the distal phalange and proximal phalange, Declan picked up his phone and began texting. He chuckled and put it down so he could continue to work on the clothes. "Looks like this box is filled and the drawers are empty. Ready to tackle the cupboard?"

It was a walk-in that was the same depth as the bathroom on the other side of the wall but narrow, with clothing hanging on both sides, making it difficult to keep from brushing against each other as they moved about. They finally agreed to work side by side after a couple of embarrassing moments.

"Is Liam going to be ready to take things over in Paris?" Kate mistakenly looked up into his eyes and felt the familiar pull.

"Absolutely. We've got a great team there to back him up, and I'm just a call away if he needs anything. It will be the same for me with Mum's job. If I get stumped, I won't hesitate to contact her. I think we'll be—" His phone vibrating drew his attention. "One moment."

Kate caught a glimpse of Alexandra's name just before he began busily texting, and the veil lifted. Maybe the arm bones this time.

"Sorry about that. Alexandra is handling the movers in Paris for me. It's not a lot since the furnishings stay, but without a car there, I couldn't manage the boxes. What were we talking about?"

Kate forced a smile. "Nothing important." Alexandra's text was a good dose of reality that his life was still intertwined with that of his ex.

Declan didn't seem to care about reality as he moved closer to Kate with a look that made her heart leap. His eyes dropped to her lips, and she froze in place, drawn to him, yet afraid of the desire she felt raging inside.

Noises below alerted them to Margaret and Tracey's return and couldn't have come at a better time. The closet space felt entirely too small.

"I-I'll go check on them." Kate couldn't get away fast enough and tried not to think about what would have happened if the ladies had not returned just then.

At the bottom of the steps, she found Margaret talking to her reflection in the hall mirror. It looked like she was greeting a long lost friend. In a way, she was. Tracey walked in behind Margaret, her face filled with tenderness and sadness.

Chapter Twenty-Six

"I wish that handsome Corbyn was here." Violet, one of Margaret's good friends, sighed and fanned herself while speaking with Kate during Margaret's going-away party. "That young man is quite the catch. I may be an old lady, but I know a good-looking lad when I see one," she continued, chatting about Declan's finer qualities.

Declan was a 'good-looking lad.' Outwardly, Kate chuckled, but inwardly, she was back in that closet with him the weekend before. It played on repeat in her head. Would he have kissed her if they hadn't been interrupted? It left her feeling conflicted.

"I can see you're thinking the same thing, Kate."

"What?"

"Don't worry, your secret's safe with me." Violet winked.

Before she could respond, their attention was drawn away by Richard with the pastor and several other men returning from loading his truck with the boxes and larger items being moved to London.

Once the men had a chance to get food, Elise moved to the front of the church reception hall and cleared her throat. "If everyone would gather around for a minute, I would like to honor my dear friend, Margaret."

Margaret was seated just to the side of Elise with Tracey standing next to her. The smile on Margaret's face beamed as she looked up at her friend and clapped her hands.

Kate looked around at Margaret's closest friends. They had all treated Kate as if she were their own granddaughter. At some point over the past few months, each one had shared stories of how Margaret and Graham had touched their lives.

There was Elise who had lost her husband seven years earlier and wouldn't have made it without Margaret. Peggy had a daughter Tracey's age and had shared stories of raising their girls together with Margaret, with years of dance lessons, family trips together—including mission trips—and girls slumber parties. Violet and her husband both had cancer about twenty years ago, but Violet's husband lost the battle, and Margaret was her faithful friend who supported and prayed for her all through their cancer and her loss. Hilda's husband had been close friends with Margaret's husband, Graham, before they were married. Graham was the one who introduced Hilda's husband to the Lord. Ruth was a single woman, never married, whom Margaret had led to Christ years before. She had joy and contentment beyond what Kate could imagine. It made her wonder if she was being called to singleness herself.

What a legacy both Graham and Margaret had left, not just through their family, but through the lives of so many others too. Kate heard how Margaret started the church food pantry and was also instrumental in sending many missionaries around the world. The school reading program had been her idea too. It was inspiring to think of all Margaret had done for others in her life. There were doubtless many other things Kate didn't even know about.

What would Kate be remembered for? She thought through her own life and couldn't recall anything special. Maybe some of her previous patients would feel differently.

"You're going to be missed, too, you know?" Ruth patted Kate on the arm. "We've all enjoyed having you around."

"Thanks. I'm going to miss you ladies." Margaret's friends had welcomed her into their group, making her feel like extended family. Maybe this was a chance to explore things Kate could become part of. "Ruth, do you have any mission trips coming up?"

Ruth's face lit up. "My next one is not until March. It will be in Bosnia with a medical team I've worked with over the years. We're currently collecting medical supplies to take. The country has so much need. It's been a year since I went. My most recent mission trip was to Rio de Janeiro with a group from the U.S. In fact, I returned just before you arrived in England. That's another group I've been working with for years."

"Rio needs medical missionaries?" Rio conjured up thoughts of posh hotels and beautiful beaches.

"Oh yes. They do not have government help for the poor like we're accustomed to. There are hundreds of slum areas called favelas just outside of the city that are run by drug lords."

"Drug lords?" Kate gulped, wondering where Ruth was going with her story.

Nodding, Ruth explained. "Yes, we do our work in one of the favelas each time we go. They are like little towns and even have churches. The group organizers used to be full-time missionaries in Rio and work with churches and the drug lords of the favela that we go to on each trip. As strange as it seems, the drug lords are happy to have medical care for the people in their favelas. We provide medical care, dental care, a pharmacy, and eyeglasses." She frowned. "No, no. I can see you're worried. I know it sounds unusual, but the drug lords make sure we're safe."

"Safe?"

"Of course." Ruth hardly took a breath before continuing. "We also have an evangelism team, and all of those seeing patients are trained to share the gospel as well. The same goes for the Bosnia trip. It also has an evangelism team and gospel training." She paused and looked closely at Kate as if reading her thoughts. "You're interested, aren't you? You would be a great addition on either trip. The Rio trip won't be until June next year, though. I can get you information on both. Would you like that?"

"I would, actually." Kate grinned at the prospect. "Could you get me information about the Bosnia trip? Oh, and how long does it usually last?"

"Ten days—Friday through Sunday the following weekend. Text me your email, and I'll send you all the information."

"Great. I should have time to work that into my schedule." At the rate things were happening with Margaret, Kate imagined she would be living at the memory care facility by then.

The rest of the party went by in a blur as Kate said her goodbyes to everyone.

Chapter Twenty-Seven

Arriving at the Belgravia London home felt different now that Kate was to be living there. Slipping from the car, Kate walked around to help Margaret. She was having more and more trouble, even with simple tasks like getting in and out of a car.

Once Tracey closed the garage door, they stepped away from the mews house, and Kate took the small building in. It was an adorable little three-story brick building painted cream with black doors to match the Corbyn estate home to which it belonged. It was flanked on either side by other similar mews lining the street. The facade included two garage doors and a small door that opened to the stairs leading to the upper apartment. Narrow iron balconies and flower boxes graced the upper floors of the building, with the third floor built into the roofline. From her previous visit, she knew it was also graced with a rooftop deck.

Several times, Tracey had mentioned that once Margaret was moved permanently into the care facility, they hoped Kate would honor them by living in their mews home.

Margaret seemed perfectly at home once they had her settled in her favorite chair. The fact that the Belgravia home had been hers for years —before she and Graham moved to Kingsdown—had much to do with her comfort level.

Chloe arrived with her two boys, and the boys busily helped

Richard unload the truck while Chloe and Kate sat with Margaret, making small talk. Upstairs, Tracey was busy arranging Margaret's personal items. The house was a flurry of motion as the family worked to get everything settled as quickly as possible.

The plan was to begin taking Margaret to the memory care facility the following week for a few hours each day to acclimate her to her future home. Kate would accompany her as her private nurse and companion. Weekends would be family time. Gradually, they would increase Margaret's time there each day until they were ready to move her in.

"Gran. Welcome home." Just as they were setting out the final dishes for dinner, Declan came through the door.

The sound of his voice set off a series of flutters in Kate's chest.

Declan greeted everyone as they sat down at the opposite end of the table, his eyes seeming to linger on hers longer than the rest.

Kate diligently focused on the conversations closer to her until James, Chloe's fourteen-year-old son, said, "Uncle C, when can I come spend the night with you in the mews house?"

At that point, it was impossible to ignore him, and their eyes met before he responded to James. The answer was irrelevant, but the revelation that he would be living in the building just behind Kate's made her stomach churn. While James bargained with Declan about his visit, Ethan, his sixteen-year old-brother, rolled his eyes and gave his two cents, or maybe in England, she should change that thought to two pence.

It wasn't until late that evening when Chloe and her family had left and Tracey and Richard had gone to bed that Declan caught up with Kate to talk. "Kate, what's going on? I feel like you've been avoiding me all night."

"I—" Kate looked around the living room as if someone might appear to help her. As much as she wanted to tell him all her feelings, there were some things that shouldn't be discussed. To admit her feelings for him would open a door that she was afraid she couldn't close. "This move has left me feeling overwhelmed. It doesn't make any sense. When I first moved to Kingsdown, I was so excited about the change and making new friends. I mean, I don't want to go home or anything. I just . . . I was so happy with things at the cottage."

Declan grabbed Kate's hand, and she flinched. "It's okay. God gave you peace before. He can give that to you wherever you are."

Kate watched him, trying to imagine the possibility. She frowned.

"I'm sorry. I'm not making light of things, but I do know . . . from personal experience that God's peace is not confined to one location."

She watched him, wondering about the times he'd needed God's peace—during his parents' divorce, the death of his first fiancée, earlier in his relationship with Alexandra, when he'd had to watch her date other men, and even now, since they'd broken their engagement. Could she really count on God to give her peace like that? "What if he doesn't want me to have peace? I have studied Galatians 5 about the fruit of the Spirit, but . . ."

"'Peace I leave with you; my peace I give to you. Not as the world gives do I give to you. Let not your hearts be troubled, neither let them be afraid.' That's Jesus talking in John 14." Declan stopped and looked down with a furrowed brow. "Like I said, I'm not trying to be flippant about this, but so many times, we don't have peace because we are letting our plans and desires overrule his, then when things happen that don't fit with our plans or things threaten to happen, we don't feel peaceful. It's one of those things that requires us each day to lay down our hopes and dreams before him and trust that he is a good Father. Though what he gives us may not look like what we pictured, it will be good."

"Some days, that's harder to accept than others." Declan's new living situation was definitely making her question God's good plans. "How come you didn't mention that you'd be living in the mews house?"

Declan grinned and shrugged. "It wasn't intentional. It just never came up. I may not be there long anyway. I'm looking for another place nearby."

"Oh." Maybe that wouldn't be so bad.

"I am looking forward to the convenience of checking in on Gran after work, though, and it will be nice to have the extra time with you."

Kate sometimes wished he wasn't so nice. It made her fragile heart hope.

Belgravia Residential Care had sections they called houses, with several specially designed for memory care. Margaret's family was already paying for her to have a room in Kensington House. It was unusual for the residents to have a room before they were living in the facility, but the head of the facility decided that as long as they were paying the full cost, it was acceptable.

Kate found the arrangement similar to the place where she had worked in Memphis, with the house functioning as a self-contained unit. It had its own kitchen, dining, and living area, as well as a sitting room for those who wanted someplace quiet.

Off of the shared spaces were the "apartments." These were a cross between a hospital room and a hotel room. Each had its own bathroom and was large enough to contain a bed, dresser, and a small sitting area. Tracey and Richard had filled Margaret's room with furniture from the cottage, which seemed to please Margaret.

Throughout the first week, Margaret was introduced to the staff and the other residents. With the exception of one female resident who had a chip on her shoulder, both the staff and other ten residents of the house made Margaret feel at home. Though for half of the residents, it was mostly through a smile that they welcomed her, since their verbal skills were limited or nonexistent. There were two male residents at Kensington House, one whose wife came and stayed with him every day, and the other a widower and consummate flirt.

In the evenings when Kate returned to Tracey's house, she did her best to avoid being alone with Declan. He was too much of an obsession. Monday, he cornered her in the kitchen when she offered to do the dishes after dinner and insisted on helping her. Tuesday, he had a dinner meeting and texted her that he was coming by the house afterwards. She made sure to be in her room before he arrived and texted him back that she was going to bed early. When he texted to invite her to a Wednesday night small group Bible study, she was thankful she'd already set up dinner with several of the workers at Kensington House. As an added precaution, she invited Hayley for a weekend visit.

After Hayley left Sunday night, talking with Declan seemed unavoidable.

"Kate, please stay up for a bit and talk with me. I want to hear about your first week at work."

Watching Declan's mom and stepdad head off to bed, she squirmed in her seat but finally nodded. All week, she had coached herself to look at him differently and distance her heart from him. Surely he didn't reciprocate her feelings and would end up reconciling with Alexandra. He was not Declan, the handsome Mr. Darcy, accent and all. No, he was just a man she knew whose path she crossed—no one special. "I like it there. It's a top-notch facility, and I'm working with some well-trained staff. The staff, aides, and other nurses seem to work well together, and so far, they've been accepting of me." Kate tapped her chin. "Oh, and dinner Wednesday was nice and helped me get to know some of the staff better."

"That's good. Do you think it's a place you'd keep working once Gran is living there permanently and your contract with us is up?"

Thinking back over her week, Kate nodded. "When Margaret was napping in her room, they had me shadow the nurse on duty so I could see what the job would entail. It's very similar to what I was doing before in the U.S. I would be in charge of two houses and spend several hours in each house during regular daytime hours. They have evening and weekend nurses as well as PRN nurses to cover when I want vacation time, so it sounds very doable. They didn't even flinch when I said I might need to take two-week-long vacations when I go home for visits."

"Sounds perfect." He relaxed into his seat.

It did sound perfect, but Kate couldn't help wondering how long she would be happy there. Would she be able to handle Declan's regular visits if he and Alexandra got back together? Even though she'd tried all week to think of him differently, just being near him now made it seem like a vain pursuit. Maybe in time it would get better.

As she looked at his handsome face, she decided maybe it would be easier if she dissected him analytically, looking for flaws. His face had a small mole on his right cheekbone just below the eye. No, that definitely wasn't a flaw. It combined with his strong jawline and gave him a dreamy quality, especially when he smiled and his dimples appeared. His five o'clock shadow was darker than his hair; more of a dirty blond. No, not a flaw either. It also accented that perfect jawline. The eyes? A dreamy blue she could get lost in. So far not helping. The eyelashes? They were longer than most men's; longer than hers. Maybe that was his flaw.

Declan ran a hand over his face. "Is there something on my face? You're looking at me funny."

"Sorry, no." Kate felt her face heat and tried to look serious. "Um, eyelashes." She pointed. "You have really long eyelashes. Longer than mine."

One side of Declan's mouth rose. "Okay? Does that bother you? Do you think I need to start getting them trimmed?"

"What?" She swallowed, searching for words that didn't sound weird. "No. Of course not. Maybe I'm a little jealous. Sorry, I just got distracted." Now she sounded like an idiot. "So . . . do *you* write? You're the grandson of an accomplished author and now head of a publishing company, but I've not heard you mention any of your own books."

"Writing is not my forte. I tried my hand at poetry but decided it wasn't anything worth pursuing. I've done quite a bit of editing, but overall, I feel my strength is in the business aspects of the company. Though I do love to read."

Kate tilted her head and analyzed him again. This time, trying to imagine him in a business meeting.

"You're looking at me funny again. What is it this time? Ear hairs?" He touched his ear. "I promise I don't have any yet. I'm not that old."

"Sorry. I guess I'm just full of funny looks tonight. Lest I scare you with any more of them, I should probably make my way to bed." She raised her arms up and forced a yawn.

With a chuckle, Declan stood and pulled her up. "Okay, sleepy head." He held out an arm, and she let him pull her into an awkward side hug.

He's just a friend. He's just a friend.

Chapter Twenty-Eight

The week couldn't move fast enough. Seeing Declan after work in his three-piece bespoke suits made it hard for Kate to stick to her plan. If she thought he looked good in his everyday clothes, that was nothing compared to his full-on British businessman attire. If Jennifer were there, she'd agree he blew Mr. Darcy away.

Tonight, Alexandra was moving back to London, and Tracey planned a dinner for her the next evening. Time for Kate to put on her big girl panties and handle whatever came.

Looking in the bathroom mirror, Kate realized she'd put entirely too much lipstick on during her little fret session. Grabbing a tissue, she began furiously rubbing at her lips. The next time, she applied it more carefully. Her big girl panties, however, could wait. She was off to meet her coworkers at a local pub. It was a timely diversion from her racing mind, and she silently thanked God that someone had set the evening plan into motion.

At ten thirty, Kate quietly returned and tried not to wake the others. Though she was only twenty-nine, late nights out no longer held the appeal they had during her college days. After ten, she was ready to be home relaxing.

As she worked her way towards the stairs, a light from the living room caught her attention. There, on one of the sofas, lay Declan sleeping. He looked so peaceful, and she couldn't stop herself from moving closer. Was it possible for him to be even more beautiful while sleeping? She relished the moment to look at him without worrying that her face would expose her hidden thoughts. "God, why won't you take this desire from me?" she silently asked.

Declan's sudden leg movement had her jumping backwards. Unfortunately, she bumped into the coffee table, which jostled a silver tea set, and Declan's eyes shot open.

"Sorry," she whispered, cringing while continuing to step back and hoping he might fall back to sleep, thinking it was a dream.

"Hey." He looked slightly disoriented as he looked around before focusing on her. A slow smile appeared on his face. "You're back?"

"I—" Her brow furrowed. Had she told him about her plans for the evening?

"Mum told me you went out with coworkers, so I wanted to wait up for you." It was as if he'd read her mind. His voice was husky, and he sat up and nodded back at the sofa. "Guess I fell asleep. Tell me about your week. We seem to keep missing each other."

Kate frowned. "I thought you were helping Alexandra move in."

"Yeah, but there wasn't too much to do. Her parents helped and hired movers as well. Plus, it was mostly furnished from when she lived here before her move to Paris. When you have a London flat in one of the best areas, you never sell." He chuckled.

"Oh." Her smile faltered.

Declan's eyes lit up, and he patted the sofa next to him. "I'm still waiting for you to tell me about your week."

Knowing her feelings for him, she decided to sit at the other end of the sofa.

"I'm not a leper." He frowned.

Kate slid over a few inches, then slipped off her shoes and curled her legs up between them. At least it would provide something of a barrier. From what, she wasn't sure. "This week, I felt a lot more comfortable with things. The nurse in Kensington House made it clear that she's waiting for me to come on with them so she can retire, which made me feel better about things. Before, I was hesitant to ask her too much, worried that I was pushing too hard for the job." Once she started talking, things just flowed out until she abruptly stopped speaking.

"What's wrong?"

"What's wrong is that I'm doing all the talking. I feel like an awful friend. You're always checking in on me, and here I am, just babbling away about myself when you've started a new job too."

He shrugged. "It's fine." He tilted his head and looked at her warily. "Do you really want to know about my boring business job?"

Throwing a hand to her hip, Kate chastised, "Of course I do. I'm sure it's more interesting than you make it sound."

Declan proceeded to tell her his day step by step until she started asking about specific dialogue in meetings. "Hold on. Are you going to tell me 'Anything I do say may be given in evidence'?"

She giggled at his use of the British Miranda Rights. "I'm just trying to determine what type of person you are at work."

When he spoke, Kate couldn't help but draw closer.

"Enough about me. Do you still think you'll be staying to work at the care facility after Gran moves there permanently?"

"Of course. Well, probably." Her eyes turned away from him. "I've also thought about finding someplace close to the beach cottage."

"It's that unsettled feeling you've been having. You need more time to heal from Mark?"

Kate froze, trying to determine her response. What could she say that was honest but didn't reveal the truth in her heart? "I haven't decided anything. I've not even started looking."

Declan's eyes searched hers, and she couldn't quite decipher everything in them. Hurt? For her? Or was that disappointment with her? He finally nodded. "Just keep praying, and I will too." He tapped her on the knee, then stood. "I suppose we should get some sleep. Sorry for keeping you up. Make sure to lock the door behind me."

He left abruptly, and Kate felt like something had changed between them.

The following week was Thanksgiving back in the U.S., and Tracey offered to have a family celebration in London. Kate met with Tracey's cook to plan a typical American Thanksgiving meal, and during their six o'clock dinner, they would FaceTime her family back home as they had their celebration at noon. Margaret was to stay at home on Thursday, and Tracey and Kate would see to the final preparations together.

Throughout the week, Declan was his usual kind self whenever he came by. He told Kate he'd been researching the original Thanksgiving and planned to share what he'd learned during their meal.

Thursday, the kitchen was chaotic. Not only were Kate, Tracey, and the cook present, but Chloe, Alexandra, and Alexandra's mom joined as well. They all wanted to help prepare an American Thanksgiving. They set Margaret on a stool at the island so she felt like part of things. With so many helpers, it was complicated to make sure everything was done properly, but they did manage it with time to spare.

All of the males trickled in gradually as dinnertime approached. Declan was the last to arrive, and Kate was thankful that she'd been too busy to think much about it. Her heart raced at the sight of him.

As everyone sat down at the table, the computer was set up on the sideboard with Kate's family on FaceTime. Kate's heart brimmed with excitement to see all her family gathered—her parents and her brother with his wife and two kids.

Declan shared the information he'd researched on the first Thanksgiving. As an American, Kate thought it would all be information she'd heard many times—the Mayflower ship landing in Plymouth just as winter approached, Pilgrims having a rough first winter with many dying, Pilgrims meeting the "Indians" in the spring who taught them what to grow in the area, Pilgrims and "Indians" celebrating their fall harvest with Thanksgiving.

What she didn't know was that the Pilgrims wanted to separate from the Church of England because of religious persecution, so they left for Holland. Once in Holland, these previously wealthy men struggled to provide for their families and felt like their children were being drawn away from God. After twelve years, they finally left Holland on a ship called the Speedwell to join with others leaving England on the Mayflower. When they departed from England, the Speedwell began to leak, and they were forced to turn back and move everyone onto the Mayflower. How amazing that after twenty-nine years in the United States, there were still things she didn't know about the long-celebrated American holiday.

Robert asked everyone to go around the table, both at Kate's parents' home and there in London, and say what they were thankful for. He said he would follow that with a prayer of thanksgiving. Growing up in a family that was Christian in name only, Kate never had a time of prayer on the occasion.

After Alexandra said she was thankful for Declan in her life, he looked at her with frustration. When it was Declan's turn for thanks, he said that he was thankful for all of the friends and family gathered there with him. Alexandra frowned when he was done and hadn't named her specifically. Kate felt her heart race at all that seemed to be unfolding.

For the rest of the meal, Kate had trouble focusing on anything but the tense looks between Declan and Alexandra. Her family on FaceTime should have been the center of her attention that evening, but even they couldn't draw her from those thoughts. Several times, she failed to respond when someone spoke to her. She tried to be present in the moment, but her mind kept spinning, trying to work out what the looks between them meant.

With more strength of mind than she thought possible and after a silent prayer, she began to turn her thoughts back to the meal, her family, and friends. It was much more enjoyable and memorable once she had the heart adjustment. By the time they said goodbye to her family, she felt back to herself.

Everyone began talking at once about the success of the event, and Chloe pulled her into a conversation about Kate's past Thanksgivings. Out of the corner of her eye, she saw Declan stand up and reach for several dirty dishes on the table before leaving. Alexandra immediately popped up, grabbed some things, and followed him into the kitchen. It was hard to ignore the tension between the two.

"We should make this an annual event," Chloe suggested as they carried platters of leftover food to the kitchen.

Kate smiled at the thought, but before she could respond, the sound of arguing stopped her. Declan and Alexandra were huddled on the other side of the room, trying to keep their voices down. Declan shook his head, and before his next words came out, his eyes caught Kate's. She saw a flash of anger before his eyes softened, then he pulled Alexandra out of the room. Kate glanced at Chloe, who was frowning, then moved forward to put away the food.

"Sorry you had to see that. I'm sure they'll be fine in a couple of days."

"Do they do that often?" Kate questioned.

"Not often, but it does happen occasionally."

The door Declan and Alexandra walked through kept drawing Kate's attention as she cleaned, and a heaviness weighed on her heart.

Chapter Twenty-Nine

"How does the chicken taste, Gran?" Declan had just finished painstakingly cutting up Margaret's food during their lunch at Kensington House.

Any other day, Kate would melt at Declan's tenderness with his grandmother, but the phone call from Mark's assistant the night before had her mind reeling and stomach clenching. Yet she couldn't hold back the smile that broke through while watching the two of them together. Margaret's trust and adoration as she looked up into Declan's eyes, and his tenderness and patience with her, were something to behold.

Kate worked desperately to keep her thoughts in the present to get through the day, but between the phone call and now Declan's presence, that seemed impossible. It was his presence that reminded her of his issues with Alexandra. In the two weeks since Thanksgiving, Alexandra had joined them for dinner at the main house twice, and both times ended with her and Declan stealing off to argue. The second time, tension was so high, they bowed out as soon as the dishes were away and went to the mews house so they wouldn't disturb everyone else. With only two more days before her trip to the U.S., she knew she'd be able to step away from the Declan worry temporarily, but there was now another issue that threatened her sanity.

Fifteen minutes later, Margaret had barely touched her food. "Eat up, Gran. You need the calories to keep your girlish figure." Grinning, Declan looked up and winked at Kate before his face fell and he reached for her hand. "What's going on, Kate?"

Despite the tingles that shot up her arm, tears long held back welled up in her eyes. How did this man continually see her, even when busy with other things? She looked around the dining area at the other workers and patients, some looking her way. Frowning, she questioned, "Can we talk about this some other time?"

"Of course. Tonight after dinner?"

She started to make an excuse but decided against it and closed her mouth.

"If you'd rather, we can take Gran home now and talk while she naps there instead of here."

Kate shook her head. "This is my last day here with her for two weeks. We should stay. You have work anyway."

"I can have my schedule rearranged." He smirked before adding, "Benefit of being CEO."

"Thanks, but really, I'll make it." The feeling of his hand still on hers was unnerving. What were the issues swirling around in her head? Part of her wanted to lay her other hand on top of his and hold on tight, but instead, she withdrew her hand.

"Okay, dinner, then we'll talk." When she nodded, he smiled and stood up, giving Margaret a kiss on the cheek before turning back to Kate. "If today gets to be too much, please don't hesitate to go back early. Call me if you need help with anything." Kate frowned. "I'm serious. Mum might be unavailable, and I'm happy to help."

"Do I look so awful that you don't think I'll make it?"

"Never. You just look distraught." He reached out and almost touched her chin before stopping himself. "Goodbye, Kate. Goodbye, Gran." With a wave to the workers and patients, he was gone, and Kate was left to swoon over the handsome man with the British accent.

At least it was a brief distraction. Once Margaret was napping, Kate turned to go check in with the staff nurse when she realized that not only would she be no help, but it would be hard to explain her bad mood and the faces she'd been making unintentionally. She stopped and texted the nurse to say she was staying in Margaret's room, then made herself comfortable in a chair before pulling open a Bible app.

Dinner was always at five thirty, and tonight, Kate had Margaret home by four. When she heard Tracey bustling around the kitchen, she led Margaret to sit at the island and washed her own hands in preparation to help.

"You sit and relax, dear. I'm just throwing together a salad for Robert and myself. We have leftovers for Mum. No need for you to do anything for our dinner. If you'd like, I'm sure Corbyn wouldn't mind your help out over at the mews house. He took off early to prepare dinner for you."

"Dinner? He's making me dinner?" Kate's brow furrowed.

"Yes, he said you had some things to discuss." Tracey stopped chopping the carrots and placed a hand on her hip. "I guess he didn't make the dinner part clear." She shook her head and smiled. "But yes, we'll take care of Mum. It looks like you could use a break. If you'd rather rest here first, that's fine too."

Just as Kate was weighing her options, Declan texted.

Declan: Dinner 5:30, mews house. Join me?

How could she say no with all the trouble he'd gone to?

Kate: Of course.

She hesitated before adding:

Kate: Need help? I'm home.

Declan: Wonderful! Yes, come on over.

When she arrived, Kate looked around the kitchen at all the food Declan was preparing. "I can't believe you've gone to so much trouble for me." Despite his thoughtfulness, it was hard to smile.

"No trouble. I thought it might be easier to have our conversation without my parents nearby."

"I smell curry."

"Yes. Seafood curry work for you? It has prawns, salmon, and mussels."

"Absolutely. Even if I still feel bad after talking things over with you, at least I'll have had a good meal."

Declan tried to smile, but worry was evident in his eyes. "Yes, there is that."

"Tell me what's troubling you, Kate." Declan had made light-hearted conversation throughout the meal, but once Kate laid her fork down and pushed her plate away, he was ready for a heart to heart. He picked up their dishes and put them in the dishwasher before leading her to the living room.

It was the first time Kate had spent much time in the mews home other than a quick tour, and she found herself drawn to its combination of old world charm and modern furnishings. Unfortunately, she wasn't there to critique the decor of the place. Her eyes finally settled on Declan, and she prayed for courage to share the pain that was breaking her heart once again.

"It's my husband Mark's mistress, Brittany." Saying the words made her cringe and heat rise to her cheeks. Just over a year ago, she couldn't have imagined those words coming from her mouth. Though their marriage was far from perfect, she thought they could work through things. She'd never dreamt that the man she'd married was the type to regularly have extramarital affairs. "She . . . contacted his assistant, the one who was so open with me about everything after the fact. Anyway, his assistant reached out to me and said that Brittany wants to meet me and apologize while I'm home for Christmas."

Even as she spoke, tears fell. The thought of facing the woman her husband had most recently forsaken his vows for terrified her. The crude things Brittany and her husband had shared and said in texts had given her too many nightmares to count.

"Kate—that was the call you received last night, and you still woke up and took Gran to Kensington House? Thank you for your commitment to her, but you must know that anyone in my family would have helped you." He shook his head. "You constantly amaze me." He looked at her as if measuring his next words. "Have you decided what you'll do?"

She took a few breaths before baring her soul. "To be honest, the thought of seeing her in person makes me angry and pains me at the same time." Her heart rate sped up, and something inside urged her on. "But in spite of all that, I feel . . . I feel like God is telling me that I need to do this. For me and for her." Frowning, she asked, "Does that sound like something God would do?"

"Ah, the question mankind has asked since being sent from the garden. Have you prayed about it?"

"Just now, I prayed for strength to tell you, but no, I think I've been so caught up in my feelings, I didn't think of it. That's terrible, isn't it? What kind of Christian forgets to ask God about important things in their life?"

"The human kind."

"You always seem to remember things like that. You seem so close to God. Sometimes I feel like I'm floundering to find my way to Him. Like I only think of him when I'm desperate. I want to be better."

"'For I do not understand my own actions. For I do not do what I want, but I do the very thing I hate.'" Kate raised a brow at Declan's statement. "That's what Paul says in Romans 7, then the very first verse of the next chapter says, 'There is therefore now no condemnation for those who are in Christ Jesus.' God knows everything about you. He knew your weaknesses before you became a Christian, yet he still chose you—and for your information, I fail as well. Too many times, I've gone to him after I've made a mess of things. It's normal for Christians to fail. Just don't get stuck in the failure. Turn it over to him, ask forgiveness and help in doing better next time."

"I'll keep working on that."

"We can start now. I'll pray first, and then you can."

Declan led her in another one of his perfect prayers. Everything he said seemed to be exactly what she needed. The way he spoke to God was so natural, not forced or fake, but like he was talking to a dear friend. She longed for that. God had already become so dear to her, too, but sometimes, she felt like she was holding back. It was silly when she considered the fact that God knew her every thought before she uttered a word.

A feeling of peace filled Kate. Declan's friendship was truly a gift from God. Just being around him gave her a glimmer of hope, and it was hard to be sad in his presence. She couldn't imagine getting through the past few months without him. Her entire outlook on life had taken a 180-degree turn.

Kate squinted at the sun coming in her bedroom window before checking the time on her phone. Six thirty on a Saturday—not when she wanted to get up after her restless night, but there was no going back to sleep. She knew without a doubt that she was supposed to meet with Brittany. It was a good feeling, not because she wanted to meet with Brittany, but because God had made his will for her clear. In fact, it was pretty amazing that he cared for her so much that he would help her with important details such as this.

She texted Declan to let him know God had given her clarity in the night. As soon as she hit send, she wished she could take it back. Six thirty was much too early to text, and unfortunately, her brain was slow to catch up to that fact.

Declan: I'll be there in fifteen. Meet me in your kitchen.

Throwing off the covers, Kate darted to the bathroom. She definitely didn't expect that. Morning breath, gross. She squinted at the mirror. Bed head and sleep in her eyes, awful. A quick ponytail, washing her face, and brushing her teeth would have to do.

Looking down, she remembered that she was only wearing a ratty t-shirt. Clothes!

Quietly, she made her way downstairs, where she found Declan in the kitchen already heating up water for tea. With no bedrooms close, they wouldn't have to worry about waking the others. Kate couldn't wait any longer to share her experience and settled onto a stool by the bar.

Declan looked at her warily, but a grin began to form when he saw hers. "You seem happy with the decision?"

She made a face. "It's not what I would have chosen, but I generally like to avoid conflict. I do feel like God has made it clear, so I'm happy about that." She paused to gather her thoughts.

"I went to bed praying for God to show me what to do, but sometime during my prayer, I fell asleep. I began to dream, and it was weird. You know how sometimes you dream that you need to go somewhere, and you can never seem to make it? Like the building you're in suddenly becomes a maze, or things keep happening to stall you from getting there? This was the opposite of that. In my dream—or I should say dreams—I went home and purposely tried to avoid seeing Brittany, but in each dream, I kept meeting her. Each time, it brought me peace. In one dream, I was praying, asking God to keep me away from her, and he actually said, 'Go to her' in an audible voice. It was so startling that I actually woke up and looked around my room. It was about three thirty a.m. when I checked my phone. Up until then, I felt like I had been wrestling with God without a moment of peace, so I finally told God 'Okay,' then tried to go back to sleep. The next thing I knew, I was waking up at six thirty. I'd slept soundly once I stopped fighting God on what he wanted from me. It sounds crazy, doesn't it?"

"No, actually. It's perfect and so like God. It makes me think of Jacob in the Old Testament of the Bible."

Kate's brows drew together. "I'm pretty fuzzy on the Old Testament. Who's Jacob?"

"He was the grandson of Abraham. Abraham was the father of the Jewish nation. God made a covenant with him that was passed down through his son Isaac and from Isaac to Jacob. Jacob had left his family's land for about twenty years, and when he finally returned, he knew he would have to face his brother who'd wanted to kill him when he left. That's a story for another time. Anyway, Jacob split his family into two camps and sent them over ahead of himself. That evening, a man wrestled with him all night. Just before daybreak, the man touched his hip joint and put it out of its socket and told him he was no longer Jacob but Israel. He also told Jacob that he had striven with God and with man and prevailed."

"Whoa." Kate touched her hip. "I guess I should be thankful I'm not limping. Wait, Israel? That's how the nation got its name?"

Declan nodded, and Kate smiled at the thought that she'd had her own encounter with God. "It's still going to be hard to face her, so I'll really need you praying about that. I'll let you know once we've set up a day." She stood up and went to the refrigerator. "I think the cook made some crêpes for this morning. Are you hungry?"

Declan smirked. "So soon after all that stress, you're ready for food?"

"I guess all that wrestling made me hungry." She found the crêpes and berries while Declan pulled out plates, forks, and honey.

Once Kate's hunger was satiated, her mind went to Declan. With all the concern he had shown her through the months, it would only be right that she was there for him too. As much as she wanted to stay out of his relationship with Alexandra, she wouldn't feel right if she didn't try to help him work things out with her. "Now that we have my plan of action figured out, what about you?"

"Me?"

"Yeah. It's not exactly a secret that you and Alexandra have been arguing."

Declan groaned. "We have."

He didn't look like he wanted to elaborate, but she refused to leave it. "I don't mean to intrude, but what's going on?"

Declan frowned and shook his head while staring at his tea. "You're right, it's been pretty obvious. It's just . . . I thought we were on the same page with just being friends, and now it seems we're not. I think you and I being so close has made her jealous of you. She's acting out and becoming clingy. I don't know." He rubbed the back of his neck.

That was exactly what Kate had been afraid of and tried to avoid. "I guess it's a good thing I leave tomorrow for two weeks." Hopefully, that would be enough time for them to work through things, either to get back together or be done for good.

"No." He shook his head. "I told her she and I need some space away from each other, so it won't matter if you're here or not. Although with our parents so close, it's going to be hard to get that space during the holidays. There are several things that our families do together that are traditions."

"Are you sure you should do that? Give each other space? Maybe you should talk things through or get counseling."

"I'm positive. We've done the talking and counseling thing, and we still ended up in this place."

What could she say to that?

Before Kate could respond, Tracey stepped in. "Good morning, you two. Breakfast crêpes?"

Kate's nerves were on edge as she looked over her luggage once again to make sure everything was packed before she went to bed. A knock on her door startled her.

"It's Declan. Do you have a moment?" he called through the door.

"Sure, what's up?" When she opened the door, he held out a present.

"I thought I was exchanging gifts with your family when I return."

He shrugged and grinned. "I wanted you to have this now."

She stepped out and joined him in the sitting area just outside her room, worried that what she had picked for him would seem too insignificant in comparison. When he laid it in her hand, she instantly knew it was a book and felt some relief. He did work at a publishing house. As she unwrapped it, her relief morphed into amazement. It was a beautiful navy blue leather-bound copy of Jane Austen's *Emma*.

"Declan, you remembered." She ran her hand across the leather before opening and flipping through it. There was artwork on a few of the pages—sketches depicting the action on the corresponding pages—which brought a smile to her face. The clothing of Austen's time period always intrigued her. "This is . . . thank you so much."

He had paid attention when she mentioned her love of Jane. She recalled the day they were in an antiques store and she saw the most beautiful mahogany George III Regency secretary. Looking at the secretary more closely, she had noticed several of Jane Austen's books sitting on one of the shelves and fallen in love with the secretary instantly, telling Declan that it seemed as if the secretary was claiming her by displaying some of her favorite books in beautiful old leather bindings. This book was one of those. "I just can't believe you remembered."

"Open to the front." He pointed to the cover.

Her hand shook as she flipped it open. Inside the front cover, he had written a note.

Throughout most of the book, Emma had no idea of her true value. I'm hoping that in spite of your past, you will realize that yours is a heart worth treasuring.

Yours in Christ, Declan Corbyn Fitzgerald

Chapter Thirty

The week leading up to Kate's meeting with Brittany had been busy, but other than her time with Jennifer and meeting Asher, she hardly remembered what else passed. There was a constant dread dragging her thoughts to dark places. Though she knew God had called her to speak with Brittany and he would get her through it, convincing herself of it moment by moment was a challenge.

Her parents' home brought back so many memories of Mark, with the pain of his unfaithfulness never far behind. In spite of the fact that God's love was better than the love of a broken man, there were still whispers in her head saying, "You weren't a good enough wife—you weren't pretty enough, you didn't fulfill his needs enough."

The words Declan had written in his gift to her—"*Yours is a heart worth treasuring*"—kept swirling in her mind, battling with the whispers in her head.

She had several people praying for her meeting with Brittany—Declan, Tracey, and Ruth, Margaret's friend from Kingsdown. Kate had been talking to Ruth regularly about mission trips and was excited about joining her in the future, but for now, she needed strength and focus to get through meeting Brittany and prayers to keep from collapsing under the resurfaced pain.

When Mark was first killed, she'd seen a picture of Brittany in the Memphis Commercial Appeal. She was a beautiful woman with long blond hair. At that time, Kate only knew her as the widow of the shooter, so she had no reason to be envious. Instead, she'd felt they shared a bond in the loss of their husbands and imagined how much worse it must have been for Brittany to learn that her husband had killed a man. She had wanted to assure Brittany that she didn't hold a grudge.

Days later, she thought she saw Brittany at a distance at Mark's funeral, but before she could make her way over to speak, one of the partners of the firm sidetracked her. By the time she was able to step away, Brittany was nowhere to be found. Wanting to send condolences and relieve Brittany of guilt, she contacted the law firm for Brittany's address but was told that the firm was taking care of sending something and that they didn't think Kate contacting her was a good idea.

She remembered looking her up on Instagram just after the murder and tried to message her that way, but the account had been removed. At the time, she'd assumed it was to avoid media attention, but after what she learned from Mark's assistant, she wondered if it had more to do with the firm trying to avoid backlash and further inquiries.

Finding out about Brittany's affair with her husband had removed any sympathy Kate previously held towards her. In fact, before becoming a Christian, she'd viewed it as karma. Even now, she was left with lingering anger and resentment. The past few days, as Kate prayed over how to respond at the meeting, she had an overwhelming sense that God was saying, "Love her. Show my love to her." That seemed to be a sticking point with Kate. She'd agreed with God on the meeting, and even planned on being civil, but show her love? Reluctantly, she shared that message with her three prayer warriors and asked them to pray for God's strength and wisdom about how to live that out.

On the day of the meeting, Brittany invited Kate to her apartment. It was in a decent part of town. Nothing fancy, but clean and nice-looking. She seemed to be using the hush money the firm had given her sparingly. From what Kate had read about Brittany's husband, he'd left behind a string of failed ventures and creditors.

Preparing herself with a quick prayer, Kate knocked on the door.

She still wondered how she would "show love" to this woman, but told God she would listen for his direction. She had the overwhelming feeling that this meeting would change her life forever.

Her thoughts were arrested when the door opened, and she saw the most adorable baby girl in Brittany's arms. Blond hair and brown eyes—eyes that had been part of her life since she was fifteen. Kate was face to face with her worst fear, one she'd not given words to. Surely, God did not call her to *this*. Her heart stuttered, and she drew back before quickly turning away and retreating to her car.

"Show my love to her," came a voice as clear as day.

Kate froze, then scanned the area before glancing back at Brittany. Did she hear it too? The voice was so strong, and she heard it from without, not just inside her head this time. "Love her." The words came again. If she turned back and did as God asked, would that finally set her free from her pain or make it worse? Was this something she could trust God with?

The world came to a standstill as her heart hung in the balance, then stopped and restarted. She found herself turning again towards Brittany. Kate saw her face full of sorrow and shame. How could she hold Brittany's sins against her when she herself had been forgiven of so much? Maybe not in ways that seemed as bad as adultery, but many other things, and it was all forgiven.

"Kate, I'm so sorry. Please hear me out. I was selfish, and I know it's too late to undo all the damage I've caused, but still, I'm sorry." Tears streamed down Brittany's cheeks, and the baby patted her face. "Would you . . . be willing to come in for a few minutes and talk?"

Brittany's voice was hoarse and not what Kate had expected. When Kate looked more closely at her, she saw a frail, thin woman, still pretty, but much different from what she remembered. She wondered if Brittany's guilt had caught up with her. There was genuine remorse in her eyes. What more would the woman say? Would it break Kate even more?

She stepped forward, silently quoting the Scripture Declan had suggested she memorize in preparation for this day. *Second Corinthians 12:9—But he said to me, 'My grace is sufficient for you, for my power is made perfect in weakness.' Therefore I will boast all the more gladly of my weaknesses, so that the power of Christ may rest upon me.*

After forcing herself to nod, Kate followed Brittany into the apartment. It was clean and sparsely furnished, with clear signs that an infant lived there.

Brittany offered Kate a seat on the sofa while she sat on a nearby chair. The tension in the air was palpable. Fidgeting with the baby in her arms, Brittany let out a shaky breath and looked up, her face filled with sadness and regret.

Kate could feel the battle within—*Forgive her, love her. Hold onto the anger, hate her.* The whine of the baby drew her attention, and those dark eyes once again held her hostage. It was like Brittany had stolen the life that should have been hers—except Mark had freely given that life away.

Brittany followed Kate's gaze and frowned. "This is Madeline." She lifted Madeline up, then cooed, "Do you want to play, Sweet Pea?" Carefully, she placed her daughter on her back on a play mat with toys dangling from an overhead arch. Seconds later, Madeline giggled and squealed in delight.

The war continued to rage within Kate, with her old self wanting to speak angry words and leave before she heard any excuses, and her new self wanting something better. God had changed her, and as she watched the child who, through no fault of her own, had been brought into the world, her walls crumbled. She looked again at Brittany. *Love her.*

Brittany coughed, then faltered. "I . . . I never set out to be . . . the other woman. Growing up, I had dreams of the handsome prince rescuing me and us having our own happily ever after." Pain reflected in her eyes, and she looked away. "I didn't know my dad. My alcoholic mother raised me along with my older half-sister. My childhood was chaotic, to say the least. We never knew if there would be food on the table, and often came home to an empty house. If Mom was home, it was rarely a good thing. She was usually either passed out or drunk and hateful.

"When Chris, my husband, came walking into the restaurant where I worked my senior year in high school, I thought I'd found my prince.

He made me feel special—told me how beautiful I was, showered me with gifts, and promised me the world. I thought that since he was nine and a half years older, he was more mature and that what we had was a love like no other." Brittany's voice gave out, and she broke into a coughing fit. "Sorry, I promise it's not contagious. Anyway, once I turned eighteen in my last semester of school, I moved in with him, and we got married.

"The first year was bliss. After that, his business failed, and creditors came calling. He became so changeable. One minute, he would brag that he had it all taken care of with his next big thing, and the next minute, he was angry at me and it was all my fault that things went wrong. We started moving from place to place and city to city to avoid creditors as his next big thing always ended in failure and left people angry. Memphis was the same thing all over again, but that time, he fought back and hired your husband."

Madeline started fussing, and Brittany moved to the floor to comfort her. "Your husband was so kind. He made me feel seen. With Chris, I had become isolated. He wouldn't let me work, because he thought that made him look bad. I had no friends and no desire to talk to my alcoholic mom or sister, who is a drug addict. I was lonely. Mark . . . he was like my knight in shining armor."

Kate fought to keep a straight face as she felt bile rise in her throat.

"Chris refused to have kids after a pregnancy scare early on, and he went to the extreme of having a vasectomy. He said he needed all of my attention and didn't want me distracted with a kid. That hurt, you know? You dream of the perfect happily ever after with your prince and eventually kids, and he took that away from me."

This hit a little too close to home for Kate in more ways than one.

After a gulp of water, Brittany continued. "Mark started coming around when Chris was out, and one thing led to another . . ." Tears ran down Brittany's eyes, and she wiped them frantically. Kate tried hard to hold her own back, but they surfaced for a different reason as the knife twisted deeper.

"I figured he was my way out." Brittany's words were practically a whisper. "I knew he wanted to have children and that you'd had trouble.

I started poking holes in the condoms, hopeful he would get me out of my marriage."

Brittany's face reddened, and she buried it in her shaking hands. Kate had the urge to flee, but felt God holding her back. "Chris . . . he found my pregnancy test and didn't tell me. He beat me, then left in a rage. He'd been verbally abusive, but not physical until that day. I never dreamt he would kill someone or himself.

"It wasn't until I received the items they'd taken off his body after the police investigation that I realized he had the pregnancy test with him." She shook and sobbed while pulling Madeline into her arms. "I'm so sorry, Kate. I never meant for any of that to happen. I'm so selfish."

Kate looked at Brittany in shock as she tried to sort through her emotions. If she'd not been married to Mark, she might feel compassion after hearing such a heart-wrenching story. Instead, she felt like she'd been pulled through the proverbial wringer. The life she had thought was mostly good, with issues in her marriage that she'd believed were minor and temporary—none of it had been real. The truth stared her in the face in the form of a little girl cooing in her mother's arms.

How could she respond to Brittany? How *should* she respond?

"Brittany, thank you for your honesty. I . . ." *What to say?* "I wish I could say it's okay, but it's not." Brittany hung onto Kate's every word and moved back up to the chair after placing Madeline back on the mat. "The truth . . . the truth, however, is that God will use and is using what you planned for evil to instead do good." The story of Joseph in the Old Testament came back to her.

"I had no idea you were religious. You must really think I'm an evil sinner. Isn't adultery like one of the worst sins?" Brittany held a hand to her chest and seemed to be breathing heavily.

"It is one of the Ten Commandments, but no, I'm not religious. I have a relationship with God, which is quite different. I became a Christian recently, after some people I work with shared with me about how Christ died to forgive us for all of our sins and I can have a personal relationship with him." The words flowed out of her mouth unbidden until she had thoroughly explained how to become a Christian.

Tears flowed down Brittany's cheeks. "You can't know what it means to me that you would share this with me. I don't think I'm ready to become a Christian, but the fact that you are being so kind and encouraging to me after all I've done . . . to you especially. Thank you."

A cry from the play mat had the attention of both women. Brittany lifted her daughter and started to walk away, then stopped and turned back. "I need to fix her bottle. I can get you some water if you'd like. Would you mind holding her?"

"Yeah . . . sure, I can hold her, but no, I don't care for any water."

With a racing heart, Kate reached out and took the fussy Madeline, placing her on her lap. What a surreal feeling to hold the child of her husband and his mistress. It should have been Kate and Mark's baby in her arms. That stung. Memories of crying herself to sleep, wishing for a little one like this, rushed to the surface.

Despite the pain, she was determined to make this little girl feel special while she held her. By the time Brittany returned with the bottle, Kate had Madeline not only content but giggling as she sang a song her grandfather used to sing to her when she was small. She even remembered the hand motions.

"Oh, how sweet." Brittany smiled while moving toward Kate. "She likes you. Why don't you feed her the bottle?"

"I can do that." Kate grasped the bottle and Madeline happily took it.

"I know you must think this is strange . . . me asking to meet with you." Tears welled up in Brittany's eyes. "Honestly, I didn't think you would follow through. I just . . . well, the past few months have been difficult. I've not felt great and have had all sorts of tests run. About a month ago, they diagnosed me with thyroid cancer."

Kate was caught off guard by this revelation and frowned.

"I'm still waiting on tests to determine what kind it is, but they said that most thyroid cancers have a ninety percent cancer-free rate after five years. Also, since I'm so young, they're hopeful, and so am I. That's the reason for my coughing." As if on cue, she began coughing. "Sorry. The thing is, it got me thinking about what I've done with my life. When my husband killed yours and himself, I felt a twinge of guilt, but I was so focused on my own self-preservation and pregnancy that it didn't fully hit. This cancer has been a wake-up call for me. I know I can't undo the past, but I do truly regret it."

By the time Kate left Brittany's apartment, she was overwhelmed. Madeline was an adorable child, but she found it painful to look at her, knowing she was Mark's. Finding out Brittany had cancer added to the nightmare. Almost as soon as she got onto the main road, she pulled into a parking lot. She couldn't get the windows rolled down fast enough. It felt like she was suffocating. With shaking hands, she reached for her phone, pushing buttons. When the familiar voice called out to her, she managed to calm her breathing.

"Declan."

"Kate? Are you okay? Why do you sound out of breath?"

"Declan, I saw her." She began to sob. Speaking with Declan brought forth all of her emotions.

"Brittany? It was hard? I'm so sorry. I've been praying."

"No, that's not it. I mean, yes, I did see Brittany, but . . ." How could she speak the words? "She has . . . his baby."

"Oh Kate. It's Mark's." He stated as if he knew.

A car blaring its horn drew her attention to the road.

"Kate? What just happened? Kate?"

"I'm fine. I'm sitting in a parking lot." She watched the traffic on the adjacent road stop and start.

"Okay. Good. I wish I were there for you. I can come. Give me a few minutes, and I'll see what flights are available."

Warmth rose up inside, and his words brought a smile to her face. "Declan, it's almost Christmas. You need to be there for your family."

"Kate, it's no problem. I want to be there for you."

"No. I won't have you change your plans. I'm not alone. I have my parents . . . and Jennifer."

"Kate, please."

"Declan, don't. It will just make me feel guilty. You talking to me is a huge help."

He was momentarily silent. "Okay, but I'll check on you each day. Now, tell me what happened with Brittany."

The pain deep in her chest that had temporarily subsided now resurfaced, and she rubbed over her heart. "Yes, Mark . . . Mark and Brittany have a baby." It somehow hurt worse when she said it out loud.

"Kate." His voice sounded strained.

"I had awful feelings towards Brittany when I first discovered she was Mark's mistress—anger, of course, but also jealousy. I was jealous that she had captured the attention of the man who had supposedly committed his life to me. I thought I was mostly over that pain. But to see their daughter, his daughter . . . I feel the betrayal as if I just discovered it. A baby . . . the thing I had longed for."

Switching the phone to speaker, she rummaged through her purse and found the tissues her mom gave her on the way out the door. Kate could barely see through her tears streaming down, and she struggled to speak again. "Yet Madeline is so beautiful and innocent. None of this is her fault. I . . ." Could she get the words out? "I held her, and . . . it was so surreal. Her eyes . . . they were just like his. I kept praying for strength to get through it, and I know that without God, I wouldn't have. I was still struggling with anger, but when Brittany told me . . ." She became too choked up to speak.

"It's okay. Take your time."

"She has cancer."

"Brittany or Madeline?"

"Brittany. I noticed she looked thin and frail, and she kept coughing. It's thyroid cancer, but she said she has a good chance. I think she said there's a ninety percent survival rate. She acted like she wasn't worried."

"It was the cancer that made her determined to apologize. From what I can tell, she sincerely regrets what she did." Kate's tears had finally subsided. "I'm left feeling a strange mixture of emotions, but mostly overwhelmed." She rubbed her forehead. "And I feel a headache coming on."

Declan prayed over her before making her promise to text once she was safely at her parents' home.

Kate's clock read 3:16 a.m., and her head continued to ache as well as her heart. Sitting up, she opened the Bible app on her phone, typed in "peace," and scrolled through the New Testament verses before stopping on Philippians 4:6-8. *Do not be anxious about anything, but in everything by prayer and supplication with thanksgiving let your requests be made known to God. And the peace of God, which surpasses all understanding, will guard your hearts and your minds in Christ Jesus. Finally, brothers, whatever is true, whatever is honorable, whatever is just, whatever is pure, whatever is lovely, whatever is commendable, if there is any excellence, if there is anything worthy of praise, think about these things.*

Chapter Thirty-One

"Kate? Are you okay?" Declan's voice comforted her almost instantly.

"I can't sleep again." Her clock read 3:37 a.m., and this was the second night it had happened since meeting Brittany.

"Still troubled about Brittany and Madeline?"

"I'm sorry, you're working. Is this a bad time?" Kate heard paper shuffling and thought of the time difference.

"It's fine. Just a minute." Muffled voices spoke in the background. "Okay. I was finishing up something with my secretary. Still troubled?"

"Yeah, but this time I dreamed that Brittany and Madeline were sitting at Christmas dinner with me and my family. In the dream, I had peace when they were there. I wonder . . . I'm wondering if I should invite them. She has no family really, but *my* family will think I'm crazy. I don't know. Is it crazy? I have such an unsettled feeling, like there's something more I'm supposed to be doing. I don't think resentment or jealousy are even part of it anymore."

"Okay. Wow. It's good that the negative emotions are dissipating, but it's a big ask to have her join your family. Let's pray about it, then in the morning, you can talk to your parents about it."

"Thanks. I could use some prayer."

"Kate!" Her mom gasped and moved to sit at the kitchen table with her. "Where's this coming from? You don't owe that woman anything. I certainly can understand feeling bad that she has cancer, but I don't know . . . and your father . . . you're his baby girl." Abby placed her hand over Kate's.

"It's hard to explain, but I feel like it's what God wants me to do. You can say no if you must, but I'm really hoping you won't."

Sighing, Abby watched Kate carefully. "Hmm." She tapped her fingers on the table and frowned. "If you can convince your father, then you are welcome to invite her."

Unfortunately, Kate was counting on her mom to help persuade her dad. It was a pleasant surprise when his response was, "That's a tough situation, but I understand your need to extend an olive branch. We should do this so you can get closure."

She was thankful both her father and mother agreed. Her brother gave her the hardest time about inviting Brittany.

"You can't expect us to enjoy our Christmas with that woman in our home, Kate. And what am I supposed to tell my kids? They're four and six. Ava and Alex, this is your sort-of cousin . . . well she would be, but *that* woman had a baby with your Uncle Mark. Oh, and her husband is the one who killed your uncle. That's crazy, Kate!"

"Cameron, this is not about you. This is my burden to bear," she'd told him. "As for your kids, just tell them Brittany is someone I know and invited. Kids don't tend to overthink like adults."

It was over twenty-four hours after that conversation before Cameron called her and said he wouldn't cause problems if Brittany came.

Brittany was skeptical, too, when Kate called her, and she questioned why Kate would want to spend time with her on Christmas Day.

"I told you before how I've recently become a Christian, and I feel like this is what God wants me to do," Kate answered Brittany honestly.

Brittany hesitated before accepting the invitation, and that night was the first night Kate slept soundly since learning Brittany wanted to speak with her.

As Kate guessed, her brother, though verbally cordial towards Brittany, was stone-faced upon their introductions. Her parents and even Allison, Cameron's wife, made Brittany feel welcome in spite of the circumstance. Doting over Madeline also came easily for everyone except Cameron. Ava and Alex's interest was particularly adorable to watch.

Before dinner, they fought over who would sit in the free chair beside Madeline, since Brittany needed to be on the other side. They made the decision that Ava would sit there during the meal and Alex during the dessert.

Throughout the meal, both children were enthralled with Madeline, especially when Brittany fed her puréed green beans and butternut squash. Madeline liked to help her mother by spreading the excess from her mouth to other parts of her face, and in the end, looked like a work of abstract art, leaving Ava and Alex giggling at the display. It entertained everyone and distracted them from the underlying tension.

Following the dinner, they gathered in the living room, and again Madeline became the center of attention when set on a floor pallet to play. Ava and Alex babbled in what they thought was baby talk and waved toys at her. Though Alex was two years older than Ava, who was four, he was more easily distracted and finally wandered off to play with his new toys.

When Brittany was ready to leave, Kate helped gather her things. The chill in the air hit Kate as she carried a diaper bag and a bag of gifts they'd given Madeline out to Brittany's car.

"Thank you so much again for your kindness in inviting me. All of you went over and above. Though I could see it was a stretch for your brother."

Kate nodded. "He's always been protective of me."

"Well . . . I could tell he was trying. I don't deserve such kindness." Tears welled up in Brittany's eyes. "I don't know how to thank you for making Madeline's first Christmas special in spite of how I treated you."

"As I said, God has been prodding me to show you his love. His love forgives all things. I can't say this hasn't been hard for me, it's just—" She stopped when Madeline reached for her.

"She wants you to hold her. She's developing a fondness for you."

Kate swallowed, then pulled Madeline into her arms. "Hey, Madeline." Madeline grinned up at her and began playing with Kate's hair.

"I—" Her words caught in her throat and she fought back her own tears. "Several people are praying for me, and it's only in God's strength that I've been able to do this. I want you to know I do forgive you. Not that I'm saying what you did is okay, but I forgive you, and I'm moving past it. I know that God wants you to know he is ready to forgive you, too, when you turn it over to him and let him be Lord of your life."

Brittany's brow furrowed, but it softened when she nervously smiled. "I'd always thought of Christians as judgmental, but I can tell you mean it. I'm really thankful." Her eyes filled with moisture, and she quickly hugged Kate before transferring Madeline from Kate's arms to the car seat. Looking back at Kate with hesitancy, she asked, "I . . . would you mind if I called you sometime?"

Almost on instinct, Kate felt the word "yes" forming on her lips, but she stopped herself, realizing that she didn't feel the anger and hurt towards Brittany like before, but instead felt at peace. This was what God intended her to do. "No, I don't mind. I'm here for you whenever you need to talk." It felt good to say that, and as she watched Brittany drive away, the worries of the previous week left as well. In two days, there would be an ocean between her and Brittany, and she didn't think the feeling of release was because of the anticipated distance, but because she had fully forgiven Brittany.

Chapter Thirty-Two

The seven-and-a-half-hour flight from Charlotte to London was overnight, and Kate struggled to get her mind to settle so she could sleep. She couldn't get the feeling of holding Madeline out of her mind.

Over the past year, the death and subsequent revelations about Mark had distracted her from thoughts of having a child, but seeing and interacting with Madeline brought her maternal desires back full force. Those desires hadn't gone away over the past year but hid in the crevices of Kate's heart, waiting for a chance to hold a child of her own. Presently, her dream of a family seemed far off. Maybe adoption was an option, but she wasn't sure about being a single mom, and doubted it would be easy for an American citizen living overseas.

When she finally drifted off to sleep, a cramp in her neck startled her awake and left her with lingering fragments of a dream in which she held Madeline while Declan wrapped a protective arm around them both. Baby giggles and coos still rattled through her brain. Declan starred as the romantic hero of more and more of her dreams, which made it hard to maintain the pretense that her feelings towards him were strictly platonic. Now she was about to see him for the first time in two weeks when he picked her up. How could she look at him without her face revealing that she loved him?

What would he think when he discovered her feelings toward him? He'd not mentioned Alexandra while Kate was back in the States, so she had no idea if they'd reconciled.

Lack of sleep heightened every negative thought, so she gathered some items to take to the bathroom and freshen up, hoping that would snap her out of the doldrums.

After quickly getting through passport control using the eGate, Kate pulled her bags to the exit where Declan waited. At the sight of him, all her negative self-talk flew out the window. Before she even made it to him, he raced over and reached for her free hand. She melted at his touch, and all the tension from travel and her overactive imagination vanished. There was nowhere else she wanted to be, and she'd never wished so hard for time to stop.

"I've missed you," he whispered into her hair. When they were jostled by a group moving past, he pulled back and grinned at her. "We should head out. I almost forgot . . ." He released Kate's hand and presented her with a bouquet of flowers.

Her eyes went wide. "They're beautiful!" She'd been so focused on his face when he approached that she'd missed them. What did they mean? She wanted to read something romantic into them, but that might be her imagination running wild. "From you?" Maybe the whole family sent them.

He looked embarrassed. Had his cheeks turned pink? "They are. I saw them at that little stand down the road from the sushi place where we like to eat. They're so bright and cheery, they made me think of you."

"They are bright and cheery," Kate gushed, at a loss for any more fitting response. Now she was the one with pink cheeks. As much as she'd unloaded her hurt and disappointments on him in the months they'd known each other, it was hard to imagine the thought of her being bright and cheery, but who was she to disabuse him of such a notion?

Declan reached over to take her suitcase and swing her carry-on over his shoulder, then placed a hand on her back. "I'm this way in the car park." He gestured with his head. "Mum has a special meal planned for New Year's Day. A belated Christmas for you."

"That's so thoughtful, but you guys already celebrated Christmas." She'd FaceTimed them just before their Christmas dinner meal, and they'd shown her the spread of food they'd put together. It was impressive.

"Mum insists. She was sad that you missed out. You've become like part of the family. Even Gran was excited when we mentioned we were picking you up today." That was an accomplishment, considering she had become barely aware of what was happening.

Soon they were maneuvering through familiar streets, catching up on the past two weeks as if they hadn't been talking nearly every day. Kate didn't mind rehashing their time apart. She loved listening to his British accent, which she'd been missing.

Now and then he glanced her way, with a smile like she was the most important person on earth. Her heart raced as he reached over and squeezed her hand. When she asked him what that was about, he said, "I needed to be sure you're really here."

Had he missed her even a fraction of how much she'd missed him? With her hand still tingling, it was impossible to keep from imagining that they were together. She eyed his gorgeous profile—honey-blond hair and blue eyes that drew female attention everywhere he went. What would it be like if he were her husband? What if they had a child and a home of their own? She kept watching him, but tried to keep it subtle.

It wasn't until they pulled into the garage of the mews house that she reluctantly brought her mind back to reality.

When she reached for the door handle, he was already out of the car and opening it for her. The tingles that worked their way through her body when he held her hand to pull her out sent a shiver up her spine.

"Cold?"

Unable to think clearly, she shrugged.

"It's definitely not short-sleeve weather like you had in Memphis." He wrapped an arm around her and rubbed up and down her arm, creating warm friction and a host of other feelings.

His familiar bergamot and musk scent engulfed her. He smelled like home—her new home. Strangely, her visit to Memphis had felt like just that—a temporary visit, but not home. "I'm sure I'll adjust quickly."

Reaching down, he slipped his hand in hers and pulled her towards his apartment door. "I have something for you, and I'm not ready to share you with the family just yet."

"Okay." She glanced back toward the big house before they entered his apartment. When he brought out a present wrapped just like the *Emma* book, she gasped. "What are you doing? You already gave me a present."

"I did." The grin on his face made her stop questioning him for fear she'd steal his joy. "Come join me." He moved to the sofa and patted the spot next to him.

"I've got a gift for you. I can just—" She started to turn back but then stopped herself. "Actually, I should wait and give it to you when I give everyone else theirs. They're all similar." She pictured the beautiful calligraphy and artwork that she'd paid Jennifer to create for each of them before settling a respectable distance from Declan on the sofa.

By the weight of the gift, she knew it was another book, and once unwrapped, discovered the beautiful lavender leather copy of *Sense and Sensibility* with navy blue embossing that she had originally seen in the store next to the copy of *Emma* he'd given her.

"Declan." Her voice was barely above a whisper. "You've outdone yourself again. Two of the books from that beautiful secretary at the antique shop." Part of her longed to go back and buy the secretary, but when she finally moved out, she would need so many other things first. An heirloom antique would leave less money for the more practical items she needed. She hugged the book to her chest. "I love it . . . I love them both, but it's too much."

"No, I saw them and had to have them for you." He smiled gently. "You are worth much more."

Her heart fluttered. How could she keep her thoughts from running wild when he spoke like that? Was there a chance he felt something for her too? How was that possible?

"Open it and look inside the cover." He touched the book, and his hand brushed hers.

"Know your own happiness. You want nothing but patience—or give it a more fascinating name, call it hope." Chapter 19, Mrs. Dashwood to Edward. Reach for your happiness; it awaits you.

Yours in Christ, Declan Corbyn Fitzgerald

Moisture in Kate's eyes kept her from looking up. He'd seen her cry too many times, but somehow he always knew the right thing to say. When a sniffle accidentally broke free, he pulled her into a hug.

"You're too good to me, Declan." Her voice was shaky and muffled by his shoulder. Feeling all too aware of his nearness, she pulled back and caught a flicker in his eyes. Was it the same as the longing in hers? It disappeared before she could be sure, and he moved away.

"I suppose I can't keep you hidden here all evening." He stood. "Let me stop in the garage and grab your luggage from the boot before we go over to the main house."

Declan's family made it clear that they had missed Kate and welcomed her back. Margaret especially touched her heart with the smiles, hand squeezes, and "bless you's." It confirmed that she was in the right place.

Excitement filled the air as the family prepared for the office New Year's Eve party. It was to be like nothing Kate had ever attended—a Regency period costume party where everyone dressed like the era of Jane Austen.

To add to the evening, there would be English country dancing. That intrigued Kate the most. She was told the 2005 *Pride and Prejudice* with Kiera Knightly presented a good example of the dances, and she looked forward to learning something new. A dance instructor would be present, teaching the dances during the party.

Tuesday, Kate went by the dress shop to have a final check for adjustments on her dress, and it now hung in her wardrobe, awaiting the party that evening. Declan had joked that he would show up during her fitting, but something made her want to surprise him with it. It wasn't as if he was her date, but things had changed between them since she returned from the U.S., and she felt like something was blossoming. *Call it hope.*

She looked in the mirror and admired her hair before finishing her makeup and slipping on the dress. The burgundy color somehow made her brown hair and brown eyes take on new depths. Earlier, she, Tracey, Chloe, and Margaret had gone to a stylist with experience creating Regency hairstyles for events such as theirs. The stylist managed to create looks that were fitting for the time period, yet still flattering to each woman.

Seeing it all come together made Kate laugh to herself. All those years ago, when she and Jennifer were obsessed with all things Regency, she'd never dreamt that she would one day live in England and attend an event where she experienced that period. She swayed and twirled, imagining herself dancing with a partner.

The image of Declan flashed before her mind, and she wondered if she might have the chance to dance with him. The thought brought a rush of excitement. *Careful, Kate*, she reasoned with herself. *Remember, Mr. Darcy does not exist.*

She snapped a quick picture and sent it to Jennifer with that very caption.

Chapter Thirty-Three

Approaching the stairs, Kate trembled at the sound of Declan's voice. She felt like a young girl on the evening of her high school prom about to see her date, but this was not prom, and Declan was not her date. The nerves, however, were very much the same.

Just as she began to descend, Declan appeared at the bottom of the stairs. Sucking in a breath, she continued, eyes on him. The look on his face had her spellbound, and she tightly gripped the rail.

"Kate. That . . . wow, you look lovely." He examined her with a penetrating gaze.

"Thank you. Regency is my look, hmm? I must say, what a fine figure you cut yourself." She'd seen the phrase in some of her Regency reading. The jacket, cravat, and top hat flattered him.

He reached out a hand as she touched the final step, and she gladly grasped it. Warmth edged its way up from their hands.

"Burgundy is your color."

"Again, thank you." She wanted to say something witty that sounded appropriate for the time period and further removed her from past recollections. If only she could capture the accent, but the few times she tried, she'd sounded like a prissy southerner. "If you keep complimenting me, it may increase my vanity." She smirked at him, happy to have managed that much.

"You are one of the least vain women I know." She frowned and tensed. "Lest you misunderstand, you are naturally beautiful, Kate." He took her hand and folded it around his forearm. "See, I have been reading up on proper Regency etiquette."

Kate wished she could stay in this moment—arm in arm, playful banter. She chanced a glance up at him and found him watching her. Everything else faded away. Could he hear her heart pounding? Could he see the love in her eyes? Despite her attempts to hide it, she suddenly wanted him to know. If she leaned up just a little more, she might even dare to kiss him. Would he recoil? What would happen to their friendship? He looked as if he might want the same thing.

A slight misstep, and the spell was broken. Two strong arms kept her on her feet, and she again felt like the nervous teenager worried about embarrassing herself at prom. "I guess I have two left feet tonight. At least I made it down the stairs safely." It was probably her imagination that he felt the same anyway.

He chuckled and resumed escorting her by the arm. "I think—"

"Look at you, Kate dear! You'll be the belle of the ball." Richard stood as they entered the living room. "Tracey and Violet are just finishing up with Margaret. They'll be ready any minute." Margaret's friend Violet had come to town to help with Margaret and would bring her home partway through the evening before Margaret became overtired.

From the outside, The Langham London was a stunning hotel. Though not built until 1865, it still held much history, and from the pictures Kate had seen, it would make a beautiful backdrop for a Regency-inspired evening.

In the lobby, they pulled out a wheelchair for Margaret. Her increasing difficulties with balance and leg control became worse in unfamiliar places and among crowds. At the care facility, they periodically used one, and she'd acclimated well.

Kate scanned the lobby and appreciated the marble columns and floor. Off to the side, a young woman and baby caught her eye. They both had blond hair. The mother smiled down at her daughter and played patty-cake. Their image blurred, and she saw a little girl with brown eyes held by a sickly-looking woman.

"Kate? Are you all right?" Declan placed a hand on her elbow and tugged at it. His eyes followed Kate's. "Let's go on into the ballroom. There's no reason to wait while they sort Gran."

"What?" Kate struggled to come back to the present and found Declan's concerned gaze upon her. "Oh." She looked at her elbow where his gentle grip held and turned to follow. "The place is amazing," she commented as they moved into the hallway.

Declan smiled, but his brow was still knit. "We don't always celebrate the new year so extravagantly, but the realization that this will be the last year Gran is capable of attending made it important to us."

"I'm sure it will mean a lot to employees and others you've invited, even if Margaret doesn't fully grasp it herself. She seems rather alert today, so maybe she will."

"That's the hope. Look, here we are." He held his arm out like he'd done when she descended the steps at the house.

The room was long, and both sides were lined with columns. A coffered ceiling and lavish wall moldings created a space fit for kings. It was easy to envision it filled with dancers.

"We also have an adjacent room set up as our dining space." Declan led her around the corner to another room filled with elegantly arrayed round tables, and they heard voices approaching.

"There you are," called out Tracey. "What do you think?" She motioned towards the room.

"It's absolutely breathtaking," Kate managed before Tracey was approached by a hotel employee to discuss plans for the evening.

Once everyone was seated, Tracey, Declan, and Chloe addressed the group and presented Margaret with an award for all of her work through the years while a light dinner was served. The short film shown after the presentation was filled with photos and video clips from the mid-1950s, when Corbyn Publishing was founded, until the present time.

Margaret and Graham made a handsome couple back in their

younger days. Their marriage had lasted through many ups and downs from what Kate had learned, and she knew from experience that was a rare thing. Watching Margaret smile, though not fully understanding, made Kate envy her long and blessed life. Hers and Graham's lives had touched many others.

In spite of everything going on, Kate's thoughts periodically drifted to the woman and child—not the ones in the lobby. Brittany and Madeline were at the forefront of her mind. She smiled and nodded at those around her and tried to push the distraction aside.

"May I have this dance?" Parker, an American writer she'd met earlier, approached her, hand extended.

He was handsome, but his touch and gaze didn't have the same effect as Declan's. A glance in Declan's direction found him leading a lithe, beautiful woman towards the dance floor. Kate tensed. According to Chloe, her name was Marion, and she worked for him at the Paris office. "Yes, of course." Parker's curious look reminded her to smile.

"What would you say if I said 'Roll Tide'?" Parker leaned in.

She chuckled. "I suppose I would answer, 'Go Vols!' So that southern accent is from Alabama?"

"Born and raised in Birmingham, with the exception of four years in Tuscaloosa for my degree. I heard you're from Tennessee?"

"Memphis, with the exception of four years in Knoxville."

"Ah, well, I won't hold that against you." He winked, then examined her gown. "Though I must say crimson is a good color on you."

"Actually, I call it burgundy." Kate chuckled. "But *I must say*, though I love the Vols, orange never was my color."

"Shall we?" He motioned to the gathering group as the dance instructor began to explain the steps of the quadrille.

With three other couples, they practiced moving through the steps. Kate couldn't keep her eyes from occasionally drifting to Declan. He smiled and laughed as he and Marion followed the instructor. Kate frowned. He'd danced the very first dance with Kate, but it wasn't at all what she'd hoped.

The types of dances from the Regency period weren't like the ballroom dancing of modern times, where apart from the occasional spin and release, one was constantly in the arms of their partner. There was very little touching. Not only that, the steps were somewhat involved and required all of her attention, leaving none for admiring him, talking, and simply enjoying the time with him. Immediately after their dance, Declan had introduced her to Tom from accounting before breaking the news that he needed to make the rounds.

"Making the rounds" meant that he danced with many of the female authors, a couple of vendor representatives, and some of the employees. She'd even seen him approach Alexandra, who had brought a date. It was clear from Kate's vantage point that Alexandra had no plans to dance with Declan. Yet throughout the night, Kate saw Alexandra look longingly at Declan. It was probably the same look that Kate wore, though she tried to hide it.

"Care for something to eat or drink?" Parker pointed towards the tables on the back wall just as the set ended.

"Yes, I think I've worked up an appetite."

"What's it like being Margaret Corbyn's nurse?"

"Do you have all night?"

"Well"—Parker looked at a nonexistent wristwatch—"until a little after midnight." One side of his mouth curved up.

"I've been working with dementia patients for years now, so that isn't new, but this is the first time I've been a personal nurse for an individual." Kate explained all that Margaret had gone through the past year and the impact Margaret had made on her community. Kate's voice caught, and moisture filled her eyes. "She's an amazing woman. I'm glad I started working with her early enough to get to know the original Margaret Corbyn before she started to disappear."

"Wow, that really puts things into perspective. I'm glad they honored her tonight." He glanced over at the dance instructor, who was calling couples to gather for the next dance, then held out his arm. "Again?"

Her eyes searched out Declan, who was leading Marion back out to the dance floor. Until now, he'd not danced with anyone twice. Yes, she was counting. Her heart sank as she nodded up at Parker and accepted his arm.

At the end of the dance, she bowed, ready to retreat to a quiet corner.

"You were awfully quiet just now."

"I'm sorry. I'm not representing us southerners very well, am I?" She glanced at Declan and Marion, who were laughing over something.

Parker's eyes followed hers. "Is there something going on between you two?"

"What? No. He and I . . . we're just friends."

"Hmm. He seems to be as curious about you with me as you are about him and that woman."

Kate shook her head, then smoothed a nonexistent wrinkle on her skirt before sneaking a look at Declan. He wasn't looking at her. Her eyes met Parker's. "I think you're mistaken."

"Okay, I wouldn't want to cause any problems. Especially with Corbyn. I like working with the company, and I don't want to jeopardize the contract for my current book. On the other hand, I *would* like to get to know you better. I'll be in town for a couple of weeks. How about dinner one night this week?"

"I—" Her eyes instinctively looked for Declan again, but he was nowhere to be found. Maybe she had imagined he had feelings for her since her return. "We could do lunch."

He passed her his phone so she could enter her number, and just as she handed it back, Chloe approached to introduce her to a local author. The rest of the night, she was swept up in English country dancing and mingling with the other guests.

The dance instructor announced the last dance of the evening at eleven thirty. Feeling as if she'd danced with every eligible bachelor that evening, Kate glanced around the room. To her surprise, Declan, looking as determined as ever, was headed straight towards her. Did he want to dance? Before he reached her, the beautiful Marion approached him. For a second, it looked like he would ignore Marion, but he turned towards her. Kate closed her eyes, forcing herself to breathe and regroup. Eyes still closed, she was hit with the familiar scent of bergamot and musk.

"Kate, will you dance with me?"

Heart racing, she opened her eyes. "Yes," she whispered.

Moments later, she found herself swept up in his arms as she awkwardly tried to follow his steps. "I always thought waltzing looked so effortless, but I guess there's a bit more to it. You seem to know what you're doing."

"I've had ballroom dancing lessons. Relax, you're already catching on." He squeezed her shoulder.

"It's because you do such a good job guiding me."

"I like guiding you. Did you know that this dance was scandalous during the early eighteenth century?"

"I recall hearing that."

"To think that we Brits were in such a state because the couples were constantly touching and so close. They would be appalled to see some of the dirty dancing that goes on these days."

"So you know all about that dirty dancing, do you?" Kate arched an eyebrow while fighting her smile.

His eyes lit up, and he smiled down at her, nearly causing her to stumble. Every place they touched, she could feel electricity. The way he was watching her, the look in his eyes—it gave her hope. It was tender, caring, filled with understanding, and what looked like longing. Or was she just imagining all of her own feelings in his look? She couldn't recall seeing Mark look at her this way—ever. Was there truly a chance for something more with Declan? Could she let down her guard?

The feeling of being watched came over Kate, and as hard as it was, she drew her eyes away from Declan to find Alexandra watching them. Her heart sank. Alexandra. Would he ever be completely over her? It certainly didn't seem *she* was over *him*. Could Kate give him a chance if there was a possibility he would end up wishing he was back with Alexandra? Kate had already spent so many years of her life in a relationship with a man who had pretended to be faithful.

Eyes back on him, she found him still watching her. "Alexandra's looking at you. She's been watching you longingly all night."

He hesitated before speaking. "It doesn't matter. I've been looking at *you* all night." His hands clenched her tighter, and he pulled her closer.

The world around them disappeared, and she was floating in his arms. What was he implying? After six months of separation from

Alexandra, could he actually have feelings for her? His couldn't be as strong as hers. "*Stop it,*" she internally chastised, "*focus on the good.*"

When the dance ended, he was as reticent to let go of her hand as she was his. People began milling about, chatting, and she feared he would move off to dutifully make the rounds again, but he stayed by her side.

A large screen came down from the ceiling in the front and displayed BBC One coverage of the New Year's Eve festivities. The countdown timer showed fourteen minutes and twenty-four seconds until midnight. Groups gathered and held hands while everyone joined in to sing "Auld Lang Syne." Anticipation began to build as waiters carried in silver trays filled with champagne.

"Five! Four! Three! Two! One! Happy New Year!" Fireworks shot off on the screen.

She looked up at Declan just as he pulled her into a tight hug. "Happy New Year, Kate." He spoke into her ear and kissed her on the cheek before pulling back and grinning.

"Happy New Year!" People greeted one another, and Kate remembered they were surrounded by a crowd.

Tracey and Chloe approached and gave them both hugs, then Tracey showed Declan her phone while discussing something in earnest. From behind, Kate felt a tap on her back and turned to find Parker leaning in. Nearly too late, she realized he was aiming for her mouth and just in time, she turned so it landed on her cheek. Preparing to let loose her southern temper, she noticed Parker looking over her shoulder as he pulled her towards him. Time slowed as she turned and saw the hurt look on Declan's face.

Confused, she stepped back to Declan and spoke to Parker. "I think I'll pass on lunch this week."

Parker's eyes moved between Kate and Declan before he bowed. "I apologize for my wrong assumption. No hard feelings, Corbyn." He patted Declan on the shoulder. "Kate seems like a lovely woman. Treat her well." As Parker turned to go, she thought she caught him smiling.

"Kate, I'm so sorry. I'll have him sent out immediately." He started to pull away.

She laid a hand on his arm. "Stay here. I'm fine."

"But Kate, he shouldn't have disrespected you that way." Her hand tightened on his arm, and she shook her head. "Okay, I'll wait and speak to him the moment I'm back in the office."

"Really, I'm okay. I realized what he was doing and turned so the kiss landed on my cheek. No harm done." She laid a hand on his arm. "To be honest, I think he was trying to get a reaction from you."

"That he did." Declan stared down at her, his piercing eyes holding her gaze.

Chapter Thirty-Four

Sunlight streaming through the window curtains pulled Kate out of her dream-filled sleep. What a wonderful dream it was. She and Declan danced just like the night before, except they were living during the time of Jane Austen's novels and engaged to be married. As reality descended and her mind stirred, she pondered that thought. Was it a possibility? What would the new year have in store?

Her discussion with Declan regarding Parker's attempt at a kiss was cut short by the chaos of everyone wanting to tell the Corbyn Publishing CEO "Happy New Year" before leaving, and she wondered what it would be like to see him today during their belated Christmas celebration with her. Something changed between them during their last dance, and she was anxious to find out what it meant for their future.

"Just lay the Christmas crackers on each plate," Chloe instructed Kate as they set the table.

"You do this every year?" Kate began placing the crackers.

"It's tradition. You have them in the U.S., don't you?"

"We do. We've had them at some Christmas parties I've been to, and my grandparents brought them to my home for Christmas a couple of times when I was little. Of course, back then, they seemed like the best surprise ever—popping noises, paper crowns, and a little toy. Just what celebrations are made of in every child's imagination."

Chloe laughed at that, and when Kate looked up from the table, she saw Declan standing in the doorway watching her. Feeling her face flush, she watched him move towards her.

"Kate. We said Happy New Year, but I feel I should say it again." Now he was before her.

"Declan." She swallowed.

"I think I'll check on things in the kitchen." Chloe quietly slipped out.

"Last night was fun." Once again, Kate found herself at a loss for words around Declan and wished she could think of something more sophisticated to say.

Declan's mouth pulled into a smile. "I hoped you would like it. Your love for Jane Austen's books inspired the theme."

Kate was stunned. "Really? I hardly know what to say. Thank you. It was wonderful, and it seemed like everyone enjoyed it."

"I imagined they would, but I thought only of your happiness when I chose the theme."

Their gazes locked, and Kate felt her heart lose its rhythm.

"Uncle Corbyn! Happy New Year!" Chloe's youngest son bounded into the room.

"James! What did I tell you about bursting in on people?" Chloe stood in the doorway.

"Mum, it's just Uncle Corbyn. I don't know why you're being so weird." James rolled his eyes. "So, are we on for gaming after we eat?" he questioned Declan.

Declan looked from James to Kate. "Don't forget we're exchanging gifts with Kate after the meal. This is her Christmas with us."

"But Uncle Corbyn, it's new years tradition."

Declan looked at Kate again, and she saw the question in his eyes. She nodded.

"Sure. Maybe we can get Kate to join us too." He smiled her way.

She raised both hands. "I know nothing about video games."

"We'll see." There was a gleam in Declan's eyes.

In some ways, the meal was similar to a traditional Thanksgiving meal in America—turkey, dressing, and cranberry sauce. But with a few differences, this became a traditional English Christmas. There were chestnuts in the dressing, which was definitely not common in the States. Where does anyone even get chestnuts? They also had Yorkshire pudding. It wasn't a pudding and definitely not sweet. Instead, it was a savory bread that was fried on the outside. Kate also noticed a red cabbage dish.

As she looked across the table, it hit her that Alexandra and her parents were absent. It seemed unusual with the closeness of their families, and before she could ponder why, Declan was offering to serve her the braised Brussels sprouts. She smiled and nodded. It was hard to say no to him, and she likely would have agreed to anything he put on her plate. His nearness made her weak, and she reveled in the attention.

For the first time since they met, she began to let her hope grow. It was a scary feeling, but the way he'd been looking at her since she had returned . . . it must mean something.

After the Christmas pudding and trifle, they gathered in the living room to exchange presents. Kate was excited about her gifts for the family. She passed them all out and asked them to wait and open them at the same time. As they all began unwrapping, Kate noticed Margaret fumbling to get a grip on the wrapping paper.

"Here. Let me help you." While Kate worked alongside Margaret, the others gasped in surprise.

"Kate, this is absolutely wonderful! Where did you find them? I've never seen such designs." Tracey ran her hand over the framed poem.

"Actually, I got permission through your cousin Liam to have my friend Jennifer in Memphis make them. She did the calligraphy and illustrations of Margaret's poems. They're all different."

"Oh my!" Tracey's hand rose to her heart, and she glanced over at

Richard's. "Indeed they are. What a precious gift." Her eyes began to glisten. "Thank you, Kate. I can't think of anything more special to me."

Each person thanked her, and Declan moved closer. "It's your turn, Kate. We all went in together to buy you something, but you'll need to come upstairs."

Kate looked at the others as if they would explain. "Okay."

Declan stood and held out a hand to her before leading her to the stairs while the others followed behind, with the exception of Tracey and Violet, who guided Margaret's wheelchair to the elevator. Once they were all gathered around the closed guest room door, Declan tied a blindfold around a startled Kate's face. It felt strange to stand in the dark with everyone watching her. She could hear Declan's deep breathing close behind and feel the warmth of his body as he guided her forward into the room. They stopped, and his warmth disappeared.

"Go on, you can take the blindfold off now." From the sound, she could tell Declan was now to her left.

Hesitantly, Kate removed the blindfold. There, several feet away, decorated with a red bow, was the very secretary that she had admired and talked herself out of. "Declan?" She turned to him.

The delight on his face matched her own. "It's from all of us, but yes, I directed them to it."

She wanted to rush to embrace and thank him but stopped herself as she looked around at the family. "Thank you! I absolutely love it. It's . . . it's just so beautiful," she gushed and moved forward to hug Tracey, Chloe, and Violet, then thank the men and boys.

"Why don't you show me how it works?" Chloe urged.

Without hesitation, Kate turned to explain the intricacies of the piece, how the desk folded down and was supported by hidden arms that slid out from beneath, and the tiny drawers that were enclosed behind the desktop when it was up. After Kate showed Chloe and the others how it worked, Chloe pointed to the middle shelf.

"It looks like there's another present," Chloe suggested.

Kate's confusion turned to surprise as she spotted a now very familiar wrapping paper around the present lying on the shelf. She looked at Declan, who just shrugged and grinned. With the gift in her hand, Kate turned to look for a seat and saw everyone leaving and the door closing behind them.

Her heart fluttered as she realized she and Declan were alone and the family was in on it. She settled on the bench at the foot of the bed. "Declan, you've already been so generous. The books and the secretary . . ." She held out the wrapped gift that she knew held another book. "Now this. I hardly know what to say anymore."

"No words are required. Just open it, and I'll be happy if you are happy."

Carefully peeling back the paper, she discovered a rose-colored leather-bound copy of *Persuasion* with sage embossing. She knew to turn directly to the inside and see what Declan had written.

"She learned romance as she grew older: the natural sequel of an unnatural beginning." Though the past is difficult to look back at, your best days lie ahead. May you be blessed with a romance like you have never known.

Yours in Christ, Declan Corbyn Fitzgerald

Pain, fear, and hope swirled within, and she hesitated to look at Declan. Could she accept whatever she found in his eyes? Did this mean what she hoped? Kate tried to calm her heart before turning to him with a look of composure that belied the storm raging inside. "What are you trying to tell me?"

Declan's brow rose with worry, but he reached for her hand and held it in his. "I hoped that maybe we could move beyond friendship. I don't think I'm wrong in believing that there's a connection between us."

She shook her head. "You're not wrong. I feel it, too, but . . ." Why did her doubts always get in the way? "You don't think it's too soon?"

He squeezed her hand. "I don't think so, but we can take things as slow as you want."

She wanted to declare her love for him right then and there, but that would be madness and surely send him running. "Okay." Her eyes went to the door. "Your family knows what's going on? I wish they didn't and we could . . . I don't know, keep it a secret for a while, until we feel more confident about it."

"My family has had an inkling about my feelings, but only Chloe knows what I had in mind. We can tell her we're still thinking things over if you prefer. In a way, it will be the truth. I'll tell her we'd like to keep things private until we figure them out. We could do some things away from home as we have in the past, but just not refer to them as dates to others. Would you agree to that?"

What was he asking her to agree to? She could hardly think straight. Date? Keep things private? "Yes, I think that's what we should do." He might have an interest in her, but she needed to make sure she wasn't just a short-lived rebound or diversion from Alexandra. Still, she couldn't deny that he had been so thoughtful with the gifts. She knew he cared for her and they had a wonderful friendship, but was it enough for a romantic relationship?

His face lit up as his blue eyes drank her in. She hoped he would always have that look of happiness when he saw her. Maybe one day it would be filled with love also. Leaning towards her, he bent down. She held her breath and her eyes fluttered closed, then she felt him place a tender kiss on her cheek. Blushing, she opened her eyes at her mistake.

"Dinner Monday night?"

She nodded, unable to speak.

"Perfect. We'll work out the details so that it doesn't seem out of the norm."

"Thank you."

"Thank *you*, Kate. You have made me so happy." His hand swept down her cheek before he quickly withdrew it. "I'd like to pray for us."

Us. The word reverberated around her mind, sending warmth through her body. When he held her hands in his and spoke to God on behalf of their relationship, she thought she would melt. Her only romantic experiences had been so different with Mark. Declan prayed that he could be honoring to both Kate and God in the way he treated her. Whatever happened with their relationship, she knew her standards would be forever raised.

"Amen." Once again, she could barely speak. Everything he did seemed perfect. He was the kind of man young girls dreamed would sweep them off their feet and give them their happily ever after. The kind she still wished would. Could they possibly have a happy ending?

Declan released her hands and stood. "We'll move this into your room today." He gestured towards the secretary.

"I still can't believe you bought this for me." She walked over and ran her hand across the burled wood on the front. "It's my first antique." Mark never liked antiques. His parents had lots of them, and he said their house felt like a museum, so he'd only wanted new things.

"I had hoped it would please you, but truly, all of us did go in on it together."

"I know, but just the fact that you paid attention—it means a lot."

He moved closer and placed a hand on her shoulder. "It's hard not to pay attention to you."

Kate forced a laugh, but her heart clung to his words.

"It's true." His hand slid up, moving to her cheek. "I know Mark made you feel otherwise, but he was a fool. You are a treasure. Don't let anyone make you feel differently." He stared deeply into her eyes, and she felt as if he were piercing her soul, leaving it forever marked as his. "You understand this, right?"

Tears began to fall as she shrugged, and he swept them away before pulling her close.

"Kate, Kate, it really is true. I'll work hard to make you see that," he whispered.

It all felt like a dream. Never, even during their best days, had Mark treated her with so much kindness and compassion. She sighed and wished she could stay in the dream, but a knock on the door brought her back to reality.

"Uncle Corbyn, are you in there?"

Declan pulled back and chuckled. "That boy's timing. I hope your thumbs are limber."

"What?" Kate looked at him with confusion.

Declan leaned down and whispered in her ear, "Game time," before turning towards the door. "We're coming, James."

"I'm out." Kate dropped her game controller, then raised her hands. "My fingers are broken and I haven't a clue what I'm doing," she declared after fumbling her way through the game. Dropping her voice to a whisper, she leaned into Declan. "I'm going to call Brittany to wish her a happy new year." She started to leave, but Declan grabbed her arm.

He furrowed his brow and stood up, leading her out of the room. "Should you maintain contact with her? I thought it was painful for you to speak with her."

Frowning, Kate shrugged. "It is painful, but it's getting easier. Also, I still can't get her off my mind. When I told her my relationship with God is what helped me forgive her, it seemed like she was curious. I've told her the basics, but I want to make myself available if she has more questions. I know it seems crazy."

She looked down and tried to remember why she wanted to do this. She pounded at her chest. "Something in here keeps prodding me and pushing me not to let this chance pass. I have to do this. I gave her my number to call, and she hasn't. I can't blame her. If I was her, I wouldn't either, but I'm not going to give up, even though it's painful."

"Oh Kate. You are truly one of a kind." He smiled tenderly at her. "Barely a new Christian yourself and willing to brave such a difficulty for your tormentor. It's the Holy Spirit, by the way . . . that feeling in here." He pointed to her heart. "I won't hold you back. It's my instinct to protect you from harm, but I know it's better for you to follow God's guidance than mine."

"Thank you." His words were just what she needed to hear. It wasn't easy to put her heart on the line each time she called Brittany. There was always going to be a deep-seated pain tied to her and Madeline, but she couldn't escape what she was feeling. "Please pray for my conversation with her."

He placed his hands on her shoulders. "Consider it done." He prayed for her right then and promised to pray while she spoke with Brittany.

His words brought calm to her heart for the task at hand. She still couldn't believe that this man was interested in her.

Chapter Thirty-Five

Corbyn Publishing was three blocks away from the Belgravia house and the opposite direction from Margaret's care center. The beautiful four-story building looked like so many of the other buildings against the shadowed street lights—white stucco with classical features like columns, pediment windows, and porticos.

Pulling her pink wool pea coat tighter, Kate looked up at the building and took a deep breath. She had been to the office building several times with Tracey and Chloe. Once she'd even met the two of them along with Declan there for lunch.

Today, Chloe was out of town and Tracey was at home having dinner with Margaret and Richard, so it was a good day for the first on-the-sly date with Declan. It was almost six in the evening, and most of the other employees would be gone. Hopefully, if anyone remained and recognized her, they wouldn't think anything of it.

Stepping into the entrance, Kate was met by the night guard, who, after confirming her name, allowed her to go up to Declan's office. That was when the nerves hit. Fanning herself, she looked around the elevator, wondering if it had any air circulation. In spite of their close friendship for over half a year, Kate had been nervous all day just thinking about their date. She peeked under her coat at the dress she'd chosen.

Was it too much? The navy blue knit crossover came just below her knees and looked elegant, but not out of the ordinary for her. She wanted to seem like herself, though she'd spent much longer than usual getting ready after returning Margaret home from the care center.

Months ago, she'd been nervous about her date with Aidan just because it was her first date since high school, and the date with Kieran had been fairly low-key. This felt completely different. She had real feelings for Declan. She loved him and was finally ready to let go of her past—she hoped.

Exiting the elevator, she found the floor was quiet, but as she moved towards Declan's office, she heard voices arguing. His door was open, and she stood back, listening. Declan and Alexandra; their voices were unmistakable. She froze, trying to decide what to do.

"—tired of the cold shoulder. I don't deserve that." Alexandra's voice softened. "Please give me another chance."

"Alexandra, I'm sorry, but I have an appointment. I really need to get going. Can we talk about this another time?" Declan sounded tired.

"Corbyn—"

Kate felt guilty the longer she stood there, and decided to knock on the door frame.

"Who's there?" Alexandra sighed as she moved to the door and frowned. "Kate?" Her voice was as cold as the look she gave. Glancing back at Declan, she added, "I'm holding you to that. We'll talk about this later." With that, Alexandra brushed past Kate.

Kate watched as Declan stared after Alexandra with a blank face, then pulled her into the office before closing the door.

Kate was at a loss. Should she apologize for overhearing? Was he still interested in their date? Would he be distracted the whole time if they went out? All the stress had built up to this moment, and now she wanted to turn around and go home.

"Kate, I'm sorry you had to hear that." She started to protest, but he shook his head. "From the look on your face, you heard enough. It's not your fault. I'd already told her I had plans. Regardless, this is not how I wanted our first date to begin." He lifted her hand and placed a kiss on it. "Can we start over?"

"Yes." The word barely escaped as she held back her competing thoughts—wanting to begin something new and wonderful with him, hoping his heart was not still entangled with Alexandra's. She dared not scare him away with the knowledge of how much she cared for him. With Alexandra still chasing after him, she needed to prepare for her long game. This would be nothing like the start of her relationship with Mark, but hopefully much more worthwhile in the end.

He studied her closely, trying to perceive if she really meant it. "I don't want you to be intimidated by her. She's part of my life, and I can't change that, but she's trying to hang on to something that's no longer there."

The tall, beautiful, model-esque woman would be intimidating even if she hadn't been previously engaged to the man Kate was about to go on a first date with. "I'll try."

He grinned. "Good. I'll make it worth your while." He tugged her towards the elevator. "You're going to love the place I chose for our date. First, though, I've got this for you." He pulled a greeting card from his suit pocket.

"A card?"

He nodded and smiled while she opened it to see laser-cut paper daisies with pink and purple flowers mixed in and the words, "Thinking of you. Today and every day."

"Thank you. It's beautiful, Declan." She flipped it over, trying to open it.

"Here." Declan reached out. "These flaps fold down."

"Oh how pretty." It popped open into a 3D floral arrangement.

"I thought it would be hard to explain a real bouquet of flowers without anyone thinking something is going on between us."

Kate smiled as she carefully tucked it into her purse. "What a unique idea. I love it." This was one card she wouldn't throw away.

Launceston Place was quintessentially British on the outside, with its shiny navy blue-trimmed traditional building in south Kensington. Its food, however, was far from traditional, based on what Kate saw on the plates being served to other guests. Composed dishes, drops and drizzles of sauces, edible flowers, and beautifully arranged foods created works of art.

"I hope you don't mind if I take pictures of my food," Kate whispered. "I hate to be that person, but everything is just beautiful!"

Declan chuckled and reached for her hand. "I'm glad you like it. Snap away. I want this to be special for you."

His words and touch warmed Kate and filled her with hope for what lay ahead. Despite the beauty and delicious taste of the meal, it was hard for her to focus on anything other than the handsome man before her. She wished to capture every moment in her heart and mind. She had hope for a future much more beautiful than her past. Everything about him was so opposite of Mark. His looks, his thoughtfulness, even his demeanor. Mark would have fussed at her for taking pictures of the food and embarrassing him.

"Are you still planning to go on a mission trip with Ruth?"

"Yes, to Bosnia in March." Kate lit up at the thought. "It makes me happy to think that I can be of use to others, and especially to have a chance to share about Christ with them."

"Kate, that's wonderful. Maybe at some point I can go with you. I won't intrude on your first trip, though."

"You could never be intrusive."

"Thank you, but I feel that you'll get more out of this first one without me."

She shook her head, and a woman carrying a baby outside the window caught her eye. That familiar feeling of longing tugged at her.

"What is it?" His eyes followed hers. "Are you thinking of Madeline?"

Not this time, but did she dare remind him of her inadequacies now that they were dating? Somehow in her excitement about finally going out with him, she'd forgotten to worry about his feelings. Her eyes found his, and the words stuck in her throat.

"What's wrong? You look like you're in pain." He reached for her hand.

Closing her eyes, she searched for the strength and words to speak honestly. "I-I may not ever be able to have a child."

His thumb rubbed circles in her palm. "I'm sorry, Kate. I know that must be hard, and you have suffered so much already because of it."

He wasn't understanding her. As hard as it was for her, she'd become used to the sadness every time she saw a mother and baby. He likely had not thought through all that dating her could mean. "But you're dating me . . ."

One of his brows raised in confusion.

No, he still didn't understand. Was it too forward of her to suggest? "If we . . . get serious, it could mean . . ."

A look of understanding filled his face, and he squeezed her hand. "Kate, as wonderful as that would be, it does not change how I feel about you. Please don't let that upset you. We take one day at a time, trusting God."

Dessert came, and with it, more doubts. If she had never come to London, would he be with Alexandra? If so, he might have a chance at a proper family. But when he spoke so kindly to her, she wanted to believe things would work out. She could at least keep praying that it would, and maybe if she kept studying her Bible, she would have the peace in all situations that Declan always seemed to have.

Chapter Thirty-Six

"This feels so domestic," Declan commented.

Kate looked down at the care center's trained dog, Albert, as it followed her, Declan, and Margaret around the indoor walking path. She smiled and warmth filled her, but she didn't attempt to speak. The thought of "being domestic" with Declan thrilled her, but she was still cautiously optimistic about their relationship. A constant underlying fear that it would never work out or something would spoil it lurked in the recesses of her mind.

With one arm, Declan supported his grandmother, and with the other, he reached to clasp Kate's hand as if he sensed her hesitancy.

The past three and a half weeks of "dating" Declan had been heavenly. He came to visit with Kate and Margaret at the care facility several times a week—sometimes for lunch, and other times during a break like today. They managed to have two more meals out, three at the mews house and two at the Belgravia home with Margaret when Tracey and Richard were out. That didn't include the times they were together with the family. Those times, they weren't able to be free about their feelings like they were when it was just them or them with Margaret. Margaret could no longer communicate clearly, so there were no worries of her spilling their news.

Even before Kate agreed to this dating arrangement, they were close, but now that she had let her guard down, their friendship began to blossom into a beautiful romance.

Declan kept urging her to make their relationship public, but she didn't feel ready. A few times, they were almost caught. Once, Chloe came by his house when they were cleaning up after dinner, and she reluctantly followed Chloe back to the main house to avoid further suspicion. Another time at the main house, Tracey ran back inside after forgetting something, and Kate barely had time to step back from Declan's hug. It left them in their current state of sneaking around.

"Gran, our dear Kate here is afraid I'm getting serious too quickly." Declan paused, and Margaret's eyes lit up as she quietly watched him. "What do you think?" Margaret smiled and patted him on the hand that was wrapped around her arm. "You think we should move forward and announce our relationship, Gran?" Margaret continued to smile. "See, Kate, even Gran agrees." He gave Kate a smoldering look that would weaken the resolve of the strongest of women.

She had to remain strong. Or did she? "Declan." She wasn't sure what she wanted to say. Was she secure enough in their relationship to take that step? "I'm almost ready. Just give it a little more time." A flash of sadness crossed his face.

"Did I tell you about my conversation with Brittany last night? She actually asked me to teach her how to pray, then she asked God to show himself to her. It won't be long now before she realizes that she wants to be in a relationship with him." Kate noticed Margaret struggling to walk. "We should slow down for Gran."

Declan looked down at his grandmother and squeezed her hand. "Are you okay, Gran?" A weak smile formed on Margaret's face. Turning, he pulled Kate's hand up for a kiss. "I love what you're doing for Brittany. You are offering the greatest gift ever to the woman who represents all of your broken dreams. I'm glad that the Bible studies I gave you for the book of John are helping her see more of who Christ is and what he has done."

"It really is a miracle."

Declan was such a good man and so kind to her, and she had an off-the-charts attraction to him. Maybe she should stop holding back and agree to make their relationship public.

He leaned down and whispered, "Don't think I didn't notice how you changed the subject. I want us to be a couple and not have to hide our feelings around family."

Margaret's sudden tug on Declan's arm pulled their attention away from one another. "Gran!"

Kate could only watch while Margaret tripped over her feet and fell before she could act. Thankfully, Declan threw his arms around Margaret and cushioned her fall, though they both went down hard.

On instinct, Kate dialed 999 and requested an ambulance, then dropped to her knees to check Margaret's pulse. "Her pulse is weak, but it's there." She reached up and gently patted Margaret's cheek. "Margaret, can you open your eyes? Margaret?"

Declan sat beside them, tenderly patting his grandmother's hand and telling her she was going to be okay. Watching him reminded Kate of all the things she loved about him. It felt like a confirmation that it was time to tell people about their relationship.

The next few hours were stressful and chaotic as the family gathered at the hospital while doctors ran a series of tests on Margaret. When they determined it was an ischemic stroke, the decision was made to give her emergency IV medication in the hope that the clot would dissolve.

It was the first hospital Kate had been in since Mark's death. The sights, smells, and even the noises sent Kate's mind to dark places—his treatment of her, his ongoing infidelity. Was she ready for another relationship and to trust another man? What if Declan was just good at covering things up? Mark had her fooled for years.

Thankfully, the family was so wrapped up in Margaret's situation that they didn't notice she was having an internal meltdown for a different reason. As worried as she was about Margaret, this emotional spiral pulled her out of the present to a place where her heart broke all over again.

Declan looked across the room with worried eyes before moving toward Kate.

She wasn't ready to talk to him in this state, even in a room full of people. "Chloe, will you come with me to the cafeteria? We can get everyone something to drink." She stepped out of Declan's trajectory.

"Sure." Chloe's brows shot up, but she nodded. "What would everyone like?"

"I'll help." Declan again walked towards Kate.

"No worries. I'm sure we can get it. They have those little drink carrier things," Kate clipped out and began taking orders. If she didn't get away from him, she might shut down. She rubbed her arms to keep from shaking.

"Kate, what's going on? You seem bothered by something other than Gran. Did Declan do something?" Chloe questioned once they were out of earshot from the room.

The hallway seemed to tilt. "It's . . . I . . . I haven't been in a hospital since my husband's death." Suddenly the chairs in the hallway looked like a very good idea, and she dropped into one, with Chloe taking the seat next to her. Closing her eyes, Kate leaned her head back against the wall, willing herself not to pass out.

"You're almost as white as a ghost. Kate, you're worrying me."

Trying to slow her heart rate, Kate took slow, deep breaths. "I'm okay," she said, only to realize the words never made it out. She felt Chloe's arm go around her shoulder to support her weight as moisture seeped from her eyes.

Warmth wrapped around Kate with the familiar bergamot and musk scent she'd grown to love. "Declan?" She opened her eyes and seeing Declan's face above her, became disoriented. Squirming, she tried to sit up, then realized her head rested in his lap with her body stretched out over several chairs in the hospital hallway. "I passed out? Where's Chloe?"

"Easy there. Let me help you. You probably need a minute to adjust." He tenderly pulled her up against his side and held her close. "Chloe messaged me when you passed out." His eyes flitted down the hall, and then he placed a kiss on her forehead.

She wished he had kissed her lips, but doubts crept back in, and she realized that would be foolish and muddle her thoughts more.

"You had us worried, but I've dealt with this type of thing before. My fiancée . . . Victoria sometimes got low blood sugar and passed out, so I recognized the signs." His brow furrowed. "This seems to be from something else, though. What happened?"

"Declan, I'm so sorry. You should be with your grandmother. I'll be fine. Please don't worry about me."

"Kate, I can't help but worry about you. I can't go back in there, knowing something is wrong with you." He stopped and searched her face. "You are not a burden. Please. I want to be here for you; don't shut me out."

Once again, it was like he could read her mind. Hopefully, he couldn't read the fact that she was questioning their relationship and still not wanting to tell others. She didn't want to burden him when his gran was in such a state.

He continued watching her closely.

"I haven't been in a hospital since Mark died, and it's awakened so much pain. It was hard being there at the time, but today when those feelings came back, so did the reminder of his unfaithfulness and deception all those years."

Her hands clenched, and she tried to distance herself from those feelings. It was easier to recall it as if it were someone else's life. "I thought I had moved past it, but it's strange how sights, sounds, and smells can evoke emotions before you have time to process what's happening. The timing is terrible. Please don't worry about me."

He held her tight and prayed for her before insisting that it was his right and responsibility as her boyfriend to be worried about her.

"Hey, how are you feeling now, Kate?" Chloe approached and set the drink holder in front of Declan for him to pull a cup of water out.

The reality of their position hit her, and Kate slid away from Declan. "Thank you. I'm feeling much better now."

Chloe's gaze shifted between Kate and Declan with an unreadable expression.

The mood in Margaret's room was somber when they returned.

Though she was stable, the staff waited for her to regain consciousness so they could evaluate the long-term results of the stroke.

Kate intentionally stayed as far away from Declan as possible, knowing his nearness would make it hard for her to think clearly about how to handle their relationship. Seeing the tension in his face increase every time he looked at her made her second-guess herself and the thoughts she had about slowing things down with him.

It wasn't that Kate doubted Declan's ability to be faithful as much as she didn't feel worthy of him. One day, he would realize she wasn't as beautiful as Alexandra or as special as Victoria, and if it was after they were married, he would feel stuck. He wasn't Mark, but she couldn't stand the thought that he might tire of her. She'd never been enough for Mark. How could she expect to be enough for a man like Declan?

As the week wore on, it became clear that it was time for Margaret to move to the care center permanently. Progress seemed nonexistent. She was awake but didn't speak. Instead, she often seemed confused. She barely moved and showed no inclination to do things like take a fork filled with food into her hand or reach for things. When they tried to help her stand to walk, she collapsed in their arms. Constant hands-on care and physical therapy were necessary. The family was disheartened, but the few times she smiled gave them some encouragement.

The vibrant and grand woman that Kate had first met upon arrival at the beach cottage was now completely gone, replaced with a shell that vaguely resembled Margaret Corbyn. It had been the same with her grandfather. Most of her Memphis patients were already so far gone by the time they moved into her facility that she never saw their previous personalities.

This was different. Margaret was like family. It felt personal, like another loss in her life.

Declan's job became extraordinarily busy the week after Margaret's stroke, and while Kate appreciated that she didn't have to face him constantly and make excuses to hold off their announcement, she also missed him. He had become an important fixture in her life, and more than that, someone she could lean on with worries and difficulties.

The times they'd spoken on the phone felt stilted the last few days, and she wasn't sure if it was real or imagined. Ever since her panic attack in the hospital, she'd had doubts that their relationship would last, and fear of a broken heart placed a shadow on her previous hopes. Maybe they would drift apart naturally and she wouldn't have to make a difficult decision about their relationship. But was that really what she wanted? Right now, God felt far away.

Chapter Thirty-Seven

"Pass the butter please, Corbyn."

After passing it to his mom, he squeezed Kate's leg under the table, and she stiffened. He'd surprised them all when he showed up in time for Friday night dinner. It was the first she'd seen him other than in passing since the beginning of the week.

In between chatter about moving the rest of Margaret's things over the weekend, Declan observed Kate and gave her a look that meant they were going to talk after dinner.

As soon as the meal was over, Declan insisted his parents go relax while he and Kate cleaned up. Just as Kate set down a pile of plates, she felt strong, warm arms wrap around her from behind. Part of her wanted to melt into those arms and never leave their safety, but another part wanted to pull away and guard her heart.

When she arrived in England, her heart was guarded by a fence that Declan had removed, piece by piece. Over the last week, her spiraling fears built it back up into a high fortified wall, much like some of the castle grounds she'd visited. She didn't even realize the wall had gone up, and though she wanted to scale it or for Declan to meet her halfway, shadows from her former life reminded her what might lie on the other side.

"Kate, I've missed you," he whispered as his hands moved to her shoulders and spun her around. "I get the feeling you're avoiding me. Have I done something wrong? You know I can't help the long hours at work this week, but you've barely spoken to me on the phone or responded to my texts."

A glimpse of his eyes showed pain, and she looked away. "Things are so busy with trying to get your grandmother's items ready to be moved." She shrugged. "And I've been talking so much to Brittany." As if pulled by a magnet, her eyes found his again. "I'm sorry."

"Don't you think it's time for us to let the family know about our relationship? It will make it easier during weeks like this when we barely see each other if we can openly be together around them."

Heat rushed to her face. She wanted so badly to say yes, but that wall —it was too high, too strong to scale or tear down. "I . . . can't. I'm not ready." The lint on his shirt held the answers to the universe.

"Kate, we can't keep doing this. Don't you—"

"The timing is all wrong, anyway. The focus needs to be on Margaret." She looked up at him with pleading eyes. What she pleaded for eluded her. Would more time allow her to figure out a way over that monstrous wall?

"I disagree."

He stared down at her, eyes begging her to give in, but she remained silent. How could she explain all she was thinking, all she felt? What could she say that wouldn't sound hurtful? He was a good man, but she couldn't agree to that next step. Neither was she ready to end things with him. Something deep within hoped for a miracle that would help her scale the wall.

He finally gave up with a sigh and turned to the sink to wash dishes. She'd never heard anyone make quite so much noise shifting dishes and cookware around, and she gingerly moved to the other side to dry and put things away. They worked silently alongside each other, but the tension was palpable. After washing the last piece of cookware, Declan stepped back, crossed his arms, and leaned against the counter to watch Kate. When she looked at him questioningly, he moved forward.

"Anything else you want to say, Kate?" He caressed her cheek.

It was tempting to agree with anything he desired when he looked at her like that and touched her so intimately, but the last fifteen minutes hadn't changed anything. She still felt as lost as when he'd first asked her. "No," she whispered.

His eyes traced the lines of her face, then he curtly nodded as if he understood everything before turning on his heels and leaving the kitchen.

What just happened? How could he understand anything when *she* hadn't the slightest clue? She wanted to take it back and call out, "*I love you*", but how could those words fix anything when she was too scared to move forward? Instead, she stood there frozen, listening as he said goodnight to his parents and left. A dull ache formed in her chest. Maybe tomorrow, answers would come.

Moving Margaret's things into the care center went quickly since they had already placed some of her furniture there for comfort and familiarity when she first started her day visits. Declan gave Kate the silent treatment except for the occasional "Excuse me" when they bumped into one another. It was obvious Chloe recognized the tension, but she made no comment as they put the finishing touches on the room. Chloe glared at Declan and made innocuous conversation to pass the time while they waited for Tracey and Richard to finish transferring Margaret from the hospital to Belgravia Residential Care Home.

As Richard rolled Margaret's wheelchair into her room, Declan stepped up and laid a bouquet in her lap. "Welcome, Gran!"

She stared at them, expressionless, and though they expected it, her reaction still pained them. Glancing from one to the other, Kate saw the anticipation that Margaret would make some improvement. Wanting to encourage them, Kate struck up a conversation with Margaret about everyday things that had happened over the week, and the others joined in.

"Chloe, you have a beautiful voice. Would you like to get us started with one of the songs we sing at church?" Kate knew that familiar music could help draw Margaret into the present and improve her transition into the facility.

They all joined in, and halfway through, Margaret's eyes brightened.

Tracey turned to Kate and mouthed, "Thank you."

"Why don't we roll her into the sitting room," Richard suggested. "There's no reason for us to all stand here." They all nodded in agreement.

Just as Richard turned Margaret's wheelchair to leave the room, a familiar voice called out, "Gran! So good to see you. I brought you these balloons and came to see your new place."

Kate's eyes flew to Declan and caught his surprise at Alexandra's arrival. She also caught his sincere smile at Alexandra and wished he were less happy to see her. When Alexandra caught him staring and winked, Kate's heart sank. Alexandra was one of the very reasons Kate held back on announcing their relationship . . . if one even remained.

When the beautiful Alexandra settled on the sofa next to Declan, Kate could say nothing. It was her own fault for refusing to tell others about their relationship. She thought she'd have time to think things over, but Alexandra's appearance made her question that decision.

Chloe's husband and sons arrived, and the room was filled with chatter. As conversations bounced around, Kate's focus drifted to what was being said on the sofa.

She caught something about dinner later that night and nearly gasped. Was he already willing to date others when they weren't officially broken up? Was it as Kate feared and his feelings for Alexandra had never subsided? The weight in her chest grew heavier, and she shifted uncomfortably in her chair while trying to act interested in the other conversations. What had she done?

It wasn't until the family was preparing to leave that she overheard Tracey mention that Declan and Alexandra's dinner was with an author. With that one comment, she felt lighter, and her smile was sincere as she said goodnight to Declan, Alexandra, and Chloe's family.

During her own dinner, however, thoughts of Declan and Alexandra's meal together plagued her. Was he enjoying his time with Alexandra? Would it make him view Kate as a poor choice? Kate couldn't get up to her bedroom fast enough after cleaning up the kitchen with

Tracey. She only hoped they didn't think her rude. Pacing around her room, she decided to call Jennifer, but before she dialed the number, a call came in from Brittany.

"I'm ready . . . I want to become a Christian." Brittany's voice was still hoarse from having her thyroid removed several weeks earlier, but her excitement was audible.

"Brittany . . . I . . . wow, that's great." Kate wracked her brain for what to say. She'd been so absorbed in her own crumbling world that she'd not even thought of God over the past two days. Shame filled her. How could she lead Brittany to become a Christian when she herself was so inadequate? She silently prayed and asked God to forgive her and work through her.

Remembering her conversation with Declan and how he'd walked her through becoming a Christian starting with Romans 10:9-10, she decided that was a good place to start with Brittany. Brittany already knew the essentials and just needed to speak those things out loud.

Twenty minutes later, after switching to FaceTime so Brittany could mouth words and not have to speak so loudly, Kate said goodbye to her new sister in Christ. It was strange to think that things had turned out the way they did, but she was overjoyed. She picked up her phone and texted Declan. He was the one who had helped her become a Christian and directed her as she shared with Brittany the past few weeks. He would be so excited.

Kate: I just walked Brittany through becoming a Christian!!!

Before she hit send, she froze. Maybe he wouldn't want to hear from her right now. He'd seemed irritated earlier, and then he'd been with perfect Alexandra. Delete . . . delete . . . delete.

Kate tapped her fingers on her phone. No, regardless of what was happening with their relationship, she had to tell him. She retyped the text and hit send before she could second-guess herself.

Several minutes passed before the bubbles popped up. Then they disappeared. That happened two more times before she received a message.

Declan: That's wonderful! You should tell my mum. She'll be excited for you!

While nothing he said was negative, she still had the feeling he was avoiding talking to her. He likely would have called her immediately after seeing news like that if it had happened before their argument. Was it possible he wasn't alone? There went her overactive mind again. Regardless of the reason, it was unlike him to not say more. She moved to her bed and rubbed her brow. The night was too special to let him get her down. Checking the time, she decided 9:24 wasn't too late to text Tracey the news.

A knock on her door a few minutes later revealed Tracey in her robe, smiling from ear to ear. "You have such a beautiful soul, Kate. This truly exemplifies how Christ called us to love our enemies." Tracey hugged her tight, then leaned back to look at her with tears surfacing in her eyes. "I'm sorry. It's been such an emotional day, but this is a wonderful way to end it. Have you told Corbyn? He'll be so proud of you."

Kate nodded but couldn't get the words out. Declan knew; he knew Tracey would be there for her when he couldn't—or wouldn't. Maybe this was for the best.

Chapter Thirty-Eight

Today was supposed to be special—Valentine's Day, the day for love—but Kate had ruined it for herself. Watching boats float by on the Thames, she delayed her arrival at the Valentine's dinner Tracey planned for the family at home. Chloe and Ian were going out on a date, but everyone else was expected—including Declan.

Last year, this day had been utterly depressing, and only a week and a half ago, Kate had anticipated the complete opposite for this one.

Declan had gone silent the past few days other than his text two hours earlier asking if she'd be at dinner. She'd ignored it and the follow-up question mark he sent. He could ask his mom if he really wanted to know, or better yet, he could have asked earlier in the week rather than leaving her to imagine the worst. She took a deep breath and tried to push away thoughts that threatened to take her down.

Pulling her coat tighter, Kate turned to go home, not knowing what lay ahead. Just as she turned onto her street, Kate's phone rang. She sighed, imagining it was Declan trying to find out where she was. Instead, the caller ID showed Brittany.

"Happy Valentine's Day." Kate tried to sound cheerful.

"It's spread . . . the cancer. I go in for more tests tomorrow." Her breath was shallow and labored. "They thought they had gotten all of it by removing my thyroid last month and with the treatment after, but apparently not. Please pray for me."

After assuring her, praying, and saying goodbye, Kate found herself inside the house. Thoughts of how confusing this must be for little Madeline came to mind. All she'd known was a sick mom. Kate covered her mouth and held back the sob that threatened to escape during her conversation with Brittany. As she walked towards the dining room, she heard laughter ring through the house.

"I'm so sorry I'm late. Brittany called and the cancer's—" The words froze on her lips at the sight of Alexandra sitting next to Declan, and she lost her train of thought. *Must act unphased.* "Her . . . her cancer has spread." Realizing she was staring at Declan, she turned to Tracey. "I'll be right back. I-I need to wash my hands."

Marching into the kitchen, Kate dropped her purse on the island and mindlessly began washing her hands. *I can do this. I can do this.* She refused to let this shake her, at least not right now. There would be time for tears later, but not in front of Alexandra, and definitely not in front of Declan's family, who had no idea they'd dated. Oh, why had she been so stubborn?

"Kate, are you okay?"

Kate turned and found a concerned Tracey entering the kitchen. "I will be. It's just a lot." She left it at that.

"I know. Brittany has had such a hard time of it. I've been praying for her, but will especially pray about this. Are you ready to join us?" Kate responded with a nod. "If you feel comfortable, you can share with all of us what you found out."

The laughter she heard earlier changed to something more somber as Kate shared Brittany's news with the others.

"Kate, I'm so sorry. Yesterday's news was wonderful, and now this." Declan shook his head and looked remorseful. Was there something more he was trying to communicate? If only they had some time alone.

Alexandra coughed into her hand, and Kate's gaze shifted, finding her wearing the engagement ring she hadn't worn in months. Was she smirking behind her hand? Today, February the fourteenth, of all days. Her heart couldn't handle much more hurt and disappointment.

After the meal, Tracey pulled Kate aside and prayed with her for

Brittany. By the time they were done, the others had finished cleaning up, and Declan and Alexandra were gone.

The week spiraled out of control. Brittany was told the cancer had spread to several organs in her abdomen, and the outlook that was once so promising now looked bleak. Margaret still made no progress, and Declan was again scarcely in Kate's vicinity. He had texted her, but she didn't have the emotional energy to hear what he had to say. Much of her free time was spent communicating with Brittany, her mom, who had been helping Brittany with Madeline, and Hayley, the only person she'd shared with about her short-lived relationship with Declan. She longed to pour her heart out to Declan. Before they'd tried dating, they'd become close friends, and sharing life's ups and downs was routine for them . . . until now.

Somehow, Brittany stayed positive in spite of her bad news, but Kate could tell she was concerned about Madeline. "God has given me so much peace about this. I trust him, regardless of what happens." That's what Brittany had said. How was it possible that Brittany, after being a Christian for only a few days and receiving some of the worst news, still gave glory to God?

Kate, however, had months to grow in her relationship with God, and felt annoyed at God. She wouldn't quite use the word "angry"— that would sound wrong. Wouldn't it? She knew she shouldn't be angry at the Creator and her Maker, but it was hard to understand how or why he would let people he supposedly loved go through so much, especially so soon after becoming Christians.

Pray. The thought crossed her mind, and she realized she'd not prayed in days. Others had prayed for her, but she'd been giving God the silent treatment.

Lying in bed, she tried to pray, but her mind began to wander. She tried again with the same result. Pressing her palms to her eyelids, she groaned in frustration. *Pray.* Still, she couldn't sleep. Climbing out of bed, she knelt and leaned against the bed. Quietly, she began speaking words to God. Thoughts flowed and flowed. She poured out her heart's desires, hurt and disappointment, and confusion about all that was happening. Rather than feeling like her words hit the ceiling, she felt comfort and warmth that she'd not felt since things went sideways with Declan. She even felt hope. Just a small seed with the promise of more.

When Kate finally crawled back into bed, she noticed that almost an hour had passed. She'd been praying the entire time. Exhaustion overcame her before she could stop and think more about the experience.

As the morning light gradually illuminated the room, a plan formed in Kate's mind. She needed to get away.

Before leaving to meet Margaret at the care center, she spoke with Tracey about taking off early and staying at the beach cottage. Tracey understood her need for a break. Margaret's stroke had taken a toll on the whole family, and she knew Kate's personal relationship with Brittany had pushed her to the edge. Tracey watched her with sadness as they spoke but had no idea that much of Kate's pain was because of Declan. It was just as well. Tracey didn't need any more drama in her life.

Next, Kate called Hayley and worked out a plan to meet up for the weekend. Though her circumstances hadn't changed, she felt relief at the prospect of the trip. The afternoon couldn't come fast enough.

Once again, Kate found herself on the train to Dover, hoping to find healing. She chuckled to herself at the thought. Many things had changed in her life over the past nine months, but she was again running from pain caused by a man.

Chapter Thirty-Nine

F riday night, Kate disembarked from the train to find a grinning Hayley.

"Finally! It's been too long. We can't wait this long between visits again," Hayley squealed while throwing herself at Kate.

Kate hugged her friend, then leaned back. "Something's different. What are you not telling me?"

Lifting her left hand, Hayley announced, "Aidan asked me to marry him!"

"What? Oh Hayley, the ring is beautiful and so perfect for you. You'll have to tell me all about it. When did he ask and where? I need details." She examined the unique antique silver ring that held a large red stone in the center and smaller ones down the sides.

Hayley looked sheepish. "He actually asked me Monday, during our Valentine's dinner."

"Hayley!" Kate frowned. "Why didn't you tell me?"

"Remember, you called me Tuesday all upset because Alexandra showed up for Valentine's dinner wearing the ring and you were also worried about Brittany? I just couldn't that day. You needed me. I planned to wait a couple of days, but your news about Brittany just kept getting worse. I'm sorry, and I promise I would have told you this weekend even if you hadn't come here. Now you know."

A tear slipped down, and Kate hurried to wipe it. "Sorry, happy tears. I'm not really mad. I do understand, and we need to celebrate. This weekend doesn't have to be all about me moping."

"How about you get your moping out tonight, then tomorrow we celebrate?"

"I like how you think, Hayley Adams, soon to be Hayley Clarke." Kate giggled through her tears.

That night, they camped out at the beach cottage with pizza and ice cream while Kate talked through all of her troubles. Not that she hadn't shared them with Hayley before, but she needed to get it all off her chest one more time. They listed and examined all of Declan's faults, yet Kate couldn't help but remember all of his wonderful qualities. Despite everything, she would forever hold him on a pedestal in her mind, and he would always own part of her heart.

"We never even kissed, but he was more romantic than Mark had been long before his death. Or maybe Mark never was romantic, and I was just an easily impressed teenager when we met." Kate sighed. She'd been doing a lot of that lately.

"You and Declan never kissed?" Hayley sounded skeptical. "A guy who looks like that? How could you hold yourself back?"

A dry chuckle escaped from Kate. "After what I went through with Mark, I wasn't about to put myself out there only to be used and tossed away, or worse . . . have him act like we were something when he was possibly still in love with someone else." She blinked back tears.

"I'm sorry."

"It's good I held back after all. Right?" It felt wrong to cast doubt on Declan's character. Regardless of what his intentions were, he was nothing like Mark—was he?

"And yet . . . I really thought he cared for me. The way he looked at me each time he saw me . . . his eyes lit up like I was the best thing he'd seen all day. It was sincere—I know it was. Sometimes, when we were alone, he hugged me so tight like he worried that if he let go, I would disappear. Then there were the kisses. I know I said we've never kissed, and that's true—never on the lips, at least. He would kiss my hand, my palm, my forehead . . . and there was that time in the car. I was wearing a sleeveless dress, and he leaned over and kissed my shoulder. It was tender and filled with so much emotion. I felt that kiss throughout my whole body. It was as romantic as any kiss on the lips."

Kate's heart skipped and stuttered as she recalled that moment. Had she so wrongly interpreted his feelings for her?

"Today is my fun day," Kate announced dryly.

"Calm down. You sound *much* too excited." Hayley looked at her somber friend.

"Sorry. Should I try again?" She pasted on a smile. "Today is my fun day."

"Now you look nauseated. Don't force it. You'll get there. We'll go walk around the property at Deal Castle, then have our spa appointments. It will be a perfect distraction."

"It's still a little . . . no, a lot cold for my taste to wander around outside."

"Well, that's Doctor Hayley's prescription—fresh air and exercise, so bundle up. We can have soup after and choose the hot stone massage to warm up. It will be invigorating."

Kate rolled her eyes. As much as she complained, between the comfort of the cottage with its reminders of happier days and the time with Hayley, she felt better already.

After walking around the castle, Kate was worn out and cold. They couldn't get inside the bistro fast enough. Hot lobster bisque, hearty warm bread, and tea followed by warm apple and black currant crumble warmed them for lunch, and now Kate was nearly ready for a nap.

The spa smelled herbal and minty, and on the massage table, dreams of a tropical oasis drew her under. She fell asleep listening to sounds of the ocean, and the masseuse had to wake her to turn over.

"Okay, Hayley, I think there was a method in your madness. I'm completely relaxed right now. In fact, I need a nap before we meet up with everyone for dinner." Kate could barely drag herself from the table to get dressed. It was as if all of her stress had been drained out, leaving her boneless and caught between wake and sleep.

"That will work great. I'll drop you off at the cottage for a nap, then I've got errands to run. I'll be back in time to get you made up for dinner."

"I don't know about you *making* me up. I'll just do my usual makeup and hair. We're supposed to be celebrating *you* and *your* engagement tonight."

"Oh no, it's girls' night, and you're going to look fabulous."

Kate didn't have the energy to argue.

Later that day, Hayley had her way, making her look like she was ready for a runway instead of dinner with girlfriends before listening to a band at the Rose and Crown.

Their friends were genuinely excited to see Kate, and after filling her in on their lives for the last three months, it felt as if she'd never left. Hayley's engagement and Mira's son, who was due in three months, were the hot topics of the evening. It took the pressure off of Kate and her woes.

After eating at the restaurant, most of the girls continued the celebration at the Rose and Crown, with the exception of Mira, who was sleepy and uncomfortable by the time they finished dinner.

"Kate, welcome back!" Aidan gave Kate a side hug.

"Thanks. I'm so happy for you two. Congratulations."

The look on his face was pure adoration as he pulled Hayley to his side. "Yeah, this little lady is going to make an honest man out of me." Underneath his neatly trimmed beard, it actually looked like Aidan was blushing. "I have a table right up front for all of you ladies."

Once they were settled, Kate recognized the Celtic band that was playing. They were regulars at Aidan's place, and she recalled they were a friendly group of guys whom she'd spoken with several times. The lead singer winked at Kate, and she laughed.

When the band took a break, the lead singer pulled up a chair next to Kate. "Hey, pretty lady, it's been a while."

Kate grinned and shrugged. "I'm glad to be back. You sounded good up there, Loch."

He nodded, then waved a waitress over and ordered a drink before turning back to Kate. "How are things in London?"

"You've been keeping tabs on me?" She didn't want to think about London today.

Loch shrugged. "Luv, it's hard not to notice when a beauty like you disappears. We'll have to lure you back, won't we, Hayley?"

"I'm all in for that." Hayley chuckled.

Loch chatted up the girls at the table and regaled them with stories about how Aidan helped his band get their start by giving them a regular venue to play in. Downing half his drink, he nudged Kate. "Hand me your phone, and I'll put my number in."

Her eyes went wide, and she froze.

Loch smirked. "Sit tight." He jumped up and ran to talk to one of the waitresses, who handed him her pen and notepad. He scribbled something and ripped off the page before kissing the waitress on the cheek, passing her the pad and pen, then dropping into the seat next to a bewildered Kate. "I get it. You don't know me well and don't want me to have your number yet, but here's mine and our band's webpage. We're playing Thursday through Saturday in London next week. Come one night on me. If you're feeling generous, I'd love to take you to dinner before the show."

During Loch's monologue, Kate tried to get Hayley's attention. Was this a setup? Hayley subtly shrugged. A closer look at Loch, and Kate realized she'd never paid attention to notice he was a good-looking man, more rugged than she was used to, but handsome nonetheless. His black hair and blue eyes made an arresting combination. Her insides twisted as she imagined Loch picking her up while Declan answered the door. Maybe she should get to know him better.

When Loch joined his band to sing the next set, Aidan filled his seat. "So, you and Loch?"

Kate shrugged, still not sure how she felt about the situation. "He gave me his number. What's he like?"

"He's one of the good ones. Doesn't mess around with girls' hearts."

Kate nodded and turned to watch Loch, pondering what she would do.

Twisting her scarf, Kate barely registered the brisk wind as she walked along the sea, calling out to God and baring her soul. To her relief, there were very few others out braving the chill. With her mouth in constant motion bystanders might think her crazy. She fell to her knees. "God, it's too much to bear!" Cold, moist pebbles and sand pressed against her hands, and she grasped at them and squeezed as if it was a battle she could win. If she just fought it harder, answers would come and problems would be solved.

Tears clouded her vision, and she lifted her hands to heaven, laughing at the fact that she couldn't even wipe her eyes with her now dirty hands. She had created this mess in her life just like the mess on her hands. She should have held off from dating Declan. Now the desire to make him jealous with Loch felt petty and wrong.

Did that mean she couldn't go out with Loch? Did she want to go out with him for who he was and not how his presence would affect Declan? If she couldn't figure that out, she had no business getting his hopes up. A few minutes of praying, then contemplating her thoughts about Loch did not help her make a decision. "God, you're all-powerful and all-knowing. Can't you make things more clear?"

Standing, she dusted off her pants and got most of the sand from her hands before dabbing her eyes with the scarf. She had a feeling that she would be finding bits of sand on herself even after changing clothes later. Funny how something so small and innocuous worked its way into her life and clung so tightly.

Time for laying down more things at the feet of God. Brittany . . . Declan? Both tough subjects. Her mind settled on Declan. She wanted him back—at least in some form. What they had before dating was good. Dating was better, but this was unbearable. Every day without speaking to him or texting with him, she felt his absence more acutely. "God, is it possible to get any of what we had back, or should I let go of this desire for him?"

Unavailable—that's what Declan had been all along, and she'd guessed it, but not been able to stop herself from leaping heart-first to take as much as he offered, despite knowing the likely outcome. Now she paid the price for letting her control slip. "God, I'm at a loss about how to repair what I've broken." She thought back to the last time she'd seen him. He looked irritated with her. It made no sense when he was the one who'd given up on them so quickly and returned to Alexandra. She would have to speak with him but was at a loss about where to start. Looking into the horizon over the sea, she found no answers to this dilemma either. She knew that whether she received answers or not, God was still with her, and she should attempt to make things better.

"God, I know you want all my burdens, and you know my thoughts about Brittany. She just became a Christian. She has a young daughter. I want to lay all these things down, but I want to fix them myself too." Kate wrapped her arms around herself and let the sound of the waves wash over her. She felt helpless, then remembered the paper she had in her coat pocket.

John 14:27—Peace I leave with you; my peace I give to you. Not as the world gives do I give to you. Let not your hearts be troubled, neither let them be afraid.

1 Corinthians 13:2—And if I have prophetic powers, and understand all mysteries and all knowledge, and if I have all faith so as to remove mountains, but have not love, I am nothing.

Hebrews 10:39—But we are not of those who shrink back and are destroyed, but of those who have faith and preserve their souls.

Hebrews 11:1—Now faith is the assurance of things hoped for, the conviction of things not seen.

Mark 9:23-24—And Jesus said to him, "If you can'! All things are possible for one who believes." Immediately the father of the child cried out and said, "I believe; help my unbelief!"

The buzzing phone in her back pocket drew her from her thoughts, and she unbuttoned her coat to get to it. When she finally pulled it out, it showed a missed call from her mom. Before she could decide what to do, a text popped up.

Mom: Brittany is going downhill fast. Please call.

Kate wondered if God was trying to tell her something with the timing of this call as she turned to go back to the cottage.

"Hey. What's going on?" Kate questioned her mom once she'd arrived back in the cottage and warmed up with a cup of tea.

"I don't think Brittany has long to live."

Kate gasped. How could things have changed so quickly? Over Christmas, Brittany had been so confident this was curable. "I don't understand."

"I know. Brittany's in shock too. She's not responding to the treatment, and now some of her major organs are shutting down. She was rushed to the emergency room today. I've had Madeline. They've got Brittany stable, but don't think she'll last long."

"Oh Mom!" Kate felt overwhelmed with emotion. "Poor Madeline. She has no idea what's going on. If she loses her mother—"

"If Brittany dies, Madeline will be put in the foster system. She said there's no way she'd let her mom or sister have her, and she'd rather take her chances."

"That's awful. So she's already making plans?"

"The doctors told her she needs to. This is hard, Kate. Madeline is a precious girl. It feels like she's my granddaughter even though she's technically not, and that reality is so twisted."

"I can tell you've grown close to her." Kate's mind tried to wrap around what was happening, and an idea pressed upon her mind. "I think . . . I think I need to go see Brittany." Her mind raced through the logistics for leaving for Memphis. "Let me talk to Tracey and see what I can work out. I know I need to be quick if Brittany is doing so poorly."

Chapter Forty

Kate recalled Tracey's words about Declan during their conversation on the way to the airport. She hadn't known how to respond. They'd kept their relationship a secret, and to admit it now that he was back with Alexandra would seem like she was stirring up trouble. Even though she was angry and hurt that he'd so easily turned back to Alexandra, she still hoped he would be happy.

Tracey was right. She did need to work things out with him. Knowing how to begin that conversation and having the courage to do it when her emotions still felt out of control around him were her greatest hindrances. Confronting him would make the end of their dating relationship seem final. Was that holding him back too?

He had texted but not made an effort to see her in person. Did he still have some romantic feelings for her? The sight of Baptist Hospital drew her back to the present.

Rhythmic beeping greeted Kate as she entered Brittany's room. She looked so frail as she slept. No one would blame Kate if she turned away from Brittany after what she'd done. Yet here on the other side of the ocean, Kate quietly sat in the chair closest to the bed and prayed. The image of Madeline playing came to mind. Madeline was happy and content when Kate left her at her parents' home. Thoughts of what would happen if Brittany never returned home skirted the edges of Kate's mind.

"Thank you for coming." Brittany's soft, hoarse voice broke into the stillness of the room. "You and your mom have been too good to me."

Tears filled Brittany's eyes, and Kate felt her throat constrict as she shook her head. "It's only through God," she choked out. This situation would look strange to an outsider and likely did to the hospice nurse who had joined them.

Brittany smiled. "True. He is so good." Kate's eyes went wide at that comment. "You know it's true. I'm at peace with death. I look forward to seeing God face to face. My only burden now is my worry for Madeline, but God is teaching me to trust him in that too."

Kate swallowed hard. She'd hesitated to bring up the subject of death, but Brittany wasn't holding back. Being here and knowing all that Brittany endured put her own life in perspective. Kate's relationship woes with Declan paled compared to dying and knowing you were leaving your daughter an orphan. *God, forgive me for my selfishness!*

"Your courage and faith strengthen *my* faith, Brittany." A sound at the door stopped her from saying more, and Brittany's face lit up.

"There's my girl." Brittany mustered every bit of energy she had for her daughter.

Madeline squealed in Kate's mom's arms. Kate had forgotten Abby routinely brought Madeline by each day after her nap. Madeline held her arms out to Brittany, who patted her lap. Kate watched as her mom carefully laid Madeline down. Brittany winced, then forced a smile and pulled her daughter close for a hug.

Madeline didn't appear bothered by all of the medical equipment and acted like the same happy-go-lucky baby that Kate had seen two months earlier. She seemed to comprehend that there was something serious happening.

"Ma-ma-ma-ma."

"Yes, Mama's got you, Sweet Pea. Did you have fun today with Grammy Abby?" Brittany nuzzled Madeline's hair, and Madeline stopped squirming to settle against her mom.

Grammy Abby was the name Kate's niece and nephew called Abby, and it was strange to hear Brittany refer to her mom that way. Kate felt like an interloper watching the mother-daughter scene. She looked at her own mom, who didn't seem to be concerned by it, before saying, "Do you need me to get you anything? Do you want privacy?"

"No, I'm fine." Brittany frowned. "I can't be left alone with her. There's always the chance she might pull at one of my tubes or monitors, so I've got to have someone nearby." Brittany glanced at Abby, who nodded.

"Okay, well . . ." Looking again at her mom and recognizing the dark circles under her eyes, Kate suggested, "Mom, why don't you go home and rest? You can send Dad in a bit to get me and Madeline." She turned back to Brittany. "How long does she usually stay?"

"Forty-five minutes to an hour."

"Okay. I can do that. You'll make sure he's got the car seat, Mom?" Kate asked and caught her mom smiling and nodding.

"Will do." With a kiss on the top of Madeline's head, Abby left them.

"Thank you. Your mom has been such a blessing, but I'm sure this is wearing her out."

Kate had not realized all her mom was doing until she arrived. It had to be much harder for someone in their late fifties to keep up with a baby's needs all day.

The buzzing of Kate's phone broke the quiet. A reminder to text Loch. In all the busyness of the week, she'd forgotten to let him know she was out of the country. She'd actually convinced herself to go to his concert before deciding on this trip. She shot off a quick text explaining the situation, and saying if he was back in London at a later date to let her know. She wondered if anything would come of that.

An hour passed quickly, and Madeline did well with the transition of leaving her mom. She'd become accustomed to Kate's dad, which helped. Later, when Abby introduced Kate to Madeline's bedtime routine, Kate had the strangest feeling, almost like déjà vu. It felt so natural and familiar.

Though Kate went to bed immediately after putting Madeline down, she struggled to wake up the next morning. Jetlag hit hard, but she'd promised her mom she would let her sleep in and get Madeline up herself. Praying for energy and wisdom, Kate crawled out of bed. Once seeing the sweet little girl with her bright brown eyes peering up happily, Kate felt renewed energy. Strangely, though Madeline's eyes were just like Mark's, Kate was hit with compassion instead of hurt or resentment each time she saw her. This innocent child was caught in a horrible situation, and in that moment, Kate knew she would do anything to make it better.

Getting accustomed to Madeline's schedule overwhelmed Kate— changing diapers, feeding her, keeping her entertained, and trying to recognize her needs when she cried. By the time they took her to Brittany, Kate wondered how anyone managed more than one child at a time. Even with her mom helping, it seemed like an impossible task. Midway through the next day, she began feeling more comfortable with the routine.

Just as she put Madeline into Brittany's arms for their hospital visit, a text from Tracey came through asking her to call. A problem with Margaret was the first thing to cross her mind, and she rushed out of the hospital room, leaving her mom to watch over Brittany and Madeline.

"Tracey, is Margaret okay?"

"Yes, sorry, I didn't mean to scare you. It's not Mum. It's . . . Corbyn. He's not himself. I hate to bother you, but he really needs to hear from you. I tried getting him to tell me what was wrong, but all I got was that he couldn't say and I need to ask you. So I guess I'm asking: what is he talking about?"

Tension worked its way up Kate's spine. She hadn't prepared for this conversation, and regret pricked her heart. "Declan and I . . . we dated." Her voice was barely a whisper. "It only lasted a few weeks. A month, really." She heard Tracey gasp on the other end of the line. "I don't know what I was thinking. I knew there was a high possibility things weren't over with Alexandra, but I let myself hope."

"Oh Kate. I had no idea. I mean, I knew you two were close. I wish you both had said something."

"That's my fault. He wanted to, but I was worried about how it would affect things if we told everyone and then broke up."

"But you can't live your life on the what-ifs."

"My head knows that, but my heart is still too raw from Mark. Anyway, it seems it turned out best now that he's back with Alexandra. When I saw his engagement ring on her finger again at the Valentine's dinner, that became very clear."

"But Kate, that's—"

"Watch out, miss!" A nurse came rushing past and entered Brittany's room, followed by two more.

"Tracey, I've got to go. Something's wrong with Brittany." Kate hung up the phone, and seconds later, Abby exited, face pale and holding Madeline in her arms.

"Mom, what's going on?" Abby was visibly shaken, so Kate reached for Madeline, who had started crying. "It's okay, Sweet Pea." Maybe using Brittany's nickname for her would help.

Abby threw a hand to her heart and started rubbing. "I think Brittany flatlined. Her heart monitor switched from regular beating to a solid beep with a red line on the display. Please pray for her. This baby can't be without a mother." Tears welled up in her eyes.

Kate nodded and began praying out loud for Brittany. "God, don't let this child be without a mom. Help us. Bring Brittany back . . . bring her back—" Kate couldn't get any more words out and instead wrapped her arms around her mom and Madeline and silently cried.

Chapter Forty-One

While waiting for an update on Brittany, Abby and Kate joined the hospice nurse. "They got her heart beating again, but she's not conscious yet." She glanced at Madeline before looking at Abby. "You've agreed to be Madeline's guardian until we can find a permanent home that's suitable. Has anything changed?"

A gasp escaped Kate before she could stop herself, and Abby looked at her with worried eyes. "I'm sorry, honey. I know it's awkward, but I couldn't turn her over to the system without knowing they have a good place for her." Abby looked back at the nurse. "Yes, I'll keep her as originally agreed. As for the other—" She glanced at Kate, then back. "I need to talk to my daughter first."

"Brittany will probably be out for a while. The medicine they gave her will likely make her groggy. Why don't you go home and talk, and I'll contact you if she wakes or things change." The nurse eyed them both warily.

Abby nodded, then patted Kate's shoulder. "We should get this little one to bed for her nap, anyway. That will be a good time for me to catch you up on things."

Kate paced the room. "You've kept all of this from me?"

"Not intentionally, dear. It all happened so fast. You were traveling here when the nurse first mentioned it during the meeting that Brittany had asked me to sit in on. When she started talking about the alternative, I couldn't bear it. You live all the way across the ocean, so it shouldn't affect you."

"No—you're right. This is all just . . ." She threw her hands up. "This is such a strange situation." She pinched her nose, feeling a headache coming on. "My dead cheating husband's daughter by his mistress being taken care of by my parents." She chuckled. "God has some sense of humor."

"This really isn't funny, Kate. This is a child's life we're talking about."

"You're exactly right. That's why—"

"Kate, that's why your father and I are considering being her permanent guardians."

"What? Like adopting her?"

"We wouldn't have to actually adopt her, but yes, she would be in our care until she's an adult."

Kate closed her eyes. "I'll do it."

"Do what? Be her guardian? We would never ask you to do that. We can even have your brother as a backup guardian. You saw how Alex and Ava doted on Madeline over Thanksgiving."

"I think that's what God wants me to do. Step in and offer to be her guardian, maybe even adopt her at some point."

"No, dear, I don't think God would ask you to do that. It's a painful situation for you. This is a big decision, and you can't take it lightly."

"I can do all things through him who strengthens me."

"What do you mean by that?"

"It's a Bible verse—Philippians 4:13. Adopting her is not a new thought. I've been feeling God nudging me towards this, but I tried ignoring it. I can't anymore. If this is what he wants, I'm sure he will give me strength."

"Kate, taking care of an infant is a huge undertaking. Not that I don't think you're an amazing woman, but it's a lifetime commitment. Please don't rush into something like this."

Kate pressed her lips together and pondered. "I'll pray about it and think about it some more, but we both know there's probably not much time left. Maybe the hospice nurse has some advice. She seemed kind and knowledgeable."

"Jennifer, you think I'm crazy, don't you?" Kate sat cross-legged on the floor surrounded by toys, Madeline, and Jennifer's three-year-old daughter Emma.

Jennifer shifted her infant son in her arms as her eyes moved from Madeline to Kate. "It does seem odd, but it's clear the two of you are comfortable with each other, and I suppose, if you're already able to spend so much time with her without her parentage bothering you much, that it will continue to get easier."

"Strangely, those thoughts are becoming fewer and further apart. Not only that, they're buried underneath my compassion for Madeline." At the sound of her name, Madeline dropped the toy she was playing with and crawled toward Kate. "Hey, Sweet Pea. You heard your name?" Kate smoothed Madeline's hair, but she was soon distracted again by Emma banging on the toy xylophone.

"Compassion can fade. Will you still be able to provide what she needs when she's being disobedient or you're tired and worn out from the busyness of being a single parent?"

Frowning, Kate shook her head. "I hear what you're saying." Her eyes drifted back to Madeline. "But this is worth it. It might not make sense to you, but I have to trust God in this."

"Okay. If that's how you feel, I'll be here for you in any way I can. I've always thought you would be a great mom. You were supposed to be one first." Jennifer's brow shot up when Kate winced. "Sorry, I shouldn't have said that. So . . . tell me, how's the search for Mr. Darcy going, and do you plan to stay in England?"

Kate rolled her eyes and sighed. "I have a confession to make." Jennifer listened with furrowed brows while Kate shared the story of how she and Declan dated, but while he was frustrated with her for not letting others know, Alexandra stepped right back into what they had before—engagement ring and all.

"Oh Kate, I'm so sorry."

"So you see, Mr. Darcy really doesn't exist. I feel sure of it now, and I think I'm okay with it." Those were the words that came out of Kate's mouth, but letting go of Declan wouldn't be as easy as letting go of the idea of Darcy. "As for the 'staying in England' thing, I'm not sure. I've got to call Tracey and see what her thoughts are if I have a child. Right now I'm still staying in her house, but Declan might be moving out of the mews house soon. That could be an option so she doesn't have a baby taking over their home. As for the long term, I really don't know. I love it there, but I don't want to have to tiptoe around Declan."

The thought that she needed to speak to Declan still burdened Kate. She'd used the excuse of the Brittany and Madeline situation to put it off, but she needed to break the ice so they could move on. Yet every time the urge to call him surfaced, she became angry again.

Throughout the night, Kate tossed and turned, her mind working through the logistics of being a mom. There were a few strange dreams mixed in that involved babies, Declan, and Mark. She still managed to wake up before her alarm and hurried to get ready for the busy day she had planned.

Kate's mom informed her that the hospice nurse texted during the night to say Brittany had awakened and was stable. Tension pulled at Kate's chest as she thought of what lay ahead. It would be a busy day if Brittany gave the go-ahead for her to be Madeline's guardian. Her parents' lawyer was at the ready with papers to sign if Brittany agreed. She anxiously waited for Madeline to wake so they could get to the hospital and see Brittany.

Red, swollen eyes greeted them when Kate and her mom stepped into Brittany's hospital room carrying Madeline. Glancing around the room, Kate noticed a tripod in the corner, but turned back to Brittany when she saw her struggling to sit up.

"Here, let me help you." Kate pushed the button to lift Brittany, then fluffed her pillows. "You gave us all quite a scare."

A weak smile graced Brittany's face as she nodded and reached a shaky arm out to her daughter. "Hey, Sweet Pea." Her words were barely audible. Brittany clasped her daughter and closed her eyes while inhaling Madeline's baby scent.

"I'd like to talk to you about something important." Kate fidgeted with the diaper bag and glanced at her mom, who urged her forward with a look. Kate had been silently praying all morning about this conversation since speaking the words out loud the day before. She had previously felt so confident, yet at the moment, she felt inadequate.

When Brittany opened her eyes and mouthed the words "Go ahead," Kate gathered her thoughts. "My mom told me that she and Dad agreed to be guardians for Madeline." Brittany nodded. "But . . ." She silently prayed for strength. "I think God is telling me to do that. Actually, I know that he is." Overwhelmed by a combination of sadness for Brittany and joy for the future she could already see with Madeline, she reached up to wipe a tear from her own cheek and noticed Brittany was crying, too, and smiling.

Brittany nodded and kissed Madeline's forehead before answering with her soft voice. Kate leaned closer to hear. "God told me—" Brittany drew in a labored breath in an effort to get the words out. "He told me you would. It's good." Another breath. "As it should be."

A mixture of elation and pain pulled at Kate. "Thank you," she whispered back.

Tears now poured steadily out of both women.

Kate wrapped her arms around both Madeline and Brittany and responded, "Thank *you*."

Abby joined the group hug and added her tears to the mixture.

Kate's pain from the last seventeen months evaporated, replaced with a different pain—a pain for all of Madeline's life that Brittany would miss and for a child without her biological parents. Knowing the questions Madeline would have in the future and the sadness that would accompany those answers squeezed at her heart as well.

When they finally separated, Kate added, "I also hope to adopt her once things settle. Do you . . . would the thought of that bother you?"

Brittany shook her head. "She needs a mother and security. I should thank you." She gasped for a breath. "Still can't believe . . . you forgive," she labored out. Her eyes found Abby. "Lawyer?"

Abby pulled out her phone. "I'll text him. We contacted him yesterday, and he's waiting to hear from us."

Paperwork filled the rest of the morning. Madeline remained calm and relaxed throughout, as if she knew life-altering things were happening.

Kate needed to talk to Tracey but didn't have time to call until they were at the house with Madeline down for a nap. They had a lot to discuss. As Kate pulled up her contacts, she saw Declan's name and hesitated before texting him first.

Kate: I'm ready to talk.

With a text to Declan done, she could tell Tracey she'd tried to reach him. Tracey didn't mention Declan as they spoke, as if she understood that the things happening with Brittany and Madeline were more important. Tracey insisted that she would love to have Madeline in their home, and they would work something out with Declan to move soon. That would give Kate and Madeline privacy in the mews house.

Tracey and Kate agreed that Kate should stay another week to have time with Madeline and see what the status was with Brittany. Then if Brittany lived for longer than expected, they would consider a long-term plan. Kate tried to keep her mind from wandering down the dark path of Brittany's death and the fallout afterwards. Periodically throughout their conversation, Kate pulled the phone back to check for a reply from Declan. Nothing.

After Madeline's nap, they returned to the hospital for more time with Brittany. This time she was lying in bed with an oxygen mask on, but she removed it before receiving Madeline into her arms. As the evening wore on, Brittany had to put the oxygen back on. Madeline's tiny hand gingerly touched it, but like the other medical equipment attached to Brittany, she accepted it and turned away to look back at the book her mom held.

"You," Brittany whispered as she pointed to Kate then to the book.

Kate gathered the meaning and pulled up a chair so she could read while Brittany held Madeline and the book. When she'd arrived earlier in the week, her mom had explained that before Brittany's surgery, she'd recorded herself reading a number of children's books and Scriptures out loud so that she could play them while showing Madeline the pictures. The recordings were a blessing since her voice had now weakened, but tonight it felt like Brittany was passing the baton to Kate.

Madeline was in bed that night by eight thirty, leaving Kate with her thoughts. She kept checking her phone. She'd started her day not really wanting to speak with Declan, but now she was angry with him for not responding and giving her that chance. In frustration, she went to the kitchen to find some calming herbal tea.

"Here you are. Madeline went down easily?" When Kate nodded, Abby continued, "You look down. How are you feeling about things?"

Kate shrugged. She'd still not told her parents about her brief relationship with Declan, and that made it difficult to explain her current problem. "I tried to contact Declan to let him know what was going on, but that was while Madeline was napping earlier, and I never heard back from him. He would have gone to sleep a few hours ago, so . . . I just want to talk with him."

Even as angry as he made her, something within still wanted to protect him. Did she still hope for a change in circumstances so that they could work things out? She couldn't imagine anything that would make her give him a second chance. Why had she let her heart get carried away? She knew better.

"Don't worry, dear." Her mom moved forward and wrapped an arm around Kate. "I'm sure there's a good reason. When we saw you two together, it was obvious that he cares deeply for you, even if it's only a friendship, as you say."

Kate felt guilt rise up, but held her tongue and kept her eyes on the kettle as she filled it with water. She hoped her mom wouldn't ask her about this again later. It would be harder to explain away his lack of response after several days had passed. It seemed obvious that he didn't want to talk. Tracey must have misread the reason for his mood. Once she had herself under control, she looked around the kitchen and noticed her father had been absent since dinner.

"Where's Dad?"

"He had an errand to run."

Kate glanced at the clock on the microwave. "At nine at night?"

"There was something I needed him to pick up. He'll be back soon. Do you need something?"

"No, I'm fine."

Needing a distraction, Kate curled up on the living room sofa and found the most recent *Southern Living* magazine. She was glad to see the March edition had arrived, because the perfect Valentine's dinner in pictures and recipes would be a harsh reminder of what happened in London. As she flipped through the pages, nothing held her interest.

"I think I'll go get ready for bed," Kate said after her last sip of tea. Another emotionally exhausting day and possibly lingering jetlag left her feeling droopy.

"I wanted to talk to you about your preparations for Madeline. There are lots of things you'll need, and shipping isn't practical, so I was thinking you could get most things there. I can come over and help, and your dad and I want to help with the purchases too. I think you'll—"

"Thanks, Mom. That all sounds really great, but can we talk about it in the morning? I can barely keep my eyes open." Kate laid the magazine down and began to stand.

"I understand, dear, but—wait, I hear your father pulling into the garage. You should say goodnight to him."

At the sound coming from the kitchen, Kate called out, "Hey, Dad. Mom said you had an errand to pick something up."

Silence, then a throat clearing.

"It was actually an errand for *someone*."

Kate's hand went to her heart and pressed down the pain as she waited, frozen in place, to see the owner of the voice coming around the corner. He was more handsome than her dreams. "How . . . why are you here?"

Declan's eyes shifted from Kate to Abby. "Abby, so good to see you again. Would you mind if I spoke to Kate privately for a moment?"

"Yes, of course."

Brett wrapped an arm around Abby's shoulder in greeting and nodded toward Kate, who glared back.

"What's going on?" Kate questioned Declan as soon as her parents were out of earshot. With everything that had happened, it didn't make sense that he would travel all this way. "I can't imagine Alexandra would be happy about you coming here."

"Kate." He smiled. "You're a sight for sore eyes." He gingerly reached for her shoulder and gave it a squeeze. "There is nothing going on with Alexandra and me. There's been a huge misunderstanding."

Kate shook her head and stepped away, letting his hand fall. She couldn't take more deception. "I saw her wearing your ring again—at the Valentine's dinner." Her eyes began watering. She tried blinking back the approaching tears, then pointed a finger at him. "That was what I was afraid of. That was why I hesitated to let everyone know about us. And why would your eyes be sore?"

Declan's face twisted in confusion, then his brows went up. "Kate, that ring Alexandra wears isn't the engagement ring I gave her. It was her grandmother's engagement ring. I have no idea why she wears it on her left ring finger, but it doesn't have anything to do with me or any other guy, for that matter. By the way, my eyes are 'sore' because I miss you."

"I don't understand." What was he implying? "She was wearing it when I first met her, while you two were engaged."

"Engaged? Wait a minute. You thought I was engaged to Alexandra when I first met you?" He stepped closer.

Now Kate was thoroughly confused and put up a hand to keep him away. "What are you saying? Are you now trying to act like you two weren't engaged? We have talked about your engagement to her numerous times, mister."

"Of course we were engaged, Kate, but it's been years. I was engaged to her at the end of university. It's been what . . ." He stopped to think. "Nine years since we ended things. I told you why. We weren't suited romantically. Victoria came after. There's been no one since, I promise. Oh Kate." He pulled her close and wrapped her in a tight hug. "Is that why you've been so hesitant with me? Kate."

He kissed her hair, then pulled back and kissed her forehead. "Kate, I've missed you so much. I was worried I had failed you when you left that weekend for Kingsdown, then came back and left for Memphis. I've been going out of my mind, hoping that it only had to do with Brittany's situation and you weren't mad at me. It wasn't until Mum mentioned your conversation with her the other day that I realized my mistake."

Kate stared at him, stunned. Was it all a miscommunication? That seemed too simple, too good to be true. She laid her head on his chest and let the stress, guilt, and sadness flow down her cheeks. She clung to Declan, fearing that if she released him, he would vanish, and she'd find that it was all a dream.

"Kate, I'm so sorry. I know you have your past to contend with, but I have mine too. You constantly saying you need more time before telling others struck a nerve. It felt like Alexandra all over again, the way she tried to string me along, and I panicked. That's why I went silent. I was wrong. I shouldn't have let so much time pass before coming after you, but I'm here now to ask forgiveness and repair what was broken."

"Forgiveness will take time." Her heart beat erratically at his declaration. "How did Alexandra string you along? You guys were engaged."

"I will keep working for your forgiveness, Kate. And yes, we were engaged, but before we officially started dating, she was such a tease with me. She knew I'd had a crush on her forever. There was finally a time that she wasn't dating anyone, and *she* asked *me* out for our first date. Within weeks, I was ready to promise her forever. While we were engaged, it became obvious that we weren't in love the way you should be with someone you marry. As we got closer, I realized how self-absorbed she was and became disillusioned with her. When I stopped fawning over her, it made *her* disillusioned with me, and we soon realized we weren't meant to be."

"But she speaks about you like you're the only man for her."

Declan shook his head. "That's the thing with her—she doesn't want me romantically when she has me, but when she sees anyone who might be a threat to her preeminence in my life, she becomes jealous and wants me back. She's tried to convince me multiple times over the last few months that she and I should try again. That was part of the reason I wanted us to open up about our relationship."

Kate swallowed the lump in her throat. "Do you still have feelings for her?"

"No, of course not. Not romantically. We've been friends forever and our families are friends, so I do care about her as a *friend*. But you have nothing to be worried about. I promise." He pulled her hand to his mouth to place gentle kisses across her knuckles.

A sigh threatened to escape, and Kate basked in the moment, heart threatening to beat out of her chest. Could she risk her heart again?

Declan lifted her face to his. "So are we okay? Can you forgive me for failing you?"

Inside, a battle raged. Part of her wanted to scream, "Yes!" but another part said men were deceitful. "I . . . I want to, but part of me is scared."

"I'm so sorry I gave you cause to worry, Kate. I'll prove myself to you. Will you give me a chance?" When she nodded, Declan's shoulders relaxed. His eyes lifted, and for the first time, he scanned the space around them. "So this is your childhood home?"

Her eyes followed his. "We moved here when I was twelve, so it holds a lot of memories."

Pulling her closer, Declan turned them around slowly. "I like seeing different parts of your life. Is your old room still the way you left it when you went to university?"

"No. They updated it when I got married. Now it just looks like a nice guest room. They still call it my room, though." Mentioning her marriage brought back thoughts of Mark. Their marriage seemed like a lifetime ago. Strange how it led to her current reality.

Declan smiled. "Is this you?" He approached a picture of her as a teenager on a horse." She nodded. "I had no idea you were a horsewoman."

Kate bit her lip before explaining. "Growing up, I rode all the time. The family of my best friend, Jennifer, breeds horses, so it was just a normal part of our lives. We even got to show them at the annual Germantown Horse Show." She pointed to a picture behind the one he'd first pointed out, which showed her riding a horse in the show. "When I started dating Mark, he often joined us for rides, though in the last few years of our marriage, he rarely rode with me." She sighed, remembering that it was another sore spot in their marriage. "Since his death, I've not ridden once." She touched the picture. "I miss it . . . riding."

"I have some connections, so we can ride back in England, but for now I'm here, and you can show me some of the places around town where you spent time. Maybe we could even go riding."

"Hmm." Kate could no longer focus on the conversation while she grappled with how to tell him her news. What would her decision mean for their relationship?

"Kate?" Declan's hand moved to her forehead, and he massaged the crease that had formed. "What's on your mind? Doubts about me?" She shook her head. "Brittany?"

Her eyes found his. "Yes . . . but also . . ." She squeezed her eyes shut. Would he still want to be with her, knowing she was responsible for a child? And not just any child, but her husband and his mistress's.

"Kate, it's okay. Take your time."

"I've decided to become Madeline's guardian." Kate watched Declan's brow furrow, then his eyes went wide.

"You mean . . . you'll be keeping her?"

Kate nodded while trying to read his expression.

"Kate, that's . . . wow." Declan swallowed hard and pulled his fingers through his hair. "You've prayed about this?"

Kate deflated at his response. "I have. In fact, God put it on my heart, but it took me several days to acknowledge it."

"Okay, wow."

"You said that."

"I did. It's just . . . quite a shock. Can I . . . The jetlag is catching up with me. Would you mind if I headed on to bed? We can talk about it more in the morning when I'm not so muddleheaded." After an awkward hug, Declan patted her on the shoulder. "Don't look so worried. I promise I'll have a better response tomorrow. Right now, I'm just too tired to comprehend things properly."

He retired to his room, leaving Kate more confused than before he'd arrived.

Chapter Forty-Two

As the first bit of daylight broke through the curtains, Kate's eyes popped open. Had it been a dream? Was Declan really here? Was Alexandra truly *not* his fiancée? It seemed impossible.

What would his response be to her keeping Madeline now that he'd slept? He spoke like everything was fine and they could pick up right where they'd left off, but he had not seemed pleased that she'd decided to be Madeline's guardian.

When Kate saw Declan that morning, he didn't bring up her future as Madeline's guardian. Nevertheless, he did join her in caring for Madeline throughout the day and didn't leave her side, even at the hospital. She was still astonished by the fact that he wasn't recently engaged to Alexandra, and had begun trying to recall why she'd believed he was in the first place. During the day, memories began to come together, reminding her of why she'd had those thoughts.

That evening, Kate felt relieved when she finally put it all together. Once Madeline was in bed and Kate's parents had disappeared into their room, she explained to Declan, "I think I know what made me believe you were engaged to Alexandra when I first arrived."

Declan quirked an eyebrow as he joined Kate at the kitchen table.

"You're going to think I'm crazy, but it was your grandmother. The weekend I first met you, Alexandra came up in our discussion just before you left, and once you were gone, your grandmother told me she was your fiancée. At the time, she seemed quite lucid, so I believed her. Afterwards, I don't recall anyone ever saying anything to make me think otherwise about your relationship. In fact, people referred to your engagement numerous times, which I took to mean in the present." She watched him for a reaction. "Then with the ring and the way she acted around you . . . it all seemed to fit."

"Wow. I guess I can see how it was all mixed up from the start." He chuckled dryly, then his face turned serious. "Sorry, it's really not funny, but sad. I feel like we lost so much time." He reached for her hand and squeezed it. "Kate, we should get married."

"What?" Kate's heart sank, and she pulled her hand away while looking around the kitchen to see if her parents had reappeared. This was not the way she'd ever imagined someone would propose to her. That was one thing she could say Mark did better.

"If you're going to raise Madeline, we should get married. It would be good for her to start things off with two parents. She's still young enough that the transition should be easy."

"Declan." Kate felt something twisting inside. "How can you say that? We just got back together. I think. Did we?"

"I never thought we broke up."

"But you . . . never mind. This is just . . ." What was he thinking? From what she knew of him, he had never been one to be irrational and act before thinking things through. "Getting married just for Madeline isn't right."

"Kate." He placed his hand over hers. "It's not just for her. Please don't rule it out. I think it could work. Why don't you sleep on it?"

There would be little sleeping . . . again . . . if she was supposed to think over a decision like this. "Declan, this is a huge decision. I don't know if I can give you an answer tomorrow."

"Being a guardian for a parentless infant is a huge decision, and it seems you made that very quickly."

That was a low blow, and she watched him as she tried to piece together her response. "I've wanted to be a mom for years. It may be an unusual situation, but I knew Madeline's father well—" She rolled her eyes. "Okay—with the exception of his mistress situation. Anyway, I knew him in ways that will help me raise her to better reach her potential. She's already responding well to me, and I've grown to love her. Also, I know this is what God wants me to do, and I'm sure I can do it. I have to follow his plan for me."

"You do, and I feel like this is what God wants me to do," he said. "I spoke with my lawyer earlier today, and there will be no issues with us getting a marriage license here, then going back to England."

Kate stood up from the table and shook her head. "I think you misunderstood what God told you. When God spoke to me about adoption—well, guardianship first—he separately spoke to Brittany and told her the same. When God sent an angel to tell Mary she would be pregnant by the Holy Spirit, he also sent the angel to Joseph and confirmed the same things. It makes sense that when something will affect two people in such a big way, he would tell them both, don't you think?"

Declan ran a hand over his face and frowned. "Point taken." He began to chuckle.

"What? I don't see how any of this is funny."

The corner of his lips turned up. "The student has taught the teacher. I hear you, Kate, though my offer is still on the table."

"Thanks, I guess, but my answer is no. I won't be 'sleeping on it.'" As happy as she was to have him back in her life, she worried that he wanted to marry her just so Madeline would have two parents.

Sleeping with thoughts of Declan's "proposal" swirling around brought more doubts. Had she been wrong to refuse him? Yet after all she'd been through with Mark, she needed to be one hundred percent sure before marrying again. She certainly didn't want to be someone's charity case in marriage.

"Why would you be willing to marry me so quickly when you've already had an engagement to someone you knew for years, and it took that engagement to make you realize the two of you wouldn't work?" Kate accosted Declan in the hallway first thing in the morning. "I'm not sure what you're trying to prove. This isn't some do-good act you can check off your list and put behind you later. As Christians, aren't we supposed to take marriage seriously with the intention of 'til death do us part!?"

"Okay, I'm sorry. Please forget I asked. I truly feel that there's something different about you and about me when I'm with you, but . . ." He placed his hands on her shoulders. "You're right, this is rushed, and you have enough change in your life. I'll be here for you to help in any way I can. I *would* like to ask that we make our relationship known from here on out, though."

Kate's heart sank. For some reason, the thought of declaring their relationship or even being in one stressed her out more than she already was. When she first saw him and learned he wasn't engaged, she was so relieved and ready to jump right back to where they left off, but after sleeping with his "proposal" on her mind, even a relationship with him felt like a burden.

"Declan . . ." Her heart sped up. Would this be the end? "I really like you . . . a lot. There's just so much going on in my life right now that I don't feel like I can make any other commitments. Would you . . . what I need right now is a friend. Can you be patient with me? Give me time?"

Declan's brow furrowed. "Kate, I—"

His voice was cut off by Madeline crying. She didn't usually wake up crying. "Sorry." Kate rushed out, dreading both the end of his sentence and what she'd find behind Madeline's door. Thankfully, it was nothing more than an arm caught between the crib rungs.

"Sweet Pea! It's okay. I've got you." She glanced back, and Declan was hovering close by. He looked so handsome and would make a great father from what she'd seen of him with kids. She internally sighed. Marriage required a lot more than attraction and potential parenting ability.

"Kate, it's so good to finally meet you. From the moment Anna and I met Brittany and she told us her story and how you witnessed to her about the Lord, we've been praying for you—and now even more so with your plan to care for Madeline. Please let us know if we or our church can do anything for you." Brittany's pastor, Ronnie, spoke to Kate outside of Brittany's room while she slept.

"Thank you." Tears threatened. "You have already done so much with the meals and the baby equipment you've loaned my mom. I know the prayers, though, are what have and will carry us through. That is all I can ask for."

"Consider it done. Right now, I'd like to pray over you."

Kate nodded and bowed her head.

The moment Kate was alone with Brittany and she woke, Brittany made it known with her rasping, broken voice that Declan would be great husband material. Brittany didn't even know about their previous relationship. How could she possibly determine his suitability in such a short time?

"I agree he's a great guy and would be a great dad." Kate shrugged. "We'll have to see how God leads. Please don't worry about anything, Brittany. I love Madeline and will see that she has all she needs."

Brittany smiled. "I . . . know. Not worried. Thank . . . you for forgiving . . . me. I'm ... ready." Her breathing became more labored, and Kate helped her replace the oxygen mask.

"I'll admit forgiving you was difficult at first, but even when I barely knew you, I knew I could do no less than our Savior has done for me. But Brittany, you must know I do truly forgive you. You are my sister in Christ." Kate wondered what Brittany's last words meant but didn't dare stress her more than she was, and instead smiled at her and fluffed her pillows. When Brittany looked over at the hospice nurse and tapped her own wrist, the nurse approached with a large gift bag.

"Kate," the nurse said after nodding at Brittany. "Brittany has been putting together letters for her daughter. One for each year until her eighteenth birthday, then a few extras that can be given on her eighteenth birthday as well. She has also put together some videos."

Kate's eyes moved to the tripod she'd noticed in the corner, and her hand moved to her chest as she took in all that this meant. "I understand."

"The videos can be shown anytime, and I know your mom already has the ones Brittany made a couple of months ago with her reading storybooks."

"Yes," Kate whispered, feeling overwhelmed as reality hit. She looked at Brittany, who was dozing off. "Thank you." Taking the bag from the nurse felt like taking on the weight of the world. "I'm going to pray over her for a few minutes, if you don't mind."

Sitting in the chair next to Brittany, Kate once again interceded for Brittany and Madeline. As much as she loved Madeline and looked forward to raising her, wouldn't it be better for her to be raised by Brittany? God could do it. With him, all things were possible. She had memorized Matthew 19:26, and read many accounts of the things he had done. "Yet not my will, but yours be done. In Jesus' name, Amen."

With visitors' hours ending, she moved to stand, but was startled by a hand on her shoulder. Warmth filled her when she saw it was Declan. Despite her determination to think of him only as a friend, she couldn't help but be drawn to him.

He reached for her hand, and they quietly said goodnight to the nurse before he pulled her away.

"You came back?" He had left with her mom several hours earlier to eat dinner while Kate stayed to discuss things with Brittany.

"I always will. I told you that I want to be here for you."

"Thank you." His sincerity tugged at her heartstrings. Could she really depend on him in this new endeavor? As they exited the ICU, Kate felt a sense of calm, as if things were falling into place.

When Declan wrapped an arm around her shoulder and pulled her into his side, she relaxed against him as they waited for the elevator. In silence, they entered, but before the doors opened on the first floor, Kate's phone buzzed. Holding it up, she saw two words from the hospice nurse: "Come back." Kate slumped further into Declan's side and gasped.

"I've got you." When the door opened, he pushed the button for the ICU floor.

As soon as they made it to the hallway outside Brittany's room, Kate's fears were confirmed. Personnel were rushing in and out of the room frantically, and the hospice nurse hurried towards Kate and Declan. "Pray!" she called while still yards away.

"What happened?" Kate asked.

"Her heart stopped again."

Frowning, Kate glanced up at Declan, who continued to hold her tightly. "I'll pray." Even while bowing her head, she felt torn inside. She wanted Brittany to live a full life with her daughter, but something inside told her that God was ready for her to come home. "God, I want her to live fully as mom to Madeline. I want you to heal her. I know you can, but I also know that your ways and plans are different than mine. I will have confidence in you no matter your will. Please help me to glorify you no matter what. In Jesus' name, Amen." Just as her prayer ended, Brittany's room went quiet.

The bag with Brittany's letters and videos felt like a lifeline as Kate waited to hear the news that could change everything. It was strange how many different thoughts and feelings could pass through the human mind in a matter of seconds. When the door opened, Kate clutched the gift bag tightly.

With sad eyes, the doctor approached. "I'm sorry. Brittany didn't make it." Other words came from the doctor's mouth, but Kate's brain couldn't seem to take them in.

Her body felt numb, and she could sense Declan holding her and moving her towards Brittany's room, where a lifeless but peaceful-looking Brittany lay. Kate reached out and clasped Brittany's hand, noticing the IV had been removed. The past few months flashed through her mind, and a weight settled deep inside as she was reminded of her new role with Madeline.

"Will you pray?" were the only words Kate could manage.

Declan's voice brought comfort, though the words eluded her, and sometime later, she found herself sitting on her parents' sofa with them consoling her shaking body. It wasn't a surprise. They'd expected it any day, yet she felt like she'd been hit with a sledge hammer.

She knew what was supposed to come next. Brittany had carefully planned her celebration of life service with her pastor, made funeral arrangements, and even had a passport in hand for Madeline, but somehow, it all seemed overwhelming to Kate. Tears welled up as she tried to clear the fuzz from her brain and think about what to do.

"Just breathe, Kate," Abby urged her daughter. Kate hadn't realized she was beginning to hyperventilate. "Right now, all you need to do is relax and rest. We've contacted Brittany's pastor to set up the viewing and service at the church, and it's being set up for three days from now. We'll take care of Madeline first thing in the morning if we need to. Whenever she sees you, you'll need to be calm. She can sense when others are upset. Your brother is bringing Allison and the boys here in two days. Tomorrow, why don't you take Madeline and Declan on a tour around town. Maybe a visit to see the Peabody ducks would be fun for both of them, and I'm hoping that will distract Madeline from the fact that we won't have our usual routine of taking her to the hospital. We're going to keep her busy the next few days, but it's also important for you to keep bonding with her and showing her that you can provide for her needs."

Kate pulled back and looked at her mom. Her mom had always been able to keep things in perspective when life became chaotic. She would solve problems and get things done while simultaneously being there for Kate, which had been especially needed after Mark's death.

"Thanks, Mom." Kate's eyes drifted to Declan sitting in the chair only feet away. His worried eyes held hers, and her heart soared with relief that he had come and was here when she needed him most.

Chapter Forty-Three

Too many thoughts raced through Kate's mind as she entered the building for her therapist appointment. Kate hadn't seen her in person since she left for England the first time and had only done phone sessions since then, with the last being just after she met Brittany. The therapist was going to think Kate was crazy with all that had happened since.

"Kate?"

Drawn from her thoughts, Kate looked up and tensed upon seeing Laura, the wife of one of the partners at Mark's law firm.

"I thought you were in London," Laura said in confusion.

"Just home for a visit." Kate wasn't sure how much she should say. She'd forgotten that Laura was the one who had recommended this therapist in the first place.

Laura nodded. "I understand the need to start fresh after such a life-altering experience. I . . ." Laura's voice shook. "Jonathan and I are going through a divorce." Her eyes fell to the tile floor. "I found out he was cheating on me."

"I'm so sorry." Kate wasn't surprised and reached out to touch Laura's shoulder. "I know how that feels." She hesitated before deciding it was time to speak up. "After Mark's death, I found out he had been cheating on me too."

A gasp escaped from Laura. "I'm so sorry. That must have been awful to discover after already suffering through his horrendous murder."

"Let's just say our therapist got to know me very well." Kate thought about the other lawyers' wives who were probably unaware that their husbands were cheating on them. "When I was looking into . . . Mark's indiscretions, I found out that the partners at the firm have no problem covering for one another's infidelity. It wouldn't surprise me if other wives are in the same situation." Laura was close to many of the wives and had always been good about initiating get-togethers for them.

Laura's hand flew to her mouth. "I never would have dreamt it. Now that I think of it, Gina is always complaining about James working so much. And so is Christina . . . oh my. I think I need to get the girls together." She reached out to squeeze Kate's arm. "Would you like to join us? I can get something together this week."

"Thanks so much for offering, but I've got a lot going on. Also, I'd rather not stir up old memories." Neither did she want to chance having to out Mark's assistant as the source for some of her information. His assistant was happily retired and didn't need to be pulled into what would surely be a huge legal mess.

"Well, it was good seeing you. You look great."

Kate knew she didn't look great after the stress and lack of sleep the past few days, but Laura was a southern woman who coated everything with honey. "It was good to see you too. I'm so sorry about your divorce, Laura." After waving goodbye, Kate rushed into the therapist's reception room, internally rehashing her conversation with Laura. Maybe she should have stopped and prayed with her? On second thought, that would have made her even more late to the appointment.

"Hi, I'm here to see Megan," Kate told the receptionist after signing in.

It took a few minutes to catch the therapist up on dating Declan, thinking she'd broken up with him and that he was engaged to Alexandra, then coming to Memphis and deciding to become Madeline's guardian. Not to mention the explanation of her connection to Laura. While she talked, her eyes trailed around the room, and she realized it had a number of Scripture verses on display. During the many hours she had spent there when she was not a Christian, she'd not fully registered what they were. She definitely hadn't appreciated them. Now the words took root in her heart, and she was again amazed at how God had been working in her life even before she became a Christian.

"I became a Christian a few months ago. Declan and Margaret were the ones who helped me understand that it is about a relationship with God and not just doing religious things."

Megan nodded. "That's wonderful. It's the best decision you'll ever make. God can give you strength and comfort even through these difficult things. You've gone through a lot this past year and a half. What is stressing you the most right now?"

"Wow, where to start? Transitioning to being the sole guardian for Madeline, moving her across the ocean, knowing how to help her as she realizes her loss." Her eyes focused on the wall as she read, *I can do all things through Him who strengthens me. Philippians 4:13.* "The other stressor has to do with Declan. Did I mention he asked me to marry him?"

"No. That's very significant. What was your answer?"

"I told him no. He said he was asking because Madeline should have two parents and he thinks it would be best for it to be right away. We hadn't even fully worked out whether we were back together. Not to mention the fact that he's been engaged twice. The first time it was to someone he'd known most of his life, but it took being engaged to realize she was wrong for him. There's no way he can know if I'm the one for him. I've already been in one marriage to a man who never loved me like he should. I'm not putting myself in that situation again."

Even as she said it, she felt the tension build inside—a mixture of pain and sadness at the loss of what could have been with Declan.

"Has he told you he loves you? Did he give any indication that he already wanted this with you?"

"No. That's the thing; he's never said he loves me, though he said he wasn't just asking for Madeline's sake. I know how hard it is to keep a marriage together without children. I certainly don't want to attempt it with a child when I'm unsure of my future husband's feelings for me."

Megan nodded. "I agree. Both of you need to make a decision to marry based on your love and respect for one another. If you don't have those things, then a child will only cause problems later. Maybe you need more time to adjust to being a mom before you make another life-changing decision like marriage. Keeping things consistent in your life can help both you and Madeline."

Kate agreed and felt like she could breathe easier with that decision.

Madeline's crying turned to sniffles as she snuggled closer to the lovey Kate sprayed with the essential oil blend Brittany had been using since she discovered her cancer. Megan agreed that the scent could help calm Madeline when she was missing her mom.

Kate squeezed Madeline a little tighter, hoping to help her feel secure. Seeing the worry in Madeline's eyes when she cried out for her mom was painful. There was no easy fix. Kate knew from experience that only time would help the sadness fade.

"I don't know how I can move Madeline across the ocean," Kate claimed in defeat as she entered the living room once Madeline had settled in her bed.

Declan frowned, no doubt worrying that he would have to tell Tracey they might be losing Margaret's personal nurse.

"What brought this on, Kate? Why would you say that?" Her mom noticed Declan's look, then turned to Kate. Abby still had no idea they had been in a relationship, but she probably suspected.

"Madeline is already going through so much change in her life. My therapist mentioned that the more things we can keep the same in her life and mine, the better."

"But we already decided I would go with you and stay several weeks until she gets comfortable with a nanny, and Declan is staying here until we leave so she'll be used to him before the change. She has her lovey, blanket, and bedding that we're taking with us. Children are very adapt-able." Abby looked at her daughter with frustration while reminding her of what they'd decided.

Declan stood and began to pace. He avoided looking at Kate, but his face couldn't hide the struggle within. His mouth moved as if to form words but clamped shut before he'd uttered a sound.

Kate's attention bounced between her parents and Declan, but she had no response. Internally, she again weighed the options. Pain and sadness seemed inevitable regardless of the decision. Staying in Memphis seemed easier. It was a place she knew more about, whereas London was still a mystery to her, adding to her unease. She felt paralyzed with indecision.

"Kate," her father, a man of few words, spoke up. "You originally left to get away from past memories. As much as I would love for you to stay, I also don't want you to hold yourself back out of fear."

It felt like too much—too much responsibility, too many decisions. Kate squeezed her eyes closed and wished she could fast forward her life several months so she could see how things would work out with her choices.

A hand touching her shoulder startled Kate. "Let me pray for you. I know this is hard." Declan's prayer was short but heartfelt. She could hear tension in his voice, like something warred within. He prayed that God would help her figure out what was best.

Soon after he prayed, her parents left them, claiming they had said all they should that evening and that it would be best for everyone to sleep on it. Perhaps more clarity would come the following day.

"Kate, it would break my heart if you stayed here, but I also know you need to follow God's lead and not mine. I won't try to hold you back if you truly feel like he wants you here, but if you do return to England, I'll do everything in my power to help you with Madeline, whether or not you and I are together."

Kate's chest tightened as Declan ran a hand down her cheek, then silently turned to go. All of the air seemed to follow him out of the room. *I won't try to hold you back.* Yet something inside her wanted him to.

Chapter Forty-Four

Kate could see Declan pacing in the back of the sanctuary as he held and calmed Madeline, who had begun to get fussy in the receiving line for Brittany's funeral. He was a natural with her, and watching their interactions made her want to tell him she'd changed her mind about marrying him. Fortunately—or maybe unfortunately— her logical side quickly won out every time her thoughts veered that direction.

It was a small gathering, mostly members of the church congregation who had been praying for and befriended Brittany. There were also a few of her coworkers. Thankfully, Brittany had put together a list of people outside the church to invite when the inevitable time came. They didn't put her obituary in the paper, according to Brittany's request. She said her family would only come hoping for money and would likely cause trouble and stress. There was also the issue of not wanting Mark's law firm to know. Hopefully, the firm was done with their manipulations over Mark's affair and death, but Brittany hadn't wanted to take that chance. All of Kate's family and Jennifer's were there to support Kate and Madeline too.

One woman stood out from the others in attendance—Mark's mother. Kate had fretted over contacting Mark's parents, but knew the right thing to do was let them know that they had a granddaughter.

It wasn't surprising that Mark's dad never responded to her message. It had been years since he'd cheated on Mark's mom and started another family. Since that time, he'd not had much interest in Mark's life. His mom, on the other hand, cared but was still distant in her own way. Since Kate had told her about Mark's infidelity, she'd pulled back from Kate even more. Yet she'd come to meet her granddaughter, the only grandchild she would ever have, and to find out about the woman Mark had his affair with. She promised not to interfere or try to force herself into Madeline's life but to let Kate determine if and when she would have contact. Kate was glad, because at the present, she didn't want to face Mark's mother on a regular basis.

The celebration of life was touching, but the full weight of the tremendous task ahead felt suffocating. Kate was struck with the realization that the last two funerals she'd attended were for Madeline's parents. Orphaned before she was one year of age, Madeline would never remember her mom or know her father. Kate hoped Madeline would not grow up feeling like an orphan and was more determined than ever to begin adoption proceedings.

"We need to buy our return flights soon, don't you think?" Declan had been subtly trying to pin Kate down on their return date when she'd not said anything more about staying in Memphis. It was apparent that he was getting anxious to make plans.

A familiar tightness formed in Kate's chest, and she stood to walk towards the fireplace. They had originally spoken of staying a week after the funeral, and it was now three days later. "You must have a lot of work waiting for you at home. I think you should go on. I'm not sure I'll be ready to leave at the end of the week, and I need more time." And maybe some space from Declan to clear her thoughts.

"But . . ." Declan rubbed a hand over his temple. "Maybe I can get

Mum to hold the reins for me a bit longer. I'll speak with her." He rose from the sofa to go.

"No." Kate answered. "It's just—I know your mom is already stressed with me not being there for your grandmother. I promise I'll be okay. You've been a great help and are so good with Madeline, but I've got my family. They can take care of us for now, so you should probably return without me. Soon enough, I'll be doing this on my own anyway."

Declan frowned but nodded. "If that's what you want, I'll go ahead and buy my ticket, but please don't hesitate to let me know if you need me back or if there is something I can do for you there." He smiled suddenly. "I can go ahead and gather items for Madeline's room. Just let me know what you would like, and I can get things ordered."

Kate bit her lip. "Thanks. I'll keep that in mind."

"You should FaceTime me every day. That way I can say hi to Madeline and she won't forget me." Declan tickled Madeline and had her giggling while he spoke to Kate.

"Yeah, I can do that," she said shakily. Her mom was driving them to the airport to drop him off, and they were nearly there.

"I'll miss you, Kate." He reached over Madeline's car seat to caress her cheek.

Kate tried speaking, but her throat constricted, and she forced a weak smile while leaning into his hand.

When they arrived at the airport, Abby stayed in the car.

After kissing Madeline on the forehead, Declan opened Kate's door and motioned her out. "I'm not giving up on us," he whispered while pulling her into a tight hug. "I hope you won't either . . . and I hope you'll come back to London. You have family there, too, though it's not by blood."

That was the first time he'd acknowledged that she was considering staying since the night she'd mentioned it, and the first time he'd alluded to them as a couple since the day after he'd asked her to marry him.

"I know," she whispered back, not to be quiet, but because her throat still felt tight. She loved the feel of his arms around her and wondered if she'd ever feel that again. He was an amazing man, but he was still a man who had never used the "L" word, and without that, they had no future.

Reluctantly, she let go and watched as he rolled his suitcase into the terminal. Despite having a precious bundle waiting for her in the car, she felt hollow. Had she made the right decision to let him go on without her? She realized she'd been praying about her relationship with Madeline, but not Declan. Kate prayed that in the coming days, God would give her clarity about the man who still held her heart.

"Doggy!"

"Emma, stop!" Jennifer called out to her daughter as she darted off the park path. "We don't know this dog, Emma. Some dogs bite." She caught up with her daughter while Kate watched the stroller.

The dog's owner stopped, said he was safe, and held the fluffy sheepdog still while Emma petted it. Madeline watched in fascination but snuggled tighter in her stroller and showed no indication that she wanted to follow Emma's lead. Once Emma was satisfied, she climbed back into her side of the double stroller she shared with her infant brother.

"When was the last time you spoke with Declan?" Jennifer asked while buckling Emma back into her seat.

"We FaceTimed two days ago. He tried to call yesterday, but I avoided him again." In only a week and a half since Declan had left, Kate had established a comfortable routine, but pressure to make a decision about her future mounted.

"Don't you think it's time you stop avoiding him?"

"I'm leaning heavily towards staying, and I don't want him to cloud my thoughts."

"How would talking to him cloud your thoughts?"

"I told you about our brief relationship, and I've also told you how I don't think he loves me—not the way he should to marry me. I'm already there, though, and talking to him will make me question myself. After all I've been through . . . I'm scared to risk my heart again."

"Kate, he's not Mark."

"I know that."

"Your mind does, but I don't think your heart realizes it yet. You keep putting up barriers to prevent things from getting serious with him. First it was his imagined engagement, now—"

"But there were real reasons that I thought he was engaged!" Kate interrupted, then caught herself when two ladies nearby looked up from their children with concern. She lowered her voice. "Those reasons were valid, and now . . . if he really loves me that way, he would have gone about things completely differently. I mean . . . he didn't even ask my dad for my hand. As proper as he is, and he didn't even do that?"

"It would have been great if he did, but . . . well, you have to admit that none of what was going on when he arrived was conventional, and it was all so sudden. You becoming guardian of your dead husband's mistress's child."

Kate bristled at Jennifer's statement.

"The mistress on the sudden verge of death. You should cut him some slack. From everything I've seen, he's very attentive to you and Madeline. Much more so than Mark had been to you in years." Memories of heated arguments over Mark's thoughtlessness pushed into Kate's mind. "And that beautiful bouquet of spring flowers he sent tells me that Declan is still trying to woo you."

Kate stared at the path ahead as she battled her conflicting thoughts. "I don't know, Jennifer. I just don't know."

Jennifer wrapped an arm around Kate. "I'm here for you. I'm also speaking truth. You need to give Declan a chance. He seems like a great guy and very sincere. I've seen the way you look at each other with longing. I know you feel something for him."

Heat rushed to Kate's face. "How could I not feel anything? He's the best-looking guy I know." They both chuckled, but sadness and fear lurked in the back of Kate's mind. Had she given up her chance at love?

"Hey, Mom." Kate continued folding clothes as Abby entered the living room and joined Madeline on the floor to stack blocks. "Where have you been?"

"Pastor Ronnie's wife, Jane, invited me for coffee. It was nice."

Kate watched her mom, waiting to see if she would add to her comments. She'd noticed them talking during the funeral, and again when they visited the church on Sunday. "She does seem like a nice lady. Their church has been a great support to Brittany and now us. I don't think we could have gotten through the past few weeks without them."

Abby nodded. "Speaking of, Jane invited us to—"

Kate was distracted by her phone ringing and Chloe's name on the screen. She held up a finger to her mom. "Chloe? Hey, what's going on?"

"Kate." Her voice sounded tight, and she spoke softly. "It's Gran. She had another stroke, and they don't think she'll make it."

"What?" Kate could hardly believe what she was hearing. If she'd followed her original plan, she would have been there with her.

"Sorry, I have to keep it down since I'm in the hallway outside of her room, but Gran is back in the hospital. We thought you should know. Declan hasn't said what your plan is since he returned, but if you want to come, you should hurry."

"Of course. I . . ." Kate's mind raced through logistics of how quickly she could get to London. "I'll see if I can get a flight out this afternoon."

"I'll have our travel agent call you, and she can set everything up."

"You shouldn't have to pay for that." The realization hit her that she would need to take Madeline. She wasn't about to be another adult that left her, and she wasn't sure how long this visit would take. The thought of another funeral pained Kate. "Also, I'll have to bring Madeline. I can't leave her."

"Then I'm coming too." Abby had moved close and was listening to the conversation.

"I can handle it, Mom. You've already done so much."

"It's no trouble, Kate. You, Madeline, your mom. We'll fly you all over. It's the least we can do," Chloe confirmed.

Within minutes, they had a flight set up for four hours later and were frantically packing so they could leave in thirty minutes to get to the airport within three hours of the flight.

It wasn't until they were settled in the waiting area at the gate that Kate was hit with the full force of what lay ahead. Would Margaret still be living when she arrived? It saddened Kate that she might not be there for Margaret's final breath. And what of Declan? Would he be mad at her for the way she left things with him? Was it possible he would give them another chance?

Chapter Forty-Five

Another hospital, another death watch—three in just a year and a half. Though to be technical, Mark was already dead when she'd arrived.

"Kate." Tracey wrapped her arms around Kate. She looked tired, like she hadn't slept. "Mum is still here, but she's not opened her eyes yet or eaten since a little before the episode last night when Chloe called you. Well, I guess it was afternoon for you."

They turned to the bed, and Margaret lay there as if resting. Relief filled Kate that she'd arrived in time, but her focus turned to the man sitting next to the bed, looking at her with a sad smile. The man who melted her heart with one glance. The man who had made her love again. Their eyes locked, and everything else seemed to fade.

"Is your mom out in the hall with Madeline?" Tracey's voice seemed far away, and Kate finally tore her eyes from Declan to turn to her. "Yes. Chloe's with them."

"Wonderful. I've been looking forward to meeting Madeline. If you two will excuse me."

With Tracey out of the room, Kate felt the tension thicken, and her eyes found Declan's again—still devastatingly handsome. So many things swirled in her mind, but she was left speechless.

"I missed you."

Kate moved closer on the other side of Margaret. "Did you?"

"Of course. I—" Declan stopped and looked down as his grandmother turned her head. "Gran? Are you awake? Do you hear me? It's Corbyn."

Margaret's eyes fluttered before opening into slits, and he pushed the button to lift the head of the bed as well as the call button for the nurse. "Kate, will you let Mum and Chloe know Gran is awake?"

Kate was momentarily frozen, her mind trying to make sense of all that was happening. "Yes," she blurted out as she moved to leave, but stopped herself and leaned down to hug Margaret. "Margaret, I've missed you." She grinned at the old woman who had meant so much to her for so many months. *Thank you, God!* He had truly given her a gift and released her from carrying the burden of not being with Margaret in her final hours.

"She's precious!" The nurses and staff in Margaret's assisted living home were overjoyed to meet Madeline as Kate helped the family move Margaret back two days after she woke.

"Thank you. I'm in the process of adopting her. Her mother recently died."

"I'm so sorry. I'm glad you were able to be there with her," said Jane, the head nurse who had been helpful and encouraging to Kate when she started working in the center with Margaret.

"I am too." Kate had told everyone at Belgravia Assisted Living that she had to return home to be with a friend who was dying from cancer. They didn't need to know the ugly details of how she and Brittany became friends.

"We're all so glad to have Margaret back. Though she doesn't really speak, she always manages to cheer us up with her sweet smiles." Jane confirmed what Kate had noticed.

Declan had hardly taken his eyes from Kate, and she wondered what he was thinking. They'd not been alone since her return and hadn't spoken about how things were left in Memphis. Since she'd arrived, he had been attentive to her and spent all his time at his parents' home, where Kate, Abby, and Madeline were staying, away from work. Hope bubbled up.

It wasn't until that evening when he finally cornered her in the hallway under the stairs. "Kate." He reached for her hand. "I'm so glad you're back. I was beginning to think the worst. Especially when you didn't return my last call."

Her chest tightened, and she looked down at their entwined fingers. Where to begin?

"I don't know what I've done, Kate, but I sense this has something to do with me. Please give me a chance to fix it."

Her eyes found his, and she stared into them, willing him to understand the words she couldn't speak. *Prove that you love me.*

He gripped her shoulders. "Kate, Sunday is your birthday, and after church, I want to take you to the beach cottage. We can take your mum and Madeline too. Will you come?"

You need to give Declan a chance. Jennifer's words came back to Kate, and she looked closely at him. She was still afraid to risk her heart, but wanted to take the chance. "Yes."

"How is Madeline adjusting to all the changes in her life?" Tracey had asked Kate to meet with her in her study while Abby took Madeline on a walk.

"To losing her mom?"

"That and to this new environment here."

"It took her about a week to stop crying for her mom multiple times a day. Now she only does it every few days. As for the trip, she's done really well the past few days, even with the time change."

"That's wonderful. I . . . I'm sorry if this seems intrusive, but Declan seems to think you're upset with him. Is that true? He said he explained to you the confusion about Alexandra, and I'm truly sorry about that."

It was hard to come up with the words to say. In her head, all her excuses sounded flimsy or silly, but she'd seen what happened when she chose her spouse without enough care. Kate shifted in the chair. "He did explain things to me, and that was a misunderstanding on my part." That much was easy to admit. "Did he tell you he asked me to marry him?"

"What?"

"Yes. It was the day after he arrived in Memphis and I told him I decided to be Madeline's guardian, which he didn't take very well. The next day, he talked to his lawyer without my knowledge, and that night told me we should get married for Madeline's sake. When I asked him to explain, he just said that she needed two parents and something about this being the time to do it, before coming back to England. He didn't say anything about loving me—didn't get down on one knee. It was just all about Madeline, though he later said it wasn't just because of her." Kate's breathing had quickened, and tears rolled down her face unbidden. "I'm sorry. I thought I had my feelings in check."

Tracey stood and hurried to Kate's side to comfort her. "Oh Kate, I'm sorry. You have the weight of the world on you, and my son's practical side made him oblivious to your emotional needs. He cares for you deeply, of that I'm sure. I'm afraid we British aren't as good at revealing our passion as Americans."

Kate appreciated the concern, but she needed to hear it from him.

"I'm glad you're going with him this weekend to the cottage. It might give him a chance to show you how much you mean to him. He told me of his invitation and asked that I move your family birthday celebration to Saturday so he would have more time with the three of you in Kingsdown. He thought you might want to catch up with friends while there."

"Oh. That *would* be nice." Could he truly care about her as much as she did him? More than anything, she needed to talk to God about it. Kate had learned that God was the most important part of any relationship, and in the chaos of the past few weeks, she had not spent enough time seeking him for answers.

Chapter Forty-Six

As Declan drove her to the early church service Sunday morning before their trip to Kingsdown, Kate stared out the window of the car, thinking about her birthday party the night before. They had invited her friends from church and work in addition to all the family. Even Ruth had come in from Kingsdown. The most wonderful surprise was that they'd brought Margaret. She may not have been able to understand what was happening, but it still meant a lot to Kate to have her there.

Only one person was notably absent the night before. "Declan, why wasn't Alexandra at the party?" Kate turned to see his response.

"I told Mum not to invite her. I didn't want anything to bother you at your party. I'm trying to be more sensitive to your feelings."

"Thank you." Seeing Alexandra would have put her on edge, even though she knew Declan wasn't with her.

"Kate, I would do anything to make your life better." He reached over and clasped her hand, then pulled it up for a kiss. "Now, I want you to have the best birthday you can remember. Wait right there, and I'll get your door."

Watching him walk around the car, a feeling rose in her chest that was different from the tightness she'd become so accustomed to.

The beach, the pebbly sand, the sound of the waves, the smell of saltwater—it instantly relaxed Kate. This had been the place where God slowly put her heart back together and gave her hope for a future. Her eyes followed Declan as he played with Madeline, and Kate wondered why she'd let her mind get clouded over the last few months. With or without Declan, she wanted to trust God, yet because of the wall she'd built around her heart, she may have lost Declan.

Kate bent down and picked up a pebble and whispered, "God, like this pebble, take my life in whatever direction you wish. Help me trust you." Then she tossed the stone into the water and watched until it disappeared.

"We're riding horses?!" Kate exclaimed when Declan removed her blindfold and she saw the sign for the stables.

"I told you I have connections. Wait right there." He hopped out of the car and was at her door in seconds, holding out his hand.

"Thank you," Kate whispered. "You keep surprising me."

He gave her a grin that would brighten the darkest day.

"Come meet my friend Ed and his wife, Josie. They've set it all up for us."

A burly man exited the stables, and after a handshake and pat on the back with Declan, he turned to Kate. "Ed MacIntyre at your service. I've heard good things about you." Ed's Scottish brogue left Kate momentarily confused as she worked to understand him. "My wife is fetching the food and will be right behind, but if you follow me, I'll introduce you to your horses. Winston and Missy. Two of my finest. Declan said you were an experienced horsewoman, and I've ridden with him, so these two should be perfect."

He looked past Kate as she admired the horses. "Ah, my lovely bride. Kate, I would like to introduce you to Josie."

After introductions, they mounted the horses and left the stable. As they trotted off, Kate recalled her birthday lunch with friends at the Rose and Crown earlier. Everyone gushed over Madeline. Mira was there and looked like she could deliver any day, though she said she still had a month and a half left. With her mothering instincts kicking in, Mira had gravitated towards Madeline.

"It still seems so strange to think that I'm a mom. At lunch today, Mira suggested we start walking the babies together after she delivered. It was like reality finally hit me. I mean, I've been taking care of Madeline, but Mom and others have been around helping. It doesn't seem like I'm her sole guardian yet. Does that make any sense?" She looked over at Declan as they led the horses down the path.

"It does. Maybe you should start spending some time with just the two of you to help you bond."

Strange feelings twisted inside. "Yeah, I think you're right. I always imagined motherhood starting in a more traditional way for me—marriage, pregnancy, then a baby. It's taking some mental adjustment to change my expectations." Would he take her comment personally since he had technically offered the marriage part? She longed for the easy conversations they used to have—ones where they could each share worries and joys freely.

He glanced over but said nothing as they continued their ascent of a hill. The view gradually opened up to more of the Dover countryside, and a castle came into view on a hill across from the one they climbed. Upon reaching the top, the Channel appeared beyond the castle.

"Gorgeous!" Kate scanned the view ahead. With early spring flowers popping up at the edges of the path and an open view for miles in every direction, she was in awe.

Declan walked his horse closer to Kate's mare and reached for her hand. "It is." He grinned at her.

"Look." Kate's heart raced and she pointed towards the shore. "A cruise ship is docked. I wonder where it's headed."

"Where would you like to be headed if you were on it?"

"Hmm. I guess France makes the most sense with it being right across the Channel. I think I'd like to visit the French countryside. Paris is wonderful, and I'd like to go back there, too, but I imagine the countryside has a completely different vibe." It struck her that if she decided to give up the job in London, it would probably be a long time before she could go back to France. A flight from the U.S. to Europe was much too long for a child on a standard week-long vacation.

"You're right, it is quite different. We should do a tour of the French countryside. It's a quick trip across to Calais, and there are some beautiful locations close by to visit. I think even Madeline might enjoy it."

"That sounds nice." She watched him closely, trying to discern if she could see love in his eyes. Today his eyes were particularly hard to read. Taking a deep breath, she looked once more across the hill. "I wish Madeline were here. I know it sounds silly since she's so young and wouldn't get much out of it, but it's gotten hard for me to be away from her. I want her to be part of everything I do." A sudden chill made her shiver. "I miss her, and I've only been away, what, an hour?"

Declan nodded. "It's okay. It's normal for parents to feel that way when their children are little, but she does need her nap, and you do need adult time." Kate quirked a brow. "At least, that's what Chloe always says. She said once her children hit preteen years, it became much easier to be away. Maybe that's why God gives preteens and teenagers such attitudes. It helps their parents let go." His eyes twinkled, and Kate chuckled. "We should head on. This way." He pointed to the other side of the hill, where the path led downward.

The descent led towards a hillside cottage. "Declan, look! Isn't it adorable?" It was partially surrounded by a low stone wall that had flower bushes surrounding it, creating a wild yet beautiful scene.

"Let's check it out." Declan turned his horse toward the cottage.

"Who lives there?"

"The MacIntyres own it and rent it out for vacationers."

"Oh, maybe we shouldn't get too close then. I would hate to intrude on someone's privacy."

"Actually, I rented it for the day so we would have a place to stop and warm up."

"That would be nice." The comment made her realize her fingers were becoming numb.

Declan dismounted his horse, opened the gate, and helped Kate down before handing her the house key and leading the horses to a small stable with hay.

"Sorry that took so long," he said as he hung her coat on a hall tree and escorted her into a quaint living room with a seating area, fireplace, and dining table set for two.

"How lovely." Kate leaned down towards the table to smell a bouquet of spring flowers.

Smiling, Declan moved to the fireplace and turned on the gas. "Here, come warm up while I set out the food Josie put together. They had this old fireplace converted to gas to make it more convenient for guests, so it will be hot in no time."

Kate stood close and warmed her frozen fingers. "Oh, this feels so nice."

Moving behind her to the dining table, Declan began laying out food he'd brought in from the saddle bags. Within minutes, he had a charcuterie plate arranged and hot tea in their teacups. "Come sit with me." He held out his hand and pulled out a chair for her.

"Thanks for all of this—the horses, the food . . . everything." Kate smiled, but suddenly felt awkward in Declan's presence. "I guess I do need to get away sometimes for adult things. Though I know Madeline's in good hands with Mom, I feel guilty."

"True, she is in good hands." He took a deep breath. "Kate, you're amazing, and I'm afraid I haven't said that enough. When I first met you —and you thought I was the gardener . . ." He smirked and waited as she chuckled. "I was immediately entranced by you. Then once I got to know you and realized all you had gone through with Mark, I was drawn to your character and strength. The way you didn't give up but picked up the pieces of your life and went on trying to create order from the chaos was admirable, but also reminded me of what I'd gone through."

"We've both gone through a lot in the romance department, considering we're still fairly young, though hitting thirty today makes me feel old." She made a horror-stricken face before turning serious. "When I came here, it didn't feel like I was creating order. I was just trying to get away from the chaos."

"Regardless, I felt we had a kinship, and you shouldn't feel old. You could still pass for early twenties."

"Hey, lying is a sin." They both laughed.

"It is, but the thing is, by the time you became a Christian, my heart felt so intertwined with yours that there was no help for me." The smile vanished from his face, and Kate froze, wondering what he was getting at.

"Kate." His voice trembled. "I've wanted to say this for a long time, but I was scared. You know my track record with women." He paused. "Kate, I love you. I wanted to tell you months ago, but I kept waiting for you to say we could openly date. In my mind, that was the sign that you were all in, and I'm sorry again that I wasn't more straightforward with you about my feelings."

Kate was shaking her head and crying. He had finally said it. Did he really mean it? "No, you can't bear the burden of that. The walls I built around my heart became so comfortable that I couldn't see that they were making it difficult for me to recognize the truth. Even now, I'm struggling to believe you have these feelings for me."

He embraced her. "Oh Kate. God made you for me. How could I not?" He released her and moved to stand by the fire.

Though the fire was still on, she felt chilled without his nearness and wanted nothing more than to hold him for the rest of the afternoon until she was sure this was real. "Declan, I'm done running. I love you too. I'm sorry I've been so foolish." She held out her hand, hoping he would sit back down, but he grinned.

"Those are the most perfect words I've ever heard, and I'm glad you're done running."

"Soon after I arrived here, Margaret asked me what I was running from. Even though she didn't know my story and wasn't completely aware of things, it was like she just knew."

"I'd say that was the Holy Spirit giving her insight."

Kate's face lit up. "Yes. The Holy Spirit."

"Look; they have some books that might interest you." Declan gestured towards the mantle.

"Declan? What an odd . . ." The familiar wrapping paper caught her eye, and she stood up next to him. "How? Is it—"

"It is." He nodded and pulled the wrapped book from between several others, then handed it to her.

"But I thought all of this was my present." She waved around the room.

He shrugged. "You're still missing part of the set. Happy birthday."

Once again, she felt warm from the inside as he handed her the gift. Her hands shook as she returned to her chair. She had given up hope of something more serious with anyone, and over the course of a day, he was once again dismantling her wall. No more running.

She slowly removed the wrapping paper, willing her heart to calm. "*Pride and Prejudice*! Oh Declan."

Reaching for his still standing form, he waved her off. "Open it."

She knew he meant for her to check for his personalization inside the cover, and she quickly flipped it open.

"You are too generous to trifle with me. If your feelings are still what they were last month, tell me so at once. My affections and wishes are unchanged; but one word from you will silence me on the subject forever."

Yours in Christ, Declan Corbyn Fitzgerald

Her heart pounded even harder as she raised her eyes to him. There he was, her beloved, on one knee.

"Marry me, Kate." He held open a ring box.

Kate's hands flew to her mouth. This whole afternoon was like a dream. He loved her, she was sure of it. Their relationship felt more real and solid than hers ever had with Mark. Barely glancing at the ring, Kate nodded. This was it—he really meant it.

"Yes," she whispered, then yelled. "Yes!" She leaned down and threw her arms around him, causing him to nearly tumble over before he placed his hands on her waist and lifted her up.

"Yes!" he repeated. "Oh Kate, this is a happy day."

"The best birthday ever." She held out her left hand as he slid the ring on. "Declan?" She looked more closely at the ring. "This is Margaret's ring."

"It is. With two failed engagements, she assured me the third one would be the charm, and I'm counting on it. After my grandfather died, she promised me I could have the ring the next time I got engaged. You and Gran are the only women to ever wear it."

"Oh Declan, this is even more special." She continued to examine the ring and was reminded of the many touching stories Margaret had told about her husband. It was a treasure that she felt honored to wear.

"I may not have had the ring when I first asked, but I was just as serious about you. Again, I'm sorry for the careless way I asked. I made it seem that it was only about Madeline, when in reality, in my mind, she was just a reason to ask for what I wanted sooner."

"Declan, I . . . this is wonderful." She still struggled to wrap her mind around what was happening. She'd hoped today he would beg her to stay and give her enough confidence to do so, but never did she dream that he would ask her to marry him.

"You need to know two important things. The first is that I *did* call your father and ask for your hand in marriage. It was through that that your mum found out we'd dated before, but she didn't lie—Alexandra was part of that discussion. I'm sorry for being the one to tell them, but they had to know why I was asking for your hand. Number two—I've been looking into office locations in Memphis. Well, actually the Germantown area where your parents live, and I've discussed with my mum having a satellite location there so that you can stay in Memphis while we wait to marry, if that's what you prefer. I don't want to be apart from you anymore. Then we can decide what to do after the wedding. So I guess what I'm also saying is that we can take as long as you want to plan the wedding so you won't feel rushed, and I want you to have the choice to stay in the U.S. if that's your preference. Does that make sense?"

Kate smiled and nodded, feeling like her heart would explode. Then she shook her head.

"What? What's wrong?"

"Thank you. That confirms how serious you are about us, but I don't want to wait a long time, and I don't need to live in Memphis."

"Are you sure? I just want to be with you wherever, and I'll make it work."

Kate grinned. "Declan, I promise that is what I want. The only reason I was unsure was because if we weren't in a relationship, I didn't know if I could handle being in places where I was reminded of you constantly, and of course, being around your family, I knew I would see you too. I'd convinced myself that you couldn't really want me, not for marriage."

"Kate, I do want you, more than you can imagine." His eyes gleamed with mischief. "I'm anxious to begin our life together, and I am inwardly thanking God that you don't want to wait long for marriage either. By the way, I think it's time you started calling me Corbyn."

"Really?" Kate felt her smile grow impossibly wider. At his nod, she tested it out. "Corbyn."

Corbyn grinned, reached for both her hands, and praised and thanked God for sending the woman of his dreams.

When he was done praying, her eyes caught the sun reflecting off the ring, and Kate remembered watching Margaret look at it adoringly on numerous occasions as she recalled her time with her husband. "This is such a treasure. Thank you." She threw her arms around him and rested her head on his shoulder.

"Kate," Corbyn said as he pulled back and gently lifted her face to his.

With the look in his eyes, she couldn't bear it anymore and leaned in, rising to her toes and wrapping her fingers behind his neck. His eyes followed her every move, and he met her halfway, their lips meeting and fitting together like two halves of a whole. His lips were soft but firm, and oxygen no longer seemed necessary. When his arms tightened around her, she felt frantic for more and sensed he did, too, until his hands moved to her face and he pulled back.

"Kate, I . . . it's time we leave." Corbyn glanced around nervously.

"Oh. What's wrong? I thought you rented it for the day."

He looked embarrassed. "I don't think it's safe for us to be here alone anymore." His hand went to the back of his neck. "I love you, Kate, and I can't wait to be yours in every way." His face colored, and he lifted a hand to her cheek. "But both of us are overcoming trust issues, and I know better than anyone that engagement doesn't equal marriage until we've said 'I do.' There's a reason God wants us to save intimacy for marriage, and I've waited my whole life. I don't think I've ever felt as strong of a pull to a woman as I do towards you, so we're going to have to be extra careful from now until our wedding day." He leaned down and pecked her lips before he released her and moved away.

Kate silently contemplated his words. "I'm sorry if I embarrassed you. I hope—"

"No, it's not what you think. You're right. It's just not something I've thought about." She was flattered by the desire she'd seen in his eyes. It was a look she couldn't recall seeing on Mark's face in years. She'd seen it the time he took her virginity and several other times when they were intimate in the years before their marriage. "But I think you're right. My eyes were clouded once by not waiting. I think . . ."

She sank back down to the chair as the realization hit her. "I think I missed the signs of who Mark really was because I had given myself to him and was too blinded by our premature intimacy." Her hands went to her face, and seconds later, Corbyn eased them away.

"Kate, no. This is a day to celebrate. We can't let Mark take anything more away from you or from us. That was your past, and you were not who you are. You've been forgiven, and we're in this together. I love you, and you will be my wife. Everyone before is the past . . . for both of us." He moved to gather their things, then turned back to her. "And, Kate, you should know that I'm not quite Mr. Darcy."

Her brow rose. "What do you mean?"

"The quote I wrote in the book, 'One word from you will silence me on the subject forever'—I could never do that. If you had not come here to England, I was ready to open that Memphis office and move to prove to you my earnestness. I might have been slow about it, but once I had everything in place, I wasn't leaving our reconciliation to chance."

Kate felt warmth build up inside, and she moved toward Corbyn. "I'd much rather have you than Mr. Darcy. I think I just fell in love with you again, if that's possible." She smiled and leaned up to peck him on the lips, and he wrapped an arm around her and held her close.After peppering her face with kisses, he admitted, "I feel the same each time I see you. I can't imagine my love for you growing to more, but it does. I love you, Kate, and hope to prove it again and again."

Chapter Forty-Seven

"Mummy?"

"Hmm?" Kate shifted her eyes from the seagull swooping down toward the water to her daughter.

"Will you read?" Madeline climbed into Kate's lap with a book from Margaret's *Under the Willow Tree* series.

"Of course, Sweet Pea." Kate held Madeline tight and rearranged her so that she could see the book and they would both be comfortable on the cottage porch lounge chair.

"Mummy, is Gran in heaven with Mommy Brittany?"

A pang of sadness shot through Kate. Then smiling down at Madeline, she thought of all the child—her daughter—had been through, and yet how strong she was in spite of it. "She is, dear. They are waiting until the rest of their family has finished all that God has for us here. Then we can celebrate together at the feast that Jesus has been preparing for us."

"Okay . . . Read, please," Madeline urged just as Kate started worrying that maybe she should have said something different to an almost three-year-old.

Smiling, Kate turned to the page where they left off the day before and began reading, imagining Margaret penning the pages as a young woman. Hers was a life well lived, and Kate was thankful to have been part of that life.

"Mummy." Madeline tugged at her sleeve, and Kate realized her mind had wandered.

"I'm sorry. Where were we?"

"In the woods." Madeline referred to the progress of the characters in the story.

"Oh yes. 'So the children continued through the woods . . .'" Kate enjoyed these peaceful moments reading to her daughter, especially at the beach cottage on weekends such as this.

A soft cry drew their attention from the story.

"Daddy, for me?" Madeline hopped off Kate's lap and catapulted towards Corbyn.

"Some of them." He held out his hand filled with flowers. "And some of them are for your mum. Easy there," he chided Madeline as she accosted him and the flowers. "Your sister is fussy enough without you poking at her." His eyes met Kate's, and he nodded towards the baby in his arm. "Kate, I think she needs you."

Kate smiled, recognizing that full feeling that indicated it was time for the baby to nurse.

"But I want to hold Margaret." Madeline reached for her sister.

"She needs to nurse with Mummy, but you and I can go put the flowers in water."

Minutes later they returned with a vase full of the flowers from the garden.

"These are beautiful. Thank you." Kate smirked at her husband.

"What?" Corbyn questioned, leaving Madeline to look between her parents.

"I'm just picturing you trimming those flower bushes the very first time I saw you."

Corbyn raised a brow. "Is that so?"

Nodding, Kate recalled that first day. "I never would have dreamt we would be here one day—a family."

"You and the gardener."

Kate chuckled. "Yep, me and the gardener." Happy tears threatened to fall. "Margaret would be so happy to see this day."

"She would. But I'm glad we were able to introduce her to our little

Margaret." Corbyn reached over and rubbed one of Margaret's feet that was poking out from under the nursing blanket.

"I still remember the words she spoke that day." Kate choked up, recalling how after months of not speaking a word, Margaret smiled and said, "More . . . Jesus."

"More Jesus—those were the last words anyone heard her speak." Declan spoke her thoughts.

"More Jesus," came a little voice from Corbyn's lap.

"That's right, beautiful. That's what we all need." Corbyn smiled over at Kate and gave her shoulder a squeeze.

Kate had come to England to escape, but instead, had been found. She was at peace, and her heart overflowed.

The End

Psalm 23 (ESV)

1 A Psalm of David. The LORD is my shepherd; I shall not want. 2 He makes me lie down in green pastures. He leads me beside still waters. 3 He restores my soul. He leads me in paths of righteousness for his name's sake. 4 Even though I walk through the valley of the shadow of death, I will fear no evil, for you are with me; your rod and your staff, they comfort me. 5 You prepare a table before me in the presence of my enemies; you anoint my head with oil; my cup overflows. 6 Surely goodness and mercy shall follow me all the days of my life, and I shall dwell in the house of the LORD forever.

. . .

In this world full of brokenness, we all have heartache and struggles. Dear reader, I have prayed for you, that through this book, you would learn tools to lay your struggles on Jesus, the one who has and will bear all for you so that you can find joy and peace in him. He is the shepherd of your soul!

Psalm 30:5 (ESV)

For his anger is but for a moment, and his favor is for a lifetime. Weeping may tarry for the night, but joy comes with the morning.

2 Corinthians 12:8-10 (ESV)

8 Three times I pleaded with the Lord about this, that it should leave me. 9 But he said to me, "My grace is sufficient for you, for my power is made perfect in weakness." Therefore I will boast all the more gladly of my weaknesses, so that the power of Christ may rest upon me. 10 For the sake of Christ, then, I am content with weaknesses, insults, hardships, persecutions, and calamities. For when I am weak, then I am strong.

Isaiah 61:1-3 (ESV)

1 The Spirit of the Lord GOD is upon me, because the LORD has anointed me to bring good news to the poor; he has sent me to bind up the brokenhearted, to proclaim liberty to the captives, and the opening of the prison to those who are bound; 2 to proclaim the year of the LORD's favor, and the day of vengeance of our God; to comfort all who mourn; 3 to grant to those who mourn in Zion-- to give them a beautiful headdress instead of ashes, the oil of gladness instead of mourning, the garment of praise instead of a faint spirit; that they may be called oaks of righteousness, the planting of the LORD, that he may be glorified.

· · ·

"More Jesus" were two of the last coherent words my mom said to me as she succumbed to Alzheimer's. What she said before and after that made no sense, but when she said those words, she patted her Bible. It was hard to hold back tears that day as I struggled to accept my own personal loss of my mother, one of my dearest friends, while simultaneously acknowledging that one day soon she would indeed have "more Jesus" and rejoice in his presence forever. "More Jesus" is my goal in life, and, dear reader, know that I am praying it is yours. There is no greater joy, and it is one that lasts for eternity. He is worthy and has sacrificed all for you.

There may be times when he calls you to big sacrifices, but know that if it is God's plan for you, he is big enough to accomplish it, and his grace is most assuredly sufficient for you. When you are weak, in him you are strong. Step into his plan for you with confidence in him, and God will be made known through your obedience.

What to read next: If you enjoyed this book and want to read more, be sure to read the rest of the series. Not Quite Mr. Darcy is book 1. You can go to book 2-**Not Quite Colonel Brandon** where you'll find mystery, meet a new friend of Kate's, and find out what became of Kieran. Or if you haven't read the prequel, you may want to read it-**Not Quite Miss Austen**. It holds Margaret's love story in her younger years. You'll find that Margaret is the thread throughout the series as she leaves a legacy that points to God. Find out more at **KimGriffin.org**

Excerpt from page 1 of Not Quite Colonel Brandon-

"Send them away! I'm not answering any questions!" came a man's shout from deep within the coastal cottage.

Megan shifted the basket of food in her arms and glanced at her friend, Kate. The yelling didn't sound like an old man's as she had imagined, and what's worse, he sounded angry.

"Hi." The dark haired, athletic-looking man at the door winced before calling into the house, "It's Kate and her friend with your food! Don't be such a grump!" He turned to them and pasted on a smile before looking back once more. "I can bring them in to say 'hi.'"

"Don't you dare!" came the gruff response.

Dear reader, thank you for choosing to read this book. Though it is my fourth to write, it was my first to officially publish. It was a journey learning the process of going from words on my computer to this, and I am so thankful I followed God's prompting into it. I have been praying from the beginning that it would touch people and point them to God. I hope it's done that for you. It is the first in the Not Quite Series. Check out KimGriffin.org for the others.

When I was deciding on the name for my lead male, I found that Declan means full of goodness or man of prayer, which were qualities that I wanted him to portray. I tried to include some weaknesses, though, because only Jesus is perfect.

Fun fact: the movie, *Heaven Bound*, mentioned in chapter 20 was filmed in my town. Parts of it were filmed at my house. In spite of some heavy themes, it is a fun Christian comedy.

I'd like to thank my best friend and love of my life for encouraging me on this journey. My husband has read every book and given me helpful feedback, even though women's fiction with romance is not a genre that interests him.

I also want to thank my Alpha and Beta readers, particularly Marla who has been a prayer warrior for me for years. Thank you, Sarah, Judith, Mariah, and Tawni. You ladies pushed me to make necessary changes in this book and gave me insight into my writing that will also help me in the future.

A huge thanks to my editor, Heather, who also nudged me along and helped make this book better.

And to my ARC readers, thank you for taking the time to read and support my writing.

Not to be forgotten is my dad who has encouraged me and my creativity all my life in all its forms. Not only that, he walked by my mom's side for almost 55 years, watching the love of his life fade away with Alzheimer's those last years. We walked that path together, but I know he bore the greater burden of it. In sickness and health, he was there until the end. Thank you. We will see her again at our real and forever home.

Above all, I thank God who has given me the creativity to write. To God be the glory. *Kim Griffin*

Free *Not Quite Mr. Tilney* novella with newsletter signup at Kim Griffin.org. For more fun and information on the Not Quite Series, check out the ***Not Quite Mr. Darcy* Extras Page** on my website by holding your phone camera up to the QR code and clicking the link or going to www.kimgriffin.org/home/books/Extras-NQMD

Kim Griffin is a former interior designer and homeschool mom who has been leading Bible studies for over 35 years and working in Women's Ministry for over 25. Several years ago, God led her to begin writing words of hope. She writes Christian women's fiction with clean romance and devotionals/Bible studies. Her desire is that her books will draw readers closer to the God who sees all of their imperfections and loves them still.

If you enjoyed this book, please consider leaving a review on Goodreads and Amazon! As an independent author this helps Kim get the word out about her books.

You can learn more about Kim and her books and sign up for her newsletter at her website:

kimgriffin.org

www.ingramcontent.com/pod-product-compliance
Lightning Source LLC
Chambersburg PA
CBHW030134310726
48970CB00005B/1434